Eleanor took a step toward Dez. "You're almost too beautiful to be human, but you're like a doughnut. I love doughnuts and I want to eat them every day, but I can't because I'll get fat."

"Yeah, but what would life be without the occasional nibble on a doughnut? Maybe just a taste." He wanted her to say yes, wanted her to toss away those crazy inhibitions that held her back.

"I could so easily, you know."

"I won't hurt you."

"That's what they all say," she whispered.

"Let's make a deal." Dez cupped her jaw, studying those delicious lips. "If things feel too much, too serious, we walk away."

Eleanor closed her eyes with a harsh laugh. "You can't walk away when the heart gets involved."

"You're thinking too damn much," he said.

Then he slid his arms around her and pulled her into his embrace. He was tired of talking. There were better ways of convincing Eleanor this thing between them was worth exploring.

Dear Reader,

In a city crumbling, weathered by time and the waters surrounding it, music is a living, breathing entity. If you've ever visited New Orleans, you know exactly of what I speak. The melding of Spanish, French and African cultures creates an essence unique from any other place, a gumbo of food, music and a way of living that's slower…and yet full of energy. It's easy to fall in love with New Orleans.

This book is a Hurricane Katrina book, yet not. *His Uptown Girl* is about healing, forgiveness and finding courage… discovering beauty among ruin. These characters grabbed hold of who they were and ran with it—they're likely the most complex and interesting ones I've written.

So come with me to New Orleans—to Uptown Magazine Street and Downtown Frenchmen Street. Listen to the *rat-a-tat* beat of jazz, blues and soul mixed with a hint of bounce. Taste the stuffed crab and andouille sausage… and don't forget a cocktail. It's the Crescent City, the Big Easy and the place where Eleanor will learn to love again, Dez will find his mojo and a young sax player will discover dreams don't fade…even when you bury them in your soul.

I hope you enjoy *His Uptown Girl.* For more information on my books and to contact me, visit www.liztalleybooks.com or write to P.O. Box 5418, Bossier City, Louisiana 71171.

Happy reading!

Liz Talley

His Uptown Girl

LIZ TALLEY

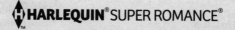
HARLEQUIN® SUPER ROMANCE®

Recycling programs
for this product may
not exist in your area.

ISBN-13: 978-0-373-71854-2

HIS UPTOWN GIRL

Printed in U.S.A.

TM www.Harlequin.com

ABOUT THE AUTHOR

From devouring the Harlequin Superromance novels on the shelf of her aunt's used bookstore to swiping her grandmother's medical romances, Liz Talley has always loved a good romance. So it was no surprise to anyone when she started writing a book one day while her infant napped. She soon found writing more exciting than scrubbing hardened cereal off the love seat. Underneath Liz's baby-food-stained clothes, a dream stirred. She followed that dream, and after a foray into historical romance and a Golden Heart final, she started her first contemporary romance on the same day she met her editor. Coincidence? She prefers to call it fate.

Currently Liz lives in north Louisiana with her high-school sweetheart, two beautiful children and a passel of animals. Liz loves watching her boys play baseball, shopping for bargains and going out for lunch. When not writing contemporary romances for the Harlequin Superromance line, she can be found doing laundry, feeding kids or playing on Facebook.

Books by Liz Talley

HARLEQUIN SUPERROMANCE

Other titles by this author available in ebook format.

To two of my favorite uptown girls:
Phylis Caskey and Cindy Lott.

You've taught me about the finer things in life, but most importantly you've taught me the value of friendship. So glad to have both you classy ladies in my life.

And to the city that never gives up, that continues to find the beauty beyond the destruction.

I know what it means to miss New Orleans.

PROLOGUE

Uptown New Orleans, September 1, 2005

LOOKING OVER HIS SHOULDER, Tre Jackson ducked between the buildings and then slid behind an abandoned car. For several seconds, he focused on gulping down the soggy air pressing in around him. *Okay. Just breathe, Tre. In. Out.*

Breathe.

His heart galloped, slamming hard against his ribs. Shadows enveloped him, but he worried his grubby white T-shirt stood out too much. He crouched to make himself smaller, peeking out from behind the grille of the Honda. The street before him looked empty, but Tre knew eyes were everywhere—eyes belonging to desperate people who could grab him, shake him down and leave him for dead.

Crazy white folks with guns.

Effed-up brothers with guns.

Police with guns.

Made an eleven-year-old kid holding shit he stole feel like he couldn't breathe too good. After all, what was one more dead black kid?

Fear washed over Tre, hard and fast, but he beat it back with the baseball bat he kept in his head. No time for thinking too much. Had to act. His mama and brother, Devontay, counted on him to be cool.

He clutched the junk he'd taken tighter to his chest, wishing he'd been brave enough to break the window of the grocery store—the place had looked empty, but Tre knew some store owners sat inside with shotguns. So he'd passed it and rooted around in a store with windows already busted. Not much anyone would want left—bunch of junk—but he'd found a weird box filled with junk wrapped inside an old shirt. It had been hidden on a high shelf. He'd grabbed it, and climbed back out into darkness. Tre had no clue if any of the stuff would score food and water in a trade, but he'd find out.

Stepping softly, he crept around the side of the old Honda, its gaping windows reminding him of the man he'd seen several blocks back. Vacant. Abandoned. Dead.

A rat ran across his grave, but Tre ignored the shiver creeping up his back. He didn't have time for no rats or dead men lying like trash in the gutter where black ribbons of sludge trailed into the clogged sewers. The water had gone down in some places, but that made it even more dangerous. Like a war zone he'd seen on TV once.

Yeah. Tre was livin' in a war zone. But he always had. Magnolia Projects ain't no cakewalk. He'd seen dudes shot. Seen bitches beat down. Kids ignored. Ain't easy living in 'Nolia. But outside the projects, there had been order.

Until four days ago.

Tre searched around for something he could use to hit somebody…if they got the idea they could mess with him. He was afraid to look in the car. He'd seen other dead people. Old folks who thought they'd be all right, but found out quick the storm wasn't like all the others.

He didn't see anything he could use, but he had the kitchen knife in the back of his pants. He'd made his mama keep the gun. G-Slim hated his mama, and G-Slim was one mean brother, quick to anger. With no soul. Better Mama and Shorty D keep the gun.

Tre stuffed the stolen bundle down the front of his shirt, hiking up his pants and cinching tight his one school belt.

Made him look kinda like a pregnant lady or one of those starving African kids, but it kept his hands free. He slid the knife from where it fit against the curve of his back and removed the cheap sheath, shoving it in the pocket of his jeans.

Time to go.

He listened hard before he moved, but the city was silent. Not like it normally sounded. No music. No laughter. No horns honking on the overpass. Like a whole 'nother place, a whole 'nother place that smelled of death…and fear.

Certain no one was about to grab him, Tre slipped out from behind the car, wishing for the third or fourth time he'd pulled on a dark T-shirt. He stepped over an old oil can and waded through muck and trash piled up on the sides of the street. Water still sat in some low areas, but he'd avoid them. He knew the way back to 'Nolia. He'd walked there from every direction.

Twenty minutes later, after ducking out of the beams of a few National Guard trucks and seeing a couple of boats with spotlights in some of the flooded streets, Tre waded through nasty water to reach the steps of his building in the Magnolia Housing Projects. He'd seen only one lone soul on his journey back to his place—some crazy dude sitting on his porch staring past Tre into the inky, still night.

Tre gripped the knife tighter as he crept toward the safest stairwell. He inched open the rusted-out door, wincing at the sound. Once he got inside, he'd be safe. The world would forget about him, his mama and Shorty D holed up like rats, sitting inside with rotten milk, the whole place smelling like shit. Even G-Slim would forget about them. About how much he hated Tre's mama. About how she'd ratted him out to that detective a month back. About getting even with her.

The air left his lungs as he got jerked backward.

"What you doin', lil' Tre?"

He stumbled, losing his balance, and the knife flew from his hand, clattering onto the cement stoop.

A bowling ball sank in his stomach. Daylight protected him in the projects. Usually, the Dooney Boys left the little kids alone, but this wasn't "usual" and night covered up stuff. Tre should have left earlier. He should have—

"Damn, son. Got you a knife. What you gonna do with that, cuz?" G-Slim asked, lifting Tre up by the back of his T-shirt.

Tre couldn't breathe. He coughed and swiped at G-Slim's arms.

The man let him go, laughing when Tre sprawled on his ass, hitting a stone planter Miss Janie had left on the stoop. She'd let Shorty D plant some seeds a couple of months ago. Now those planters held weeds and dirt. "What you got in your shirt?"

Tre almost pissed his pants. G-Slim had killed some Chinese guy a couple streets over when he wouldn't pay for some smack. Tre's friend had seen the dude's brains and stuff. "Nothin you want."

"How you know?" Another smile. And it wasn't no good smile. Nasty and mean. Tre scooted back, teetering on the edge of the stoop, his heart tripping on itself with fear. He tried to think about how to get away, but his mind wouldn't work. Tears filled his eyes and he forgot how to be hard. How to pretend he was brave.

G-Slim peered down at Tre. "Where's your mama, boy?"

"She 'vacuated."

"Why you still here?"

Tre tried to swallow but his mouth felt full of sand. "I—I didn't wanna go. Mama took Shorty D on the bus, but I ran away 'cause I ain't leavin' Big Mama."

G-Slim stared at him, and Tre prayed the man bought the lie. His grandmother had already left before the storm, but

G-Slim didn't know that. And he didn't know Shorty D and Mama were still on the third floor.

In the moonlight, Tre could see only the whites of the man's eyes. But he knew what lay in their coal-black depths. Revenge. "That so?"

"Yeah. I's going back to get Miss Janie's horn and then I'm going to Big Mama's."

G-Slim moved toward him. Tre shrank against the rough brick, feeling around for the knife, hoping somehow he could save himself. Maybe G-Slim wouldn't kill him, but maybe he would.

A gun fired, the shot hitting far above Tre's head. He squeezed his eyes shut as dust fell on him.

"Get your janky ass away from my boy," Tre's mom said from the doorway. Tre opened his eyes, shocked to find his mother standing on the stoop in a stained T-shirt. Talia's braids were ragged, but both her gaze and the gun were steady.

G-Slim held up both his hands as if Tre's mama was the police. "Whoa, now. I ain't hurtin' your boy."

"I'm going to blow a hole in you a truck can drive through if you don't back the hell up off my boy," she said, eyeing G-Slim as if he was a cockroach sitting on their table. "Get upstairs, Tre."

Tre moved quick as a snake, bolting through the space between his mama and the doorway.

"Oh, that's how it is, bitch?" G-Slim said, his voice not sounding the least bit scared. G-Slim was hard. He'd been in prison a couple times, always out because no witnesses would testify against him…because they knew they'd bleed their life out on the street.

"That's how it is, Gerald," Talia said, her voice firm but sad. Tre felt the tears on his cheeks. He hadn't even realized he'd started crying. And his pants felt wet. Maybe he'd peed them. He couldn't remember.

"Go on then," G-Slim said. Tre couldn't see him, but he imagined he'd dropped his hands and turned toward Talia. G-Slim wasn't afraid of a bullet. He wasn't afraid of Talia. He'd beat the shit out of her many times before declaring her a waste of space. G-Slim didn't even give Talia anything for Devontay, and G-Slim was Shorty D's daddy.

"Oh, I am, and you better stay the hell away from me and my kids. I got plenty of bullets," Talia said, inching back through the door. She didn't take her eyes off the banger in front of her. "Tre, get your ass upstairs like I told you. 'Bout that time, baby."

Tre turned and ran up the stairs two at a time, the bundle of stolen goods thumping against his belly. He and Mama had planned for every scenario in regards to the storm and G-Slim. He knew what he had to do even though it made him feel sick. His job was to get Shorty D out of 'Nolia. Mama had gotten bad sick over the past days, and she'd told Tre he had to be the man. It was up to him.

He ran into the apartment, ignoring the smell of vomit and spoiled food. Shorty D stood in his baby bed in the corner wailing, a lone sound in the still of the building. Most folks had left. Gone with the National Guard. Like they should have done. But Talia wouldn't leave because she said the old people had to go first. And she hadn't found Aunt Cici.

Tre pulled out the bundle from his shirt and ran to the closet. They had a place they hid stuff. G-Slim had used it to hide drugs, but now Talia used it to hide the gun, bullets and other stuff they didn't want anyone to find. Tre lifted the wood subfloor and jabbed the bundle into the space between the aged joists, tucking it in good, slamming the board back into place and tugging the tired green shag carpet over it. He'd just backed out of the closet when Talia came through the front door, sliding the dead bolt into place and doubling over in pain.

"Get Devontay and go. G-Slim ain't waitin'. He mad and we ain't got time."

"Mama—"

"You do what I say, Trevon."

"Yes, ma'am," he said, grabbing Shorty D, who still cried. Tre jabbed a pacifier in the toddler's mouth and Shorty stopped whining. "Come on, Shorty. We gonna play a game. Gonna be fun."

Tre dragged his brother over the bed's rail and sat him on his hip. He grabbed the dirty cloth diaper bag sitting on the table, shouldering it as he moved to the bedroom, sparing a parting look at his mother, and at the room where his only worthwhile possession sat on his bed—his saxophone. Couldn't carry it with him. Shorty D was too big as is.

"I'm scared, Mama."

"No time for scared. You's a man now."

"Come with us," Tre said, shifting his brother to his other arm. He didn't care that the tears fell on his cheeks. G-Slim would kill his mama if he got hold of her. Talia wasn't strong enough. He couldn't believe she'd fired a gun and stood up to G-Slim earlier.

"I'll come when you safe. Go. Now."

Tre moved quickly because it was all he could do. He flung open the closet, stepping over his few pairs of shoes, pulled the air-conditioning vent from where it sat under a makeshift shelf. It was a false front, put in by whoever had the apartment before them. The hole led to a small space in the wall, which led to a similar vent in the apartment next door—Miss Janie's apartment. No one had ever questioned the vents, though the projects didn't have no air-conditioning.

Shorty D fussed as Tre scraped his head on the crumbling drywall. "Shh, Shorty, shh."

The toddler quieted and laid his head on Tre's shoulder. Tre patted his brother's back and pulled the grate into place. For a moment, he paused, trying to hear his mother. Trying to decide if he really had to take Shorty D and go find a policeman.

Then he heard the door break open and his mama scream. Gunfire made him clap his hand over Shorty D's mouth.

More gunfire before his mama yelled, "Run!"

Tre choked back a sob as he punched in the grate in Miss Janie's apartment, pushed past a small cabinet hiding the secret entrance and headed for the window and the ancient fire escape.

Shorty clung to Tre as if he knew what was going down, as if he knew his life depended on holding on.

As if he knew his father was next door killing their mother.

Tre set Shorty D down so he could open the crumbling window. G-Slim would figure things out soon enough... unless he was dead. Tre couldn't count on that so he snatched up Shorty D, climbed out onto the iron scaffolding and shut down his mind, focusing on simply breathing.

Just breathe, Tre. In. Out. Breathe.

CHAPTER ONE

New Orleans, 2013

"HOT GUY AT TWO O'CLOCK," Pansy McAdams said, craning her head around the form mannequin and peering out the window.

Eleanor Theriot rolled her eyes and swiped her dust cloth over the spindles of the rocker she knelt beside. "You think half of New Orleans is hot."

"No, I'm just optimistic."

"Or need a good optometrist."

Pansy didn't turn her head from whoever had drawn her attention. "I have perfect vision, thank you very much, and this one is worth the drool I'll have to wipe off the glass."

Eleanor pushed past Pansy, who'd plastered her nose to the window of the Queen's Box. Eleanor could only imagine the picture her friend and employee presented to passersby. Pig nose.

But no actual drool.

"Let me be the judge," Eleanor said, playing along. Pansy had spent the past month reminding Eleanor of her resolution to get back into the dating game. When Eleanor had examined her life, as everyone is wont to do on New Year's Day, she'd discovered her home felt empty, and most of her lingerie had been purchased from a wholesale club. Time to start dating again, to start claiming a new life for herself outside widowhood and motherhood. Up until now, Eleanor had been good at ignoring the male sex—hot or otherwise—but today,

Eleanor felt game. Maybe it was the phone call earlier from her mom, who had cut out an article about healthy living for the premenopausal woman.

Not that Eleanor was going through menopause.

Yet.

So an innocent ogle sounded…harmless.

Across the street, in front of the place where tradesmen had been streaming in and out like worker bees, was a pickup truck. Leaning against the side of that truck was someone who made her swallow. Hard.

Pansy *soooo* didn't need glasses.

The man resembled an Aztec prince. Like his honeyed skin should be twined in gold and turquoise, bedecked in a feathered headdress. And a loincloth. He'd be breathtaking in a loincloth.

"Told ya," Pansy said, shouldering Eleanor out of the way. "He could eat crackers, chips and freakin' beignets in my bed any day of the week."

"Not sure your husband would appreciate an extra bed-mate."

"Eddie lets the dog sleep with us. What's one more hairy beast?" Pansy straightened the ceremonial Mayan mask that sat next to the silver candelabra in the window display before sliding off the edge of the window stage, her long body loose and loping. Pansy was over six feet tall, flat-footed and thin to the point of painful, but she had a sharp sense of humor and a heart that was big, fat and full of good cheer. Like Santa Claus in Olive Oyl's body.

Eleanor glanced again at the man standing beside the pickup, peering at his phone. He wore well-worn jeans and a long-sleeved T-shirt. His face had a sort of sexy Brad Pitt thing going on with sensuous lips, but his jaw was hard, nose straight, brows dark and drawn to a V as he tapped on the phone. His skin was a creamy café au lait and his hair jet-black, clipped close to his head. Broad shoulders and narrow hips finished off the visual treat. A damn chocolate cupcake from Butterfield's Bakery wasn't as tempting as this man.

"Hey," Pansy whispered over Eleanor's shoulder, making her jump. "You should go get him and see how you like sleeping on cracker crumbs."

"I already know I don't like sleeping on cracker crumbs."

"With the right guy, you'll never feel 'em. Trust me."

Running a hand over a well-crafted Federal chest of drawers, Eleanor turned to Pansy and wiggled her fingers. "Dust."

"Chicken."

Eleanor wasn't going outside to talk to a guy leaning against a work truck. She wasn't that kind of girl. Never had been…even if she was determined to get out there…wherever "there" was. "No way."

"Candy ass."

"Calling me names won't work. Get the lemon oil and let's make sure our pieces up front look pretty. Tourists will be pouring in with Mardi Gras weekend coming up. I could use some sales."

Pansy propped her fists on angular hips and narrowed her piercing blue eyes. "Come on, El. What will it hurt to do a little flirting? You'll probably never see him again and you need to get your feet wet. Beyond time, sugar."

Yeah, it was way beyond time. That's what her daughter, Blakely, had yelled at her over a month ago—to get her own life. But Eleanor wasn't going outside and getting her feet wet with some random house painter. Even if she'd never see him again. Even if it was harmless, silly and somewhat daring. "I'm moving on, Pansy. I am. I even checked out that eHarmony site last night, but I'm not the kind of girl who goes up to a random guy and says, uh, I wouldn't even know what to say."

"Pretend you're locked out and need a screwdriver or something to jimmy the lock. I'll hide in the back."

"Jimmy the lock? Who are you? Nancy Drew?"

Pansy faked an elaborate laugh. "You're so funny. Share it with the sex god across the street. Unless you're…chicken?"

Eleanor looked around the antiques store that had been her salvation, first after the hurricane and then after the sex scandal, and felt the security she always did when she really thought about who she was. Did she want to be another relic of the past like the beautiful pieces in her store? Hmm. Pansy was right. Blakely was right. She needed to step out and get a life. "Okay. Fine."

Pansy froze. "Really?"

"Yeah, what'll it hurt? Not like I'll see him again."

Pansy pulled Eleanor to her, snatching the ponytail holder from Eleanor's hair. "Ow!"

"Hold still," Pansy said, tugging strands of Eleanor's hair around her face and studying it critically.

Eleanor batted her hands away. "Jeez, Pans."

"Let me grab the coral-rose lip gloss I bought at Sephora. It will look nice with those new red highlights you just put in."

"I'm—"

"Shh," Pansy said, pressing a finger against Eleanor's lips. "He's a little out of your league so we need to prepare you for—"

"Please." Eleanor pushed past her friend and tucked her shirt into her new gold Lilly Pulitzer belt. "He'll be gone before you could perform all that magic. Besides, he's *not* out of my league. Forget the lip gloss."

"Whoa, that's my sassy girl," Pansy called, scurrying to the back of the store, thin arms and knobby knees moving so fast she resembled a clumsy puppy. She sank behind the counter, leaving only her eyes visible. "I'll hide back here so he buys the story."

"This is nuts," Eleanor proclaimed.

Pansy's hand emerged over the register, shooing her toward the door. "Just go."

Taking a deep breath, Eleanor pushed the glass door, ignoring the dinging of the sleigh bells affixed to the knob, and stepped onto Magazine Street, which had started waking up for the day. She shut the door behind her, slapped a hand to her forehead and patted her pockets.

Damn, she was a good actress.

She started toward hunky painter dude, looking both ways before crossing the street 'cause she'd learned that rule when she was seven years old. The closer she got, the hotter—and younger—the guy looked.

God, this was stupid. Pansy was right. The man was out of her league.

Too hot for her.

Too young for her.

She needed to go back to her store and abandon the whole ruse, but as she began to turn, he lifted his head and caught her gaze.

Oh, dear Lord. Eyes the color of smoke swept over her and something shivery flew right up her spine. It wasn't casual or dismissive. Oddly enough, the gaze felt…profound.

Or maybe she needed to drink less coffee. She must be imagining the connection between them. It had been almost twenty years since she'd tried to pick up a man, so she was out of practice. That was it. She imagined his interest.

He lifted his eyebrows questioningly, and she tried to remember what she was supposed to ask him. A horn honked and she turned her head.

Yeah. She stood in the middle of the street like a moron.

The Aztec sex god turned his head and nodded toward the car. "You gonna move?"

"Yeah," she said, stepping onto the sidewalk. She licked

her lips, wishing she'd put on the stupid lip gloss. Not only did she look stupid, but her lips were bare. Eleanor the Daring was appalled by Eleanor the Unprepared, who had shown up in her stead.

"Can I help you?"

You can if you toss me over your shoulder, take me to your temple and play sacrifice the not-exactly-a-virgin on your stone pillar of lust.

But she didn't say that, of course.

"I'm looking for a screw," she said.

DEZ BATISTE LOWERED his phone and stared at the woman. "I beg your pardon?"

"Huh?"

"You asked for a screw?" he repeated.

She turned the color of the red tiles that framed the doorway behind her. "No. I didn't ask you—uh, I meant a screw-*driver.*"

He almost laughed because he could see where her thoughts had jumped to…which was kind of cute.

He'd parked in front of the club five minutes ago, pissed he couldn't get his damn contractor to show up. He'd dialed Chris Salmon three times, but hung up each time he heard the voice mail. He wasn't in a good mood, didn't need some woman bothering him, but when he'd really looked at this one, he had put his bad mood on pause.

"A screw*driver?*"

She nodded and a chunk of hair fell from behind her ear. She pushed it back.

"At first I thought you were propositioning me." He smiled to let her know he wouldn't bite. At least not hard.

Her face turned even redder. "Heavens, no. I just got distracted, uh, by that car." She glanced at the antiques store across the street and rolled her shoulders.

"Why do you need a screwdriver?" he asked, liking what his questions were doing to her. Why? He hadn't the foggiest. There was simply something about her that made him want to peel away layers.

"The stupid lock to the store is messed up, and I'm locked out. No one else is here yet, and I don't have an extra key."

He glanced inside the truck. "Don't have one out here, but I can check to see if anyone left something you can use inside."

She caught her lower lip between her teeth, drawing his attention to the perfect pinkness of her mouth. Soft. As if she'd been painted upon canvas and intentionally smudged. Her fire-streaked hair with a stubborn flip fell to her collarbone, which was visible beneath a shirt the color of ripe watermelon. "I suppose I could ask Mr. Hibbett at Butterfield's. He might have one."

Not wanting to miss an opportunity to make friends in the area, he held out a hand. "I'm Dez Batiste. Let me unlock the door, and we'll see if there's something you can use. Wouldn't want to bother Mr. Hibbett, would we?"

Her gaze lifted to his. "Batiste? As in the guy who wants to open the nightclub?"

His fascination with the woman immediately nose-dived. Five months ago, he'd chosen to roll the dice on an Uptown location for his nightclub rather than a place on Frenchmen Street. Tremé might be the hottest jazz scene in New Orleans, but Dez was pretty sure his old neighborhood near the Garden District would welcome the upscale club opening in less than a month. However, there had been opposition to Blue Rondo from some of the merchants. He'd recently received a letter from the Magazine Street Merchants Association questioning the judiciousness of opening a business that could potentially harm the family-friendly atmosphere. It hadn't been "welcoming" at all. More like holding a veiled threat of ill will. "I'm Dez Batiste, the guy who *will* open a nightclub."

He started to lower his hand, but she took it. "I'm Eleanor Theriot, owner of the Queen's Box." She hiked a thumb over her shoulder toward the large glass-front store directly across the street from where they stood.

"Oh," he said, noting the warmth of her grasp, the sharpness in her gaze and the scent of her perfume, which reminded him of summer nights. He knew who she was, had seen that name before. On the bottom of a complaint to the city council. One of his friends had scored a copy and given him a heads-up.

She dropped her hand. "I assumed you were a worker or something."

"Why, because I'm ethnic?"

Her eyes widened. "No. That's insulting."

He lifted his eyebrows but said nothing.

"You're dressed like you were coming to work or something." She gestured to his old jeans and faded T-shirt, her face no longer as yielding.

Okay, he *was* dressed in paint-streaked clothes, and the truck had Emilio's Painting plastered to the door, so maybe Eleanor wasn't drawing incorrect conclusions. Because though his grandfather was black, his grandmother Creole and his mother Cuban, Dez didn't look any distinctive race. "Yeah. Okay."

For a moment they stood, each regarding the other. Dez regretted the shift in mood. He'd wanted to flirt with her, maybe score her digits, but now there was nothing but a bad taste.

"I'd wondered about you, a renowned New Orleans musician returning to open a club in the old Federal Bank," Eleanor said, glancing up at the crumbling brick before returning her gaze to him. Those green eyes looked more guarded than before. "So why here in this part of New Orleans? Aren't there better places for a nightclub?"

"Uptown is where I'm from," Dez said, folding his arms

across his chest and eyeing the antiques dealer with her expensive clothes and obvious intolerance for anyone not wearing seersucker and named something like Winston. "What? I don't meet your expectations 'cause I'm not drunk? Or strung out on crack?"

Her eyes searched his, and in them, he saw a shift, as if a decision had been made that instant. "And you don't have horns. I'd thought you'd have horns…unless they're retractable?"

She didn't smile as she delivered the line. It was given smoothly, as if she knew they were headed toward rocky shores and needed to steer clear. So he picked up a paddle and allowed them to drift back into murky waters. "Retractable horns are a closely guarded musician's secret. Who ratted me out?"

Eleanor locked her mouth with an imaginary key.

"Guess a screwdriver wouldn't help?"

She shook her head.

Again, silence.

It was an intensely odd moment with a woman he'd resented without knowing much about her, with a woman who opposed his very dream, with a woman who made him want to trace the curve of her jaw. He'd never been in such a situation.

"Just two things before I go back over there and walk through that very much unlocked door," she said with a resolute crossing of her arms.

"Really? The door's not even locked?" He arched an eyebrow.

"A ploy to come check you out dreamed up by my not-so-savvy salesclerk. Totally tanked on the whole thing from beginning to end. It's pretty embarrassing."

"I'm flattered. Thank your salesclerk for me."

Her direct stare didn't waver. "Oh, come on, don't even

pretend you're not the object of a lot of 'Can I borrow your pen?' or 'Do you know what time it is?'"

"Wait, those are pickup lines?" he asked with a deadpan expression. There was something he liked in her straightforwardness along with the soft-glowy thing she had going. Not quite wholesome. More delicate and flowery. This woman wasn't lacquered up with lip gloss and a shirt so low her nipples nearly showed. Instead she begged to be unwrapped like a rare work of art.

He shook himself, remembering she was a high-class broad and not his type.

"Maybe not pickups per se, but definitely designed to get your attention," she said, sounding more college professor than woman on the prowl. Or maybe she wasn't really interested in him. Perhaps she'd known who he was in the first place and wanted to goad him, size him up before he made trouble.

Dez leaned against the truck he'd borrowed from his neighbor since his Mustang was in the shop. "So what did you want to tell me?"

"One." She held up an elegant finger. He'd never called a finger *elegant* before, but hers fit the billing. "I oppose the idea of a nightclub in this particular area. All the business owners here have worked hard since the storm to build a certain atmosphere that does not include beer bottles and half-dressed hookers."

He opened his mouth to dispute, but she held up a second finger.

"And, two, this little—" she wagged her other hand between them "—thing didn't happen. Erase it from you memory. Chalk it up to midlife crisis, to a dare, or bad tuna fish I ate last night."

"What are you talking about?"

She frowned. "Me trying to check you out."

Something warmed inside him. Pleasure. "I don't even remember why you walked over."

A little smile accompanied the silent thank-you in her eyes.

Dez answered the smile with one of his own, and for a few seconds they stood in the midst of Magazine Street smiling at each other like a couple of loons, which was crazy considering the tenseness only seconds ago.

"Okay, then," she said, inching back toward her store.

"Yeah," he said, not moving. Mostly because he wanted to watch her walk back to her store and check out the view.

"So hopefully I won't see you around," she said lightly, turning away, giving him what he wanted without even realizing it.

"Don't count on it," he said, playing along.

She didn't say anything. Just kept walking.

"Hey," he called as she stepped onto the opposite curb. She turned around and shaded her eyes against the morning sunlight. "I'm going to change your mind, you know."

"About?"

"My club and the reason why you came over here."

He straightened and gave her a nod of his head and one of his sexy trademark smiles, one he hadn't used since he'd left Houston.

And from across the street, he could see Ms. Eleanor Theriot looked worried.

Good. She should be…because he meant it. His club wouldn't draw hookers or anyone who would smash a beer bottle on the pavement. Nor would it draw the sort of club-goers who would break windows or vomit in the street. No rowdy college crowd or blue-collar drunks.

Blue Rondo was different—the kernel of a dream that had bloomed in his heart when everything else around him had fallen apart. The idea of an upscale New Orleans jazz club had sustained him through heartbreak and heartache. Had given him sanctuary when the waters erased all he'd been, and the woman he thought would be his wife had turned into someone he didn't know. Seven damn years wasted and all he'd held on to was the dream of Blue Rondo, the club named after "Blue Rondo à la Turk," the first song his father had played for him when he'd been a boy.

And no one was going to take that away from him.

Not when he'd risked so much to get here.

Not when he'd finally faced his past and embraced New Orleans as his future.

So, yeah, she could strike number one off her list.

And as Eleanor stood staring at him on the opposite side of the street, he knew she could strike number two off, too. She may not want him to remember her "attention-getter," but his interest was piqued.

Straightforward eyes the color of moss.

Lush pink lips.

Ivory satin skin.

Color him interested.

Dez tucked away that idea, turned and contemplated the faded building behind him—the old Federal Bank that would house his dream. He sighed.

Another wasted morning.

He could have slept in after a late night in the Quarter playing with Frankie B's trio. They'd stretched it out until the wee hours, playing sanitized versions of tourist favorites, and he'd made plenty of dime. The city had started seeping back into him.

Dez checked his messages once again. Still no Chris. So he pulled up his schedule. He could spare a few hours cutting tile for the bathroom floors before he needed to head back to the place he'd leased a few blocks over and grab a shower. He had another gig at seven o'clock that night, but wanted to stop in and talk to a couple friends who'd opened some places in the Warehouse District about glassware and distributors.

Dreams could come true, but only with lots of work.

He pulled his keys from his pocket and headed toward his soon-to-be jazz club.

ELEANOR BACKED INTO the glass front door, spun around and yanked it open.

Pansy's head popped up from behind the counter like a jack-in-the-box. "What happened?"

Steadying her nerves, Eleanor closed the door and flipped the sign to read Open. "Nothing."

Pansy slid out. "Nothing?"

"He's cute," she said, busying herself by straightening the collection of early-American brass candlesticks displayed on the shelf of a gorgeous cypress cupboard.

Eleanor didn't want to look at Pansy until she got her emotions under control. Dez Batiste had stirred up so many things inside her—anger, embarrassment…desire.

He'd been so damn sensual. Like a jungle cat, all powerful, sexy and dangerous. His body had been at once tight and muscular, yet he moved with a loose-limbed grace, a sort of lazy insolence. Up close, he'd been droolworthy, with stormy eyes contrasting against deep-honeyed skin, with his manly jaw contrasting with the poutiness of his mouth. Just utterly delicious like a New Orleans praline.

And he'd allowed her some dignity, playing along when she stupidly admitted her crappy attempt to engage him. It had been admirable, and somehow made him even sexier.

Pansy loomed over her like a winged harpy. "Cute? That's all I'm getting? Cute?"

"What? You want a play-by-play?"

"Duh."

"Fine. I said 'hello' and he said 'hello' and I felt stupid. And he said, 'I'm Dez Batiste,' and then I said—"

"The Dez Batiste?"

Eleanor stopped fiddling with the candlesticks. "The Dez Batiste who's opening the nightclub. The Dez Batiste you threw your panties at back in '04. The Dez Batiste who—"

"OMG!" Pansy clasped her hands and ran to the window. "Can't believe I didn't make the connection. He's more filled out than he was back then. Seems taller, but then again he stayed at the piano the one time I saw him. Oh, but the way he played. Like he made love to that piano. I swear to God, I'd never seen anything like it. I got wet just watching him."

"Pansy." Eleanor made a frowny face.

"Oh, don't be such a Puritan." Pansy glanced at Eleanor. "But I'm not kidding. I felt guilty looking at Eddie for the rest of the week, but don't worry, I didn't throw *those* panties."

"Too much information."

Pansy laughed. "Uh, right. He was too young anyway, but I did have some of those *The Graduate* fantasies."

"The man's trying to bring in a bar when we just got rid of Maggio's. Don't you remember wading through puke to open the store? Or how about the night you worked late and someone broke into your car? Or maybe you'll remember the drunk asleep in the alcove who pooped by the garbage bin?"

Pansy twisted her lips. "But it's Dez Batiste. He's back in New Orleans. And I can't imagine that he'd—"

"A bar is a bar. It's not going to bring us business. It will only be a headache. Trust me."

Pansy walked toward the register. "You need to get laid."

"You need to do your job," Eleanor said, heading for the rear of the store and her small office, which was crammed into a room the size of a coat closet. Damn Pansy for not being on her side.

"I do my job every day," Pansy called, her tone slightly

hurt but more perturbed. Pansy didn't take crap off anyone... not even her employers and friend. "And you still need a good f—"

"Don't say it," Eleanor growled, slamming her office door, blocking out Pansy and her unwanted advice.

Eleanor sank against the door and gave a heavy sigh.

Sweet Mary Mother of Jesus, she'd been such a fool.

Dez Batiste.

He wasn't what she'd expected. Oh, Pansy had raved for days after finding out Dez Batiste and his partner had bought the old building across from them. Oddly enough, Eleanor had prayed for someone to snap up the old bank with its pretty mosaic tiles flanking its doors and the interesting fresco reliefs trimming the upper floor. But she'd hoped for a yarn shop or an organic health food store.

Not a nightclub.

Run by a hot young jazz musician.

Well, she wasn't going to think about how hot he was or the sort of challenge he'd flung back at her.

He'd change her mind.

Huh.

Not likely.

Even if she'd likely have erotic fantasies about him all night long.

Pansy was right. She needed to get laid.

CHAPTER TWO

TRE JACKSON LIFTED the heavy bookcase with ease and placed the piece where Mrs. Dupuy indicated it should sit in her husband's den. The bottom slipped a little on the slick Oriental carpet, but settled snug against the ornate baseboard.

"Perfect, darling," the older white lady trilled, clapping together hands with fingernails tipped in fancy white polish. She then ran one hand along the aged wormwood that had been painstakingly restored. "Tommy loves pieces with history, and it's perfect."

Tre stood back and nodded, though he had no idea why anyone would want some old piece of furniture with marks and grooves all in it. He just didn't get white people. Why buy something old when you could have something new, something solid steel, something that wouldn't rot? But rich white ladies strolled into the Queen's Box and dropped crazy money on old stuff all the time.

But he didn't have to understand antiques junkies to do his job. For the past few months he'd been working for Eleanor Theriot, and he wasn't sure how it had happened. One minute he was standing there looking at the help-wanted sign, the next he was filling out a W-2. Crazy stupid to be working for someone who could have him arrested in the blink of an eye, but he'd needed a job…and that sign had called out to him.

Mrs. Dupuy turned toward him, handed him two twenty-dollar bills and gave him a weird smile.

This particular crazy white people habit didn't bother him

so much. Rich ladies always tipped good unless they were real old. Real old ladies—black, white or purple-polka-dotted—didn't part with money too easy. He bobbed his head. "Thank you, Mrs. Dupuy."

"Oh, no. Thank you, Tre. And please tell Eleanor she made a good find with that piece. Exactly what I envisioned," she said, smiling at walls the color of blood and sweeping a hand toward blossomy drapes. "Now if I could only find an antique secretary's desk to fit between those two windows. You tell her to be on the lookout, you hear?"

"Yes, ma'am. I will." He slid toward the wide double doors that opened to the marble foyer. Mrs. Winnie Dupuy was a lonely woman, spending much of her time shopping for things her too-busy husband might like. Which meant she could talk a blue streak if someone took up the other end of the conversation. Tre wasn't. He had another delivery to make and it was across town. Had to get going if he wanted to make his brother's game on the West Bank later that afternoon.

"You want a drink or something? I can get you a Coke or…maybe something stronger? Bourbon maybe? Or vodka?" Mrs. Dupuy asked, cocking her head like a little bird. She wore a pink dress that showed off her bosom and little clicky heels that rat-a-tatted on the hardwood floors. A strange bored-housewife gleam in her eye made him hurry his steps. She followed, running a tongue over her top lip then biting her lower. "Or if there's something else you want? Something not on the menu maybe?"

It wasn't as if he hadn't had fantasies about a little something-something with a client or two. Some of the women he made deliveries to were fine, but Mrs. Dupuy was too skinny, too straight, and her husband was a judge. Besides, he had to get to Devontay's game in three hours.

Better not even think about it.

"No, thank you, Mrs. Dupuy. I gotta get back to the—"

"Oh, sure. No problem," she said, looking nervous, as though she knew he could read her thoughts and suddenly her unstated invitation was too real. She followed him out the room into the foyer and opened the large door painted black as sin. Sunlight tumbled in like a smack of reality upside the head. Mrs. Dupuy blinked, appeared confused. "Well, thanks again."

"Sure," he said, stepping onto the brick stoop.

The door shut behind him softly, like an apology, as he walked to the delivery van. He didn't really blame Winnie Dupuy for not wanting to feel so empty. He knew what it was like to feel as if no one cared, to want some simple comfort, a human touch. He didn't fault her…but he couldn't oblige her and still be the man he wanted to be.

The man he'd promised his mama all those years ago.

The van was warm, which was good, considering a cold wind had picked up. New Orleans wasn't cold in February, but it wasn't warm either. The seat felt good against his jeans. He'd just pulled out of the driveway when his cell rang.

It was Big Mama—she always called this time of day.

"Yo, Big Mama, you get your applesauce cake yet?"

"I've done got it, sugar. Merlene had some with me, though she ain't as fond of it. You workin'?" Big Mama's voice was still frail. His grandmother had been sick a long time and he hated she had to be in the nursing facility. But what could he do? Neither he nor his aunt Cici could take care of her.

"Yes, ma'am. I'm getting off in a few hours for Devontay's game. They playing at Erhet today."

"You gonna call me and let me know how he do, ain't you?"

"Yes, ma'am. I know you'd skin me alive if I didn't." Tre smiled as he swerved around the oncoming traffic and headed toward the store on Magazine. Luckily, he had only one more delivery, and it was a Queen Anne settee. Since the delivery was on the West Bank, Eleanor said he could take the van over the bridge—as long as he locked it up tight—and make Shorty D's game.

"How's Cici getting on with that new job? She going in on time, ain't she? I worry about her."

"Yes, ma'am, she doin' fine." Kind of. His aunt had missed work a few weeks ago and had to plead with the shift manager to put her on probation. Since then, she'd done good, making it on time every day, but he was worried because she'd started hanging with her former girls, going out, leaving Kenzie with him. Tre had threatened to call Child Protective Services if she went out anymore. He didn't like threatening his aunt, but his cousin Kenzie needed a mother who wasn't strung out and banging with the 3-N-G, a local street gang that hung on Third and Galvez.

He wasn't worrying Big Mama about Cici or anything else. Her health wouldn't tolerate no worrying. He wanted her to get stronger so maybe she could come back and breathe some life into that rambling house of hers where they all lived. Things weren't the same with Big Mama gone. It had been too long since he'd smelled greens and hocks cooking and tasted her fried corn bread. Been too long since he'd heard her laughter in the kitchen and felt the tenderness in her faded hands.

"The doctor says maybe I can come home 'fore too long. They still working me to death, but I'm walking pretty good now. Maybe won't be long, chile."

Big Mama had fallen and broken her hip almost seven months ago. After extensive surgery, she'd done well, until the pneumonia had set in several weeks later. She'd been in a nursing facility ever since, determined she wouldn't live out her days at Plantation Manor.

"That's good. You keep doin' what they tell you. Dr. Tom said you'll be home to dye Easter eggs for Kenzie."

Big Mama cackled. "Lordy, that's in two months. I need to see that baby hide her eggs. Gotta make her a dress, too."

Tre drove through the alley between the Queen's Box and a vintage clothing store, and put the van in Park. A loading platform on his right led up to rusted double doors. "I've got to go now. Got to make another delivery before I can get out of here."

"Tre, you don't worry about me. You got enough to worry about. Try to take some time for yourself, chile. You not even twenty years old yet."

He felt a hell of a lot older. "I know. I got time."

His grandmother huffed but didn't say more, and after promising again to call her about Devontay's game, he hung up.

Pocketing the keys, he slid from the van, careful to lock it. As he came around the side of the van, Eleanor met him.

"Hey, Tre, we need to talk if you have a minute."

He looked up, sensing what was coming. Winnie Dupuy had called. "Yeah?"

"Mrs. Dupuy called me a few moments ago." Eleanor held tight to the door, looking embarrassed. "Is there something you want to tell me?"

"No, ma'am."

"Oh, well, she said you made her feel uncomfortable. Uh, like in a sexual way." Eleanor stared him in the eyes and he could see her discomfort, but she didn't shy away. He, at least, liked that about her.

"No, ma'am."

Eleanor looked hard at him and nodded. "She's lonely."

Folding his arms over his chest, he met her gaze. "Yeah, I guess she is."

For a moment they were both silent. Her studying him. Him bearing her scrutiny, defensive on the outside, hoping she believed him on the inside. As the seconds ticked by,

Eleanor's posture changed. Relief gathered in him because he knew she'd worked out the facts rather than jumping to conclusions.

"Winnie propositioned you?"

"What you mean?"

Eleanor rolled a hand, still looking as though she'd rather clean toilets than have this conversation with him. "Make a pass? Come on to you?"

"Why you think that?"

"Because the more I think on it, the more I see the flaw in this accusation. Winnie's husband ignores her, she's lonely and you're awfully nice-looking," she said, holding open the heavy steel door and jerking her head toward the black yawn that led into the back room. "She's a good customer, but I don't necessarily believe you'd have to hit on older ladies when you've likely got plenty of girls your own age blowing up your phone."

The knot in his gut unraveled as he started up the steps. Eleanor believed him over Winnie Dupuy. The thought startled him, put a dent in the shield of mistrust he kept between him and his employer. Between him and everyone. "Did you just say 'blowing up my phone'?"

Eleanor made a face. "Blakely says that all the time. Guess it seeped into my vocabulary without me noticing."

Tre didn't smile much, but he had to smile at her admission. He hadn't yet met her daughter, since Blakely was away at college, but from the way Eleanor talked about her, she had attitude to spare. He liked a girl with attitude. Someone who wasn't all mealymouthed. His Big Mama had always said to never trust mealymouths. They're the sneaky ones.

"I'm sorry Mrs. Dupuy accused you of something so awful."

He shrugged. "Don't matter."

Eleanor stopped him, pressing a hand to his shoulder. He flinched, but didn't pull away. "It does matter."

"She just embarrassed is all."

He met Eleanor's gaze and an understanding lit in them. He knew she saw he tried to be an honorable man—the kind of man Big Mama would be proud of. The kind of man who didn't screw lonely old white women just 'cause he could. He had pride, integrity and respect for himself.

Eleanor could see all that in his gaze.

The dent grew wider.

"Maybe so, but I'll take care of it. She can't make those kinds of accusations against my employees and think it's okay. Go ahead and wrap the Queen Anne and get it over to the Wilkies. Sign out for three o'clock and then you should be able to make Shorty D's game."

Devontay's nickname sounded funny on Eleanor's lips. "Thank you."

Eleanor closed the door and started for her office. "Oh, and tell Shorty D I'll buy him a Tastee doughnut for every point he scores."

Tre shook his head. "He scored ten last time."

She smiled. "I know. I'll plan on picking up a dozen."

ELEANOR SHRUGGED OUT of her khaki pants and tossed her new T-shirt on top of the laundry hamper in the corner of her bathroom. Fragrant lavender perfumed the air as her bath filled, automatically soothing her, pulling her mind away from Winnie Dupuy's tirade, Blakely's request for more money and her mother-in-law's message on the answering service. Margaret Theriot didn't like to be ignored. Or so she said.

So many people giving her grief.

And no one to take it away.

Eleanor eyed the old claw-foot tub, hoping her best bath salts would do the trick. Her day had been longer than most because she'd had to run errands after work, including the dreaded grocery store. Before she could blink it was a quarter of eleven o'clock and past her bedtime.

She snorted as she grabbed her toothbrush. "God, you're acting like an old person, Elle. In bed by ten o'clock is sealing your doom, baby."

She didn't respond to her own taunts. What could she possibly say? Then the cell phone sitting on her dressing table buzzed. She picked it up and eyed the number. Margaret. Again. Shouldn't her mother-in-law be in bed?

She tossed the phone down, peeled off her underwear and put her hair in an old scrunchy. No friggin' way would she let Skeeter's mother ruin the most precious time of the day: her cocktail bath.

Grabbing the highball glass, she sank into the tub and used her big toe to turn off the hot water.

"Ahhh," she said to the wall on her right.

The wall said nothing in return…as well it shouldn't. After all, she'd only started on the drink.

The swirl of the water around her felt like a sweet embrace as she slid down, burying her nose in the soft bubbles as the phone jittered again. And then again. Then the home phone jangled in the hallway.

"I'm not answering you, damn it!" she called out, studying the chipped polish on her left toenail as she took a sip of her vodka tonic.

Vodka tonic—one of the many good things her late husband Skeeter Theriot had taught her to love. Every night before they'd gone out to art exhibits or political fund-raisers, they'd indulged in the drink and conversation about what they should say, who they should pander to and why they needed to keep the goal in mind.

Ha.

An illusion built like a house of cards.

But the past didn't bear dwelling upon, did it? All that hurt and bitterness was supposed to be locked up, chained with determination and dumped in the nearest pit of forgotten dreams.

Eleanor closed her eyes and focused on the good things she had in her life—a store, a healthy daughter, another year before she turned forty. And Nutella. A whole new jar in the pantry.

She'd just grabbed the handmade green-tea soap and a soft cloth when the doorbell rang.

"Really?" she said to the ceiling, blowing an errant bubble off her shoulder. "All I want is a bath. And a drink. And some blasted peace!"

She stood, grabbed her plush terry-cloth robe and padded to the door, not bothering with the water streaming down her legs. She'd mop it up once she dealt with whatever person continued to lean on her doorbell. Eleanor stomped down the stairs, shouting, "Coming!"

When she peeked out the door peephole, her heart stopped.

A uniformed police officer stood beneath her gas lantern porch light, hat in hand. A cruiser was parked in her drive.

With a shaking hand, Eleanor set the crystal tumbler on the late-nineteenth-century telephone table next to the door. A cannonball landed in her stomach; her mouth suddenly became a desert. Last time a policeman had stood on her porch, she'd learned her husband had been murdered...by a mistress she hadn't known existed.

Please, dear God, don't let it be Blakely. Please.

Eleanor tugged the belt tighter and turned the lock, pulling the door open. Cold crept in, matching the fear in her heart. "Yes?"

"Eleanor Theriot?"

"Yes?"

"We've been trying to call you on your cell and home

phone," the officer said, his dark eyes shifting away from her disheveled appearance.

"Why? What's happened?"

He read her fear. "No one's hurt. Nothing like that—"

"What then?" Eleanor fussed with the collar of her robe and peered around the police officer as if he might be hiding something horrible behind his back.

"Someone vandalized your store. Some guy from one of the other businesses hit gave us your numbers, but you didn't answer. I was in the area, so dispatch sent me over."

Sweet relief stole over her. Blakely was safe. This was not about her daughter. But then realization hit her. Her store had been vandalized. What did that mean? Broken windows? Items stolen? Her heart skipped a beat. "I'll head down there. Thanks."

"Dispatch said other merchants are on-site, so you have time to, you know…" he stammered, nodding toward her. She looked down at where her robe gaped and jerked it closed.

"Thank you for coming by," she said, as he backed down the front porch steps and turned toward the open door of his police car. She shut the door, twisted the lock and scrambled up the gleaming stairway.

Fifteen minutes later she pulled her Volvo to the curb in front of her store and hopped out, clad in an old sweatshirt of Skeeter's and a pair of jeans. Her teeth chattered as she approached the glass glittering beneath the streetlights.

"Damn," she breathed, surveying the damage. Whoever had vandalized the store had done a bang-up job. Like serious bang-up. How had no one seen him…or them?

"Got me, too," said a voice over her shoulder. She turned to find Dez Batiste standing behind her. He wore a beat-up army surplus jacket and straight-legged jeans that fit him like sin. In the lamplight, his skin seemed darker, making him appear more dangerous, and it finally hit her who he resembled—that wrestler-turned-actor who'd done a movie in a tutu. She couldn't recall his name, but she and Blakely had gone to the movie a few years back.

She peered across the street to the spidered glass in Dez's window. "How did this happen? And why didn't my store alarm go off?"

"Don't know," Dez said, his gray eyes probing the depths of her store. "You sure you set yours?"

"Always," she said automatically, even as her thoughts tripped to the actual process of locking up. She always set the alarm before slipping out the back and slamming the dead bolt into place. But she'd been distracted by a last-minute customer who wanted a rush delivery…and by her failed attempt at stepping outside herself to flirt with a man she opposed enough to pen a letter to the city council, a man who now stood before her very much doing his part within the community she wanted to protect. She swallowed the guilt. "At least I usually do."

Dez propped his fists on his hips, making his shoulders look even broader. The planes of his rugged face were exotic in the glow of the streetlight. "Wouldn't have mattered. They think it was kids driving by and shooting pellet guns, so an alarm wouldn't have changed the outcome. Mr. Hibbett has a street cam, so maybe the police can get the license plate off the tape or something."

Maybe they would…or not. Didn't really help the short-term situation. She needed lumber to cover the gaping holes and prevent the current open invitation to her stock. After Hurricane Katrina, and the looting that had followed, she was more cautious than probably necessary, which was why the whole not-setting-the-alarm thing didn't make sense. She slid her phone from her back pocket and started dialing Pansy's number. Her husband sometimes helped with big deliveries and lived close by. Eddie would have plywood ready for storms in his storage shed. He would let her use some until she could get the glass company to come out in the morning. "Better see if I can get some lumber to patch this up."

"Don't worry. I've got plenty left from the remodel," Dez said, jerking his head toward his bar across the street.

She hung up before the call could connect, and nodded. "I'd appreciate it. It would keep me from troubling Pansy and Eddie. And since we're already up…"

Mr. Hibbett approached carrying a toolbox. "Sons of bitches busted my stained-glass rooster. If I get my hands on those little bastards, I'll plant them in Cemetery No. 1."

"I'm sorry, Mr. Hibbett, but Eddie can probably fix it. Let's see how many whole pieces we can salvage and we'll call him tomorrow," she said, giving Mr. Hibbett a pat on the shoulder. The older man had been on Magazine Street for over twenty years, and ran one of the best pastry shops in the Crescent City. Butterfield's, with its sunny decor, delicious cupcakes and strong coffee, was a local favorite, and the stained-glass rooster had been created by Eddie, who was a glass artist. Somehow the fearless visage of the fowl was welcoming.

Mr. Hibbett shook his head. "Maybe so. I'll gather the pieces. Here's my toolbox if you two want to get started on boarding up your windows. I still have to fetch the video loop for the detective."

Dez took the old-fashioned toolbox from the man and set it by her door, which fortunately hadn't been hit. "Let me grab some plywood and I'll be back."

"I'll help you," she said, stepping over the shattered glass and following his broad shoulders.

"I can probably get it myself if you want to stay here."

"And do what?"

"Sweep up the glass?"

His suggestion had merit but for some reason she didn't want to be alone. Which was stupid. The perpetrators were likely random kids, and there was little danger with a police-man standing yards away. Dez must have sensed her hesi-tation because he waved his hand. "Come on, then. I might need an extra set of hands after all."

She followed him across the street, wincing when she saw that the vandals had knocked holes in his art deco door and the one large window that had earlier held the name of the place—Blue Rondo.

She stopped and stared at the ruined window. "That sucks."

Dez looked at the destruction. "Yeah, but it can be fixed."

He opened the front door and stepped back so she could pass. When he reached past her to flick on the light switch, she caught his scent—something woodsy and primal that suited him, and made her very aware of how masculine he was. Of how long it had been since she'd been close to a man she found attractive. Hunger stirred within her. She wanted to touch him, breathe him in.

Light flooded the room and she squeezed her eyes shut against the startling brightness.

"So here we have Satan's lair," he said, wryness shadow-ing his voice along with humor.

She opened her eyes, wondering how he could be jovial when what he'd been working on had been damaged. "Okay, I've never actually called it Satan's lair."

"Den of iniquity? Palace of prostitution?"

Eleanor snorted, shifting back a step because Dez's pres-ence overwhelmed her. "I never said any of those things, Dez. Besides, we don't have time to wade into those waters right now. Maybe another time."

His gaze flickered over her worn jeans and ragged sweat-shirt. She didn't flinch, but a silly voice that sounded a little like her mother's whispered she should have taken a bit more time to fix herself up. At least a brush through her hair.

Shut up, voice. It was an emergency.

"Definitely," he said, with not quite a purr in his voice. Okay. Nothing in his voice indicated he wanted to strip off her clothes, but her fragile ego needed to cling to something, right?

"So where's the plywood?"

He jerked his thumb at the bar. "In the back. Stay here."

With the grace of a jaguar…or maybe just a natural athleticism…Dez disappeared behind the bar, giving her time to look around the club.

Clean gray walls met tiles that glowed with metallic patina, making a unique pattern of charcoal and onyx. Several black tables were piled in a far corner, awaiting placement. Cool cobalt-and-gold-glass pendants hung from the ceiling, above where the tables would eventually sit. A covelike stage with plenty of room for a good-size band was on her left, with a grand piano created by the gods sitting front and center. She'd never thought to see a Fazioli in a club across from her shop, but then again, she'd never thought there'd be a jazz club in her sedate block of Magazine either.

"A Fazioli?" she asked Dez when he returned lugging several sheets of plywood and then sliding them onto a piece of cardboard.

He glanced at the piano, and in his gaze, she saw incredible pride. "Yeah, that's my baby."

The piano didn't look like a regular piano, but she'd known exactly what it was, having seen it in a magazine once. The design was called M. Liminal, and it had a futuristic appearance that seemed at odds with the art deco…yet oddly right.

"I hope you have a crazy-good alarm system."

He slid the boards closer to her. "Who do you think called the police? I was playing a gig on Frenchmen when I got the call from the alarm company."

"Thanks for being Johnny-on-the-spot," she said, walking toward the piano. "This piano's beautiful in a weird way."

Dez leaned the plywood against a support column and joined her next to the stage. "It was a gift."

Eleanor ran a hand over the shiny silver top. "Some gift."

His gaze shuttered as he stepped onto the platform. "Yeah."

He lifted the lid and ran his fingers over the keys, his hands masterful, playing a light run of exceptional beauty. How ironic to see such exquisiteness in the chaos of destruction.

Something shivery skipped up her spine, and the moment felt prophetic, as if there was always the possibility of beauty in the midst of ruin, a truth held tightly in a city crumbling away.

The click of the lid jarred Eleanor from her musings, from her appreciation of the man before her.

"We better get back. It's late," he said, his voice sounding faraway, as if he, too, felt something in the moment.

She glanced at the Timex on her wrist. 11:56 p.m. "Morning's one blink away."

Looking up she caught his gaze and her stomach trembled at the raw desire she saw in his eyes. This time she didn't have to imagine the invitation. The moment crackled with electricity, making her lean toward him rather than take the steps toward the door. For a moment, she wanted something she shouldn't with a man who was so far away from her normal kind of guy he was completely off the charts.

His gaze slid to her lips.

Instinctively, she caught her bottom lip between her teeth.

"Y'all coming?" The voice at the door grumped. Cranky Mr. Hibbett.

Eleanor blinked the intense moment away. "Uh, sorry. I'd never seen a Fazioli before." She pointed to the piano as the older man, whose fuzzy eyebrows knitted together, waved a hand at her and headed toward the leaning plywood.

"Bah. Stare at pianos later. We've got work to do."

Dez leaped off the stage and grabbed the opposite end

of the boards, helping Mr. Hibbett maneuver them out the club door.

Eleanor stood there like a fool, watching.

What was wrong with her?

She scratched her head, jerked the ugly scrunchy from the ponytail and scraped a hand through her hair, wishing she didn't feel so inept, so awkward, so…old.

Dez Batiste was too young for her. Too hip. Too cool. If she wanted to get back into the dating pool, it would be better to don a conservative tankini and slowly descend the steps into the water. Not bling it out in a string bikini and do a swan dive off the high dive into deep waters.

'Cause that's what Dez Batiste was.

Deep waters in a string bikini.

She needed a nice sedate man who sipped Scotch and talked about the stock market. With gray around his temples and an enviable golf handicap. A guy who wore Dockers and Ralph Lauren. Her type of guy.

Right?

Right.

So Dez could haunt her fantasies, but he wouldn't be part of her reality. Because he was a young, hot musician and she was a middle-aged mom and antiques dealer.

God. How boring was that?

Sounded as if she'd given up.

Dez popped his head back inside. "You coming?"

She wished.

"Oh. Sorry. Flashback of Katrina," she said, hurrying toward the door.

Actually, she hadn't been thinking about Hurricane Katrina, and the way her store had once stood with gaping black windows, the debris from the looting scattered around the sidewalk. She hadn't been thinking of the empty display case holding the moniker for her store, but Dez didn't have to know her little moment wasn't about the past. And he damned sure didn't need to know she wanted to rip off his clothes and have her wicked way with him.

"I understand," he said with a reassuring nod. "Not easy to be reminded of a time when we all felt helpless, but we're not helpless any longer. Let's get the windows covered, give the police a report and then move forward. Everything here can be restored easily."

"Right."

As she passed him, he reached out and patted her shoulder. As though she was his maiden aunt.

Exactly.

She'd totally imagined the thing they had had a few minutes ago. One-sided desire felt by a woman who'd been sidelined too long.

"You okay?" he asked, his eyes kind, searching hers.

"Yeah, I know this vandalism is easily fixed, but—"

"Can we get on with this without all that touchy-feely crap? I want to see the back of my eyelids in the next century," Mr. Hibbett complained.

Eleanor retwisted her hair into a ponytail. "Lead the way."

After spending the next forty-five minutes boarding up the broken windows, signing the police reports and sweeping up, Eleanor turned to where Dez stood across the street, depositing the last of the glass fragments into the curbside garbage can.

She walked across and studied the wood covering his window. "Thank you."

Dez dusted his hands. "Of course."

"I'm opposed to a nightclub in this particular vicinity, but beyond that, you were a good neighbor tonight."

His gray eyes swept over her once again. This time she didn't worry about the way her hair fell out of the pony and the fact her crow's-feet were probably deepened in the shadows. Because he wasn't attracted to her. And he wasn't an option.

"I'm still determined to change your mind. My club will help the neighborhood. All it takes is seeing things in a new light. Maybe one of my patrons will see a table in your window and come back the next day, or pop back by Butterfield's for morning coffee, or remember she needs party invitations from that kinda strange dude. You have to try things from a new angle. Step outside your expectations."

His words echoed those of Pansy, who constantly nagged her to expand her mind and see possibility. But Eleanor wasn't good at breaking out of the safe cubby she'd created for herself these past years. She knew she needed to take chances like she knew she needed to clean out her front closet…but some things were easier when ignored.

"Maybe so, but I still have doubts. We've worked hard to make these couple of blocks of Magazine reputable and safe." She peered around at the scene that made her words false. "Or as safe as it can be."

"Right," he said, surveying the freshly boarded windows, giving her a nice vista of hard jaw and broad shoulder.

"This could have happened anywhere, but feel free to convince me otherwise." She almost groaned at the suggestion he must convince her. Sounded as though she'd issued a challenge. Like she wanted to spend more time with him.

You're overanalyzing. He's not into you, Eleanor, baby, so forget about the imaginary vibes. Stick to your guns on the opposition to the club and finding Mr. Fortysomething with silver temples and a pet wiener dog.

"Well, I've got a bath to finish and some z's to catch. Good night," she said, walking backward.

Dez's gaze sparked. "I'll take that image with me."

Good God. He had a dimple in his right cheek—a small one that begged to be kissed. Her body thrummed at the

thought of placing her lips in the slight indention…and on
other parts of him. Eleanor stopped in the middle of the street.
"Flirting will get you nowhere."

Or maybe it would get him a free ticket into her bed.

"You seem like the kind of woman who needs a little flirting in her life."

"Me?" she asked.

"Oh, definitely."

Undeniable purr. No mistaking his intent. Dez had tossed
out a sexual overture, and suddenly she climbed on a roller
coaster, embracing that pent-up expectation as the car ticked
up the incline, knowing the plunge would soon take her belly
away.

"Well, then, I—" Eleanor didn't really know what to say.
She hadn't flirted since Bill Clinton's administration. Maybe
she needed to buy *Flirting for Dummies*. "See you later."

And then she hurried back to her car like some buttoned-
up virgin who'd just caught the eye of the football captain.
Pathetic. Screw *Flirting for Dummies*. She needed a copy of
Cosmopolitan, stat.

Beneath the feeling of being sort of lame was the cele-
bration she wasn't a withered, used-up old hag just yet. The
hot guy liked her. The hot guy thought she needed some
flirting…and maybe more. So, yeah, there might be hope
for Eleanor Theriot.

CHAPTER THREE

DEZ SLID ONTO a worn stool and held up a finger. "Scotch and soda."

Bigmouth Sam waddled toward where Dez sat at the end of the bar. Sam wagged his head like an old hound dog. "That's heartache medicine. You got a sweet thang I ain't know about?"

Dez tapped the bar. "Nah, just need something to make me forget about the money falling out of my pocket."

Bigmouth Sam swiped the bar with a damp cloth and leveled bloodshot eyes at him. "Hate to say—"

"I told you so," Dez finished for his friend. Bigmouth Sam had run the Bigmouth Blues Bar on Frenchmen Street for over forty years. The bar was an institution, frequented by musicians and tourists alike, revered for its strong drinks, smoked oysters and sassy-mouth waitresses wearing short skirts and tight T-shirts that read Open Wide. And that was the icing for the serious cake of music that was served nightly. The older man had talked a rare blue streak trying to stop Dez from opening a club. He'd said it would suck out his soul and take his money with it.

Maybe Big Sam was right.

But Dez was as stubborn as he was talented and couldn't be convinced. He knew this about himself and accepted it. Besides, he wasn't all the way alone in the venture—Reggie Carney, a Pro Bowl lineman for the Saints, was his silent partner. Somehow, having a partner, one with some clout, comforted. "Guess I'm a slave to my mistress. I don't want a different gig at a different place every night."

Johnny Durant elbowed his way between Dez and a pretty-decent-looking coed and called to Sam, "Give me a Heiney and put Dez's drink on my tab. The tips are hot tonight, my man."

Dez held up his glass, clinking it against the icy bottle Sam handed Johnny. "Get it while it's good, bro."

"Damn straight," Johnny said, downing several gulps. Perspiration glistened on the man's brow. Most drummers who played like Johnny D would be drenched by now, but Johnny was a cool cat, sliding out easy tempos, his voice verging on a croon, his songs tight with a traditional bass line. "You got any new stuff yet?"

Dez's gut twisted. Everybody wanted new stuff from him. Didn't matter where he played, who he ran into, what he delivered behind the piano, everyone wanted something new. Something different. Something revolutionary.

But Dez had run out of new long ago.

Everything started with the storm. After years of collaboration on other people's albums, Dez had written some good solo stuff. His turn in the spotlight had been washed away by Hurricane Katrina. He'd been in the studio cutting the demo two weeks before the storm hit. And then everything, the only recording that had tasted like magic, that had the whole music scene in New Orleans buzzing, had been destroyed. The entire studio had been under five feet of water. No demo. No debut.

His grief had lasted for almost a year, and every time he tried to write music, he failed. He couldn't feel it anymore. What had once flowed in him like life's blood had vanished.

Old standards weren't a problem. Those melodies weren't

his. He hadn't poured his soul into those runs, into those words, so he'd gotten a gig playing at a hotel bar in Houston, subbing in for other bands when he could get the work. The few visits home he'd made to fulfill his obligations with a youth music program called Second Line Players or to back up Trombone Sonny at a festival or two, only filled him with a weight he couldn't explain or drink away.

And then he'd met Erin Garcia.

And shut himself off from his dreams, jumping into a life he'd never imagined—a life of grilling burgers, going to movies and making love on Sunday mornings. He'd gone to work overseeing her father's upscale restaurants, paying a mortgage on a house they'd bought together, taking the dog for a walk every night, scooping up poop and convincing himself he could walk a new path and forge a regular-Joe life.

But even that couldn't make him whole again. Eventually, he'd realized he couldn't take his city out of his bones nor could he pretend to be someone he wasn't. Maybe he had more of his rambling daddy in him than he thought... at least when it came to settling down with one woman. Or maybe he'd hidden long enough from who he was...a songwriter and musician.

"Come play with me, man," Johnny D said, jarring Dez from his thoughts. Johnny jerked his head in the direction of the old upright standing in the corner awaiting a loose-limbed rollicking New Orleans rag.

"Nah, man, I ain't in the mood," Dez said, downing the rest of the Scotch, willing the fiery liquid to wash away the memories, as well as the image of the shattered glass outside Blue Rondo.

"Horseshit. You're always in the mood. Let's go," Johnny said, slapping his shoulder and disappearing into the crowd, heading for the stage.

Bigmouth Sam jerked his head. "This crowd wants a beat, but do 'Take Five' for last call."

Dez slid off the stool. "I want to find my bed, man."

Bigmouth Sam grinned. "Yeah, but you's a Batiste, and music's in that blood. You ain't turnin' down hittin' that piano any more than I'd turn down hittin' Beyoncé if she's standin' here wantin' it."

Dez snorted, grabbed an almost-empty bottle of Crown and turned. "Beyoncé's married and so are you."

"You think thatta matter to me? Hell, naw. And I charge for that drink."

"It's my fee for playing," Dez called over his shoulder, slugging back a few gulps of the Crown as he made his way to the piano. Several ladies eyed either him or the bottle of booze appreciatively. Maybe he'd take one of them home… or maybe he'd just go back to his place uptown and enjoy the peace of his bed and the cool satin sheets he'd bought a few weeks ago.

Johnny had started without him, backed up on guitar by Jose Mercury, who played enthusiastically if not technically sound. Denny Jay handled the bass and Carl Van Petzel took a break from the piano at a nearby table. He held his drink up with a grin as Dez passed him, sat down at the bench and joined in on "Where Y'at?" settling into the groove, letting the music flow through him. It wasn't like before, but he allowed the chords to wash over him, heal him, soothe those pains he'd never faced with the sweetest of balms—music.

It was the only way to feel again.

Maybe the only way he'd ever get back to his own music. Ever since the waters had come and tried to wash New Orleans away, Dez hadn't been able to find what had made him who he was—the man who could create, tying beats and chords together with reckless abandon that somehow worked to create a distinctive sound of funk, jazz and blues with a thread of Bounce.

The fact of the matter was Dez Batiste could play the piano, but he'd lost his mojo.

ELEANOR SET THE PHONE on the desk as Blakely outlined all the reasons she needed a new Valentino bag, and picked up the freight slips on the new shipments from England. Two tables had been damaged beyond repair and she'd need to file a damage claim with the shipping company.

"Mom? Hello?"

Eleanor picked up the phone. "Yeah?"

"Were you even listening?"

"No. Because I'm not buying you a new purse. Too much money and you're lucky you have the Louis Vuitton. Your grandmother's a generous woman, and I do not want you asking her for this money. It's not a necessity."

Silence sat like a bullfrog on the line.

"Blakely?"

"Yeah?"

"Are you listening to me?"

"No. Because you aren't telling me what I want to hear. I know it's selfish, but I really love it—it's shiny pink with the cutest bow."

Eleanor rolled her eyes. "And you're a Phi Mu. Everything must be pink."

"Of course," Blakely said with a smile in her voice, something that gave Eleanor a dollop of joy. She missed teasing Blakely. She missed a lot about having her daughter home… at least the daughter she used to know. This one seemed so distant, so not like the Blakely she'd raised to be smart, selfless and independent. "But Grandmother would—"

"Honey, Margaret and Porter already pay half your tuition." And, Lord, didn't Margaret love to remind Eleanor. Didn't matter the Theriots had paid the full bill on their other grandchildren, Margaret liked to remind Eleanor of the power they still possessed over her life in the form of their grand-daughter, the last vestige of their precious angel of a son Skeeter.

"Fine," Blakely said, her voice showing not total accep-tance, but at least acknowledging the truth in Eleanor's words. Blakely had turned nineteen several months ago, and had sud-denly fallen victim to the spoiled New Orleans debutante her grandmother pushed her to be. Eleanor had done her best to ground her daughter, but it was hard for Blakely to resist the lavish gifts, the fancy school and the convertible BMW sent her way. The Theriots had money, position and shitty self-control when it came to their grandchildren.

"So, how'd you do on your last psychology test?"

"Okay," Blakely hedged and Eleanor could almost see the panic in her daughter's eyes. Blakely had always been a B student in high school and wasn't a serious academic. "Hey, Mary Claire just texted me. We have to set up for the Kappa Alpha mixer, so can I call you later?"

"Sure. Have fun. I love you."

"You, too," Blakely said, hanging up.

Eleanor sighed and tossed the new invoices down onto the desk as Tre passed by.

"Hey, Tre?"

The boy stopped and shifted backward to look into her office. "Ma'am?"

"How was the game?"

His normally guarded expression softened as it always did when he talked about his younger brother. "He did good. Only seven goals, but he had a lot of assists. Word's out about him and they double-teamin' him."

"That's great." She really liked Tre's ten-year-old brother, Devontay "Shorty D" Jackson, who possessed more swagger than any hip-hop star and wore sunglasses à la Usher. Brash, funny and hiding a sweet heart behind his bravado, Shorty D was a favorite at the Queen's Box. "Bring him by for doughnuts tomorrow after school."

"Yeah. I'll do that," Tre said, glancing about as if he were in a prison warden's office. Always guarded to the point of looking hunted, Tre was the opposite of his younger brother. Tre graduated from St. Augustine, a traditionally African-American boys' school, over a year ago and was saving up for classes at Delgado Community College in the fall. So far, he'd been a good worker—respectful, industrious and trustworthy—but Eleanor still didn't know him well because he rarely talked about himself.

"No deliveries this afternoon, but Pansy wants to rearrange the back room with the brass bed and steamer trunks, so if you'd give her a hand…"

"Sure."

The phone rang and Tre backed out of the office, heading up front to where Pansy conversed with a customer who wanted a Tiffany-style lamp with a peacock shade. Eleanor answered the phone, hoping it was the guy from the glass company. "The Queen's Box."

"Well, about time you answered my call. You'd think you'd have more respect for your husband's family."

"Margaret," Eleanor said, closing her eyes and banging a fist softly on her desk. Why hadn't she checked caller ID?

"Yes. Your mother-in-law. Or have you already forgotten so quickly?"

"How could I?" Eleanor purposefully made her tone light…for her daughter's sake. Blakely never saw past her grandmother's veneer to the controlling nutcase beneath the cashmere sweater sets. Years ago, after a heated discussion with the Theriots, ending with Blakely in tears, Eleanor had promised to tolerate Margaret's meddling, if only to keep the peace. "My shop was vandalized last night, and I've been quite literally picking up the pieces."

"When will you let that store go? It's been nothing but trouble—a complete money pit—and Skeeter left you more than comfortable. Why don't you spend your time more wisely, working with the family charities and taking care of your daughter?"

Eleanor gritted her teeth and begged her temper to take a hike.

"What's that noise?" Margaret asked.

"What? Oh, nothing. We've been over this before, Margaret. The Queen's Box belongs to me. The insurance money and Skeeter's trust have been set aside for Blakely when she's of age. I can earn my own living."

Barely.

"Stubborn mule," Margaret quipped.

"Meddlesome cow," Eleanor returned, slapping a hand over her mouth.

"What did you say?" Margaret squeaked.

"Oh, I didn't mean you, Margaret. Sorry. I was talking to Pansy about an item someone wants to buy," Eleanor said loudly, hoping like hell Pansy would hear and save her.

Like an angel, Pansy appeared in the doorway, holding up a finger to whoever stood at the counter.

"I found the cow creamer set! Sorry to bother you," Pansy yelled.

"That's okay. You didn't know I was on the phone with my mother-in-law," Eleanor said, pointing to the phone before slapping her hand once again over her mouth, this time

to prevent laughter. Pansy grinned before ducking out. Sometimes it was a blessing that Pansy was nosy.

"You talk very loudly, don't you?" Margaret said with ice
in her voice. Eleanor wasn't sure the older woman had bought
her white lie.

But did it matter? Blakely was no longer living at home,
and thus, the uneasy peace she'd kept between herself and her
former in-laws seemed not as important. The Theriots made
her unhappy, and she was tired of allowing their machinations
to affect her outlook. Margaret knew how to suck the joy out
of the happiest of occasions. "I wanted to discuss Blakely's
upcoming debutante season. I'm taking her to New York over
spring break to shop for her wardrobe. I've already purchased
airfare and secured a room at the Seasons."

Eleanor closed her eyes and counted to ten. Margaret knew
very well Eleanor was taking Blakely and a few of her friends
to the beach over spring break. She'd told the woman last
weekend when she'd dropped by to help plan a bridal brunch
honoring one of the Theriot cousins. Margaret's presumptu-
ousness was another attempt to gain control of Blakely's life.

"If you remember, Blakely and I already have plans. The
cottage in Seaside I booked for a long weekend? I can't—"

"You'll have to cancel, of course. The parties will begin in
the summer, and since I'm chairing the benefit for St. Jude's
this year and Justine's getting married, I won't have another
chance to get away. We must have Blakely looking her best.
She's—"

"My daughter," Eleanor finished, steel creeping into
her voice. Eleanor knew very well Blakely was a Theriot
and didn't begrudge her grandparents that disclaimer, but
Blakely was also a Hastings. Eleanor's family was intelligent,
hardworking and didn't suffer put-on airs. Eleanor would
be damned if she let Margaret turn Blakely into a soulless,

snobby bitch. "I don't mind you spending time with your granddaughter, but I'm standing firm on this. Ask Blakely about the last half of the break. Perhaps you can work something out."

For a moment there was nothing but cold silence on the line.

"I should have called Blakely in the first place," Margaret finally said with a sniff.

"No, you were right to call me."

"But she's old enough to make her own decisions, isn't she?" Eleanor knew there would be trouble. And probably a new Valentino handbag on Blakely's arm as part of the bribery.

"Maybe so, but we have to keep what is best for Blakely in mind."

Margaret sniffed. "I always keep what's best for Blakely in mind, Eleanor. It takes a village."

What should have sounded reasonable sounded snide. Margaret liked to be thought a strong Christian woman, a philanthropist, a most judicious person, but beneath her well-moisturized skin was a despot, tripping on her own power and determined to organize the world according to her wishes. Eleanor had learned long ago Margaret got what she wanted.

"I have to go now, Margaret. Pansy has her hands full."

"Really? I heard you had little business these days. The antiques market isn't what it used to be," Margaret said, feigning camaraderie but driving her barbs in all the same. "I'll give Blakely a call. Bye."

Eleanor didn't bother saying goodbye. Just clicked the button to disconnect.

"How's the devil incarnate?" Pansy asked from the doorway.

"Still alive," Eleanor said, grabbing her keys. She needed

a drink and then maybe a walk down the back of the Target store to shop off the bargain end caps. Retail therapy and booze cured anything. "Can you close for me today? After last night and dealing with family, I need a—"

"Afternoon in bed with a hot guy?" her friend teased.

The image of Dez Batiste popped into Eleanor's mind. Good gravy, she was deranged to think about the hunky pianist.

But was deranged such a bad thing anymore?

Last night while lying in bed, she had mulled over Dez's words about seeing life from a new angle, and had decided that she would burst out of her safe box built of tasteful linens and blouses that covered her from throat to waist. Of course midnight decrees looked different in the light of day.

"So order him up," Eleanor cracked with a smile. "Until then, I'll console myself with vodka and extra olives."

DEZ HAD SPENT the entire morning and half the afternoon working on the tile in the bathrooms, stopping only because he'd run out of black tile. Which was just as well since his stomach growled with the intensity of a wolverine.

Dropping the boxes of alabaster tiles he'd need to return on the bar, Dez brushed off his shirt and searched for his cell phone. Across the street a flash of color caught his eye so he moved toward the newly installed thick-paned glass. Never before had he looked for movement across the street.

But then again never before had he known a beautiful woman that ran an antiques store across from him.

Eleanor Theriot had been on his mind for the past twenty-four hours, and he couldn't figure out why.

Sure, she was beautiful.

But not his usual type.

In fact, she was about as far from his usual type as possible. His type wore hoodies, motorcycle boots and big ear-rings. He liked dark, overblown beauties who drank straight from the beer bottle, wanting a good time and little else. Erin had been the grown-up version of this party girl—spoiled, sexy and three years younger than he. She'd been his match, or so he'd thought, until things crumbled beyond repair. He was man enough to shoulder the blame for the demise of their relationship because he never should have tried to hide from himself.

Opening the door, Dez found the flash of color was indeed Eleanor, clad in black pants, a bright green cardigan and high-heeled boots. "Eleanor."

She turned, her purse over her shoulder, keys in hand.

"Wait up." He didn't know why he'd opened the door and called out. Couldn't think of a good reason to stop her from wherever she was heading other than he wanted to see her... maybe touch her. He definitely wanted to taste her.

Turning, he spied his phone, grabbed it and locked the door before jogging across the street. "Where you headed?"

"For a double martini."

"That bad of a day?"

"It's always a bad day when I have to deal with my former mother-in-law."

"If you're drinking, I'll join you," he said.

She paused as if thinking about it. "Not sure I should be seen consorting with the enemy."

"Is that what I am?"

She shrugged. "Well, I *am* the president of the Magazine Merchants Association, and there has been opposition to the nightclub."

"But the association can't stop me from opening."

"True, but we don't have to like it."

Did that mean they would cause trouble? He couldn't see

Eleanor clasping a torch and leading villagers armed with pitchforks to the club door. "No, you don't."

"Ah, well. I'm heading to the Bulldog."

"Should I be the designated driver?" He held up his keys.

She shook her head, looking a little trapped. Maybe he shouldn't press her, but something in him wanted to spend more time with her, wanted to figure out why the attraction was so strong.

Dez put his hand on the passenger door. "It's smart to know your enemy better, right? So let's see, I already know you're divorced and civic-minded."

She clicked her key fob and the Volvo SUV chirped to life. "Civic-minded? Yes. Divorced? No."

"Wait, you're still married?" His hand fell from the door handle.

"No." She gestured he should climb into the passenger's seat, waving at the strange dude who owned the stationery shop. "See, I'm already busted."

He hesitated to open the car door because he drew the line at messing around with married women. Once he'd slept with a barfly he hadn't known was engaged and it had left a bitter taste in his mouth.

She gazed across the top of the car at him. "You do know I'm widowed?"

"Was I supposed to?"

Pressing her lips together, she shook her head. "My husband was Skeeter Theriot."

"Skeeter? You don't look like a Skeeter's wife."

"He was a New Orleans Theriot. Actually he was running for the U.S. House of Representatives when his mistress killed him and then herself. You didn't see it in the papers... for, like, weeks on end?"

For a moment he could only stand and stare. How did one

respond to an admission like that? "I don't pay attention to politics much. Sorry."

She stood still as a puddle, her face unreadable. "I am, too."

Then she opened the door and slid inside. Dez stared at the streetlight festooned with a Mardi Gras mask, grappling with that tidbit of information. Eleanor had been married to a man who had cheated on her and then been killed by his mistress. Heavy shit.

So did she still love her husband? Was she grieving? Or maybe mad as hell at the bastard? He couldn't read her enough to guess.

Leaning over, she peered up at him from inside the car. "Are you coming or not...? 'Cause I really do need a drink."

He climbed in. "Think I need one, too."

Pulling away from the curb, Eleanor performed a perfect U-turn and drove down Magazine toward the Business District. Silence reigned as she kept her eyes straight ahead and chewed on her bottom lip. Finally, she pulled into a vacant spot in front of the Bulldog Bar and Grill.

"I don't know what we're doing," she said with a heavy sigh. "This is weird."

She sat, hands dangling on the steering wheel, lips glistening from the constant attention she'd given them as they drove. Again, it struck him how soft she looked, like a Monet painting, slightly out of focus but begging for contemplation. Pink lips, delicate throat, velvet skin. She made him want to breathe her in, explore the feminine curve of her neck. Relish her essence. "I thought we were going to have a drink. Get to know each other better."

"Yeah, but why? So you can change my mind?"

"Actually I hadn't had lunch and I figured any bar in New Orleans worth its salt has a burger on the menu."

She shook her head. "Don't play games. I'm too old for you. Too—"

"Too old for me? What? You're thirty-three, thirty-four tops?"

The groove between her eyes deepened. "No, I'm thirty-nine."

"Really? Don't look it."

"Yeah, really." Eleanor seemed put out. "This is stupid."

Dez tried not to laugh. He really did. But she looked so adorable, so flummoxed at the thought of admitting her age.

"What are you laughing at? This is serious. I'm too old for you, and you're too...too—" she waved a hand at him "—sculpted and hip."

Sculpted and hip?" He leaned his head against the seat, a deep belly laugh welling up within. "That's the strangest word combination ever."

"Stop," she said, punching him on the arm. "You know what I mean. We're from two different worlds. This is a Volvo."

Dez couldn't stop laughing. Her reasons were so funny. He was sculpted and she drove a Volvo?

"Dez," she said, her eyes plaintive.

He stopped, pressing his lips closed. "Huh?"

"Why are you laughing?"

"Because you're funny...and beautiful...and I really want to kiss you."

Eleanor's eyes widened. "You do?"

He clasped the back of her neck, drawing her to him. Her hair was silk, her neck small. She came to him willingly, breathing notched up. With his right hand, he brushed an errant strand of hair from where it stuck to her lip gloss. Wild horses couldn't drag him from kissing Eleanor.

With his lips hovering close to hers, he stared her straight in the eye. "I wanna kiss you 'cause I totally dig old ladies."

Her mouth fell open just as he intended and he took full advantage.

"Mmm," she said, struggling for only a moment before succumbing. Desire, hot and heavy, raised its head in his belly. She tasted like spring rain, healing and fresh. Cupping her jaw, he drank from her, thrilling when her tongue met his. Pulling her closer, he embraced the essence of Eleanor... and wanted more.

She broke the kiss, pulling back, her breath quick and her eyes clouded with passion.

"I'm *not* an old lady," she breathed, her eyes crackling. "And if this is some crazy 'needing a mother' thing, climb out, buddy."

"You think I'd kiss my mother like that?"

"God, I hope not," she said, swallowing hard and looking out the window, avoiding his gaze. She pressed a hand to her chest and sucked in a deep breath. "I can't believe I did that."

"You didn't. I kissed you."

Her eyes met his. "But—"

"I kissed you because you're all I've been thinking about since last night, because you're beautiful, desirable and sexy... even if you are a few years ahead of me. You think age matters that much?"

She searched his gaze. "It should."

"Age is a number."

She gave a wry chuckle. "Spoken like a man who brushes convention aside."

"I brush aside what doesn't make sense. You're a woman. I'm a thirty-year-old man. Not a kid."

"God, this is silly. Let's go get that drink and slow this down a little."

"Why?"

"Because I'm thirsty," she said, tugging on the door handle. "By the way, I hope you have your fake ID."

He opened his door. "What?"

Her teasing gaze met his over the top of the car roof and he caught a taste of a mischievous Eleanor. "I'm not contributing to the delinquency of a minor."

"If you're going to contribute to the delinquency of a minor, I'd rather it be for something more exciting than a tequila shot."

"Yeah?" She arched one eyebrow.

"Oh, lady, you're so in trouble."

Eleanor shook her head. "We shouldn't be doing this."

He gave her his best charming smile. "We're just having a drink. Relax, okay?"

"Feels dangerous, Dez. Like we should stop this right now."

"But where's the fun in that?"

CHAPTER FOUR

TRE STARED AT CICI sprawled on the couch and shook his head. Passed out in the middle of the day, which meant she hadn't gotten Shorty D up for school. More important, it meant she'd missed work again, and this time the manager of the Pet Pro wouldn't give Cici the benefit of the doubt. Three strikes and you're out. That's how it worked in life. Everywhere.

He kicked the couch. "Get up, Cici. You missin' work."

She didn't move.

"Cici," he said, kicking harder. Twice. Three times.

"Mmmf…" she groaned, throwing an arm over her face. She still wore the clothes she'd gone out to the club in—a bright blue skintight shirt and a skirt that rode over her thin thighs. "Damn, Tre, I tryin' to sleep."

"You missed work. Kenzie's been crying for an hour straight, and it's my damn day off. I shouldn't have to do your job for you."

Cici smacked her lips and groaned, rolling over as if she could hide from his words. "I don't give a shit. I'm sleepin', bitch."

"Bitch?" he said, anger curling in his gut. "That's all you got to say to me? Callin' me a bitch?"

Cici didn't say nothing. Just nestled into the back of the couch, dismissing him. She was still drunk. Probably high, too. He beat down the fury inside because Kenzie needed to be dealt with. Along with his brother.

Tre grabbed the empty beer can tottering on the edge of the

scarred coffee table and walked toward the bedroom where Cici slept, where her three-year-old daughter stood wailing at the threshold. "Come on, baby girl."

He scooped up Kenzie, ignoring the snot pouring out of her nose, and strode into the kitchen. After tossing the beer can in the trash, he sat his cousin on the counter, shoving a dirty cereal bowl aside. Kenzie didn't stop crying. He figured if his mama was a drunk ho and ignored him, he'd cry, too. "You hungry, baby girl?"

Kenzie immediately stopped crying. Sniffling, she rubbed her eyes. That meant she was.

Tre grabbed a paper towel, wiped Kenzie's face and looked for a sippy cup in the nearly empty cupboard beside the sink. There were obviously none clean.

Shorty D came in holding a bag of chips and a game controller. "Ugh, she stinky."

Tre hadn't noticed, but, yeah, Kenzie needed a diaper change. Panic rose in his throat as he surveyed the sink full of dirty dishes, the stack of unpaid bills, the toddler sitting in her own crap, and his brother, who'd stayed home from school for obviously no good reason.

What the hell was he doing?

All those dreams he'd woven in his mind, wearing a nice business suit, with a sweet ride in the driveway of a condo in a nice Uptown neighborhood, were so ridiculous…so damn far away he couldn't even taste them anymore. The money he'd squirreled away in an old Nike shoebox in his closet laughed at him—it wasn't enough to buy the books he'd need for college much less pay for a semester of tuition.

And the only thing he'd taken pleasure in, his music, was gone. The saxophone rescued from his bed many years ago by the police had been sold last summer.

His life was shit.

"What you doin' home?" Tre asked his brother, giving

Kenzie a somewhat stale granola bar from a box sitting on the counter.

"I didn't get waked up and missed the bus. Besides, I don't feel good this morning," Shorty D said, picking up a drinking glass sitting beside the sink and squinting at it to determine if it was clean.

"You look fine to me so go get dressed. You're going to school."

"No, I ain't," Shorty D said, not even looking at his older brother.

"Yeah. You are. You already missed three days this semester and I saw that progress report. You gonna get held back."

"Nah, I ain't." Shorty D went to the fridge and grabbed a two-liter bottle and poured a glass of soda. "Ms. Barre don't even take roll some days. We don't do nothing in her class no way."

Tre grabbed a package of diapers he'd picked up at the dollar store the day before and walked toward the bathroom, Kenzie in his arms. "You're going, Shorty."

Something set Kenzie off and she started screaming in his ear, drowning out the curses Shorty D popped off. Pieces of granola dropped onto his clean T-shirt as Tre realized he'd left her sippy cup on the counter.

"Yeah, yeah. I could use a drink, too," he said, walking behind the couch and kicking it as hard as he could. "Get the hell up, Cici. I gotta take Shorty D to school since you didn't do it, and your baby needs to be fed."

Cici's reply wasn't fit for Kenzie's ears, but that never stopped his aunt. Disappointment filled him. This wasn't good for no one. His mother's younger sister had fought against her addiction problems ever since she'd been Shorty D's age. Tre's own mother had led her sister into a life of drugs, booze and prostitution. Talia had kicked her habit before Shorty D had been born, but Cici never could pull that monkey off her back.

Cici had Kenzie while in jail, and he and Big Mama had been taking care of the little girl, waiting for Cici to get clean and straighten the hell up, but it was a daily fight. And with Big Mama not in the house to pray over Cici, fuss at her and force her hand, Tre was just plain tired of fighting for his auntie.

He cleaned up Kenzie, combed her hair into two puffy ponytails and put her in a clean dress Big Mama had sewed. The dress was too small, but Kenzie liked the funny green frogs on it. He tied green ribbons in her hair with looping lopsided bows. After brushing her teeth and finding her shoes, he dragged Shorty D's clear plastic backpack from under the coffee table. With sorrowful brown eyes, Kenzie watched her mother as she slept on the couch, its stuffing peeking out the arm.

Cici's snores made him want to punch his aunt.

Lazy-assed bitch needed to go back to jail. He didn't need nobody else to take care of.

"Maaa?" Kenzie asked, touching her mother's face, making Tre's heart hurt. He pulled the small girl back but not before Cici's hand slapped the child's hand away. Tears trembled on Kenzie's lashes, and she stayed away as if she understood there was no hope left in the woman.

Tre jerked his thoughts away from the pain and sadness— two feelings he had no use for. A man can't change the world around him...only himself. He had to keep moving, sheltering Kenzie and Shorty D because they were innocent. They shouldn't have to pay for everyone else's selfish choices. Yeah, life wasn't fair, but he'd do his best to even it up for them.

Shorty D appeared in the doorway of the living room, wearing khaki pants that sagged too low to meet dress code and a wrinkled school-uniform shirt. Normally, Tre would make his brother change, but today he had to choose his battles.

"Let's go," Tre said, picking up Kenzie, settling her on his hip before pushing out the wooden door of the old house in Central City. He stepped off the porch, wishing he'd grabbed his shades because the sun wanted to battle him, too, but he didn't turn around. The bus would stop at the end of their street in five minutes.

"Shorty D, today, son."

"I ain't your son." Shorty D slammed the door as laughter bounced across the street. Tre turned his head to see Grady Jefferson and Kelvin "Crazy Eight" Parker leaning against Grady's Charger, a new 2013 model with twenty-inch rims and a custom paint job.

"Damn, son. You runnin' day care or what?" Crazy Eight called out, his laugh high and clownish. Tre didn't like Crazy Eight much, but Grady was cool.

"Yo," Tre said, giving them a nod as Kenzie turned her little head toward the two gangsters. "What up?"

Crazy Eight giggled again but Grady nodded. "A'ight. Later, bro."

Tre nodded, ignoring the knot in his gut. Grady ran with the 3-N-G boys and he'd mentioned a couple times about some easy ways Tre could earn money. Tre had always resisted the thug life, but lately he wondered why he bothered. He told himself it was because he'd made his mama a promise to take care of Shorty D, but couldn't he do that a lot better with a roll in his pocket?

He kept his chin high as he marched down the street, pretending like he wasn't carrying a little girl who should have been potty-trained by now, followed by a ten-year-old who had remembered to grab his shades and who kept darting glances back at Grady like he was the man.

Tre couldn't blame Shorty D.

Grady looked cool as shit.

Tre would want to be him, too…if that kind of life didn't lead to prison or getting his ass shot by a rival gang.

"Hurry up, Shorty D. You already late."

"Man, this is bullshit. I'm tired of school and livin' like this."

Tre didn't say anything, because he couldn't make things better for Shorty D at present. The kid had to go to school. Cici needed to beg for her job so they could pay the electric bill. And Tre had to figure out some way to get Big Mama strong again so she could take care of Kenzie. The woman who'd been minding his little cousin while Cici worked had just taken her own job. She'd told Tre he'd have to find someone else by next week.

No one to help him and he needed to make more money than what he did lugging furniture around town for little more than minimum wage.

He pulled out his bus pass and said a small prayer.

God, help me through another day. Help me be strong and be the man You want me to be. And, please, God, help me say no to Grady when he asks me to ride with him.

As he reached the bus stop at the corner of Carrollton, he caught the exhaust as the bus pulled away, heading toward the city and away from them.

Shorty D looked up at him with a smirk. "Now, that's some bullshit."

"Watch your language around this baby girl."

Shorty's eyes were an old man's as he slid off his sunglasses. "Like she ain't goin' find out soon enough."

Maybe God was tired of listening to Tre.

Maybe, despite his best intentions, life *was* some bullshit.

ELEANOR LOVED THURSDAYS because it was delivery day, and today she was getting a new carton from the Cotswolds.

However, the carton arrived late. There were only twenty minutes left before closing time, and the afternoon was dead.

Maybe just a peek? She shoved the keyboard back and pulled her screwdriver and hammer from the bottom drawer.

"Hey, Pans," she called out her open office door. "Want to open the crate and see what's inside?"

She accidentally dropped the screwdriver and rooted under the desk for it. Grabbing it, she emerged to find Pansy staring at her thoughtfully.

"Creepy Gary said he saw you and the jazz pianist climbing into your car together the other day. Is there something you want to tell me?" Pansy asked, bending over Eleanor's desk, dropping her pointed jaw on her folded hands and batting her eyes like a deranged debutante.

"No."

Pansy narrowed her eyes. "No?"

"Why does everyone make a big deal about going for a drink?"

"Uh, because your girl parts haven't been oiled in a decade, and you went for a drink with sex in a pair of tight jeans...."

Eleanor leaned back in her chair. "Oh, Jesus, Pans. It's liquid and they pour it in a glass."

"Is he circumcised?"

Eleanor stiffened, causing her office chair to shoot upright. "What?"

Pansy giggled, doing a little finger-pointing thing that accompanied a jaunty wiggle. "Come on. Spill the beans. What's he got down there?"

"You're seriously cracked."

Pansy dropped into a wing chair with carved cherubs etched into the wood. The dressing chair had been damaged in Hurricane Katrina, but Eleanor couldn't bear to part with it even if it were no longer worth kindling. "That's why you keep me around."

"Who told you that? Your dusting skills and witty repartee with the customers are the only things that keep you gainfully employed."

"You call this gainful?"

"As gainful as it gets, chickadee." Eleanor rose from her chair and tugged one of Pansy's farm-girl braids. "Let's go see what Charlie sent us this month."

Pansy sighed, but struggled to her feet. "Right-o," she said in a bad British accent. Charlie Weber was a buyer from England who scoured auction houses and estate sales for the perfect antiques for Eleanor's store. The man had a notoriously good eye for spotting masterpieces beneath grime and paint, even if his stuffiness and fondness for responding with *right-o* drove Pansy bonkers whenever she talked to him on the phone.

"Just one crate today, but there should be an eighteenth-century cupboard inside along with some rare French books. Charlie said he wasn't certain about the quality, but several were first editions. And there's a painting he found in a widow's attic that could be a—"

"You're a pro at avoiding things, you know that?"

Eleanor moved some empty cardboard boxes aside and ignored her friend.

"So you're not even going to tell me about Dez? About the drink? It shocked the hell out of me when Gary sidled over and spilled those delicious beans. Didn't know you had it in you."

Eleanor spun. "Why? Like I can't do something…atypical? Besides, it was a drink."

"With sizzling-hot Dez Batiste. So is he still the enemy?"

"Having a drink with him doesn't change the opposition I have for the club he's opening. I needed vodka and Dez wanted to convince me his club could be an asset to the community. That's it. Practically a business meeting," Eleanor said, not daring to meet Pansy's gaze. The woman could have been Sherlock Holmes had she been male, British...and a fictional character. She didn't want her friend to see how much her odd afternoon escape with Dez had affected her. Even now she couldn't sort out what it had meant.

"So did he?"

Eleanor studied the nails in the crate. "Did he what?"

"Change your mind?"

"No." But he'd made some good points.

"Oh," Pansy said, holding out her hand.

"What?"

"The hammer and screwdriver. I'll break the fingernail this time."

Eleanor handed Pansy the tools. Pansy had better leverage with her height.

While her friend struggled with the crate, Eleanor allowed her mind to drift back to her strange afternoon at the Bulldog pub. Back to the way Dez looked gulping down the bitter German beer, his neck strong, masculine, nicked by the razor. The way his hands had cupped the mug, the flash of his teeth, the hum of electricity between them, unacknowledged but allowed to hang in the air. She'd wanted to touch him again, but didn't.

It had all felt too dangerous.

Had there been three or four years between their ages, she might not have worried. She might have asked him to come to her house for supper. Or a drink. Or a roll in the bed she'd slept in alone for too long.

But she was eight years and nine months older than him.

Too much to bridge.

Even for mere sex.

Maybe it didn't matter—just like Dez said—but she saw the difference in the way they approached life.

He ate a double cheeseburger with hickory bacon along with a side of fries and a hearty beer to wash it down. Dez wasn't far removed from the buff frat boys her daughter chased, who didn't know what statins were and had never thought about cholesterol intake.

And then the phraseology he used. Some of the words she wasn't familiar with. He knew the music played in the bar. He caught the eye of college girls. He dressed like a twenty-something…even if he was nearly thirty-one.

As she sat there, discussing the weather, the Saints and the music scene with Dez, she felt more and more he wasn't the man to take her first steps back into the dating jungle with.

But she'd enjoyed their conversation.

He didn't probe into her background, asking about Skeeter, wanting to know about the bipolar secretary who had shot him dead in the Windsor Court hotel room. Dez didn't even ask why she needed a drink so badly. No talk of the past. Just football, food and music. She tried his Cajun fries and a sip of his beer. He made fun of her vodka martini with six olives, and inquired about purchasing a rice bed like the one he'd seen in the store window of the Queen's Box when he'd first visited the building he'd purchased.

Light, inane talk.

Heavy, meaningful glances.

They wanted each other…that never faded away. But, still, Eleanor couldn't think it was a good idea.

"Hello?" Pansy said, huffing and puffing and not successful at opening the crate. "Little help."

Eleanor spotted the crowbar they'd been looking for over a month ago on the ledge of a high window. "There it is."

"What is?"

"The crowbar. Tre must have left it up there…I've been meaning to ask him about it. Let me get a step stool." Eleanor turned, but stopped. "Hey, Pans."

"Yeah?"

"Why do you think I should sleep with Dez?"

Pansy lifted her thin eyebrows. "Left field, darling."

"I know."

Her friend let go of the wooden crate, her eyes settling into seriousness. "Because you need someone fun to take a running leap into the land of living with."

"I have been living."

"Well, yeah, technically. But it's been five years since Skeeter was killed, five years since you thought about anything else other than the store or Blakely. I wanted you to get out there long ago, but I understood you wanted to feel stronger, to be at the right place in your life before adding any more drama. But—"

"I'm not getting any younger?"

Her friend snorted. "Eleanor, you're a beautiful woman. Everyone can see that, but you hold yourself back, allowing only those close to you to hear your laughter, to see your bold side, to feel the fullness of who you are. You guard yourself so well no one wants to step close to you."

Eleanor knew this about herself, but hearing the truth out loud made her wince.

Yeah, she'd been hurt.

When Hurricane Katrina had struck the coast, she, Blakely and Skeeter had been in Hilton Head on vacation. Skeeter had gone to play golf and meet with a potential campaign manager about his forthcoming bid for the U.S. House of Representatives. Eleanor had gone to scour the antiques shops of Savannah. Blakely had taken her best friend, Mary Helen, with them, intending on playing on the beach, making friendship bracelets and shopping for school clothes. A whole week away from the steaminess of New Orleans…and then disaster struck.

At first they'd been dismissive and relieved they weren't in town. But then when the levees broke, they'd watched in horror as their city came apart. For three whole days they didn't leave the TV set, glued to the death and pain rampaging in the streets they'd trodden. Images of looting on Magazine Street had torn Eleanor's heart into two tragic pieces, and she'd known, standing right there on the jute rug of the overpriced beach house, her dream had been smashed like the windows of Butterfield's...for she'd seen the ruin of her neighbor's bakery on CNN.

And knew the Queen's Box had received the same callous treatment.

But what really broke her heart was realizing the moniker for the store—the beautiful lacquered box from Marie Antoinette's private collection of boxes—had likely been stolen.

Skeeter had bought it for her in place of an engagement ring. They'd married quickly after finding out Eleanor was pregnant with Blakely. A simple, friend-filled wedding had been followed by a honeymoon in Europe where Skeeter had surprised her with the gift, purchased from a reputable dealer. She'd never missed the sparkle of a diamond, not when she had such a beautiful box to place in the window of the hardware store she'd inherited from a great-uncle. The engagement gift became the symbol of the new venture store—the Queen's Box—her dream come true.

It had sat in a display case in the window, beckoning passersby, greeting old friends, representing the authenticity of her marriage with Richard Ellis Theriot, third son of Porter Theriot, former mayor of New Orleans. But as she'd suspected, it was gone, a horrible omen of what lay ahead.

Depression, desolation and distance...which led to betrayal.

"Eleanor?"

She jerked her gaze to Pansy, blinking against the memories blinding her future. "I don't want to be that victim anymore, Pansy. But I also don't want to be foolish. Dez Batiste feels like foolishness."

"And what's wrong with a little crazy if it amounts to naught? It's Mardi Gras...have fun with him until Fat Tuesday and then swear him off for Lent. What's it going to hurt?"

"He's like king cake. Delicious, but I know I'll regret it," Eleanor said, running a finger over the chimes of a grandfather clock awaiting repair. Turned out four-year-olds were hell on the inner workings of a clock.

"Everyone has regrets. I have them, but I embrace them because I'd rather have memories than nothing at all. That's part of living. Why do you care so much about what other people think? You're no longer a politician's wife. You no longer have reporters stepping on the backs of your shoes. No one cares if you have hot sex with the fine-ass man across the street and drop him a week later."

For a moment, silence hung between them as Eleanor mulled over her friend's words. "So just sex?"

"If it's *just* sex, then you're not doing it right." Pansy smiled and yanked Eleanor into an embrace. "Stop thinking so much. Be naughty. Have fun. Stop looking for reasons to hold yourself back."

Eleanor squeezed her friend and stepped back. "He's not my type."

"Exactly. Besides, smooth, sophisticated and unfaithful didn't exactly work out for your last go-around."

"You're a laugh a minute."

"Seriously. You fell in love with Skeeter because he charmed your panties off with his very safe, desirable lifestyle. He had money, position, and you were looking for a daddy."

"No, I wasn't."

"Sure you were. Trust me. I took a psychology class in college."

"You went to college?"

"Two semesters before I abandoned my career goals and my clothes in Eddie's '69 VW Wagon."

They both laughed.

"But in all seriousness, your parents were too busy running their school to be—"

"They were good parents, and they're still good parents."

"But clueless. You were looking for guidance and there was the older, not-so-wise-but-you-didn't-know-that-yet Skeeter Theriot with his old money and new BMW. You didn't stand a chance."

"But choosing to date a guy opposite of my mistake isn't a good enough reason. I'm not sold on sleeping with Dez... if he's even receptive." But Eleanor knew he was. It might have been a while since she'd been "out there" but she hadn't missed those signals.

At the sound of the front door, they both lifted their heads.

"I'll get it," Eleanor said, dusting off her hands. "This can wait."

"Can it?" Pansy asked, obviously speaking about more than the shipment. "Don't try to make everything so perfect, Eleanor. Get dirty."

"I don't like to get dirty. Besides, Dez is too—" Eleanor clamped her mouth closed because as she glanced into the store, Dez Batiste stood next to the chiffonier wardrobe with the speckled beveled mirror.

"Gorgeous," Pansy finished for her, craning her head around Eleanor's for a look.

Eleanor swallowed. "Exactly."

"And you should totally have sex with him."

CHAPTER FIVE

DEZ TOOK A HARD LOOK around Eleanor's store, and decided he liked the rambling, homey feel of the place. Many of the antiques dealers on Royal Street had a fussy aloofness that made passersby steer clear, expecting prices higher than a cat's back, but the Queen's Box exuded warmth trimmed with the scent of beeswax and eucalyptus—like his great-aunt Frances's parlor, but not as stuffy.

"Hey," Eleanor said, stepping out of her office with a cautious smile.

Another woman followed and he assumed her to be an employee, since he'd seen her come and go each day. She was almost as tall as he was, with sloping, thin shoulders, an endearing gawkiness and a wide smile full of the devil.

"I'm Pansy McAdams," the woman said, stretching out a hand and giving him a once-over. Appreciation shone in her eyes, and he decided he had an ally in Pansy. "I saw you play Tipitina's with the New Birth Brass Band back in '04. You were such a baby."

He took her hand. "Good to meet. You caught that gig? That was one of the ones that got me noticed."

"You were brilliant on that Dixieland rag you played. Spontaneous and inspiring—I was blown away," Pansy said, dropping his hand and spinning toward Eleanor. "Hate to go, but I don't want to be late."

Dez held out a flyer. "Before you go, take one of these.

Late notice so I'm trying to spread the word." He handed the purple paper to Pansy.

She scanned the flyer. "You're playing with Trombone Sonny at the Priest and Pug before the Endymion parade? Meow."

"That's what it says," he joked, pointing to the heading. "Yeah, I'm trying to drum up some excitement for Blue Rondo before we open the doors mid-March, and with that many people lining the street before the parade, it's a perfect time. The owner's a friend and offered to front the cost as a welcome. Several other New Orleans guys will be there. Gilly Sanchez may drop in. Goin' to be jammin'."

He watched Eleanor as he put special emphasis on the "welcome" part of his response. He really wanted her to relent on her position regarding his nightclub.

Eleanor held out her hand and he gave her a sheet.

"So this is music for the entire family?"

He gave her a flat stare. "You *have* been to a bar before, haven't you? It's not exactly family-friendly, right?"

"Of course," she said, her eyes flashing a color somewhere between the shade of emerald glass and the soft fir trees sold at Christmas, "but being that you want to create an image the association—"

"Really? You think I'm into pandering to stuffed-up old goats afraid to let go of their outdated ideas?" He stopped admiring the woman's eyes and gave his full attention to her argument, which was as thin as tissue. Disappointment soured his stomach. The past few days had shown him a different side of Eleanor, one he hadn't anticipated, based on the letter to the city council he'd snared. In his mind, he'd repainted her the opposite of an uptight, obtuse business owner, thinking she'd let go of the idea Blue Rondo was a mistake for the neighborhood.

"Look, I respect your ambition, but the other merchants

and I have worked hard to come back from obscurity after the storm, some of us from near bankruptcy. Maybe we'd all feel better if you go to the next merchants' meeting in a few weeks and tell us more about your business. This isn't personal—it's about the community. There are significant ramifications to having a bar in a historic building within these particular blocks of Magazine."

"Now I see it," he said.

"What?"

"The politician's wife."

Pansy laughed. "You got her pegged. Sometimes a skunk forgets it stinks."

"I do not stink." Eleanor's frown deepened in conjunction with the narrowing of her eyes. "And I'm not a politician's wife any longer. I'm merely trying to do the job for which I was elected, and that means not allowing my personal preferences to color my actions on behalf of the elected board."

He gave her a slow smile. "So your personal preferences have changed?"

A strange look crossed her face. "What? Oh, well, that's not what I meant. In any situation—not just yours—I have to be unbiased and act in the best interests of the merchants."

"So you haven't changed your mind?" he asked.

"I have—" Eleanor snapped her mouth closed. "I hate when people twist my words."

"Just wondering where I stand is all." Irritation made her somehow more desirable. Maybe he could kiss the exasperation away.

Pansy, a grin as big as a tuba on her face, waved. "As interesting as you two are, I have to jet. Eddie's show's at six o'clock and I have to pick up the cookies for the reception."

Eleanor nodded. "Fine. I'll be by after I close."

Pansy hiked a canvas bag onto her shoulder and addressed Dez. "Why don't you stop by if you get the chance? My husband does fantastic glass art. His show is at Marvel's gallery over on Maple."

She pressed her hands against the front door. "In fact, why don't you escort Eleanor? It's not dressy or anything."

Before he could answer, Eleanor's assistant disappeared out the door.

Eleanor rolled her eyes. "She's been trying to fix me up with any man who walks through the door."

"Lucky I'm the last one through for the day," he said, walking over and flipping the Open sign to Closed. He turned around. "Just in case there's some other man thinking he'll get to do the honors."

The ever-present attraction fired between them. A flicker of pleasure played at her mouth. Ah, sweet lips he wanted to taste again. No…needed to taste again. Her eyes slid to his lips as if she'd maybe had the same naughty thoughts. Then she jerked her gaze away. "Who said I wanted to go with you anyway?"

Eleanor turned from him and busied herself with something at the register. He got it. The thing they had going between them—a wisp of something new and exciting—was scary, almost too much to take in. Eleanor wasn't anything silly as a nervous mare or a skittish virgin, but somehow she felt close to one of those ancient depictions. She was a woman who teetered on a decision, torn between what she wanted and what was expected.

And maybe needed a little convincing…

He set a few flyers on the desk, longing to reach out and slide a hand along her stubborn jawline, wanting to trace his tongue along the delicate shell of her ear, bury his nose in hair that smelled seductive, like mandarin and vanilla.

In his head, music started.

Dez froze as the almost-forgotten feeling came back. Words, desire, music. Was he getting his muse back? Years upon years, the little inner voice inside him, his guide who brought forth the perfect lyrics, had been defiantly silent. The loss of his album had weighed him down, unyielding and tainting his creative consciousness.

But just now—those realizations about Eleanor and wanting to kiss her—had appeared to him like music. He could hear the notes to accompany the words.

Hope sprang loose inside him. Maybe it wasn't merely being back in New Orleans…maybe it was in the curve of Eleanor's cheek, in the slight dimple in her chin, the hollow at the base of her neck, or the depths of those mysterious eyes so full of uncertainty.

She stared at him, her eyebrows arched. She waited for him to speak.

"So will you hand these out to interested customers?"

She eyed the stack he'd set down. "I'm not sure that's a good idea. I'm as conflicted about Blue Rondo as I am about you."

"About me?"

Pushing her hair behind her ear, she swallowed. "This thing we've got between us, whatever it is, I think we better stop it before it gets out of hand, you know?"

He shook his head. "No, I don't know."

"Yes, you do." She grabbed the cash from the register, shoved it in a bank bag and slammed the drawer shut, twisting a key and pocketing it in the fuzzy cardigan she wore. Ignoring him and the stack of flyers, Eleanor took the bank bag and disappeared into her office.

He followed.

She closed the safe in the wall as he walked in. He went to her, not giving her room to maneuver. "Why are you putting definitions on flirtation? On the possibility of what could happen?"

"Because we need them. *I* need them." She turned to him,

her eyes pleading. "I'm not used to doing this. It's like I'm parking my ass in foul-ball territory, knowing I'm going to get smacked in the head."

"Or maybe it's like knowing that the dance will end but enjoying the time on the dance floor. If you want comparisons I can do this all day. Ultimately what it boils down to is you're one of two things—either embarrassed because I'm a little younger and my skin's a little darker, or still in love with your cheatin'-ass husband."

Her eyes widened but she didn't respond.

"So which is it?"

"Neither one of those and a smidge of both," she said, rubbing her fingers against her eyes with a huge sigh.

"So that means…what?"

"I don't know. I'm ready to start over again, but I'm not sure my debut can be with you. We're not even remotely from the same world and—"

"You can't handle someone who's not white and younger than you?" He couldn't keep the disappointment out of his voice.

She stepped toward him, her eyes deepening. "You're almost too beautiful to be human, but I'm afraid of you."

"Afraid?"

"Of this turning into something I can't handle. I've got shaky legs and it feels like a new world. But, Dez, wanting you is not the issue."

"But what's life without taking chances?" He closed the gap between them and traced one finger down her cheek. Her breath quickened.

"I don't remember," she said, refusing to meet his eyes, refusing to make that connection he craved. "But being totally honest, I don't think I can handle being hurt right now…not when I finally feel strong enough to want something more than my empty bed each night."

He slid a finger beneath her chin and tilted her head up. Finally, her gaze met his. In those depths he saw the fear. "I won't hurt you."

"That's what they all say," she whispered, an ironic little smile tilting her lips. "I don't want to be a victim, and I don't want you to have to protect me. Doesn't seem fair to—"

"Let's make a deal." He cupped her jaw, studying those delicious lips. "If things feel too much, too serious, we walk away."

Eleanor closed her eyes with a harsh laugh. "Now here's where my age gives me the upper hand. You can't walk away when the heart gets involved."

"We won't let our hearts get involved."

"Sure. You can tell yourself that, try to trick yourself, believe you won't fall to pieces…because things are just casual. But suddenly, it's not. And if one person doesn't feel the same then—"

"You're thinking too damn much," he said, lowering his head and kissing the pulse fluttering above her collarbone.

She exhaled and her head fell back as a small shudder trembled through her. He slid his arms around her, pulling her into an embrace. He was tired of talking. There were better ways to convince Eleanor this thing between them was worth exploring.

Her hand found his shoulder, and she held on tightly to him as he kissed his way up to the ultimate goal.

By the time he'd made it to her mouth, he knew the convincing was over.

She wanted him.

Her mouth met his, hungry and demanding. She slid one hand up to his jaw, the other to his belt.

Well, then.

But it wasn't his belt she was after. Her hand dipped under his T-shirt and slid over his stomach up to his chest. Her hand was cold against his heated flesh, but he didn't give a rip-roaring damn—Eleanor had touched him. Everywhere her hand went, heat followed. He cupped her ass and pulled her against his hardness, grinding his hips a little, showing her how absolutely crazy she made him.

She pushed against his chest, making him step back, hitting the corner of her desk. He stopped a pencil box from falling and when he returned his attention to Eleanor, she'd tugged the fluffy cardigan sweater from her shoulders, dropping it to the floor, giving him bared shoulders to taste.

He pulled her to him, and worked on touching the deliciousness of her bare skin while she did remarkable things with her tongue, stroking his lower lip before returning to the depths of his mouth. She tasted like toothpaste, fresh and warm.

And then she broke the kiss again.

Gazing up at him, she smiled sexily. "Well, aren't you good at convincing a girl to shut her mouth?"

"I don't want your mouth shut," he said, tugging at the camisole tucked into her pants.

She helped him, grasping the soft cotton hem and lifting it, revealing a light orange-colored bra and a vista of soft honey-eyed skin. After whipping it over her head, she said, "Okay, no more thinking."

He reached for her, but she stepped back. "Go up front and lock the door. That shirt better be off when you come back. Jeans, too."

He dropped a kiss onto her shoulder blade. "Yes, ma'am."

Her answer was to unbutton her pants and slide them down smooth legs, giving him a tease of matching postage stamp–size panties.

"Damn, you're one sexy woman."

Pleasure shone in her eyes, urging him to hurry. He exited

the office, cursing himself for forgetting to twist the lock on the front door in the first place.

Just as he reached for the lock, a woman reached for the doorknob from the outside. Quickly twisting the lock, he pointed to the Closed sign.

The blonde looked surprised then shook her head.

He jabbed his finger at the sign and mouthed, *Sorry.*

Again, the young woman shook her head.

Twisting the lock again, he opened the door about a foot. "We're closed."

"Who *are* you?" she asked, crossing her arms, clearly perturbed.

He didn't know who the chick was or why she was so adamant. "I'm Dez and the store's been closed for almost fifteen minutes now."

The blonde's clear blue eyes slid down his body before her gaze traveled back to his face. She was incredibly lovely with long legs clad in tight jeans, and blond hair tumbling over thin shoulders. She had a sort of elegant confidence in the way she carried herself, and a face that likely made angels weep at her beauty. If he hadn't already held the most interesting, sexy, challenging woman in his arms moments ago, he might have been more appreciative…even if she were too Erin-like.

"Where's my mom?"

"Pansy?"

"No. Eleanor Theriot. She owns this store," the woman drawled, sounding annoyed and much younger than he'd previously thought.

"I didn't know she had a daughter." Color him shocked. Color him very shocked. Eleanor had a full-grown daughter? How had she forgotten to mention that?

"Well, she does. Is she here?"

"Dez," Eleanor called from the back.

Shit. Eleanor was in her underwear.

He slammed the door closed, twisting the lock. The girl started banging on the door as he lurched toward the back of the antiques store where Eleanor stood in her underwear, looking like a gift from the freaking gods. Bitterness choked him. Frick.

"What's wrong?"

"Your daughter's out front."

Her face paled. "Blakely? She's here?"

"If she's an angry blonde chick who says her mother is Eleanor Theriot, yeah."

"Oh, shit." Eleanor grabbed her pants, and while hopping on one foot and jabbing the other into the leg hole, she looked for her tank top thing. It was inside out, on the floor. He picked it up and flipped it right side up as Eleanor buttoned her pants. "What's she doing home? She's got class tomorrow."

"I didn't know you had a kid."

Eleanor shoved her foot into the clunky-looking shoes she'd kicked aside. "I never told you about Blakely? I swore we talked about her and Ole Miss."

"She's in college? When did you have her? In high school?"

"I thought I told you." She shook her head before tucking strands behind her ears. She grabbed the cardigan from the floor. "How do I look? Do I look like I was about to have sex with a guy I've known for, what, five days? Oh, my God. I'm the worst mother ever."

He made a face. "You look fine."

The banging on the front door got louder. "Oh, my God. Did you lock her out?"

"Yeah. You were in your underwear and I had a hard-on."

Eleanor brushed past him, muttering a mantra of "shit, shit, shit."

He adjusted himself before following behind her, not knowing whether to laugh at Eleanor or be pissed she hadn't even bothered to tell him she had a daughter who looked at least twenty years old.

Eleanor swung open the door. "Blakely!"

"What the hell, Mom? That dude locked me out," Blakely said, stomping into the store and dumping her oversize purse onto a random dresser-looking thing to her right. Then she swept back her hair and hit him with a pissed-off glare. "Who *is* that?"

"That's Dez," Eleanor said, clutching the cardigan between her breasts and knotting up the fabric. "He's opening a bar across the street."

Blakely ignored her mother, who gestured weakly at the door. "The piano guy you pitched a fit against a month ago? That's him?"

Eleanor nodded. "Yeah, we're—"

He started to fill in the blank with the word *lovers* but knew Eleanor would probably stroke out if he did. Besides, they were almost lovers, and if he wanted to make it more permanent, he better keep his mouth shut.

"Friends," he finished for her. "Actually, I was helping your mom move a table in the back. Pansy had to leave early."

Blakely tossed her head. "So why did you have to lock me out? That was total crap."

He shrugged. "Honestly, I didn't think a woman as hot as your mother could possibly have a daughter your age."

"Well, she does. Even if sometimes people think we're sisters."

Eleanor remained silent, watching the exchange between them.

He extended his hand to Blakely. "Think we better have a do-over introduction. I'm Dez Batiste, owner of Blue Rondo, which will open in about a month, God willing."

Blakely raked him up and down with her gaze before arching her eyebrows and taking his hand. "I'm Blakely Theriot and I'll take that do-over."

As her hand closed over his, a silent alarm screeched in his head. "Nice to meet you, Blakely."

"What are you doing home, honey?" Eleanor asked, her eyes widening as she obviously picked up on the same vibe. Blakely looked at him as though he was the last scoop of ice cream in the carton…and she was hungry.

"Duh, Justine's bridal shower. Grandmother would flip if I didn't show."

"But that's not until Saturday—I thought you were driving in tomorrow night."

"I was, but Nikki's having a party on Friday night, and all my sorority sisters were dying to come to the Endymion parade Saturday night. Since I didn't have any tests this week and my Friday lab got canceled, I invited them to crash with us this weekend. Thought I'd come early and help you with the shower and stuff."

"Oh," Eleanor said, biting her lip. "I wish I had known. I could have stocked the pantry."

"I thought you'd be happy to see me." Blakely assumed a Little Girl Lost expression. It was obvious to Dez she knew how to play any situation to her advantage.

"I am," Eleanor said, releasing the knot she'd twisted in her sweater and holding out her arms to her daughter. Blakely gave her mother a quick hug before turning to him.

For a moment none of them spoke.

It was awkward, so he shifted toward the door. "Guess I should be heading out. Don't forget to hand out the flyers."

"What flyers?" Blakely asked.

Eleanor waved her daughter's question away. "We'll talk about it later. Right now, we've got to get to Eddie's show."

"Ugh, I so want to grab a bite, go home and shower before I go out tonight."

Eleanor frowned but covered it up nicely. "You'll hurt Pansy's feelings if she finds out you're here and don't come by."

"Fine." Blakely sighed, sliding her eyes to Dez. "Are you going?"

"I may pop by. I have a feeling that once Pansy expects you, you better show."

Blakely nodded, clasping her hands behind her back and giving him a flirty smile. "Now I've got a good reason to go."

Uh-oh.

He stared at Eleanor, who glanced at her daughter and then at him with the same *oh, shit* expression in her eyes. "Mr. Batiste likely has other plans, honey. He's busy with the remodel. I'm sure—"

Blakely shot her mother an annoyed look. "But I bet he's not too busy to walk over to the gallery with me. It's not too far and I'm dying to stretch my legs after that long car ride." She gazed at him with big blue eyes that scared the crap out of him.

Eleanor opened her mouth, but snapped it closed as Dez opened the door. "Sure. Let's take a walk. Eleanor can meet us there." He gave the woman he'd been about to get naked with an *I got this* look, hoping she understood he'd put Blakely where she needed to be with regard to him.

"Perfect," Blakely said, scooping up her purse, pulling out lip gloss and sashaying past him. "See you in ten, Mom."

He followed Eleanor's daughter. "We'll get back to that desk later, Eleanor. And that's a promise."

"I thought you said y'all were moving a table?" Blakely said, giving him a flirty smile.

He glanced at Eleanor, but her eyes had shuttered, and now he wasn't so sure there would be the kind of later he wanted. And that sucked.

ELEANOR WATCHED THE DOOR swish closed and swiped a shaking hand over her face.

What the hell had she been thinking?

Having sex with Dez Batiste in her office like some reckless, horny single woman?

Oh, God. Was she a reckless, horny single woman?

No. It was a toe dip into insanity that had thankfully been interrupted.

Relief and disappointment met and swirled in her gut. Half of her wished she were still in her office, using Dez to get over the barren stretch of desert that was her love life for the past five years, and half of her wanted to high-five her daughter for good timing. Having sex with Dez would have been a mistake—a hot and no doubt rewarding mistake—but a mistake nevertheless. She couldn't handle being the cougar antiques store owner who diddled the younger, gorgeous musician. The very thought sounded tawdry, like a half-baked prime-time television show. And beneath that obviousness was the feeling things could get out of hand with him quickly.

The man looked like a heartbreaker.

And that brought to mind her daughter's blatant interest in the same man.

Eleanor locked the door, wondering what Dez was going to do to dissuade Blakely's attentions. Her daughter was much like her former husband—single-minded in her determination to get what she wanted. It was both a wonderful quality and a concern.

Eleanor turned and a movement to her left made her scream.

"It's me, Mrs. Theriot."

Pulling her fingernails out of the invisible ceiling she'd tried to clutch, Eleanor exhaled. "Oh, Tre. Good Lord, you scared the devil out of me."

Balanced on her young deliveryman's hip was a little girl

with fuzzy braids wearing a too-small dress. Shorty D stood beside him, his backpack hanging low on one shoulder, a cocky grin on his face.

"What's up, Mrs. T?" Shorty D said.

"I saw you had company so I waited. Used my back door key and hoped I could find you here before you left. Sorry about scaring you," Tre said, rubbing the back of the little girl, who sucked on her fingers.

"That's okay," Eleanor breathed, trying to stop her galloping heart. Double thank-God Blakely had interrupted her and Dez. She could have scarred some children with the naughty things she wanted to do to Dez. "I'm good, Shorty D. How are you?"

"Cool. Thanks for the doughnuts. Hit the spot." He patted his stomach.

She tried not to laugh at how grown-up Shorty D talked. He wore pants that sagged a bit too low and tennis shoes that had seen better days months ago. "Anytime. I like rewarding those awesome baskets you shoot. You keep playing like that and every high school in the city will be trying to get you to play for them."

Shorty grinned. "I'll go wherever they have the most doughnuts."

"Hey, Mrs. T. Can I talk to you?" Tre spoke, jerking his head toward her office.

Obviously something serious was afoot. Tre never came in after hours and the worry on his face seemed too much for a kid who was the same age as her daughter. She didn't know who the little girl was. Could be Tre's daughter, she supposed, but he'd never mentioned having any children on his employment application…only his brother, for whom he was unofficial guardian.

"Sure. I don't have much time because Eddie has his show tonight, but I can talk." She moved toward her office, hoping there was no evidence of her near insanity with Dez moments before.

Office looked the same as always.

Huh.

Somehow she expected it to show some small indication she'd tossed out all sense.

Tre set the toddler down next to Shorty D at the threshold and handed his brother his iPhone with earbuds. "You can play Ninja Jump, but you have to make sure Kenzie don't mess with nothing. Got it?"

Shorty took the phone with a nod before tugging on the little girl's arm. "Come on, Kenz. You can help me."

Tre watched as the two settled on the desk chair behind the counter, giving another grave nod to his younger brother.

"So, what's wrong, Tre?" Eleanor asked, moving a few papers around, trying not to be overly concerned with the atypical actions of her employee.

"Yeah, uh, I hate to ask, but you think I can get an advance for this week?"

"An advance?"

Tre straightened and she wished she hadn't repeated the request. Tre was proud, reminding her of a young Morgan Freeman. He had a sort of confidence that allowed one to trust him, and she figured he'd rather have a tooth yanked out with no pain medication than to ask for help. Things had to be bad for him.

"Yeah. Won't happen again, but I need to find someone to watch Kenzie and I got to pay them."

Eleanor nodded. "Of course, Tre. You can have an advance."

He nodded and shot his gaze anywhere but near her. "Thanks."

"Tre?"

He still wouldn't look at her. "Is Kenzie your daughter?"

His eyes widened. "No, she's my little cousin. My mama's sister's girl."

"Oh, okay. I just never heard you speak of her. Let me grab my checkbook." Eleanor didn't know how to breach Tre's defenses. The boy didn't trust her and she'd never given him reason to feel the way he did. If she could get him to open up, she might be able to help him solve his problems. She felt like he needed someone on his side, but thus far, he'd been unwilling to be anything but polite.

Several minutes later she thrust a check toward him. "That should cover what I'd pay you for the next two weeks. Will that be enough?"

His dark eyes flickered to the paper and he nodded. "Yeah. Thanks."

"Tre, is there anything more I can do? You're not in trouble, are you?" She hated to ask it, but she couldn't seem to stop herself. Maternal instinct whispered in her ear she could help, that she could at the least fix something for someone.

But Tre withdrew even further.

Yeah. Good job, white woman. Think you can fix years upon years of poverty. Of hunger. Of need. Of out-and-out racism?

"I'm good. Appreciate it." Tre turned toward the half-opened office door, making her feel uncomfortable for being so presumptuous. She should have kept her stupid mouth shut.

"Okay, sorry. I'm not trying to meddle. Just thought maybe you might need someone to talk to." She offered up a smile, hoping he'd see she wasn't trying to manage him, and he nodded, his handsome face softening a little at her words.

"You a good lady." He folded the check and tucked it into his back pocket.

"Thank you," she murmured, rising and coming out from around the desk.

Tre moved into the store, jerking his head toward Shorty

and Kenzie. The kids looked up from the flashing screen as he approached. "Let's roll."

"Hey, Tre. You want to ride with me to Eddie's show? Pansy's got cookies from Butterfield's, and it's casual. I know they'd love it if you came, and then I can drop you by your house."

Tre shook his head. "I ain't got time tonight. Gotta get Kenzie home and fed."

"Please," Shorty D whined, jumping off the chair. "Eddie's my boy and Kenzie wants some cookies, don't you, Kenzie?"

The little girl just sucked on her fingers and looked up at Shorty.

"She don't want no cookies," Tre said, taking the little girl's free hand.

"I wanna see Eddie's shit. He said he'd show me some-time."

"Watch your language, Shorty D," Tre said, kneeing his brother into motion.

"It's no trouble," Eleanor said, grabbing her purse and turn-ing out the lights in her office. "I'm heading over. My daugh-ter came home unexpectedly, and I want you to meet her."

"Yeah," Shorty D said, nodding as he followed Eleanor to-ward the back. "I hate ridin' the bus at night. Freaky-deaky people on there always drunk and stinkin' and stuff."

Tre sighed. "Okay. Whatever. Only this once."

Eleanor smiled at Shorty D as he jerked his elbow in and hissed, "Yesss!"

She winked at him. "You just want cookies."

His wide smile was answer enough.

CHAPTER SIX

TRE SURVEYED THE PEOPLE gathered inside the cramped art gallery. Some were well dressed, others looked as if they smoked pot and created crap for a living.

Like Eddie.

Eddie McAdams was a bear of a man, with a full beard streaked with gray and a belly that spoke of extra helpings of Pansy's cooking. Tre had already sampled her crawfish corn bread and some lemon pie things in the few months he'd worked at the Queen's Box. Pansy wasn't as good of a cook as Big Mama, but she was good enough to make Eddie fat and happy.

"Don't touch," Tre told Shorty D for the seventh time since they'd followed Eleanor through the creaking double doors of the former church that now served as an art gallery. Kenzie looked around wide-eyed as Shorty D scoped out the refreshments table and eased toward the plates of sandwiches and cookies sitting beside a bowl of pink punch.

"What?" Eddie said, flinging his heavy arms out wide. "You brought my man Tre? Oh, yeah, baby. Now we talkin'."

Tre shrank back because Eddie was going to hug him. The man liked to touch people—slaps on backs, arms around the shoulders or just out-and-out bear hugs.

Tre lifted his hand for a five. "What up, Ed?"

Eddie's high five smacked his hand so hard it startled a few people nearby. The artist grinned and reached out, grabbed Shorty D's nearly bald head and turned him from the refreshment table. "And you brought my man Shorty D. What's happenin', lil' bro?"

Shorty D spun and performed some kind of complicated handshake with Eddie. Kenzie squirmed and held out her hands to Shorty D so he could pick her up. Baby girl didn't share her older cousin so much.

"And who's this beauty?" Eddie asked, bending down to peer with copper eyes at Kenzie.

"This my cousin Kenzie."

"Oh, but you're a looker, little one," Eddie said, reaching out and plucking Kenzie from his arms. Kenzie's dark eyes widened and Tre knew she'd start wailing at being surrendered to a white-bearded giant who was more Jerry Garcia than Santa Claus. But she didn't. Just stuck her fingers in her mouth, slurped, studying Eddie.

"Let's get you a cookie, yeah? Pansy, get over here and look at this little sprite I found."

Pansy stood on the other side of the gallery, but turned when Eddie called her. She wore a cotton dress that fell to the floor. It had a weird tribal pattern, which didn't look right on her, but somehow suited the occasion. Pansy crossed the room to stand beside her husband. "You brought Tre and Shorty D." She tossed a glance at Eleanor, who'd stood beside him, oddly silent.

"Yeah. Tre came by and I pretty much forced him to come, using cookies as bribery," Eleanor said with a smile, though her eyes searched past Pansy and Eddie. Probably looking for her daughter.

Pansy smiled down at the ten-year-old, who Tre suspected was already on his second cookie. His brother was a pro at sneaking things and working people—his smoothness scared Tre at times. "Have as many as you want, Shorty D. In fact, I have a bunch more in the back and I'll send a bag home with you."

Shorty D wiggled his eyebrows. "Now, that's what *I'm* talkin' about."

Pansy laughed and turned to Eleanor. "So I saw Blakely arrive with Dez."

Pansy said it like a question.

"Yeah. I had no idea she was coming in for the whole Mardi Gras weekend. The last time I talked to her, she'd pleaded to being 'so over' the parade thing. But here she is, bringing sorority sisters with her."

Pansy's eyes narrowed and some unsaid communication obviously occurred between the two women. Tre suspected it was over Dez Batiste.

Tre knew Dez from the Second Line Players. When Tre was in middle school, he'd participated in the program and Dez had been the one to place Tre on the list that helped him get a scholarship to St. Augustine, enabling him to attend the historic African-American Catholic school and participate in the Marching 100, the famed New Orleans marching band. With its precision, discipline and support, the band stamped its mark on Tre. The principles he'd learned at the school stuck with him, keeping him strong when the wind blew him near to the ground. But things had been so bad lately, he wasn't sure he could hold out against the life he could lead, a life that would buy bread, new shoes and respect in his hood. He'd wanted more for Shorty D. More for himself, but things weren't working.

Dez had been a shining star for him years ago. A man who, though he didn't look black, was the son of a racially mixed father and Cuban mother. He'd been raised several streets away from the projects where Tre had scratched out an existence. Dez hadn't gone to St. Augustine; instead he'd attended Ben Franklin and the NOCCA program for the arts. But once Dez had experienced success, he hadn't turned away from his roots. He hadn't turned his back on boys he could help in his hood—Dez had been cool like that.

But for some reason Tre didn't want to run into Dez now.

He wasn't sure why. Maybe he was embarrassed he no longer played the sax. Maybe he didn't want to come across as some punk who barely made a living moving furniture and went grocery shopping with food stamps. Shame engulfed him, and his pride was hard to swallow when confronted with a man who'd beaten down obstacles and hammered out a future on the very instrument he loved. Something Tre couldn't do 'cause he had sold his horn and had to support two kids who weren't even his.

A few people shuffled around the exhibits mounted on tall white rectangles, and suddenly Dez was in his line of sight, standing near a fine blonde girl that could only be Eleanor's daughter, Blakely.

Dez and Blakely looked good together. His golden skin offsetting her lightness. His hardness emphasizing her softness.

"Eleanor," Dez said, coming over. Tre hadn't seen Dez since his freshman year at St. Aug, and the man looked different. He hadn't lost his swag, but he looked as though life had given him a few licks. Shit, that bitch Katrina had given them all a few blows, leaving them dizzy, broken and feeling around on the worn earth for some traction.

Blakely was fine, that was for sure. But she looked like every rich chick he'd ever seen. Shoulders straight, hair down her back with a sort of *eat shit and die* attitude that a brother couldn't touch. But she was a dime—perfect ten.

"Hey, Mom. Took you so long I was starting to worry you'd already taken up old-lady driving," Blakely said with a sassy smile. On the surface, the words sounded teasing, but there was an edge to her tone, a sort of *I'll show you*.

Made him wonder about Blakely.

About why she felt threatened by her mother.

Then Eleanor glanced at Dez and something fired between them. Then Tre knew. Dez didn't want Blakely. He wanted Eleanor.

"Your mother is far from granny driving," Pansy said, wrapping Blakely in a hug after introducing Eddie to Dez. "She scared me silly the other day when she drove me to the pharmacy. Mario Andretti ain't got nothing on her."

"Who's that?" Blakely laughed, true warmth flooding her blue eyes as she returned Pansy's hug. "Besides, you're already silly, Petunia."

"Ha, ha, monkey girl," Pansy said, wrapping an arm around Eddie, who'd turned to talk to a couple who wore business suits and looked moneyed up. "Have some punch and sandwiches. I gotta go mingle and drum up some sales for Eddie."

Eddie set Kenzie down with a smile, leaving Tre and Shorty D standing with Dez, Eleanor and Blakely.

"Give me Kenzie," Shorty D said, his voice reflecting boredom...or hunger. Probably both. "I'm gonna go get us a plate and sit her over on that couch."

Shorty D grabbed the little girl's hand and wove through a few old white hippies to the nearby table. Tre could see the couch from where he stood. When Tre returned his gaze to the others, he saw recognition in Dez's eyes.

"Dez, Blakely," Eleanor said, "this is Tre Jackson. He works with me at the Queen's Box doing our deliveries and helping keep Pansy in line."

Blakely stuck out a hand. Her smile looked genuine, and he wondered if he'd imagined earlier the animosity between her and Eleanor. "Hey, I'm Blakely. Sorry I didn't get to meet you at Christmas."

He took her hand, catching a whiff of perfume, which smelled like a sample he had once been handed in the mall. "Good to meet you."

Dez held out a hand. "And we've met before."

Tre shook Dez's hand, which was hard, strong and callused. "What's up?"

"Trevon Jackson. You played the hell out of the sax."

Tre withdrew his gaze and begged the sucking wound inside him to remain hidden. The thoughts of his short-lived music career always burned more when he was around someone who created music, around someone who had the pleasure of putting his emotions into notes.

When Tre sold his horn, it had felt as if someone had cut off his arm. But he'd gotten over it for the most part. He wasn't quite whole, but he was managing. "Yeah. I played back in the day."

Dez lifted his eyebrows. "You don't play anymore? You were one of the most talented guys I'd met."

"Nah," Tre said, tearing his gaze away again. He didn't want Dez to see the lie in his eyes. "I'm done with that."

"Tre is saving to go to college next fall. He's going to study business," Eleanor said, sounding somehow proud of him, which made him feel like such a fraud. He was no one worth being proud over.

"That's good," Dez said, slapping him on the back. "But I'd love to riff with you. Why don't you bring your horn and we'll play on your breaks or after work?"

"Nah, dude, I sold my horn a while back. Don't have time to mess with that no more. Gotta work, you dig?"

"Damn, that's a shame," Dez said.

"Yeah. Maybe one day I'll take it up again. If I get the time."

Blakely tilted her head. "I have a saxophone you can have. Daddy bought it for me when I was, like, in the sixth grade. I thought I wanted to be in orchestra. Turns out I'm not good at music. It's been in my closet for years."

Eleanor frowned. "I thought I donated it after Katrina,

when so many of the schools were looking for instruments and trying to bring back their programs."

"Nope, I saw it over Christmas on the top shelf," Blakely said. "You must have forgotten about it."

Eleanor smiled. "Well, for good reason. It was meant for Tre."

Everyone smiled at him as if they'd bestowed upon him the greatest of gifts. But he didn't want their damn charity. He'd been living with people giving him shit for so long it made him feel sick to think about taking something else, especially since the check Eleanor just wrote burned in his pocket.

"Naw, it's no big deal. I ain't playin' no more. In fact, I'm going to take on an extra job on weekends if I can find something. No time for blowin'. Thanks, though."

Dez studied him for a moment, looking as if he was weighing Tre's words. Finally, he nodded. "All right, but if you change your mind, I want to blow with you. You were tight on that thing, and my man Johnny Zeber's looking for someone to work with since his regular guy went to L.A."

Hope fluttered in Tre's heart but he beat it down.

Hadn't he learned a long time ago that hope was a dangerous thing? Good things don't happen unless a man's willing to shave off part of himself, unless he's ready to bend and give way to evil. Trevon Jackson wasn't meant for music. He wasn't meant for luck. He was meant for facing shit flung at him, scraping it off and moving forward.

'Cause standing still wasn't an option. He had to keep moving forward so the life he didn't want didn't catch up to him.

DEZ SHUT THE FRONT DOOR to his Uptown apartment and tossed car keys onto the black granite bar.

Hell of a night.

And he was so close to having Eleanor beneath him, loving her, taking a small piece of pleasure to knit into his soul

In the darkness of his roomy place, his piano occupied the middle of the room, beckoning him to give it some well-deserved attention.

He strode across the carpet and plinked one finger on the ivory keys. This piano wasn't as pure as the Fazioli, but rather well loved and well played, a gift from his grandmother, who had received it from a wealthy paramour back in her wilder days, before she fell in love with a tuba player at a gig in the Quarter and gave up her life of crooning ballads and running with Mafia boys. A full-out grand piano with mellow strings, and smoothness gained from seasoning.

Dez sank onto the bench, his fingers striking keys, creating a haunting melody he'd never put together before.

Huh.

He tugged off his jacket and tossed it onto the leather sofa, wiggling his fingers, allowing the passion to wash over him, take him to a place where he could create. It was like waiting for a wave, paddling slowly, searching for just the right crest, just the right color of water.

His fingers returned to the keys and he allowed the melody to return, playing the same progression. A tweak here and there, and then, yes, it worked. He played the same chords over and over, letting the fire pour from his fingertips, building crescendo, pulling back to play softly when necessary. Over and over he played, the magic weaving around him, absorbing into his pores and spilling onto the keys, becoming one with his instrument.

And all the while he thought of Eleanor.

Of her smooth skin, so soft, smelling as a woman should. Of her green eyes, the fear within, of her giving herself to him. Yielding while at the same time wrapping him in her essence, demanding he give forth to her.

Eleanor.

His fingers flew across the keys too fast. He slowed,

reached out and grabbed the blank sheets awaiting the music that hadn't come for years. A black charcoal pencil sat beside it, freshly sharpened, awaiting use.

Minutes later, he had three stanzas of soft, plaintive notes. Notes that begged for surrender.

During the next three hours, those notes grew and wandered a bit along the melody before gathering at the chorus, and by the time day crawled over the windowsill, Dez Batiste had written his first song since Katrina.

And it was beautiful, powerful and so full of angst that tears had streamed down his face.

The words to accompany the piece had floated nearby, and he knew he'd write them down, but not now. His body felt depleted, and his fingers shook with exhaustion. He needed food and sleep, and then when his body had recovered, God willing, he'd find the words to go with the chords he'd created. They were there, hovering in his soul like small birds with rapidly beating wings.

Dez dropped his head onto the piano and allowed the heaviness of life, of sheer exhaustion, to soak into him. One yawn. Two.

He slid from the bench and fell onto the sofa, shoving his jacket to the floor. He'd close his eyes for a few moments and dream of Eleanor.

And of the future that didn't seem as empty as it once had.

ELEANOR PLACED THE TRAY of sandwiches on the low coffee table, which was surrounded by a group of Blakely's sorority sisters. "There's the last of them."

"Thanks, Mrs. T," one of the girls said, choosing a small cucumber sandwich and popping it into her mouth before picking up a pair of tweezers and turning toward Eleanor's daughter. "As soon as I shape up Blakely's eyebrows, I'll do yours if you want. I'm really good at it. I worked at the MAC counter last summer."

"Uh, no, thanks, Caroline. I think mine are okay," Eleanor said, folding herself into a straight-back chair beside the big-screen TV in the den, watching four girls prep for a night on the town.

Caroline surveyed her and raised her own awesomely sculpted eyebrows. "If you say so."

"Do you think I need some reshaping?"

"Uh, yeah." Caroline smiled before angling in on Blakely like a deranged scientist.

"Owww," Blakely said, jerking away.

"Don't be a baby."

A redhead who Eleanor couldn't remember the name of said, "Yeah, stop being such a baby."

"Screw you," Blakely said, jutting her face at Caroline. "I'm not the one who cried when Margaret Ann got engaged."

"You're such a bitch, Blakely," the other blonde in the group said. Eleanor was certain her name was Reese because she reminded her of the actress who shared the same name.

"You know it," Blakely said with a laugh. "Oh, and check it out. Across from my mom's store is this nightclub, and the guy who owns it is on frickin' fire."

"Ooh," Reese said, looking away from the compact mirror and grabbing a sandwich and another swig of some obnoxious energy drink. "Do tell."

Eleanor's heart dropped into her still-chipped toenails. Blakely talked about Dez as if he was a decadent chocolate.

Okay, he kinda was.

She eyed her bare feet and then the metallic nail polish sitting on the table next to the sandwiches.

"He's so hot—looks like the Rock. Swear to God."

"Oh, my God. I would so do the Rock," the redheaded girl said.

"You'd so do half the Sigma Nu frat house, Darcy," Blakely said, clearly trying not to cringe as Caroline plucked away. "But this guy, Dez, is like honey. He's, like, part Creole, part white and full-on yummy. That whole ethnic thing is so hot."

Eleanor wondered how many times the girls could fit *hot* into their description of Dez. It could be a drinking game. A shot every time they said *hot*.

"So you gonna go after this hot guy?" Reese asked.

Blakely shrugged. "I don't know. He's kinda older."

"Yes, too old for you," Eleanor chimed in, relinquishing her role of gargoyle in the corner. She couldn't handle much more of the Dez talk, not after watching her daughter make an idiot out of herself at the gallery.

"Mom, he's not that old. I'm in college, in case you didn't get the memo."

The other girls cast looks at one another, nodding their heads as if being in college made it okay to do whatever one wished.

"How old is old, Blake?" Reese asked.

"Like maybe thirty or something. But he's seriously hot. I mean—"

"Smoking," Darcy finished for her.

"And y'all haven't even heard the best part," Blakely said, smoothing a finger over her eyebrows because Caroline had moved on to lip liner. "He's a musician."

Darcy squealed. "He's in a band?"

"Not a band. He's a jazz pianist."

"Okay, that's enough," Eleanor said, rising and pointing a finger at her daughter. "You stay away from Dez Batiste. He's too old for you and too experienced. Stick with frat boys."

Blakely rolled her eyes. "Frat boys? Please."

"Davey Weiss thinks you're the cat's meow, Blakely, and his daddy owns a shipping company," said Reese.

"So?" Blakely's gaze caught Eleanor's, and she saw in

their depths rebellion, which Blakely had never shown before. Where was her sweet girl who made bracelets from parachute cord and sang in the school choir? "You didn't stick with frat boys, Mom. You were my age and daddy was Dez's age."

Eleanor felt as though she'd been hit in the face with a wet towel.

Dear Lord. Blakely was right. She'd been nineteen the day she'd met Skeeter Theriot at the Blind Gator bar in Midtown. Sipping on a beer, wearing ripped jeans and a white shirt that had embroidered little mirrors on it, Eleanor had had big dreams of being a historian and little protection against the charming assault launched by one of the city's favored sons. Skeeter had been wealthy, smooth and entitled. Eleanor had been easy pickings.

Her fate had been sealed, and she'd found herself wedded and painting a nursery while trying to finish up her degree in history at Tulane. She'd been twenty years old when she'd delivered Blakely. Twenty-three when she finally got her degree. Twenty-seven when she opened the Queen's Box, her little hobby that she managed to grow into a business. At thirty-two she'd sat through Hurricane Katrina. At thirty-four she'd found out her husband was dead at the hand of a mistress she'd never known existed. And now at thirty-nine, she stood looking at her daughter on the precipice of adulthood.

Yeah, age was only a number, but it was a number that added up to life not being as picturesque as a nineteen-year-old girl envisioned. Prince Charming often turned into a toad far too quickly, and dreams of a career often withered on the stalk.

"You're right, honey," Eleanor said, scooping up the empty sandwich tray and wadded-up napkins and heading toward the kitchen. "But I was stupid. You don't have to be."

She walked out, not bothering to hear Blakely's argument. Having a nineteen-year-old daughter was harder than she'd ever expected. She and Blakely had always had a good relationship, and even when Skeeter had been killed, they'd maintained openness with each other, a sort of "us against the world" attitude that had been a small measure of comfort during a media attack that literally had them hiding in their house for weeks on end.

They'd been a team, but it had changed last summer when Blakely had spent two months in Europe with her father's family. When Blakely had returned, she'd been different. There was a distance Eleanor couldn't bridge, and the gulf had widened during the fall of Blakely's freshman year at Ole Miss.

Eleanor hurt and mourned for the daughter who had once picked her daisies and turned down invitations to parties so she could go see Gerard Butler movies with her mother. And even scarier than the distance was Blakely's new focus on the "right" friends and the "right" clothes. That scared Eleanor because it felt as if Blakely was turning into a Theriot... and not in a good, philanthropic kind of way. But in the way that allowed one to talk out of both sides of her mouth...like her father.

Eleanor slid the tray into the dishwasher as Blakely appeared in the doorway, lips glossed, moccasin boots past her knee. "We're heading out, Mom. Don't wait up."

"You sure?"

"God, Mom. I'm not ten anymore."

"Hey, honey," Eleanor said, walking toward her daughter.

Blakely watched her with a guarded expression and Eleanor's heart pinged. She lifted a hand and brushed her daughter's golden hair from her face. "You're the best thing I've ever done."

Blakely looked away. "Mom, you have to think that. You're my mother."

"No, you are, but don't grow up too fast, okay? It's fine to date frat guys and enjoy being nineteen."

"Yeah, okay," she said, stepping away.

"I love you, Blakely. That's all I've ever done. Remember who you are, sweetheart."

"I know who I am," her daughter said. "Remember, don't wait up."

CHAPTER SEVEN

DEZ FOUGHT OFF a dull headache as Chris Salmon went over the plans for the last stage of the renovation. After many calls and Dez's threat to contact his attorney, the contractor finally showed up early Friday morning with an apology. And the special reclaimed wood to install on the wraparound bar at the back of the club.

"So three weeks ought to do it," Chris said, propping a work boot on the iron bar rail Dez had found in an old railway station in Plaquemines Parish.

"Three weeks has to do it. I'm opening on March fifteenth."

Chris made a face. "Isn't that a bad-luck day or something?"

"The Ides of March?"

"Yeah. Don't people get killed on that day?"

Dez smiled. "No, it's a movie. Oh, and I guess it was bad luck for Caesar. Hmm, maybe I should figure out a drink— Ides of March martini. I like it, and that would be a great signature drink we could build into our history."

Chris shrugged and waved his men inside. "You creative types. I don't get you."

"You don't have to. Just use *your* creative abilities to get this place ready to roll. The interior decorator Reggie hired will be by to consult with you this afternoon about the paint colors for the bathrooms and the location of art that needs electrical, so stick around. I gotta go rehearse for the gig tomorrow. I got my cell."

Chris nodded and snapped on safety glasses. "I'm bringing the fam on Saturday. We always watch the parade off Telemachus at my uncle's law firm, so I'll walk a few blocks to hear your debut back into the scene."

"Cool. I'll look for you."

After a handshake, Dez slipped out the front and nearly ran into Eleanor.

"Oh," she said, stepping back and putting a hand over her heart, drawing his immediate attention to her breasts. "I've got to stop running into people."

He grinned. "Feel free to run into me anytime you want."

She tried to frown, but it didn't quite reach her eyes.

"Need something?"

She swallowed. "Sort of. Thought I'd be neighborly and warn you. Blakely found one of the flyers, so she and her girlfriends might be stalking you at that concert you're having before the parade tomorrow night."

"I'm hoping for a big turnout, but I doubt they will be able to get in anyway. She's nineteen, and I know they're carding at the door."

Eleanor frowned. "No, you don't understand. She's a determined girl, a college girl and way too young for—"

"You're warning me? That's cute."

"Cute? It's not cute. She spent last night talking about nothing but you—I don't think I've ever heard the word *hot* used so many times in a sentence. Look, just be aware and keep your hands off her. I don't want her making the mistake I made."

Dez pulled the door closed, grappling with the words Eleanor had thrown out. She thought he'd be into her daughter? What in the hell was wrong with her? He thought the message he'd given Eleanor in that back room was a pretty strong indicator. "Damn, I know you just didn't imply I'd hook up with your daughter."

Eleanor jerked her chin up. "I'm not stupid. I know Blakely's effect on men. She's young and beautiful."

"Really?" He stared hard at her.

"What?" she asked, her eyebrows drawing together. "What did you think I would think? You went with her on that walk. And from what I saw did nothing to dissuade her attraction to you."

"I wanted to give you time to get it together, and I did nothing more on that stroll to the gallery than ask questions about you. If that encouraged her, I don't even want to know how she responds to sincere romantic interest."

Eleanor remained silent, but in her eyes he saw what he didn't want to see—insecurity. As much as he wanted Eleanor, he wasn't rescuing her. "Know what? You're not the woman I thought you were."

Not bothering to hear what she had to say, he fished his car keys from his pocket and headed to where the Mustang was parked several yards down the street. Inside, his gut churned equal parts anger and disappointment. He wasn't going to waste his time on a woman who had to be convinced she was desirable. Eleanor tugged at him with a strange pull, but he couldn't bog himself down with a woman with esteem issues. Been there, done that with Erin. He wasn't stupid enough to take on a relationship that required more of him than it did her.

"Wait, what are you talking about?" Eleanor said, dogging his footsteps, her voice portraying honest bafflement. "I thought you—"

"You thought wrong."

"I drew a logical conclusion. Blakely is beautiful, young and pretty much what every guy wants. I have eyes."

He turned. "I'm not interested in your daughter, Eleanor.

I thought you knew I was interested in you. Pretty sure I was emphatic about that when you were half-naked."

Her eyes widened and she swiveled her head, glancing around the street. "I think it's best if we forget about that moment of insanity."

"Know what? You're right. I'm not into convincing a woman she's desirable."

Her gaze slid away for a second before meeting his again. "You don't understand."

"Guess I don't."

She paused, seemingly searching for the right words. "Issues in the past have tempered who I am. I'm trying to work through them, but I own the fact my husband's cheating on me with a younger woman skewed my thinking, made me feel a little less. Something like that makes you careful. Makes you feel not so…desirable. I'm trying, Dez, but it's hard." She shook her head, pressed her lips together and closed her eyes.

"I get that, but this isn't about the past, Eleanor. This is about here and now."

"But I've only known you for a few days. You don't know me. You don't know my situation. Everything's happening too fast."

Dez almost felt sorry for her. Almost. "I don't have to know your situation or put parameters on things. I'm not asking you to marry me. We're not entering into some complex agreement that says if we do this, then it means that. What we started between us wasn't about forever."

She flinched. "I know."

"I don't think you do. You've spent so long being overly careful about what you say and do, you've forgotten half the fun in living is going with your gut. There are some things in life that are meant for pleasure, fleeting, but worth it."

Anger flashed in her eyes. "I haven't had that luxury, Dez. Ever since I became a Theriot, I've been placed on a slide, shoved under a microscope, poked, prodded and tortured. I always had a daughter to protect, a family's reputation to uphold. I couldn't elevate myself over their well-being just so I could 'feel' something pleasurable."

"Aren't you tired of being a martyr? Aren't you tired of worrying what everyone else thinks, Eleanor?"

"I don't care what everyone thinks."

He cocked one eyebrow.

"Okay, maybe a little. I don't *want* to care, but I know what everyone will think about the aging Eleanor taking up with the young, hot pianist. They'll call me a cougar and stuff, and that sort of makes me feel dirty."

Dez smiled, wishing he could understand her world better. He'd never lived cautiously, so he couldn't judge her for not being able to disassociate with who she'd always been. "Feeling dirty is half the fun, babe. In fact, it's a lot of the fun. But I'm not going to corner you at every opportunity and try to convince you we'll be good together. I'm not into begging."

"I never asked you to."

"No, you warned me away from your daughter like I regularly sleep with any woman who crooks a finger at me. Your opinion of me is pretty low, just like your opinion of Blue Rondo. But, know what? You're wrong on both accounts, and it makes you come across as a judgmental, pompous Theriot who can't see outside the little world of prejudice you've built."

Her mouth fell open.

But he didn't regret his words. She needed to be shaken out of her box, the one she'd constructed to protect herself from getting hurt.

"What the hell are you implying? I'm not a racist."

"Never said you were. *You* just said that. I said you were prejudiced against me as a younger entertainer who obviously sleeps around…and prejudiced against a nightclub that's obviously going to bring in prostitution, drugs and violence."

"That's not fair, Dez."

"Maybe not, but it feels that way to me. You're making assumptions based on, hell, I don't even know what you're basing them on," he said, backing toward his car, not in retreat, but in an effort to end the conversation. "But actions really do speak louder than words."

"God, Dez," she whispered.

"Hurts, doesn't it? Life isn't something you can put rules on. It's something you do. Either you want me. Or you don't. Ball's in your court, and I'm hoping you can see past your Volvo, Eleanor. When you get brave enough to listen to your own heart, come find me."

He gave her a sardonic smile and climbed into his car, feeling justified in his words. He felt like someone needed to wake up Eleanor to who she was. Hopefully, his remarks would sink in and settle into her soul, making her question her motives and her actions.

Or rather inaction.

If he never saw her again, except from across the street, he'd live with that repercussion even if the thought made his gut clench. Eleanor had inspired the music in him again, and he didn't want to lose that…or the possibility of something more with her.

Yeah, he'd regret it, but he'd regret stepping into a relationship where he had to convince someone of his worthiness. The years he'd spent with Erin had taught him an important lesson about women—he couldn't fix them.

So he wasn't making that mistake with Eleanor.

He wanted her with a need so intense it hurt, but he wasn't lying on an altar to be used and abused, marginalized as something he wasn't. He thought more of himself than that.

Dez wanted Eleanor.

But she had to want him, too.

TRE SAT ON THE BENCH at the bus stop, balancing Kenzie on his knee. He'd gone to three day cares in the area near their house, and wouldn't let a dog stay at any of them…much less the three-year-old sucking on her fingers.

"Kenz, time you start using the toilet, baby girl. We need money, and diapers ain't cheap, you know."

Kenzie looked at him with bottomless eyes and kept slurping.

Damn. Kenzie needed to learn to talk, too. She should be saying lots of words by now. Hell, when Shorty D was three years old, he never shut up. He worried about her. What if something was wrong with her? She was too little and would hardly eat sometimes. Maybe he could bring her to that clinic Cici had taken her to back in the fall, and talk to the nurses or doctors there. Last time they'd said Kenzie needed to eat more, and had given them a book about nutrition. But going there would have to wait until next Thursday, since he'd taken today off to look for a seven-day-a-week day care.

Tre felt someone sit down, and turned his head to find a woman about his age settling her purse on her lap. She wore a tight skirt that fell past her knees, a bright yellow jacket and overly large sunglasses. Her glossy pink lips pursed together as she gave him a cool glance. Or at least he thought it was kind of cool since he couldn't actually see behind her glasses.

"What up?" he said, acknowledging her presence.

She lifted her eyebrows. "How would I know? That particular greeting doesn't make much sense."

He didn't know what to say to that. She was definitely his age, give or take a few years, but she talked funny. Like she was from up north or something. So he didn't say anything else. Just glared back.

Shit, she was fine, but he wasn't whack. And he wasn't taking any shit off any uppity shorty with a badass attitude.

But Kenzie stared at the woman with fascination. Probably because her jacket was so bright.

"Hey, little angel," the woman said, wiggling her fingers at Kenzie, showing she at least didn't have ice running through her body.

Kenzie smiled.

Tre couldn't believe it. The kid rarely made any expression. "She likes you."

"Of course she does. Babies and children in general have good instincts about people. She can tell I like children."

The woman continued to flirt with Kenzie, playing peekaboo and making silly faces. The woman didn't like him, but she certainly liked Kenzie.

"Does she talk?" the woman asked.

He didn't say anything for a moment. Just watched traffic whiz by and wondered why this woman asked him such stupid questions. Wasn't any of her business, was it?

"Did you hear what I asked?"

He turned to her. "Yeah, I heard you. I just don't care to answer a person who acts rude when I ask her 'what up?'"

She slid her glasses down her nose and angled a firm gaze at him with eyes the color of strong coffee. "You're dogging me for correcting a greeting better suited for someone with gold teeth and britches down to his ankles. I'm a lady."

Tre almost laughed. She was funny. "Okay. You a lady. How do you do, lady?"

She smiled. "Very well, thank you. And you?"

"Oh, I'm ever so lovely. Fine day, is it not?" He affected a British accent. He might be from the hood, but he wasn't stupid.

She laughed, and it sounded like little bells ringing, the way Christmas sounded. Light and hopeful. Kenzie clapped her small hands together, which made the woman, who'd at first looked cold as an icicle, smile. "Where'd you learn to talk like that?"

"Finishing school for young black men with britches down to their ankles," Tre said, giving her a rare smile.

"You look nice when you smile," she said, turning her knees toward him. "I'm Alicia."

"Trevon. And this is Kenzie."

Alicia smiled. "Well, your daughter is precious."

"She not my daughter. She my cousin."

"Oh," Alicia said, nodding. "Well, you're a good cousin. I can tell by the way she keeps looking at you."

"She don't talk much. I been worried about that." Now, why had he said that?

"She's very tiny. Does she go to school?"

He shook his head. For some reason, he wanted to keep talking to Alicia, but the bus rambled toward them with the squealing of brakes. He shifted Kenzie to his hip and stood, standing back so "the lady" could find her bus pass and board first.

As she passed him, Alicia acknowledged his manners with a nod of her head. "Thank you."

He inclined his head and followed her up the steps, not even bothering to keep his eyes off her rounded backside, which was plump and made for a man's hands.

Kenzie whined a little, but he shushed her, found a seat not too far from Alicia and settled the little girl back in his lap. He'd left Shorty D with the lady next door because Cici had miraculously kept her job and had to work that morning. He could manage Kenzie a lot easier than Shorty D, plus he'd wanted to see the day care facilities firsthand.

"Hey, Trevon," Alicia called out, catching his eye. "You gonna ask for my digits?"

Inside he grinned. On the outside he played it cool. "A lady like you don't call a phone number digits, does she?"

Alicia shrugged. "I call it what it is. They are digits so it makes sense. I'm practical that way."

Tre appreciated practical in a woman. Alicia felt like a little bit of something delivered to him. Like maybe God was tossing him a life preserver in the midst of choppy waters. He didn't know why it felt that way, but it did.

He pulled his phone from his front pocket, shushing Kenzie when she fussed, and passed the phone to Alicia.

A woman his grandmother's age tittered like a bird, her eyes sparking at what she believed the start of something romantic. It sort of made him embarrassed, but not embarrassed enough to not pass his phone.

Alicia went to work pressing icons on his screen, looking as though she knew her way around an iPhone, the one indulgence he allowed himself.

A minute later, giggling granny passed it back to him. "Ooh wee."

He slid his eyes toward Alicia, and she smiled the kind of smile Shorty D used when he got his way. That smile filled him with edgy anticipation.

When should he text her?

Wait, she was an old-fashioned girl…maybe he actually needed to call her. Should he ask her to meet him somewhere? Maybe the movies?

The bus rattled along Carrollton, taking him closer to the old house his grandmother had lived in her whole life, closer to Cici, Shorty D and bills that would go unpaid, but somehow felt lighter.

He saw his stop ahead and pushed the button, tossing Alicia a nod before he climbed off with Kenzie and a battered diaper bag. As the bus pulled away, he caught her eye for several seconds, and it felt like something in a movie. And then the moment was over. He pulled his phone from his pocket and pulled up his contacts.

Alicia Laurence.

He clicked the info and saw she'd put something in the company field.

Lighthouse Center for Special Needs Children.

A profound presence settled around him, and he looked up at the sky dotted with ruffled clouds and whispered, "Thank You, Lord."

CHAPTER EIGHT

DEZ STOOD on the wooden deck of the Priest and Pug Pub and counted off a sound check for the technician. Since the day was such a nice departure from winter-weary grayness, and Carnival was in its prime, Ray, the pub's owner, had suggested they do the gig outside, which pleased Dez. Most people liked the confines of playing the piano in a room with four walls, but Dez liked the freedom to release his notes into air, letting them rise over the treetops, reach the ears of those walking down the street or hanging out the wash.

He wasn't so sure the surrounding area liked it, but it *was* Mardi Gras weekend, and one could taste the excitement in the air.

Already parade-goers lined Canal Street, their coolers and tents bright with decorations honoring the festivities. The eating and drinking appeared to have started early. He'd even glimpsed some second-line dancing in the street, people of all ages, colors and sizes taking up the challenge to dance, reveling in the sunshine and being alive.

Strains of traditional Mardi Gras music filtered over the wood fence surrounding the back patio of the Priest and Pug, and Dez found himself singing about the Audubon Zoo.

The sound guy laughed and joined in. "They all ax for you."

"They even inquire about ya," Dez sang, smiling at the silliness. But, whatever. It was Mardi Gras—a time for absurdity, eating too much king cake and drinking too much Abita beer.

"We good?" Dez called to the guy who gave a thumbs-up.

"Yo, you ready, brah?" Ray said, sneaking up on them, followed by the guys Dez had hired to play with him at Blue Rondo in a few months. Kyle Barre, Champ O'Rear and Little T Sparks worked the horn section, with Champ subbing in at guitar when needed. Big Eddie Guerrero handled drums. They were a good fit for him, young but still moderately experienced. They'd had some problems with negotiating money, but finally settled on a schedule that would expand with the success of the club. They were good guys who would hopefully grow with Dez as he tried to rebuild the reputation he'd left behind years ago.

"Trombone Sonny comin'?" Big Eddie asked as he tightened the various parts on his drum kit.

"He'll be here for about half an hour at the beginning of our second set. He's riding on one of the floats as a celebrity."

Champ snorted. "Wish I was a smooth baller like Trombone Sonny. I'd be rollin' in dough and chicks."

"Don't we all," Dez said.

Big Eddie gave a big guffaw that scared the bejesus out of a few waitresses wiping down tables. "Who you kiddin'? You pretty as a little bitch."

Dez waved off his band and jogged to where Ray had moved to greet a man wearing a silk suit. "What's up?"

"Hey, Dez. This is Thomas Windmere."

"I know Tom," Dez said, shaking the hand of his former manager, clamping down on the flipping in his stomach.

"Good to see you, Dez."

Dez would say it was good to see Tom, too, but it wasn't. Tom had been his manager long before he'd signed on a young Andrew "Trombone Sonny" Jefferies. After Katrina, when most managers would have the courtesy, hell, the conviction to remain with their clients who'd lost everything, Ol' Tom had met up with Trombone Sonny on tour in Oregon and put his eggs in the basket of a young up-and-comer. Sure, he hadn't dropped Dez, but he might as well have. So Dez dropped him first. "Yeah. How you been?"

"Busy. Trombone Sonny's really got momentum. His sound has caught the attention of a lot of big names. He's opening for Kid Rock next week at the Bowl then he's off to Germany for a tour."

"Good for Drew. He's a great artist and deserves success. I appreciate him coming out here and tossing me some of his talent."

"So you're not working on an album?" Tom asked.

"No, just working on the club. I think it's going to be a unique venue and bring some of the talent into an area that also has a strong musical identity."

Ray laughed. "You sound like a politician."

Dez stiffened. No way was he even close to taking up anything in the realm. He was an ambassador for music and for his new business. Nothing more. Or less. "Just a businessman trying to do something good for my community."

"And yourself," Tom added.

"That, too."

Dez didn't want to continue the conversation tinged with animosity. He needed a positive vibe going for the gig, and trading barbs with his former manager wasn't going to get him anything more than a red ass. No sense hating on Tom because he'd swum in another direction, leaving Dez to sink into oblivion. No sense in hating on Drew for taking the hand held out to him. That was business. No sense in living in the past. Dez had a future to claim. "Need to take care of some things. Tom, wish you and Trombone Sonny the best. Later."

Dez went back to the stage and rechecked the mics and tacked the set list to the stage. The band had indulged in oyster po'boys and draft while he chatted up Ray and Tom, and Dez needed to get some food before they started.

An hour and a half later in the middle of Trombone Sonny's tribute to the Mardi Gras Indians Wild Magnolias, Dez had forgotten about Tom, old resentments and the uncertainty of all things in his life. There was nothing but the music.

Until Eleanor walked in.

ELEANOR PUSHED THROUGH the throng of people standing on the huge weathered deck, happy for Dez that the Priest and Pug was packed. Standing room only…not that there were many seats anyway other than the stools clustered around tall bar tables, and even those were filled. People tapped feet, clapped hands and shouted into each other's ears as they swigged beer and enjoyed the gift of a beautiful day and soul-stirring music.

After sitting through the shower brunch for her niece Justine, Eleanor was more than ready for a drink and a reprieve from the world of monogrammed napkins and Limoges china. She still wished she hadn't been talked into helping host the shower at her mother-in-law's Garden District mansion. Justine's mother, Courtney, despised her, blaming the whole Skeeter scandal on Eleanor's depression after the storm. Somehow, everything was Eleanor's fault in the Theriots' eyes.

Margaret had been in rare form, simpering over Justine, playing the generous matriarch, tittering, glittering and whittling Eleanor down with her smiling barbs.

"Oh, I remember when you got married, Eleanor. Of course, we weren't able to have a shower, were we? And you picked out that dated china pattern they didn't even carry in Dillard's, for heaven's sake."

Along with, "Skeeter would have loved to be an usher with his cousins. Oh, if things had been different. I miss him so much."

And finishing with, "Oh, and my final surprise for all my girls. Ta da!" Then she'd passed out pink shopping bags to Justine, Courtney, Blakely and Eleanor's other niece, Harley. Bags containing pink Valentino purses.

Of course, Eleanor didn't get one—not that she would want it anyway—because she had never been one of Margaret's girls. Even Blakely had noticed and given her a hug over the slight. Yes, Margaret always got her digs in—this time twofold. Blakely got the bag she'd begged for last week and Eleanor was made to feel like the redheaded stepchild of the Theriot family…just as she'd always been.

So after sitting at the shower, listening to the lacquered New Orleans society ooh and aah over overpriced gifts, Eleanor wondered exactly what held her back from Dez.

This?

Thin, judgmental women she didn't really like anyway?

Or was it merely because Dez was younger? Or that his skin wasn't the color of a frog's belly like Skeeter's? Did it matter he made his living playing a piano? Was she throwing up roadblocks because as the president of the Merchants Association she was supposed to protect the integrity of her block? There were lots of reasons Dez was the wrong person to introduce her to a new life as a nearly fortysomething single lady, but none were bigger than the fact she wanted him.

Over her, under her, in her and around her.

Her sojourn to Margaret's hadn't been the straw that broke the camel's back in regard to Dez, but it helped her realize she was tired of worrying about how her actions affected others. She was tired of thinking about Blakely's feelings over her own happiness. She was really sickened of Margaret, and had decided after helping throw Justine's shower, she was done with any leftover obligations to Skeeter's family. They sucked the joy out of her life, and she was done with toeing whatever line they set.

So she was ready to line her toes up on the end of the diving board and secure the ties of her bikini before diving into the deep waters of modern-day dating. Screw wading into the waters in her sensible one-piece suit. If she were going to take the plunge, might as well do it with the finest man she'd seen in a decade.

Eleanor only hoped she didn't belly flop.

So she'd gone home, washed her hair, painted her toenails a bright lime-green and put on her skinny jeans. Then she'd sprayed her favorite perfume right between her breasts, tugged on a sexy lace bra and tight sweater, and headed out to the Priest and Pug.

She didn't even care that she was going to support the man who she was supposed to oppose. The Magazine Street Merchants Association would have to freaking impeach her.

Eleanor wanted Dez to know she wasn't afraid to take what she wanted…and she wanted him. Just as he was. For a little while. For as long as it worked for both of them.

So when she shoved through the crowd of people, wearing her favorite pair of cowboy boots with the turquoise trim that matched her sweater, she gave him a smile that would leave no doubt.

"Hey, how's it going?"

Eleanor turned to find an overweight man with beer trickling down his chin grinning at her. "Oh, hey. Going good."

"You here alone?"

How did she answer that? Was she here alone? Technically, yes. But futuristically, she hoped not. "I'm waiting on someone."

"Yeah? Why doncha come wait with me a little while. Let me buy you a drink."

"I don't think so," she said, keeping her eyes on Dez, who seemed to notice the interaction. His dark eyebrows lowered and his gaze narrowed, but he didn't stop hammering the keys of the piano.

"Aw, come on. A pretty lady like you don't need to stand here without a drink." The man's hand brushed her waist, giving her creepy crawlies in her stomach.

She grabbed the man's wrist and pushed it back. With a smile, she said, "Hands to yourself."

The drunk leered at her. "You know you like it."

Eleanor blinked at the obtuseness of the man. Was this what it was like "out there" in dating land? Getting mauled by drunks who thought women liked clammy, meaty hands of strangers touching them? She brought the heel of her boot down on the top of the man's tennis shoe.

"Yeow!" he yelped, stepping back as fast as a scalded cat.

"Oops. Sorry," she said, not bothering to smile this time.

"Bitch."

"Thank you," Eleanor said, refusing to scamper away even though she wanted to move elsewhere on the patio. She wouldn't give the man with the wandering hands the satisfaction of watching her flee. And she'd never been called a bitch before, well, except when Blakely might have muttered the insult under her breath. Eleanor decided she didn't mind being called a bitch.

The thought made her smile.

And big, drunk and misogynist took off to find other woman to molest.

She cut her gaze back to Dez and he smiled, maybe even chuckled a little, before diverting his attention back to the instrument, which he mastered so well. And at that moment, she knew she'd made the right decision by coming to his gig.

Ten minutes later, when Blakely and her friends arrived, she wasn't so sure. For one thing, she didn't know how they'd gotten inside the bar when they were under the age of twenty-one. Maybe the bouncer looked the other way on a day when the streets were packed and breathing like a live organism. Or Blakely could have scored a fake ID. Wouldn't put it past that savvy group of girls to be prepared with someone else's driver's license.

Of course, Blakely looked much older than nineteen. Her lanky body, which had seemed so awkward a few years ago, had rounded out with curves in all the right places. A sophisticated application of makeup highlighted her strong bone structure. Her aura of self-assurance gave her added maturity, so she looked in her mid-twenties, rather than clinging to nineteen.

As she and her friends moved through the crowd, men turned and looked. Hell, women did, too. Her beauty drew the eye, and her freshness made Eleanor shrink toward the perimeter.

But the bright turquoise of her sweater caught her daughter's eye. Blakely frowned and wove toward her, leaving her friends at a table full of college-aged guys.

"Mom, what are you *doing* here?" she shouted over the thrum of music.

"Me? What are you doing here? You're not even old enough to get in," Eleanor said, tugging Blakely into a less crowded area. "You said you were going to Emily Serio's grandmother's place to watch the parade."

"We are…later," she said, her eyes flickering toward the stage where Dez and his band seemed to be ending their set. "But I told Dez I'd come hear him play. Wow, he's, like, really good."

Eleanor didn't bother looking at the stage. Instead she studied her daughter. Studied the way she licked her lips and the spark of desire in her blue eyes.

What the hell did a woman do when she and her daughter wanted the same man?

Arm wrestle for him?

"Yes, he's good, but as previously stated, he's much too

old for you," she said, taking a less physical, more rational approach. She didn't care if she and Dez didn't work out; Blakely wasn't going to make the mistakes her mother had made. She wasn't going to date a thirty-year-old man.

"But too young for you," Blakely said, returning her gaze to her mother. "Is that why you're here? Because you're into him?"

Well, hell.

Eleanor really didn't know how to answer that one.

Thankfully, she didn't have to, because the object of their desire headed toward them, looking hotter than a two-dollar pistol, in a pair of tight jeans and a short-sleeved gray T-shirt with some kind of British-looking screen print on it. Motorcycle boots completed the look, and the mirrored sunglasses propped on his head and simple silver crucifix at the base of his throat only made him look almost untouchable. Like he belonged in an ad in *Glamour* or something. He had an essence that made a girl sigh.

He stopped next to Blakely and the girl sighed.

Exactly.

"Hey, ladies," he said, holding up two fingers to the bartender, who must have been directly behind Eleanor. He turned to Blakely. "How'd you manage to get in?"

Her daughter smiled. "I have my ways."

He arched an eyebrow at Eleanor. "You came."

Not yet.

Eleanor shook herself, dumping her dirty thoughts and focusing on the predicament in front of her. "Yeah, thought about that old saying about friends and enemies."

"Oh, keeping your friends close, but your enemies closer?"

Blakely shook her head. "It's family. You're supposed to keep your family closer...or something like that."

The irony wasn't lost on Eleanor. She gave a fake laugh.

"Guess I'm covered both ways. Family and friends. Right here. Right now. Besides, Dez, I don't consider you an enemy."

"I hope not," he said, his voice lowering a few octaves.

Narrowing her eyes, Blakely turned from Eleanor and smiled brightly at Dez. "So if you're not watching the parade anywhere, I'd love for you to join me. A friend's family has a prime spot and there will be a keg and stuff."

"Well, that sounds cool, but I already have plans."

Of course he had plans. What had Eleanor expected? Dez to wait around on her while she decided if she would or wouldn't...if she could or couldn't? Suddenly she felt stupid.

"Oh, well, that's cool. I'll give you my number if you want to hook up later and go out." Blakely flipped her hair over her shoulder, trying for nonchalance.

"That's decent of you, Blakely. I appreciate the invitation. Relay that to your friend."

"So what about you, Mom? You going somewhere to watch the parade? Are you, like, here with anyone?" Blakely looked around as if she expected someone to pop out and give Eleanor a better reason for standing in a bar watching Dez play.

"No," Eleanor said, as loud music blasted through the speakers. "I'm not with anyone. Just felt like getting out. Haven't been to a bar in forever and I thought I might be supportive."

"Of someone you've been grumping about for months?" Blakely cracked, smiling at Dez as if they'd established it as an inside joke.

"Dez is my friend."

"She's trying to keep me closer," Dez said, sliding an arm around Eleanor, pulling her to him and delivering a charming smile.

Oh, he so didn't know how close she wanted to keep him. His eyes dipped to her neckline and grew smokier than they had previously.

Okay, maybe he did.

Finally, Blakely picked up on the currents and twisted her lips. A little furrow appeared between her beautiful eyebrows, and Eleanor saw the lightbulb go off. The frown, however, stayed.

"Why don't you come with us, Mom? Mrs. Serio will be there, and y'all can drink wine and gossip or something. I know she'd like you to come," Blakely said, slipping her hand inside the new purse she'd received earlier to extract a container of pink lip gloss and apply it without the aid of a mirror. She smacked her lips and smiled. "I'd hate to leave you here by yourself, and I think Emily's uncle Bobby will be there. He's had a hip replacement, but he's back to playing tennis again. You love tennis."

"Not really into tennis, but you go on ahead, honey. I'm not even sure I'm staying for the parade. I might drop by Pansy's house later. She's thinking about putting up some vintage wallpaper and wants me to look at the backing. I'm fine. You go and have fun."

"Okay," Blakely said with a shrug, before turning to Dez and leaning forward to kiss his cheek. "Good seeing you, Dez. You were superb."

Dez gave her an awkward hug, shooting a puzzled glance to Eleanor as if to say, *What the hell?*

She didn't know what to say to that either. In fact, the whole exchange had felt like something in a movie, rife with tension, underlying electricity, and ringed with disappointment. A more awkward moment hadn't existed.

Okay, it had.

Hell, Eleanor knew awkward. Only she had never felt it with her daughter competing over a man.

That thought had the doubt creeping back in.

Did she want to head down that one-way street? Dez wasn't interested in Blakely, but Blakely was interested in him, and if her daughter knew how close the two of them had come to having illicit sex in the back of the Queen's Box, the gulf that existed between mother and daughter could well become an ocean. Even though Dez struck something inside of Eleanor that smoldered out of control, she didn't think scratching that particular itch was worth ruining the relationship she had with her daughter…even if nothing would or could happen between Blakely and Dez.

She wasn't going to choose sex over her daughter.

Hadn't Blakely said what had been hanging out there for the past few days?

You're too old for him.

How many more flashing warning lights did she need to get the message? The capricious free spirit in her, that small piece of herself she'd smothered with reason and judiciousness, had been locked in a closet for many years for good reason. Living selfishly, with little thought of repercussions, wasn't what was required of Eleanor.

She was stupid. She was crazy. She was—

"I have one more set, Eleanor, and then we can go," Dez said, taking the two beers a waitress handed him, giving one to Eleanor and clinking his bottle against hers. "Wait for me."

He'd totally taken the decision out of her hands while simultaneously letting Blakely know why he wasn't going to be "hooking up with her later."

Because he was going to be hooking up with her mother.

Dez winked and jogged to the stage, leaving the two women in uncomfortable silence.

"Mom?" Blakely turned a hurt expression on her. "You're not seriously going out with Dez, are you? You're old enough to be his mother. My God. That's, like, icky."

It was at that moment, with Blakely clutching the thousand-dollar handbag Eleanor's mean-ass-bitch former mother-in-law had bought her, looking as if someone had kicked the puppy she'd never even wanted in the first place, that Eleanor decided listening to her capricious free spirit was long overdue.

Dez wanted Eleanor.

And she wanted him.

As a friend, as a lover and maybe not anything else, but at that moment, it was enough for Eleanor to reach out with both hands and grab hold of him.

Screw convention.

Because she'd be damned if she gave up a chance to feel whole again because her daughter thought it was improper.

For once, Eleanor was going to take what she wanted, even if it meant Blakely had to swallow it down like bitter medicine.

"First of all, unless I ovulated at seven years old, it's highly improbable I could have given birth to Dez. Second, I've spent my life taking care of you and your father, worrying about what everyone else wanted. I'm tired of being just a mother. I'm tired of being just Skeeter Theriot's poor cuckolded widow. And I'm really tired of trying to please everyone else and never myself. So honestly, honey, I love you, but I couldn't give a rat's ass if you approve of who I date."

And with that said, Eleanor turned away from her daughter, stomped across the deck and parked her thirty-nine-year-old ass on an empty stool until Dez finished his last set.

CHAPTER NINE

USUALLY DEZ LINGERED on a set, playing drawn-out solos, proving his command of the instrument, giving Champ leeway to do the same, but today he hungered for something more than his ass on a piano bench—he hungered for the woman sitting on a stool, legs crossed and eyes resolute.

He'd seen the angry words between her and Blakely, and the resulting flash of resentment in Eleanor's eyes made him silently applaud her.

His fingers found the keys, falling into the grooves perfectly, the music gliding, dripping, filling the bottom of his soul. The movement of his fingers was as natural as breathing, and the anticipation of having Eleanor all to himself at the end of the gig built inside him, fueling the desire simmering beneath the surface.

Eleanor had chosen him.

Simple as that.

He'd never come between a woman and her daughter, but he could see Blakely through a stranger's eyes. Blakely was like so many women who'd flitted in and out of his life—charming, beautiful and bold. But she came with baggage. Underneath the beauty lay a strong will to manipulate, and immaturity requiring time to temper. It was a time thing. Blakely may look like a woman, but inside she was very much a girl.

It baffled him that Eleanor thought he'd drop the attraction he felt for her in trade for her daughter. Blakely was beautiful, but in a glossy-magazine way. Filler advertisements.

He refocused his attention on the complicated run at the end of the last song, and ten minutes later, after resounding applause, stood next to Eleanor.

"You ready?"

She'd been nursing the beer he'd handed her. He took the warm bottle and set it on the table, nodding his thanks to those who called out their appreciation for the music.

"You can leave now? Don't you have to pack up?"

"It's not my piano. The guys are packing up our gear, but I'm done and ready to go play with you."

He didn't mean it the way it came out, but the way Eleanor's eyes widened, and the way the heat flared between them, was satisfying.

"Okay, then."

He helped her off the stool, taking pleasure in touching her, inhaling the scent of her hair. "Let's roll."

After thanking Ray for the third time and introducing his "neighbor" to the bar owner, they made their getaway. Blakely was nowhere to be seen, and relief settled in his bones. They walked out of the Priest and Pug and right into chaos.

The crowds had thickened along the streets and the music bled into a cacophony of jazz and hip-hop. Everywhere people milled about in funny hats and laden with ropes of shiny beads. Beer flowed, children laughed and New Orleans made ready for one of their favorite parades. Endymion delivered more throws—the goodies tossed from the floats—than any other parade, and in less than an hour it would roll past where he and Eleanor stood. Ray had erected a tent, and though Dez wanted nothing more than to take Eleanor back to his place and peel off her tight jeans, he also wanted to savor the evening with her.

He remembered the words he'd tossed at her days ago. *You*

seem like the kind of woman who needs a little flirting in her life. She also seemed like the kind of woman who needed some time before they moved forward.

Eleanor needed lots of foreplay.

And Dez reveled in foreplay.

"How about we catch the parade here? Ray gave me some tickets for the spread of food he's putting out. I haven't been to a parade since before Katrina."

Eleanor looked around, and for a moment he saw alarm creep into her gaze. It was a very public place, but also a place they could fade into the crowd. She nodded.

He slid his hand down and captured hers, marking her as his…at least for the moment.

Her face relaxed. "Actually I haven't watched a parade in a while myself. Like most locals, I choose to stay out of Mardi Gras traffic. So, yeah, we're here. Let's watch the parade."

They moved toward the large tent bearing the Priest and Pug sign and got in line behind several other patrons wearing wristbands. When they reached the table, a woman took their tickets, wrapped a band around their wrists and handed them a beer. "All you can eat. Have fun."

Dez dipped out jambalaya and barbecue shrimp while Eleanor went for the oysters and fried chicken. She didn't hold back, and not one leaf of lettuce touched her plate. He even liked the way she ate. Oysters and beer? Right up his alley.

"We don't have chairs," she said, scooping up extra napkins and glancing about.

Dez followed her gaze. "We don't need 'em. Come on."

He led them to a curving oak tree set back several yards from the street. In front of them were ladders with old-fashioned carpenter boxes set side by side like soldiers along the parade route, awaiting parents who would climb them and seat small children on top so they could see the elaborate floats roll by without getting trampled. The ladders were a brilliant idea, but hard to see around. However, Dez knew that if he and Eleanor sat back several yards from the street, they could still see the festivity unique to the Crescent City.

Spreading his jacket, he indicated she sit.

"I don't want to—"

"Sit already. I'm starving."

She plopped down and spread a napkin in her lap. Just like the lady she was.

He lumbered down beside her, balancing his beer and plate. "Perfect."

She watched the screaming kids chasing one another, the adults laughing and eating Popeye's Chicken out of the box, and the sun dropping behind the row of houses lined up across the neutral ground. She nodded. "It *is* perfect."

They dug into their food, taking a few moments to ooh and aah over the savory dishes, tossing back beer and waving at the kids who played hopscotch on the sidewalk nearby.

It was one of the better meals he'd had in a while.

"Look." Eleanor jabbed a finger to their right. "Here come police cars. Won't be long now."

He wiped his mouth and stood, offering her his hand. Instead of taking it, she shoved her empty plate into it and smiled. "Thanks."

He took both of the plates but couldn't find a nearby garbage can. Finally, he spotted one near a port-a-let, but when he turned back, Eleanor was gone. He scanned the area and found her tossing stones and playing hopscotch down the sidewalk in her blue-and-brown boots.

Several little girls watched in silent admiration.

"What're you doing?" he asked, smiling as the little girls eyed his approach.

"She's playing with us," one girl said, looking at him like he was an idiot. *Duh, can't you see, big dumb man?*

He arched an eyebrow.

Eleanor turned and hopped back, her breath coming in short puffs. "Needed to work off that fried chicken."

He held out his hand and she took it.

"Thanks for letting me have a turn," she said to the same little girl who had answered him seconds ago.

"No problem," the girl said, picking up the rocks and handing them to her friend.

Eleanor waved goodbye and in her manner, Dez could see the mother she'd been to Blakely—calm, fun and loving. Didn't take a rocket scientist for him to see she liked kids and could be silly. In every minute he spent with her, he grew to admire her more and more.

Eleanor walked back to where she'd left his jacket and picked it up, handing it to him. "I couldn't resist the challenge Lucy threw down."

"Lucy, huh? She sounds like a Lucy."

"Thank goodness she didn't have a football," Eleanor joked. "You ready to go?"

"No. Are you?"

Tilting her head, Eleanor studied him. "I can't figure you out. You do understand I picked up the challenge *you* laid down."

"Yeah, but I'm not ready to let go of this moment," he said, and tugged her to his side as two fire trucks sounding their sirens rolled down Canal Street, signaling the start of the parade.

"See? I don't know how to respond. You're different than any other man I've been around."

"And you've been with a lot of guys?"

"Uh, isn't that, like—" she crooked her fingers into little quotations marks "—a 'date three' question?"

"I don't know. I don't have rules for—" he crooked his own fingers "—'dating.' I figure you got married young and hadn't spent a lot of time with different guys. You had Blakely when you were, what?"

"I turned twenty years old a month before she was born," she murmured, stopping them at an open area on the sidewalk as a high school band marched along the parade route followed by a team of Clydesdales pulling a beer wagon.

"And since your husband died?"

"I've been on one date, which really wasn't a date. We attended my high school reunion together so we wouldn't have to deal with the recently divorced classmates on the prowl," she said, keeping her eyes on the parade bearing down on them. As he looked up the street, he could see the thousands of throws being tossed from both sides of the first float. "I thought you said you didn't need to know my past."

"I don't, but I wanted to affirm something."

"What? That I'm a loser?"

He sighed. "This again?"

"It was a self-deprecating joke," she said, rolling her eyes with a smile. "So what do you need to confirm?"

"That you need time."

"What if I don't want time?" She turned and stared him in the eye. "What if I want to take you home, strip you naked and make you scream my name?"

"I'd say, 'taxi!'"

A smile curved her very delectable mouth. Her teasing struck a match, but he wasn't ready to set the kindling they'd laid aflame. It was enough she'd taken the step toward him. No need for either of them to misstep before they'd even started.

"So, in all seriousness, you don't want me in that way… uh…right now?"

He curved an arm around her, drawing her into the hollow under his arm. She felt good beside him, like a perfect-fit good. And she smelled like vanilla and something else he couldn't place, but it was sexy, soft and inviting.

He was a fool.

The only thing he should be doing was hauling her to his car and then up to his bed.

"If we weren't in front of a million people, including those little ones back there, I'd show you how much I want you, but I don't intend to spend the evening in jail." He jerked his head toward the uniformed officer leaning against the street sign at the intersection on their right.

"And here I was looking forward to getting dirty."

He pulled her tighter to him. "You know how after Thanksgiving, you start humming Christmas carols and wanting to do festive things?"

"Huh?" she said, reaching up to grab a plastic cup thrown off another fire truck rolling by.

"Bear with me." He snatched a pair of beads from the air and hung them around her neck. "I like that feeling. Anticipation."

"Like the Carly Simon song," she said, before wagging the cup. "Hey, we don't have a bag to store throws."

"Give it to those kids."

Eleanor placed the cup at her feet. "So that's what you're doing? Building anticipation?"

"Yeah. I like soaking in moments, enjoying the stage I'm in every minute of every day. For a little longer I want to feel this newness between us. To savor the way you feel beside me, laughing, playing hopscotch, catching—"

Her hand shot up and she grabbed a pair of purple and gold beads.

"—beads," he finished.

She turned to look at him, nearly getting conked in the head by a Frisbee. "I don't know what to say, but that's kind of beautiful."

He reached up to catch another big strand of beads. "I'm thinking we better save the serious convo for later."

"Ow," she said as another cup hit her shoulder. "I think you're right."

For the next hour they were pelted with coins, beads and other throws, even netting a big stuffed bear for Lucy. After dumping off their loot with the girls' family, they walked hand in hand back to the parking lot behind the Priest and Pug.

"So, are we calling it a night?" Eleanor asked.

"What do you want to do?"

She wrinkled her nose. "I don't know. No one ever asks me what I want to do. My life has been a lot of what I have to do."

"Then I definitely think you need to decide."

"That may be the single most romantic thing a man has ever said to me."

ELEANOR STOOD IN the parking lot, staring up at the most gorgeous creature she'd ever had the pleasure of kissing, and closed her eyes.

What did she want?

A successful business? A better relationship with her daughter? World peace? She wanted to have wild, passionate sex with Dez, but she also liked being with him, having his attention focused on her. Something good curled round her insides at the realization he had tossed the ball in her court yesterday and that it had stayed there. He wasn't pushing her, using his appeal against her. Quite frankly, he was giving her space.

"How about coffee?" She cracked an eye open.

"I like coffee."

"There's a CC's close to my place, and they have really good caramel brownies," she said, wondering if a brownie could satisfy the craving that had set up shop inside her, hanging out an open-for-business sign.

Probably not.

"I'll follow you. Where're you parked?"

She pointed down a narrow side street.

"Let me walk you to your car."

Wrapping an arm around her, Dez walked beside her. They were surrounded by the chatter of thousands making their way back to cars and houses. The chilly night air settled on them, and Eleanor was glad for the warmth of Dez's arm. He smelled good—clean laundry mixed with sultry cologne. She took a couple of extra deep breaths so she could memorize the scent of him.

Several minutes later, they approached her Volvo parked beneath a fluorescent streetlight. Safety first. She always parked under a streetlight just as her father had taught her years before.

"This is me."

He released her so she could pull her keys from her pocket and unlock the doors, but he didn't move away. His hip brushed hers, a constant reminder of his maleness, of the fact she wanted him. No, needed him to help her move forward. To help her live again.

Eleanor turned so her back was against the door, and tilted her face at him. "We're still on for coffee, right? I mean, if you want to go back to your place or something, that's okay, too."

He peered down, his gray eyes strangely bright in the dimness. "I want to take you home."

Her stomach flopped. "But—"

"I stand by my initial plan. Your daughter's home this weekend. We could jump into bed and have a really good time there, but for some crazy-ass reason, I want to take my time with you."

Eleanor swallowed because the way he said *take my time with you* sounded sexier than anything she'd ever heard. She gazed at his mouth and swallowed again. His lips were made for kissing…or taking his time leisurely traveling down her body. "Oh, well, those are good points."

The air crackled between them, and he leaned in, setting a hand on the car door. His gaze dropped to where the pulse in her throat galloped, and her body changed from cold to scorching in .09 seconds. Or some other crazy-fast speed. She didn't follow NASCAR.

"You know what I like, Eleanor?" he asked, his fingers lightly tracing her jawline before he slid one finger down her throat to the edge of her sweater. "I like foreplay."

She inhaled, closing her eyes. "Oh, I'm really glad you said that."

He chuckled.

"Seriously. Because sex therapists cite lack of foreplay as the leading cause of women failing to climax."

He didn't respond so she opened her eyes.

"It's true," she said.

His grin widened. "How long have you been holding on to that tidbit?"

"I thought it was widely known," she said, studying the smooth expanse of male flesh visible at the base of his throat. No crinkly hairs present or weird bumpy things. Just smooth skin the color of caramel.

"Climax won't be a problem because I'm a very determined man."

She lifted her gaze. "Are you?"

"Uh-huh," he said, lowering his head and catching her lips with his.

For a moment she stayed perfectly still, receiving his fairly chaste kiss…at least chaste for a man who claimed her upcoming orgasm was a sure thing. Please let it be a sure thing… eventually…when he got through with foreplay.

She opened her mouth to him and an avalanche of need toppled onto her. One moment she was sane. The next, she was stark-raving mad with the need to have this man beside her, around her, in her. It had been too long.

His leg moved in between hers as if he could read her mind, and the chilly steel of the car pressed into her back, giving her the strange sensation of a cold backside and a gradually warming front side.

Angling her head so the kiss deepened, Eleanor wound her hands around his neck and pulled him closer. Oh, he tasted so deliciously warm and filled up the empty spaces inside her.

She wanted the kiss to go on forever.

"Yo, get a room," someone called out, followed by laughter.

Dez smiled against her lips before breaking the kiss. "Freaking powder keg."

"Hmm?" she asked, swearing at the pink creeping into her cheeks.

"If someone tosses a match our way, we're going up in flames, sweetheart."

"Too late," Eleanor said with a rueful smile, fanning herself. Dez stepped back and cool air took the place of his warm body.

"Okay," he said. "Let's go get coffee before I change my mind. CC's on Jefferson, right?"

"Right."

He dropped a kiss onto her forehead. "Drive safe."

Eleanor unlocked her car, slid inside and cranked the engine. Her headlights illuminated Dez walking away, and her heart clinched. She didn't want him to go.

Damn. When had this happened?

Total crush on Dez Batiste.

She cocked her head as she shifted into Drive. Probably happened the day she met him.

CHAPTER TEN

TRE WIPED THE SWEAT from his brow as the old lady next to him passed the offering plate for the third time that night. She eyeballed him as he passed it to the man next to him just as he'd done the two times before. Guilt pricked his conscience, but he couldn't spare a nickel, much less anything of the paper variety.

Whew. It was hot in the church, and he wished they would open up the double doors and let some cool night air inside. But there seemed to be an unwritten rule for revivals—everyone has to sweat—so maybe the heat blasting through the wall vents was intentional.

The choir members occasionally threw up their hands and shouted, "Praise Jesus." From her place in the front row of that group, Alicia caught his eye and smiled.

Yeah. There was that—Alicia smiling at him. Guess he'd stay and sweat.

He could have been hanging with his boys on the parade route since a sober Cici, feeling guilty about the past month, had taken Kenzie and Shorty D to the parade, and had told him to have fun on his own. The one time he could feel like a nineteen-year-old dude and here he was sitting on a pew, sweating and trying to pay attention to a fat preacher who kept waving his hands and shouting about sin and evil and the devil creeping into the heart. And it was all because when he finally got the nerve to call Alicia and ask her to go out, he'd told her to pick the place. He'd never expected the choice to be the Second Greater Zion Baptist Church of New Orleans.

It had taken him a day and a half to call her. The phone had gone to voice mail and he'd hung up. But she'd called him right back...and acted like she didn't remember him.

But he could tell she did.

After a few minutes of talking about Kenzie and where she worked, Alicia had said, "So?"

"What?"

"You calling me just about your little cousin, or is there something more you wanted to ask me?"

"Damn, girl, you may be a lady but you ain't scared, are you?"

"I'm not scared of too much, Trevon Jackson. Are you?"

He felt his throat close up because he knew fear was something he beat back every day. "I ain't afraid of you."

"Good. So when you taking me out?"

"When you want to go? You pick."

And she had.

So here he sat on a pew, shifting and recrossing his legs, sweatin' buckets.

"Boy, you got ants in your pants," the old lady to his right hissed, showing him crooked teeth beneath a bristly mustache. She cackled and slapped his thigh.

He shifted again. Away from her. The man to his left grunted as he bumped him.

Thirty minutes later, Tre finally stood up and clapped at what he prayed was the closing hymn.

Please, God, let this be over. Soon. Amen.

And twenty minutes later, it finally was.

Alicia grinned at him, having shed her choir robe. Not one bead of sweat dotted her upper lip—a lip that was thankfully bare of anything resembling a mustache. In fact, her lips looked really good, made him want to embrace the sin in his heart and do bad things to her body. "How'd you like it? Good message, huh?"

He snorted. "I feel holy."

"Yeah, and you're sweating. You wanna go outside?"

"Is the preacher Baptist?"

She squinted her pretty brown eyes. "Huh?"

"You know. Like 'Is the Pope Catholic?' It's a joke," he said, grabbing her hand and pulling her behind him as he moved through the sweating masses toward the double doors.

"Oh, yeah. A joke," she laughed, tugging against his hand before he could reach the doors leading into the cool night. "I need to tell my mama and daddy you're going to take me home."

He stopped. "I can't take you home. I ain't got no car."

"Well, I got one, so I'll take you home."

Tre kept walking. "If you got a car, why'd you ride the bus the other day? That don't make no sense."

Alicia tugged on his hand again. "Any sense. And my aunt borrowed it because hers was in the shop. It was fate. Now, you *do* want me to walk out that door with you, don't you?"

If she knew what he wanted her to do with him, the church would fall down around their ears. God would smite him down for the lust in his loins…which was a close relative to the evil in his heart. Or maybe not. He wasn't sure of God's position on wanting a woman. After all, the Big Man upstairs had made them damned delicious.

"Tre? You listening?"

He jerked his gaze to the small fireball standing a few feet away, right next to the preacher who kept wiping his brow with a soggy rag from his back pocket. "Sorry."

"Tre Jackson, this is my daddy, Reverend Cornelius Jamison, and this my mama, Snookie."

Damn. Her daddy was the preacher. But didn't have her last name. Tre's head screamed, "Get your ass outta here, Tre."

But his feet stayed planted on the red carpet covering the middle aisle. His hand jutted out to grasp the hand of the man who looked at him as if he was a cockroach on his kitchen counter. "How you do, sir?"

The older man shook Tre's hand with forced vigor. "Nice to meet you, young man. Lee Lee told us you have a cousin who might go to her center."

Okay, news to him. He was a charity case, all right. "Uh, yes, sir. Uh, Kenzie been having a few problems with some things."

Tre jerked his gaze to Alicia, who smiled as if they'd already spoken about Kenzie and the Lighthouse Center...which they really hadn't. All Alicia had said was they would talk about it later.

"That's wonderful," Alicia's mother said, extending her hand. The woman wore her hair pulled back and earrings so big it was a wonder she stayed balanced, but her smile was genuine and warm. "My sister Evelyn and Alicia have worked so hard to help so many little angels. We're so proud of what they've accomplished in just a year. I'm so glad you found your way to them."

He didn't know who Evelyn was or exactly what Alicia did at that center, but her mama used *so* so much. He nodded and smiled like a blessed fool.

"Alicia tells us you work for a store down on Magazine Street." This from Rev.

"Uh, yes, sir. I work at the Queen's Box, doing deliveries and other things for Mrs. Theriot. I'm saving for school in the fall." He looked up to make sure the roof didn't fall in on him. Well, it wasn't actually a lie. Just more like something that wasn't going to happen, but he didn't want Rev. Jamison to know that. He didn't want to look like he was a bum.

"Good, good," the reverend said, nodding his bulldog head.

Fathers always wanted their daughters to date men with jobs. And men who went to—

"And where do you attend services?"

"I go to St. Peter down on Cadiz." He hadn't been in over a year, but Reverend Jamison didn't have to know that. "My Big Mama's in a home and I haven't been in a while, but Pastor Greer been a blessing to us."

"I know Ernie Greer very well. A fine Christian man, and you are blessed indeed to be one of his flock."

Tre nodded gravely, accepting that he was going to burn in hell for lying to a man of the cloth.

"Well, we're going to go get some ice cream and then I'm taking Tre home," Alicia said, smiling at her parents.

For a moment, Tre wondered if he'd shifted into some alternate universe. He'd once read a book in school about a boy who'd gone back in time and this felt like that. No knights or round tables. But going for ice cream and meeting a girl's parents? Felt about the same.

"You two young people have so much fun," Snookie said, her ruby lips curving into a plump smile and her dark eyes twinkling. "I remember when Cornelius took me for root-beer floats at Frostop. Those were the good ole days."

Alicia rose up on tiptoe and kissed her daddy's cheek before grabbing Tre's hand and pulling him down the aisle, calling out goodbyes to all the folks tossing *good-night* her way. Seconds later, they burst out the door, the cold air wrapping round them with icy fingers. Stars overhead winked as headlight beams illuminated the asphalt lot outside the old church off Airline Highway.

"Brr, it's cold. Come on." Alicia hurried toward the silver-blue car sitting near a cyclone fence covered in a tangle of dead vines, pulling her keys out and unlocking the doors. He had no clue what kind of car it was. Wasn't new, and looked like a Honda or a Toyota. Not flashy, but not a clunker.

He slid inside as she cranked the engine and turned the heater to High.

"Good Lord, it was hot up in there, but the cold creeps in fast," she said, fiddling with the channels on the radio. She pushed several presets until she found Kanye, and the bass thrummed low, mimicking the confused emotions rolling in his gut.

This was a mistake.

A preacher's daughter, ice cream and going to church didn't reflect his swag. Hell, Crazy Eight would laugh himself dead if he could see Tre dressed up in a monkey suit going for ice cream.

The lights in the car dimmed to black and Alicia's hand found his thigh. He reared back in the seat as she turned, leaned over and kissed him.

Her lips were soft and tasted like strawberry lip gloss, and her quick, light hands moved up his chest to twine about his neck and brush against his closely shorn hair at the nape of his neck.

It was all he needed to pull her tight against him and take over. Her hair had been pulled back into some bun thing at her neck and her small skull fit the span of his hand perfectly. He nipped her mouth open, and then took full advantage of the warm mouth offered to him. He slid his left hand around to cup her waist, stroke her back, impeded by the jacket nipped tight at her waist.

"Mmm—" she said, breaking the kiss and capturing his hand before he could move around front and unbutton the scratchy wool. "Wait. Uh, we in the parking lot of my daddy's church."

He inhaled and then exhaled. "Damn, girl."

She laughed. "I've been wanting to kiss you since I saw you holding that baby girl on that bus bench." Alicia settled back into the driver's seat and shifted the car into Drive.

Tre couldn't stop the smile that came to his lips. "You a surprise, Lee Lee Laurence. Why your name different than your daddy's anyway?"

"Because I was married for a year."

"Married?"

"Yes, but now I'm divorced."

"Divorced?"

"You going to repeat everything I say?" Alicia shook her head. "It was a dumb idea I had when I was eighteen. I'm twenty-one now...and divorced."

"Fine. You're divorced. So we going for ice cream?"

She slid her light brown gaze to him as she pulled out of the parking lot. "What you think?"

He didn't know what to think. He only knew what he hoped—that his divorced angel would give him something wonderful to think about in the weeks to come. That she would make him forget about the shithole that was his life for a few hours. That she would smile and love him and give him something good to hold on to. "I think I need something stronger than ice cream."

Her grin got bigger. "Here's the thing. I'm a Godly woman and I don't mess around with men who are looking to hit it and quit it. You get me?"

"Yeah. I get you."

"Good. So we going to have some fun. Maybe not the fun you want, but it'll be the fun you get. Because I ain't no ho. And then you going to come to church tomorrow morning and show me and my daddy that you a good man. You can bring Kenzie, too, 'cause we got to talk about her and how me and Aunt Evelyn going to help her. Then you going to call me later and take me to the Zulu parade 'cause my uncle Delroy is one of the captains this year. Then we'll see after that."

He didn't know what the last statement meant, but he didn't care because at that moment, he knew he'd never met anyone like Alicia Laurence, and for some reason, God only knowing, it was meant to be like this. That's all he knew and that was good enough.

"Let's roll, then."

Alicia's response was to press the accelerator.

ELEANOR CUT THROUGH several streets, trying to avoid all the traffic around Canal Street, but was blocked at every turn. It felt as if the world actually wanted to prevent her from getting to the coffee shop and Dez.

Which wasn't true, of course.

It was merely self-doubt whispering that idea.

But even under the whole "maybe I shouldn't do this" thing, happiness beat in her heart. The past few hours had been the most pleasurable she'd had in a long time. Dez wasn't what she'd expected. Sure, he was confident and in control, with a sexy alpha maleness that sped a girl's pulse, but romance also beat beneath the overtly male facade.

I like foreplay.

Damn, those words made her stomach puddle.

Okay, it puddled a little lower than her stomach. Those whispered words were such a turn-on. Anticipation buzzed in her stomach, driving her crazy. Made her hot enough to turn on the AC. She angled the vent at her face. She had to get some coolness, some calmness, or she was going to burn out of control thinking about sex with Dez.

Absurd.

But she cranked the AC higher.

Her phone chirped a happy tune in the cupholder.

She picked it up and took a deep, steadying breath, gathering her composure. "Hello."

"Mrs. Theriot?"

"Yes?"

"This is Sergeant Baglio down at the Third Precinct. I've got your daughter here and—"

"Blakely?"

"Yes, ma'am. Margaret Blakely Theriot? We picked her up on a drunk and disorderly half an hour ago. She's not exactly cooperating, but we managed to find your number from her cellular phone and thought we'd give you a call."

"Oh, my God," Eleanor breathed, her hands shaking so hard she stopped the car in the middle of a street. "I don't— I mean, what do I need to do? Does she need a lawyer? Can I come get her?"

"Why don't you come on down here, and we'll decide how to proceed. You'll likely have to post bail. This is a courtesy we usually don't extend, but she's crying uncontrollably and, well, circumstances being what they are…"

"I'll be right there." Eleanor clicked the phone off and tossed it in the seat next to her, turning into a driveway to her left and reversing out. Dez had been following her, thank God, because she didn't even have his cell phone number.

"Hey, what's up?" he asked, rolling down the window, his eyes worried. "You okay?"

She shook her head. "No. They just called from the police station and Blakely was arrested."

"What?"

"Something about a drunk and disorderly. I'm sorry but I have to go."

"Are you okay to drive?"

She nodded. "Yes. I'm just angry and scared for her. What's wrong with her? To do something like this? I don't—"

"All right, all right." He pressed his hand into the air in a soothing manner, his voice mimicking his actions. "Deep breath, and remember, she's okay."

Eleanor sucked in the air and exhaled. Any other time and she would have felt as though Dez patronized her, but she knew he only tried to give her perspective. It wasn't the end of the world, and Blakely *was* safe. It was, however, the end of their evening together. "I wanted to spend some more time with you."

"We have tomorrow. And the next day. And the next. Right now, though, you need to take care of your daughter. Do you need me to come with you?"

"No. I'm fine. I'll be in touch."

"Sure. Let me know if you need anything, okay?"

"Thank you," Eleanor said, inching the car forward as a pair of headlights appeared in her rearview mirror. "You're a good man."

"Nah." He smiled with a wave. "I'm just trying to get you into bed. Later."

He pulled away, and oddly enough, his flirty words gave her a strange comfort, as if there were lightness left in the world even as she faced something that was definitely a drag on her soul. And that said a lot, considering her soul felt rock bottom in regards to Blakely.

Eleanor pressed a button on her phone, pulling up directions to the Third Precinct on Paris Avenue, and sped away. Twenty minutes later after cursing the traffic, she pulled into the station parking lot right beside a white Mercedes she knew belonged to Porter Theriot. Damn it, her in-laws had beaten her to the station.

She parked, and then hurried toward the glass doors. She'd just begun to climb the steps when Margaret and Porter pushed out the doors, a silent, soggy Blakely between them.

"Oh, honey," Eleanor said, raising her arms to her daughter, who started crying when she caught sight of her mother.

"Mom," Blakely cried, falling into Eleanor's arms, smelling like booze and faintly of vomit. "I don't feel good. I wanna go home."

"You *are* going home," Margaret said, with a sniff. "To our house, where you will be taken care of properly."

Eleanor clasped Blakely tighter. "No, she's going home with me. I'm her mother."

Porter wagged his head. "Now, Eleanor, no need to cause a scene. We need to get out of here and take care of your daughter. This isn't a power struggle. Blakely needs to come first."

"Of course," Eleanor said, tucking a hank of her daughter's hair behind her ear. Blakely cried harder, fisting her fingers into Eleanor's shirt. "But she can get that at home in her own bed. I appreciate you coming here, but I can handle this."

"Can you?" Margaret said, stepping down so she was level with Eleanor. They were the same height and thus their gazes lined up. Margaret's cold blue eyes resembled the winter sea. "Because Blakely tells us you were on a date with a black musician who is a decade younger than you. That doesn't sound like much control. It sounds like a woman who has lost her ever-loving mind."

Eleanor felt the familiar anger burble inside her. Normally, she ignored it and avoided ruffling Margaret's feathers, but not tonight. When she'd sat in Margaret's house and made the decision to go out with Dez, she'd taken her life back from the Theriots. No more.

She patted Blakely's back and disentangled from her. "Go on to the car, honey."

Blakely straightened and blinked. "Huh?"

"The car. Go to the car."

"But, Mom, I don't want you and Grandmother to fight. I'm really sorry. I am."

Margaret patted Blakely's upper arm. "Don't you worry a bit, sweetheart. Your granddaddy has already talked to the D.A., and the charges will be dropped. Everything will be okay. You know Grandmother takes care of you."

"But I don't mean that. I mean about Dez." Blakely swayed

a little and her bloodshot eyes beseeched. "He's not what you make him sound like, Grandmother. He's not trash or anything. I like him, so don't make it sound like he's bad or something. 'Cause he's not."

"Of course not, dear," Margaret said, her voice patronizing. "I'm sure the boy is nice, and I'm certain your mother will put a stop to the shenanigans going on between them if only out of consideration for you and the family."

"Go to the car, Blakely," Eleanor said through gritted teeth. Her stomach tightened as anger burgeoned into full-fledged fury. Dez had nothing to do with the trouble Blakely had brought on herself—he was a diversionary tactic her daughter used to force the attention off her inappropriate behavior and onto her mother. Besides, who Eleanor went out with wasn't any of Porter's or Margaret's goddamned business.

"Okay," Blakely said, stumbling toward the Volvo with its headlights shining on the police department sign out front.

"Go with her, Porter. I need to speak to Eleanor," Margaret said.

Porter took his granddaughter's elbow and helped her down the steps, giving the floor to his wife of over fifty years. Margaret did the heavy lifting in their relationship.

When they were out of earshot, Margaret whirled on her. "This is a disgrace, Eleanor. An utter disgrace. I highly doubt your management of anything anymore. First, you lose control of your husband, and now it's Blakely. And associating with a street musician? Surely you can find someone decent to scratch your itch, dear."

Eleanor curled her hand and shoved it into her back pocket. She wanted to deck Margaret right on the steps of the New Orleans Police Department, but she wouldn't. Because Blakely needed her...and that meant she couldn't occupy the jail cell her daughter had vacated minutes before. But she wasn't taking any more shit from Margaret. "I don't give a flip what you think. What happened with Skeeter had nothing to do with me. He made the decision to screw his bipolar secretary. And Blakely made the decision to drink too much and act like a fool. I'm not responsible for everyone I care about so don't lay that crap on me."

Margaret's face tightened.

"And as to my personal life, it's none of your business who I date. I don't need the approval of the Theriot family, and I only tolerate the shit you dole out because I love my daughter…and she loves you."

"Your language tells me all I need to know. Of course, that was evident the day my son brought you home. One would think you'd learned some polish these past years, but still you prove daily exactly what you are—Northshore trash."

"My language has nothing on your actions, Margaret. I may talk dirty, but you live dirty. Stay out of my life, and tread lightly with Blakely."

"Don't threaten me, Eleanor. I've tolerated you for the past twenty years and I've reached my limit. Go ahead and slum around with your young musician, but leave Blakely to me. She is a Theriot, and I won't let you ruin her like you did my son." The older woman pursed her lips, her gaze hard as the iron her father had milled into a fortune years ago.

Margaret had never wanted for anything, and had spent her entire life manipulating the people around her to suit her needs. Eleanor had often succumbed to Margaret's wishes because it was easier than fighting her. But Eleanor no longer wanted Margaret's strings attached to her…or to her daughter. If she didn't handle Margaret's machinations now, this very moment, she'd lose Blakely. "You're nothing but a cold-hearted bitch. Don't tell me how to take care of *my* daughter."

"If you want to play games, Eleanor, I'll play them. But be forewarned, I always win. If Blakely is the prize, I have the advantage, and you know it."

A vise squeezed Eleanor's heart because she feared her former mother-in-law's words were true. Blakely enjoyed the shine the Theriot name and the money gave her, especially in the past few years when social status became a selling point for getting into college, sororities, social clubs and all the right mansions lining St. Charles. Blakely liked her unlimited credit card, monogrammed sheets and valet parking for her BMW.

It didn't help Eleanor had claimed Dez, tossing her daughter's needs and wants aside so she could honor her own. Blakely's actions this very night were likely a result of unspoken jealousy, a subconscious way to needle her mother.

Panic rolled in her stomach at the thought of Blakely claiming the Theriot life over the simple, honest lifestyle Eleanor had worked to give her. "Fine. You do what you must do, but remember this—I may no longer be part of your family, but I know enough Theriot business to put some of you in prison. So be careful about what you do and say regarding Blakely. If you profess to love her, you won't do anything to undermine me or destroy my relationship with her."

Margaret shrank back at Eleanor's insinuations. "How dare you!"

Eleanor stepped forward. "No, how dare *you*."

"You don't know anything about Porter."

Feeling power over Margaret was like snorting a line of cocaine, not that Eleanor knew what that was like. But Porter did. "Tell it to the *Picayune*."

She said nothing more. Just turned on her heels and walked toward the car where Porter stood watch over Blakely, who slumped in the passenger seat.

"Thank you, Porter," Eleanor said, opening her door and giving him a nod. Poor Porter. The man was tolerable, and had been the only voice of reason she had in Skeeter's family. She had no intention of bringing the skeletons of the Theriot family into the light, but Margaret didn't have to know that. It had been low and petty to suggest that she would, but somehow Eleanor didn't care. For once, it felt good to be mean.

"Good night, Eleanor. Take care of our girl."

"I will." Eleanor slid into the car and seconds later was on her way to the house she'd shared with the Theriots' youngest son for fourteen years, before he'd bopped his secretary, given the woman reason to think he loved her and then died at her hands. Eleanor both loved and hated the house they'd shared together, just like she both loved and hated the man who'd given her a daughter and his name. Sometimes she wondered if she should sell the house and start over, but Blakely cried each time she mentioned it, so she'd stayed.

"I'm so sorry, Mommy," Blakely said, smacking her lips, her head hanging to the side, obscured by her tangled blond hair.

"I know, baby. So am I."

CHAPTER ELEVEN

DEZ'S PARTNER in the club, Reggie Carney, had a certain presence about him—one that made lesser men nervous. Of course, most men *were* lesser, because at six foot five inches and three hundred and twenty-six pounds, Reggie Carney towered over the city, larger than life as a man...and as a New Orleans Saints offensive guard.

"I don't like this crap the designer brought in. Too old-school twenties. Freakin' feathers? Looks shitty," Reggie said, picking up a peacock feather lying on the aged bar now shiny with a new patina. In his hemp hoodie and brown cords, he reminded Dez of a fairy-tale giant...holding a feather.

"You hired her," Dez muttered, trying to pull an errant nail from the corner of the restored bar with a hammer. The contractor had missed it and the metal head would definitely snag clothing.

Reggie was supposed to be a silent partner...who hadn't gotten that memo. But since the scourge of NFL defenses was on the money in regards to what the designer had brought in, Dez didn't feel too irritated.

"Guess we can call someone else. Tiffany recommended her, and usually my girl's spot-on," Reggie said.

"Tiffany's a stripper, Reggie."

"Well, *I* like her style."

"'Cause there's so little of it."

Reggie snickered. "Exactly."

Dez finally pulled the nail loose, wishing the thorns in

his life were as easily removed. That night was the quarterly meeting of the Magazine Street Merchants Association, and he was slated to speak in favor of his business. He wanted to join the group, but first he needed to help them see his establishment would draw a sophisticated crowd and meet their mission of a safe environment…and the peacock feathers and tacky metal wall art weren't helping.

"Hey, what about that place across the street?"

"What place?" Dez asked, tucking the hammer behind the bar and straightening. He needed to call the suppliers and get them to bring another box of glass tumblers, and he had to call the state about the liquor license. Reggie would help him there. In a state crazy about football, a Saints player could probably borrow the governor's wife for a night. A liquor license was gravy.

"That Queen's Box place."

Eleanor.

Saying her name in his head was like taking a deep breath.

It had been over a week since he'd seen her. Mardi Gras had passed with the usual crowds and cleanup, and he'd turned to his work at Blue Rondo, trying to put last Saturday night at the Priest and Pug behind him, but her laugh, the way the moon shone against her hair and the way she leaned into his touch haunted him.

Each night after a much-needed shower, he sank down on the piano bench, and like water from a drain spout—hard, fast and abundant—the harmony swelled and the sacred words tumbled from his conscience. He thought of Eleanor, and the music flowed, the words emerged.

All the doubts about being with her—Blakely, her past, the fact he had a business about to open—waned in that moment. The barricades on the path to wherever the hell they were headed became mere potholes, easily stepped over or avoided. Because his body craved her touch, his soul her smile, and his music her passion.

"Dude?" Reggie jarred him from his thoughts.

"Huh? Oh, the Queen's Box?"

Reggie jabbed a finger toward the store across the street. "Yeah. That place. Over there."

"It's an antiques store. Not sure you're going to find what you envision over there," Dez said, moving some boxes from the end of the bar, heading back toward the storage room, shoving Eleanor and thoughts of her soft body onto the back shelf of his mind.

"I'm going over to take a look anyway. Never know what I might find," Reggie called.

Dez heard the door close. "Shit."

He wasn't going over to the Queen's Box because he didn't want to see Eleanor until after the meeting that night. Somehow settling things with the association cleared a path to her. He felt like if she saw how Blue Rondo fit into the community, she could see how he fit into her world. Tonight, he'd prove he belonged in both.

He hadn't called her or stopped by her store. His second sense told him she needed some breathing room after the ordeal with Blakely. Or maybe he pulled back because things between him and Eleanor felt too difficult? No sensible dude waded into a tangle like Eleanor, no matter how much his body demanded gratification. But he knew what he and Eleanor had between them was more than desire, even if he didn't want to admit it yet.

If he had any smarts, he'd let Eleanor slide away. He should forget about the complicated antiques store owner and get an uncomplicated girl like Tiffany who would screw his brains out and not ask for anything more than a cup of coffee in the morning.

Of course, he didn't want uncomplicated.

He wanted the complexity of the buttoned-up, Volvo-driving Uptown woman with the drama-queen daughter and the dead husband who made her overly cautious.

But for the time being, Reggie would have to handle Eleanor and the decorating scheme. At this point, he was ready to staple the damn peacock feathers on the wall and say to hell with it.

Twenty minutes later Reggie was back, carrying several pieces of art and a weird-looking board with holes in it.

"Dude, you're *dating* that store owner?" Reggie asked, setting the pictures on the end of the bar and propping his hands on his hips like a disgusted parent.

"What?" Eleanor had said they were dating?

"I asked that lady out and she said she was dating you."

Something in his chest vibrated. Eleanor had claimed him in a very public way. In front of Dez's business partner. In front of Pansy and maybe Tre. "We went out last Saturday night."

"Dude, I feel like a punk. Why didn't you tell me you were bumping uglies with the neighborhood-watch president?"

"She's the president of the Magazine Merchants Association. Not neighborhood watch. And we're not bumping uglies."

Reggie snorted. "Why not? She's a sweet piece of ass, bro."

Dez tried not to be offended at Reggie's nonchalant words, but when it came to Eleanor, she wasn't the kind of woman a guy casually disassembled in front of his boys. He couldn't brag about how he'd bang her soon or any of that other stuff guys sometimes blew smoke about in locker room camaraderie. "We're friends. She's cool."

"Friends?" Reggie lifted an eyebrow. "'Cause she didn't make it sound like friends. She looked kinda serious."

"Yeah? Good to know," Dez said, picking up one of the pieces of art Reggie brought over. "What's this?"

"Something the skinny gal suggested. She said it had soul, but it looks like a bunch of weird bottles to me."

The colors were good, and there was a nice cubist quality to the bold-colored glass bottles that were set against a background the color of mustard. Would probably look good against the cool gray walls. The other painting matched, but was a different size.

"I liked that skinny chick, too. She's tall and I didn't have to look down on her part or anything."

Dez jerked his gaze up to his friend and business partner's. "Huh?"

"You know, I didn't have to look down at the part in her hair. Most girls are short and I'm always looking—"

"I get it, but Pansy's married."

"Ain't that the way it is. One's hung up on you and the other is hitched. Guess I'll give Tiffany a shout tonight." Reggie smiled, showing that such a fate suited him fine. "Hey, check out this riddling board. We can put empty bottles in it. Thought it was cool."

Dez opened his mouth to agree at the same moment the front door banged open. A sign came toward them followed by Tre Jackson.

"Mrs. Theriot said to bring this over and see if it fits over the bar," Tre said, placing the sign down and swiping his brow. "Whew, this heavy."

Dez walked over to the large metal sign with the words Dew Drop Inn across the top. It was bright red with various shapes rising from the bottom to form a skyline of brass horns. He had no clue where it had come from, but he'd never seen anything so perfect in his life. "Reggie, you gotta see this."

His partner moved to stand beside him. "Hot damn, that's sweet. Is that from *the* Dew Drop Inn?"

"I don't know. What's the Dew Drop Inn?" Tre asked, eyeing the huge metal sign.

"Oh, my lawd," Reggie said, slapping his forehead. "A New Orleans legend, a club for the brothers, you know?"

Tre looked at him blankly. "So where you want it?"

"Where in the hell did she have this?" Dez asked.

Tre shrugged. "Dunno. I got it out the back. She got this funny light in her eyes when Mr. Carney asked about stuff for the club, then she snapped her fingers and called me back. She said something about getting it out of an old advertising place."

"It's perfect," Dez breathed, running a hand over the weathered metal. "Let's lean it against the bar."

Reggie wasted no time showing off why he'd made the Pro Bowl a year ago, and hefted the sign as though it was his granny's suitcase, placing it gently against the wood of the bar.

"Show-off," Dez grumped, crossing his arms and eyeing the space above the bar. He sensed Tre slipping toward the door and turned. "Hey, Tre, I been meaning to catch you."

Tre stopped, his eyes questioning, his stance tense. The kid was always jumpy, as though he expected someone to throw a punch at him at any moment. "Yeah?"

"You said at the art gallery the other night you were looking for some extra work?"

"Yeah?"

Conversationalist the kid wasn't. "So I gotta staff this place and thought you might want dibs on some shifts."

"I ain't old enough, am I?"

"You have to be over eighteen."

Tre nodded. "Okay. Yeah, I'll think about it."

"And think about taking that horn Blakely offered you. I've never seen a kid who could blow like you, and you were, what, in junior high?"

Tre inclined his head.

"Freaking amazing."

Reggie spun at Dez's words and regarded Tre with new eyes. Nothing Reggie liked more than a young kid with musical talent. Reggie played football for his living, but his passion was playing bass and working with inner city kids in the Second Line Players, a weekly program that preserved New Orleans' musical traditions. It's where Dez had met the football player. "He's that good?"

"He was," Dez said.

Tre wouldn't look at them. "I'll check into it. Mrs. Theriot done brought the horn and set it in front of me like she was my mama or something. Determined to give it to me."

"Then take it. Damn, man, you gotta have something in life. Can't take care of your brother and cousin and work all the time without having something to take the edge off. Better music than booze or drugs."

"Yeah. Okay."

"Good. We'll plug you into the work schedule and when we're done, we'll blow for a while."

Tre nodded and slipped out the door.

"Well, damn if there ain't a whole lotta surprises in that antiques store across the street," Reggie said shaking his head. "That kid really any good?"

"He blew my freakin' mind when I first heard him. He was only eleven years old and played like he'd been sprouted from the womb with a horn in hand. Freaky."

"Hmm." Reggie stroked his chin. "I already liked that kid—he knew who I was but he didn't ask about the Saints or football. Know how often that happens?"

"Hmm?"

"Never. Kids like him always want an autograph. A pic on their iPhone so they can post to Instagram or whatever that crap is Gemma's on all the time." Gemma was Reggie's twelve-year-old daughter, who lived with her mom in Dallas. Reggie spent the spring and summer in Texas and would be leaving once the club opened. His friend rolled shoulders the size of boulders, and glanced around the club. "You know what else I like? This club. The vibe is good here, and I can see it really taking off in a big way. And now I found a kid with golden lips. Good day, my friend, good day."

Dez laughed. "Opportunist."

"I like money in the bank. Besides, I've been hankering to find someone new, someone who can really feel the music. It's like rubbing a lamp and finding a genie to shake things up. I wanna hear this kid play, so call me when he comes back."

If he came back.

Something about Tre made Dez sad. He didn't know the kid's story, but Tre wore enough of his life for Dez to see things weren't easy for the boy. Not many kids his age would shoulder the burdens Tre carried. Selflessness was a rarity on the streets of New Orleans.

"We'll see," Dez said, thinking his words covered a lot in his life. He wasn't building his house on sand, but he wasn't on a firm foundation yet. Too many balls up in the air, each with the potential of clonking him on the head.

The last thing he needed was a lump of regret. Too much remorse already in his life.

He glanced out at the street between him and Eleanor, and wondered if he should keep that particular ball in hand.

Only one way to find out…and that meant putting it into play.

ELEANOR PASSED THE PLATE of sugar cookies toward Kristina Simoneaux, and picked up the agenda. The meeting of the Magazine Street Merchants Association convened at the Kitchen Counter, a lively breakfast and lunch place owned by Mr. Michigan that closed in the late afternoon, providing a perfect establishment in which to hold their quarterly meetings. About twenty people were present, but most came for the cookies and company.

"So the funds for the new Christmas wreaths will come from the renewal grant?" the recording secretary asked, pen poised above her notebook.

"Correct," Eleanor said, moving her finger down to New Business. "Okay, we have a petition for membership from Desmond Batiste, who would also like to say a few words. Dez?"

Eleanor had tried to keep her eyes off him all evening, but now it was impossible.

Dez stood, dressed in pressed khaki slacks and a white button-down shirt rolled at the sleeves and open at the throat. The man took business casual to a new level. Several of the women on the board leaned forward. Mr. Hibbett, the treasurer, crossed his arms and nodded to Dez.

"Good evening," Dez said, his gaze traveling over each member of the six-person board. Eleanor tried to remain passive, but the warmth in those eyes felt like a match struck against her skin. She uncrossed and recrossed her legs, swallowing hard.

He is just another potential member of the association. You do not want to strip him naked. You do not want to lick his stomach. You do not want to chain him to your bed.

Crap.

Keeping her distance in front of her colleagues wasn't going to work if she kept imagining the wicked things she wanted to do to him.

And have him do to her.

Dez turned away from the large table where she sat and faced the other members present. "I'd like to thank the board for allowing me to address you this evening. My name is Dez Batiste and I'm the owner of a new jazz club opening in less than a month, the middle of March to be exact. I know many of you have reservations about having a nightclub in the middle of a shopping district and inside a beloved icon, but tonight I'm going to prove to you that Blue Rondo will complete the picture of a restored Magazine Street."

As Dez spoke about his venture, Eleanor watched him charm his audience. Several business owners nodded as he made salient points about diversity, others remained impassive as he discussed business hours and the implausibility of his patrons taking up parking for their customers. As he spoke, Dez moved, talking with his hands, his posturing expressive, his words passionate—all that he was spread out on the table for the merchants who'd worked so hard the past seven years to rebuild the street shattered by desperation. A warm certainty burrowed in her heart, a strange feeling of fear and excitement.

Not for Blue Rondo or the association.

But for her and the man who loved his community and his music so much he wanted to overlap them and bring forth something good from the ashes of his world.

How had she not seen this? Why had she been so afraid of what Blue Rondo might bring? Maybe her own fears had tangled into something that stopped her from imagining a better community…a better Eleanor.

After making points about what the club could do for the area, and how he'd already had contacts in the State Department of Tourism who were featuring Magazine Street in a national campaign for the fall, Dez finished with, "So each of you must know I care very deeply for this community and want to help it grow into a vital, thriving center for the arts, music and commerce. You have my pledge I will carry forth your mission."

With a nod, Dez resumed his place in the back of the restaurant, next to Reggie Carney, who'd slipped in while he spoke. She almost smiled at the irritated look he shot the football player, but reined in her emotions enough to say, "Thank you, Mr. Batiste."

A low hum broke out when the others caught sight of the New Orleans Saints player, and if Eleanor had a gavel, she might have used it. Since she didn't, she cleared her throat and finished out the agenda, ignoring the buzz in the room over Dez and Reggie, pretending it was any other meeting.

Didn't work, but she dealt because if Eleanor was good at anything, it was dealing.

After days of not seeing Dez, the thought of taking things to a new level with him had cemented in her mind. She'd missed him, but appreciated the space he'd given her to deal with Blakely, the police and her mixed-up emotions. The first order of business—Blakely—had been the hardest.

The morning after Blakely's drunk and disorderly arrest, Eleanor had sent her daughter's hungover friends back to Oxford before sitting her daughter down for a little chat.

It hadn't gone as well as Eleanor would have liked, but she'd hammered out her complaints to her nauseous daughter.

"Who are you?" Eleanor asked Blakely as her daughter curled up on the overstuffed sofa in the family room.

"What do you mean? I know I screwed up, but I really can't handle a lecture now, Mom. I feel like shit."

Eleanor sat on the other end of the couch, tucking her sock-clad feet under her. "Blakely, you're not the same. This kind of thing, it's not you. You pushed a policeman and knocked down ladders. In essence, you made a fool of yourself. Not to mention it was dangerous—you could have hurt someone."

"Mom, I was drunk."

"Even when you're under the influence, you know what you're doing. I've been drunk. Inhibitions may loosen, but you don't pull away from the core of who you are. I didn't raise you to act like a spoiled brat."

Blakely frowned. "Is this about the purse? I'll take it back if that makes you feel any better. Or maybe I should trade in my car for a crappy used Toyota like you had. Or maybe I should just go to Delgado. Would that make you happy?"

Eleanor stared hard at her daughter. "That's not the issue. Your behavior is."

"And yours isn't? You went out with Dez."

"So?"

"Jesus, Mom. You and him are like hot sexy lava meets cold cream. It doesn't work. It's wrong."

"Look, young lady, I don't need your permission to date Dez. Or anyone else. You said over a month ago for me to get a life, so I am."

"But I didn't mean with someone like him."

"This is not about Dez, Blakely. This is about you. About getting arrested, about trading in the sweet girl who gave her Christmas presents away one year, who won a service award, who—"

"Doesn't think she has to be freakin' Gandhi or Mother Teresa 24/7, Mom. I'm not spitting on homeless people or boiling puppies, for God's sake. I'm just having fun and enjoying being young and, well, privileged. You act like it's a sin to have nice things. It's not like you don't wear designer clothes or drive a high-end vehicle yourself. Little hypocritical, aren't you?"

And then Blakely had stomped off, packed her belongings and left without another word.

Her daughter's anger and harsh words had wounded Eleanor…but also strengthened her resolve to claim a life for herself. She'd started down a different road and was committed to seeing it all the way to the end…even if claiming herself risked losing her daughter. Something told Eleanor she couldn't back down without cementing her fate…without

Blakely, the Theriots and everyone else in the world getting the message Eleanor didn't value her own desires.

So tonight Dez would be coming home with her…if he, uh, didn't have any other plans, and if he still wanted to show her how good he was at foreplay.

She swallowed hard and refocused on Mr. Hibbett's report about how the NOPD hadn't apprehended the hooligans responsible for the damage done to the stained-glass rooster.

Several minutes later, after shaking the hands of the many members who'd attended the meeting, including ones who'd once spoken out vehemently against him several months before, Dez stood beside her.

"So I submitted my application for the association online. Just an FYI." No gloating in his voice. No *told ya so* in his gaze. He'd done what he set out to do—not merely gain entrance into the association, but win over his detractors.

And he'd won over one of his staunchest—the president of the Merchants Association.

"Oh, okay. I'll make sure it gets taken care of," she said, giving him a smile. "You did it, huh? Worked them right into the palm of your hand."

He tilted his head slightly. "You're not angry, are you? I know you're still not sold on Blue Rondo, but I hope I can prove to you and everyone else it won't turn into something contrary to your mission. Scout's honor."

Eleanor narrowed her eyes at the three fingers he held up. "Were you a scout?"

"No, but I wanted to be. I always liked those neckerchief things."

"I can't imagine you in a neckerchief."

"You really don't want to know what I imagine you wearing," he said, his voice smooth as a satin sheet.

"Oh? Probably nothing, right?"

His eyes glittered. "Wrong. I was thinking support hose. I have a thing for them."

Eleanor nearly choked. "Oh, do you? Well, aren't you a lucky boy. This old lady has a drawer full of them."

"I hope so." His smile teased, and the intimacy between them warmed her, which was shocking considering Mr. Michigan had turned off the heat earlier that day. Her teeth had actually chattered at the beginning of the meeting, but now sheer waves of heat radiated down her spine.

"Do you want to come to my house for a late supper?" She glanced around because asking Dez to her house made her feel so naked, so bared to him. All of her—what she wanted, what she needed—spread in front of him. Her turn to lay it out in front of him.

"I've already eaten."

She blinked, trying to recover. "Oh."

"But I'd still like to come by…for a drink?"

Relief blanketed her. She'd been afraid he'd changed his mind after last Saturday night, after Blakely, whether intentionally or not, had trampled the flame they'd kindled. Looking from the outside in, she knew she looked like trouble—her doubts, her inexperience, her family baggage. What man wouldn't run from that? But Dez wasn't running yet.

Eleanor needed Dez.

Needed the crackling energy tempered by his practical, easy nature. She basked in the desire he felt for her as much as she cherished their friendship. Eleanor had awakened from a cocoon ready to spread her wings and take flight as someone new. She didn't want to live as Eleanor the faded. She wanted to live boldly, not afraid of flapping those wings and taking off into the unknown.

And she knew Dez Batiste could—how had Margaret put it?—scratch that itch.

"So let's go," Eleanor said, smiling at Marcie Gorman

and giving a wave, but heading toward the front door. No way would she get stuck talking to the salon owner. Marcie always wanted to try Botox on folks...and new hair colors.

Dez shook another few hands, but in two minutes, he emerged on Magazine Street, his expression relaxed, but a purpose in his step. She watched him from inside her Volvo before pulling away and heading toward her house.

She beat him there by a good five minutes, which gave her enough time to turn on a single lamp, light a few candles and take a shot of vodka.

Coughing and wiping the tears from her eyes, she hurried to the door as the chimes rang. For a crazy moment, she wondered if her daughter might be standing on the other side. Like maybe Blakely could sniff out her mother about to get naughty with Dez, but when she opened the door, there was only Dez.

Dez.

With close-cropped dark hair, smooth honey skin and deep gray eyes. Broad shoulders, lean hips and not a wrinkle on him anywhere. Her Aztec prince.

Despite the pretty hefty shot of vodka she'd taken minutes ago, her mouth grew dry. "Hey."

"Hey," he said, propping his hands on the door frame and leaning toward her. "You gonna let me in?"

She swallowed. "Yes, of course. I'm sorry."

She fanned a few imaginary bugs away from the flickering lanterns beside the door and swung the door wider. He passed by her, brushing her hip with his hand, making her suck in her breath. Thank God there weren't really any bugs buzzing around her porch. She might have added protein to her diet.

Closing the door, she turned the lock.

CHAPTER TWELVE

THE SOUND OF the dead bolt snapping into place echoed in the foyer of her house. Eleanor pressed her lips together because even though she hadn't intended it to sound like a decision, she knew it had. Done deal. Eleanor wanted Dez, and she would have him that night. In the house she'd shared with her husband.

God. It felt weird. It felt…somewhat freeing.

Beyond time to step forward.

She tried to tuck away the anxiety churning in her gut, but it insisted on staying and pricking at her, shredding her nerves.

Dez turned. "Well, that says a lot, doesn't it?"

"I always lock men in my lair. Well, of course, you're the first one, so I'm setting a precedent."

Smiling, he turned toward her formal living area. "Jesus, you're making me nervous. Let's have that drink."

He read her like an open book. And just why was she so nervous? It was just sex. People had it every day, and she'd already shucked her clothes in front of him two weeks ago. No big deal.

Breathe, Eleanor, breathe.

She sucked in a deep breath and gestured to the back room. "I'm not trying to make you nervous. But, yeah, a drink sounds good. Come on back to the family room."

Family room? Why had she called it that? Yes, perfect. Remind herself that once a family occupied that room, playing Barbie dolls, watching Saints games and putting up the Christmas tree. She'd never ever imagined herself seducing a younger man in a room with curtains she'd made from vintage toile found in South Hampton.

"Nice house. Very elegant, very you."

The right thing to say—very her. Exactly. This was no longer a house for a family. It was Eleanor's house—which sounded strange and a little lonely, but was exactly what it was.

"Thank you. It's an old house with lots of character. I tried to let that show through in my decorating."

Oh, Lord, she sounded as if she was on the Tour of Homes, Garden District edition. Decorating? Like he cared?

They entered her family room, which flowed into the kitchen. Eleanor went immediately to the bar and poured herself another vodka, splashing a little tonic water into the glass. "What would you like?"

"You."

She turned to him, her heart galloping with funny little hitches. "And would you like that with a twist of lime?"

He smiled, his teeth brilliant against his tanned skin. She loved his smile. It seriously made her pulse race and her breathing ratchet…or maybe it was his words doing that. He wanted her. "If you're into kinky stuff, sure."

"Oh, my good gravy," she breathed, quickly downing her drink, trying not to cough at the fiery path it tore down her throat. She needed the courage. She needed the numbness. No, not numbness. She wanted to feel Dez all around her, drink him up, meld him with her body and fill the holes left in her so long ago.

He was what she wanted.

It just felt awkward initiating what she desired in the room where she'd once been a different Eleanor—wife and mother and sewer of toile curtains.

"I'm sorry about this." She rolled a hand, fluttering it against her stomach. "Feels so weird. Such a new part of my life."

Dez approached her, his hands sliding to her elbows. "We don't have to do anything."

"Yeah, we do. You don't understand. This isn't like taking medicine or pulling off a bandage. I think about you all the time. Hot, dirty, sexy thoughts without a twist of lime. You drive me crazy, so it has to be tonight. The Blue Rondo thing is settled with the association. There is no longer anything between us."

"Blue Rondo had nothing to do with us."

She nodded. "Actually it did. I opposed Blue Rondo because of a preconceived notion of what it was…just like I had this notion of who you were. But I was wrong. You helped me see the world differently. And tonight when you talked, I remembered why I want you in my life. So I need you tonight. I need you giving me something I haven't had in such a long time—a touch to bring me back to life."

"Damn," he breathed, his mouth brushing against her hair, his hands sliding up her arms around to her back, drawing her to him.

"Is that okay?" she asked, hating the vulnerability flooding her. Maybe she'd asked him for something he couldn't give. Dez couldn't heal her, but he could help her start the voyage she'd put off for too long.

"We're sharing dreams, baby. You don't know the things I've imagined doing to you."

She set her empty glass on the sideboard. "Yeah, I kinda do. My imagination has been working overtime. All I think about is you. Your body touching mine. Your mouth doing things I can hardly imagine."

Her breath came out in pants, which might have been a

little embarrassing if she hadn't been so fired up and ready for Dez to touch her.

The "mmmm" he issued rumbled his chest, vibrating against her breasts, making them tighten, the place between her legs ache. She reached up and slid a hand along his jaw, enjoying the rasp, the strong line declaring him a man, and very much what she needed.

Eleanor lifted her gaze to his. "Is it okay if we skip the drinks?"

"Show me your bedroom."

And that was all it took for her to leave Eleanor Theriot, purveyor of toile curtains, behind and become Eleanor Theriot, sensual, strong despoiler of young musicians.

That thought made her smile, mostly because it was untrue. There would be no despoiling, but something inside her accepted who and where she was in life at that moment…and it gave her peace.

"Follow me," she said, glad she'd gambled and pulled out her prettiest underwear after soaking in a bath of green tea and chamomile. She smelled good, and the high-cut lacy panties made her feel desirable.

Dez's hand stayed on the small of her back as they climbed the stairs, as if he didn't want to break their connection. Somehow it was both comforting and a turn-on.

She didn't bother flicking the light switch as she entered her bedroom. Instead she turned and stepped into his arms, twining her own around his neck and pulling him close enough to count his heartbeats…close enough to savor the erection prodding her belly. A sweet ache vibrated inside her as her blood heated, an automatic, guttural response to something she'd been denied far too long.

Dez lowered his head and grazed her throat with his lips. Goose bumps sprouted on her arms, traveling up her neck, and she dropped her head back so the man had room to work.

"You're so sexy," he breathed, his mouth skimming her ear before nipping her earlobe. "Feel so damn good."

His words were all she needed to take the next step. She broke free, stepped back and grabbed the hem of her sweater. Pulling it over her head, she shook her hair before kicking off her serviceable beige pumps and unbuttoning her pants, shimmying so they pooled at her feet. She kicked them out of the way and stood before him in her lacy undies, bra and the gold chain Blakely had given her for Christmas. Eleanor was totally ready for all that was about to transpire.

His gaze moved hungrily over her in the dim moonlight streaming through the drapes. She felt beautiful.

He did that to her—made her feel beautiful and strong—and she knew beyond doubt that making love with Dez was the absolute right thing. No matter what happened down the line, she would always have this moment.

This sweet, exquisite moment…right before she licked his stomach and kicked things up to raunchy.

DEZ STOOD ON SOFT CARPET in scant light studying the beauty that was Eleanor. He'd seen her in the harsh light of her office, and knew every viewable inch of her was lovely, but the moonbeams falling softly on her hollows and dips made her mystical. Her light hair, streaked with flame, darkened with the absence of the sun, but the luminosity of her skin glowed, beckoning his touch. She was fluid, warm poetry, and he wanted to draw near and immerse himself.

Quickly, he unbuttoned his shirt, tossing it atop Eleanor's pants. He tugged off his T-shirt, unhitched his belt and, after disengaging them from a very erect barrier, allowed his pants to fall to his feet. Shoes, socks and another kick until he stood in his boxers, noticeably tented but not caring it was a ridiculous look on a man, because nothing could mar the moment between them.

He loved the way Eleanor watched him, her eyes hungry, her breathing elevated. It was a sacred moment—two lovers baring themselves, preparing for something beautiful, magical and satisfying. No doubt it would be good. He knew this the way he knew the piano.

Dez reached for her and the words didn't matter. No more poetry or magic. Just sheer raging lust for the woman he'd wanted ever since she'd enraptured him on the sidewalk outside Blue Rondo.

"Ah," she sighed as their bodies met, fitting perfectly, bared flesh against bared flesh. "So good, so very good."

Her words inspired, and he bent, tasting her lips. She tasted like coming home, a vague wonderful rightness, mixing past and present with the hint of a future.

Eleanor opened her mouth, her tongue darting out to meet his. He slid his hand to cup her head, taking the kiss to a new level. He teased her, withdrawing to nibble at her lips, allowing his hands to dip down to the curve of her waist, stroking lightly along her flesh before deepening the kiss again, establishing a rhythm, a precursor of what would follow.

Eleanor groaned, breaking the kiss, moving her hands to his stomach, stroking, exploring, scorching a path as she learned his body. She seemed to particularly like his stomach, which made him glad for all those daily sit-ups.

"Yes," he groaned as her fingers threaded the scant hair trailing down his belly. His erection leaped in response against the heat of her stomach. "Bed. Now."

Eleanor walked backward, unwilling to break the contact between them, her silken arms vises around him, her warm, wet lips nipping at his before returning again to the depth of his mouth, tasting him, devouring him. The back of her knees hit the bed, and they tumbled onto the plumped quilt, a tangle of arms and legs.

Beneath him, she felt even better than before, a soft place on which to land.

He cocked one elbow on the bed and lifted his head to admire her spread before him. Her hair spilled in a satin halo about her head, fiery strands catching the moonlight. Lips glistened below eyes pooled with need. He felt himself grow harder even as his heart softened with tenderness for this beauty in his arms.

Here was a woman the way God intended her.

Lush, soft and made for a man's hands.

Dez trailed a finger down the silky skin of her throat to the lace holding a small, plump breast.

"Oh," she inhaled, closing her eyes before opening them again as he teased the softness at hand. The green depths of her eyes shimmered with vulnerability and need. "That's so nice."

He slid his thumb over her erect nipple, earning a gasp. "Just nice?"

Not a man to settle for "nice," he bent his head and sucked her nipple into his mouth through the satin.

"Oh," she moaned, her hips automatically lifting, inflaming him, teaching him to play with fire. His erection lay hot and heavy in the curve of her hip and the rocking motion unfurled fully the desire curled inside him.

He increased the pressure of his mouth, not caring he might damage the fine lingerie, as his other hand found her other nipple and played it through the satin.

Eleanor's hands grasped his shoulders, wandering frenzied along his back, pressing him ever nearer to her.

"Beautiful, beautiful," he murmured, lifting his head, sliding his lips along her throat, inhaling her scent, tasting her skin. He found her lips again and she sighed before tangling her tongue wildly with his.

Minutes ticked by as they allowed passion to fill to the brim, slosh over, dampening them until they forgot time.

Eleanor's hands pushed at his chest and reluctantly he lifted his head from the stiff nub he'd laved with attention.

"Gotta get out of this," she said, pushing away the errant strands of hair stuck to her cheeks and reaching for the clasp on her bra. Seconds later, her breasts were free.

And ready for his pleasure.

Oh, and it *was* his pleasure.

He caught a rosy erect nipple and tortured it with his teeth and lips until Eleanor writhed. Moving his head to its twin, he gave equal attention, pleased with her sighs, with the way she stroked his shoulders and held him to her.

"You are so beautiful," he murmured against the plumpness, sliding his lips lower to her soft belly, ringing her navel with his tongue.

"Oh, my," she muttered, head thrown back, hips grinding now against his chest.

"Yes, oh, my," he murmured, one hand sliding down brushing the angular bones of her hips on a journey to her thighs. "'Oh, my' is exactly right," he said, tugging the lace at the top of her panties with his teeth.

"Dez," Eleanor moaned, moving her hips. "Please."

He lifted his head, glancing at her as she writhed against the half-dozen fluffy pillows on the bed and felt satisfaction. Yes, this was what this woman needed. Certainty made a home in his gut…right next to the lust raging a bit lower. He wanted to sink inside her, bury himself to the hilt within her body, but not yet. No, not yet.

Eleanor needed more.

Trailing his fingers slowly up her thighs, he brushed against her damp heat, inhaling her scent, feeling the need balled up inside her, matching his own.

"Dez," she said, pushing against his shoulders.

He chuckled, dropping kisses along the sensitive skin above her panties. "Just trying to take 'nice' to 'hot damn.'"

Hooking his fingers on either side of her panties, he slowly pulled the satin from her skin, sliding the sexy bit of nothing down her thighs so he might reach the sweetest part of her. Teasing her with small kisses for several minutes, he finally tasted her.

"Hot damn, hot damn," she moaned, tightening her fingers around his head, holding him in place as he continued to taste her, to love her in the most intimate of ways.

"Exactly," he said, sliding over her, dropping between her thighs, pulling her bottom to him, lifting her so he could render her speechless.

Didn't take long before she shattered against him, her cries bouncing off the tasteful ecru walls as she came completely undone.

Three times.

Panting and shoving her hair from her eyes, she lifted herself onto her elbows and looked down at him. She blinked several times. "Whoa."

And that made him smile.

"Yeah?"

"Oh, yeah," she breathed, reaching for him. He allowed himself to be pulled to her body, dropping onto her, finding the fit intended for man upon woman as she kissed him with an open mouth. His erection within his boxers bobbed at the entrance between her thighs.

"Hold on a sec," he said, pulling away from her.

"No," she said, her arms grasping air.

"Condom," he said, reaching for his pants, finding his wallet and pulling out the plastic package.

"Oh," she said, watching him as he pulled his boxers from his body and came back to where she sprawled on the bed, knees in the air, feet on the coverlet, beautiful in a way almost unfathomable. Who would have thought the little buttoned-up antiques store owner could be so wanton and sexual, so damn achingly gorgeous and hot that his heart squeezed within his chest?

Her eyes traveled the length of his body and he saw the admiration…the sheer desire brimming in the emerald depths.

"You're almost too much," she said, reaching for him, capturing his erection in her soft hands.

"Shit," he breathed as she stroked his length with an almost reverence. "You're killing me."

"Really?" she breathed, drawing him to her. "'Cause if that's what's happening, I better jump on this fast."

He closed his eyes as she very teasingly took care of protection, sheathing him with the condom. Eleanor might have been agreeable to let him take the lead earlier, but now she showed her skills, using every inch of herself she could to tease, tantalize and take him near the edge.

After several minutes of her very excellent ministrations, he found himself on his back and Eleanor rising above him.

"I've been dreaming of having you this way," she said, her eyes soft, a small smile of victory curving her delectable lips.

"Have you?" he asked, reaching to cup her breasts as she straddled him. "Is it as good as imagined?"

She guided him into her, sinking down. "Ah."

"Sweet—" He lost words as she began to move, closing his eyes, straining against immediate climax.

Finding some measure of control, he stilled her hips and opened his eyes. "Eleanor?"

She gazed at him with heavy-lidded eyes. "Oh, it's so much better than I could have dreamed. You're perfect."

And with those words, they began to move in harmony. Thrust and parry. Ebb and flow. As two became one in an ancient dance of passion and beauty, Dez embraced the emotion coursing through him, rising and wrapping Eleanor in his arms, turning her so he rose above, reversing the power, setting the tempo.

Beneath him she was everything he'd ever imagined in a woman, from the tiny wisps of hair trailing along her hair-line, to her toes curled against the back of his calves. She ensconced him in sheer, liquid want, raging so hard and fast, he couldn't control himself.

He hadn't much endurance left. It had been a long time since he'd been with a woman, and he wanted Eleanor with an irrational desire. He needed to watch her come, needed to see her face as he took her, so he slid a hand between their bodies and found what he knew would tip her over the edge.

"Dez, oh, oh, oh," she cried, the muscles inside her tightening as he drove into her. He felt the tension gathering, mimicking the pressure inside of him. He increased the tempo, pulling her tight against him. Finally, her inner muscles clamped down and she shattered against him. With a rough cry, he, too, went over the precipice of desire, and allowed the waters to crash over him, wave after wave of pleasure shaking his body.

And it was sheer, incredible splendor.

An intense thing of beauty.

"Oh, Dez," Eleanor said, holding him tight as he collapsed on top of her, breathing hard, finding the perfect spot to rest against the salty sweetness of her neck.

"Damn," he breathed, finding no other words to describe how incredible the moment had been.

She nodded, and said nothing as they lay spent beneath the vaulted ceiling of her bedroom. The moment couldn't be described in words…perhaps not even in thoughts. He'd never expected the profound emotion spilling over between them. Yes, it had been hot, dirty and all the things he'd envisioned when he thought about making love to Eleanor, but yet, there had been something else. A realness between them, a sort of opening and mingling of all they were. Totally unexpected, but brilliantly accepted.

Seconds ran into minutes, and still they lay, quiet and tender in one another's arms.

He didn't want the moment to end.

"Dez?"

"Mmm?"

"My arm's asleep."

He shifted off her, rolling to his side, giving her a sleepy satisfied grin. "Sorry."

She smiled at him. "You were right."

"About what?"

"Dirty is so much fun."

CHAPTER THIRTEEN

"THESE ARE DELICIOUS," Eleanor said, scooping up a forkful of scrambled eggs, and sighing.

"They're just eggs," Dez said, clad in nothing but orange boxers bearing little green palm trees. His bare feet had small tufts of hair, which she thought pretty sexy. If, you know, a gal was into thinking feet were sexy. Normally she wasn't, but at that moment, everything about Dez was sexy, including the way he stirred scrambled eggs.

"But they're really good."

"You're just famished from all the sex we had."

Eleanor laughed. "Probably. And I've never heard a guy use the word *famish*."

"I minored in English lit. Thought it would come in handy as a lyricist. I know lots of words. Big vocabulary along with my big—"

"Ego?" she finished, eyeing his buns in the fairly fitted boxers.

Dez flashed a smile. "Among other things."

"So where did you go to college? I never heard you talk about it."

He scraped fluffy eggs onto a plate, grabbed a fork and joined her at the table. "I went to LSU for two years before dropping out to go on the road and do session work."

For the next few minutes they chatted about college and the things they loved and didn't about the traditional classroom. Eleanor loved talking with Dez because he was a good listener. Skeeter had been a brilliant conversationalist, but never really listened. He always seemed to be thinking of his own next point, so it was refreshing to sit at the breakfast table and carry on inane conversation with no overtones.

Of course she wanted to ask, "What now?" but she didn't want reality to intrude upon the perfection of the night…and early morning. It was as if they'd wrapped themselves in an invisibility cloak, and disrupting the folds in any way might drop it to the floor, leaving them naked and exposed.

And not in a good way.

Dez cleaned his plate and eyed hers. She slid it toward him and he finished it off.

"So tell me about Skeeter."

Eleanor nearly choked. If that wasn't a slap of reality, she didn't know what was.

"Skeeter?"

"Your husband. I was in Houston when all that went down, so clue me in."

"I thought you didn't need to know about him." She didn't want to talk about her late husband. Or Blakely. Or the fact she had to take a quiche to the Young Women's Business Owners Open House later that night. Reality knocked and she didn't want to relinquish the small world in which they'd existed for the past ten hours.

Dez shrugged. "I don't. If you don't want to talk about your past, that's cool."

Eleanor set down her mug. "It's not that I don't want to talk about Skeeter—well, actually I don't—but that whole mess made me raw and it still…"

"Chafes?" His gaze probed hers.

"Yeah, but I'm over Skeeter if that's what you're asking. No grieving widow here."

"I didn't ask if you were still in love with your husband. I asked what happened between you two. At some point, we have to decide about us. Understanding what you went through might help us figure out how to proceed."

How to proceed? How would her past help her with her future with Dez? Skeeter's murder-suicide had nothing to do with them.

Irrational panic knocked on the door of her mind. A future with Dez didn't compute. Didn't make sense. Scared the woolies out of her. "Maybe we shouldn't proceed."

His eyes shuttered and he turned his body slightly away from her. "So this was a one-night stand?"

She stared at her coffee mug. "I don't know. I mean, I—" She grappled for the right words, but they weren't there. Eleanor had no experience with doing the morning-after thing, and she hadn't really thought beyond having sex with Dez.

His eyes gave her nothing to go on.

Eleanor hated the sudden discomfort hanging between them. "I don't know. I've never done this."

"Were you just using me?"

"Oh, God, no." She grabbed his hand, wanting him to understand she'd never see what she shared with him as tawdry.

He pushed his plate toward the center of the table and folded his arms. "So tell me about Skeeter."

"I don't want to talk about Skeeter."

"Too bad." Dez's jaw set and his eyes no longer resembled gray flannel.

"I don't want to talk about the past."

"From the past we learn. I need to know more about you. You need to know more about me."

"Fine. I'll tell you about Skeeter, but you have to tell me about whoever gave you that expensive piano."

"What does that have to do with anything?"

"Humor me."

"Fine," he said.

"Fine," Eleanor huffed, rising and grabbing her empty cup. "But I need more coffee."

Two minutes later, she inhaled the French Market brew and blew out a breath. "Skeeter was the only man I had slept with until you."

His eyes widened slightly, but he didn't say anything.

"I met him at the end of my freshman year at Tulane. He was older, charming, and before I knew what hit me, I was pregnant. At first, he wanted me to take care of it, which shocked me, but his family is extremely high-minded when it comes to their reputation, and a secret abortion seemed too big a stain on Skeeter's past, so after having my family of educators vetted, they decided Skeeter marrying a Louisiana girl from middle-class roots would play well in the polls for both Porter and Skeeter, so like a dumb sheep, I found myself bedded then wedded to a Louisiana Theriot.

"And I can't lie and say Skeeter and I had a horrible marriage. We didn't. We got along well and I loved him. Everyone loved him—that's what made him a perfect candidate for the U.S. House of Representatives."

Eleanor took a deep breath. "But things changed after Katrina."

"For everyone," he said with a nod.

"Yes, but I had trouble, which led to some, well, let's just say I had to have medical intervention."

She paused for a moment, the shame of the depression she'd suffered engulfing her. The months after the storm had been difficult, and for a while, she'd borne it beautifully, but then like the levees that broke, emotion overwhelmed her. She couldn't sleep, she couldn't function, her mind raced… and then suddenly all she wanted to do was lie in bed. Eleanor had checked out. "You know what? I don't want to rehash this. It's a bad memory."

"Okay."

"That's it? You're done trying to understand my past?" she asked, tilting her head, trying to see inside his gaze to the thoughts within. "Why do you care?"

"Because."

"Sounds like a child's reasoning."

He frowned. "Sometimes a child's reasoning is best. I don't know where we're heading or what specifically we have going on between us. Right now it's just a 'because.'"

Eleanor looked down at her now empty plate. Was "because" ever a good enough reason? Or did it merely mask what neither of them were prepared to declare—a definition on what they had. "I suffered from severe depression for almost two years. Took a long time for me to get my medication straight and for therapy to work. It was during that particular hell that Skeet took up with his secretary. Now I can step back and see the situation. Skeeter needed to feel like a man and Shellee gave him—"

"That's no excuse."

She shook her head. "No, but it's the truth. Skeeter wasn't a bad man, but he was a weak one. So he gave in to lust and it led to…his death. Shellee believed he loved her and would leave me. But she forgot who she was sleeping with—a politician. No way Skeeter was going to abandon his family when he mounted a campaign. Once my medication worked, I got better. Skeeter tried to end their relationship, and Shellee refused. Then she made sure he couldn't have what he always dreamed of—a seat in the U.S. House of Representatives. End of story."

"But?"

"I was left to face the music…and not the good kind you make." She smiled ironically. "The press had a party with the murder-suicide. They camped outside our door, jostling me for interviews, haunting Porter and Margaret. We could hardly plan the funeral without some reporter lurking behind the floral sprays at the funeral home. I'm surprised they didn't pop out of caskets. 'Mrs. Theriot, can you comment on your husband's alleged affair with Miss Genoa?' It was crazy and made me protective of Blakely and my own privacy."

He studied her, his eyes no longer intense. She saw no pity within their depths, merely an understanding. "You're cautious."

"Of course, which is why this whole thing between us scares the hell out of me. I didn't date because I wasn't ready."

"But you are now?"

"I thought I was. You were supposed to help me get my feet wet, but it's feeling more like I'm up to my neck in you."

"Why?"

"Because."

His lips tipped up. "See? That word covers a lot."

"Yeah, so does that help define 'us'?"

"You don't want a relationship."

She studied his bared chest faintly swirled with dark hair, the muscled breadth of his shoulders, the definition of his biceps, and her mouth nearly went dry. "I don't know. All I know is you make me happy."

"And that's enough for now?"

She nodded. "I think so."

"So…we date?"

"Does it have to be a definition? Maybe we can be exactly what we are now? Friends. With benefits."

Dez arched his eyebrows. "Not exclusive?"

Something pinged in her chest at the thought of Dez doing what he'd done to her with another woman. Her eggs nearly came back up. "Well, *I* can't handle another man, so I'm going to say mutually exclusive friends with benefits?"

"It fits both our lives right now. I don't want anything serious either—too much going on—but I enjoy being with you, and the benefits, whoa, those benefits are nice. When we end, I hope we'll stay friends. It will be better since we're business neighbors."

"Of course." Her words sounded hollow. Was this how people did things? So nonchalant about sex and relationships? Something told her it wouldn't be that easy for her. She wanted to pretend Dez was just run-of-the-mill, but her heart pushed toward extraordinary. Keeping it casual on the surface was much easier said than done. What if she fell in love with the hot, young musician? How could that ever work?

It wouldn't. Or maybe…

She struck the possibility of something more from her mind as she picked up the dishes and headed for the sink. If there was one thing Eleanor had, it was self-control. As long as she set the parameters, she could toe the line…even if it was in the deep end of the pool in her string bikini.

Eleanor Theriot wasn't up for love.

But she was up for exploring a new world with Dez.

TRE LIFTED THE BOXES, stacking them into neat columns in the crammed storage room of the Queen's Box. He purposely ignored the Plexiglas display case on his right. That case worried him like a gnat buzzing around his head, reminding him of what had once sat inside—a fancy box owned by the queen of France. The queen who'd gotten her head chopped off. Tre hated that display case. Wished Eleanor would put it away already.

"Hey, Tre," Pansy called out, not seeing him because of the tall clock that waited for the specialty guy to come fix it. "Tre! Where are you?"

"Right here," he said, stepping from behind the clock.

"Shit!" Pansy jumped and drew back a fist. That was the difference between Pansy and Eleanor. Eleanor always looked like she was going to faint. Pansy always looked like she was ready to beat the hell out of someone. "You scared me."

"I see."

She narrowed her eyes. "I think you like doing that. Men and power tripping."

"Nope. I was already standing here."

"Whatever," she said, waving a hand. "Some girl called and said to tell you the paperwork went through and there's a spot. She said you would know what that meant."

Tre nearly closed his eyes with relief, but didn't want Pansy to see him act like a little bitch, so he nodded. "Thanks."

She lifted her eyebrows near to her hairline, but he didn't say anything more. "Well?"

"Well, what?"

"Ugh, men."

At this he smiled, mostly because his heart was about as happy as it had been in years. Alicia. God had sent her to work miracles in his life. "So you said before."

"Fine. You don't want to talk? What else is new?"

He didn't answer. He rarely answered.

"Well, Eleanor said you were free to go over to Blue Rondo. Something about working for Dez. Oh, and you're to take that horn out of her office. She said she's sick of looking at it." Pansy spun around on a foot the size of a boat paddle and walked out, letting him know she was mad he wasn't sharing whatever news he'd received.

He had to call Big Mama and let her know Kenzie had gotten into the Lighthouse program. Alicia's aunt had taken Kenzie to the community clinic to see a new doctor. The little girl had learning disabilities brought on from something called FTT—Failure to Thrive. It qualified Kenzie for additional testing, and Cici could take parenting and nutrition classes. Alicia's message meant they had room and money in the school to take in his small cousin. Like a bird singing, Tre's heart soared. Finally, a break in his life.

And not just a break for Kenzie. His date with Alicia last

Saturday after church had been the bomb. They'd grabbed a bottle of sweet red wine, driven out to Lake Pontchartrain and made out beneath the stars. Usually, if he was with a girl, he liked a side of freaky, but Alicia acted like a lady. She was into him, but she didn't give nothing up to him. And though he'd been stiff as an oak tree when she'd dropped him by his house, he sort of liked her more for not climbing on him and giving him that part of herself.

Most dudes he knew would have dropped a bitch if she hadn't given it up, but Tre wasn't most dudes.

That night it had been easier than ever to walk by Grady and his boys and not stop.

Alicia had liked him despite the fact his kicks were older than shit and he didn't have a ride. In fact, she seemed to like him more because he wasn't frontin'.

Wiping his brow on his shirt, he grabbed his time card, punched out and left the storage room. Eleanor had come in and left again, and the case holding the saxophone sat on her desk, looking as new as the day it had been bought. He stepped into her office, looking over his shoulder despite the fact he wasn't stealing it, and picked up the horn.

The handle felt good hooked beneath his fingers, and something inside him sped up at the thought of a bright shiny horn.

And it would be bright and shiny.

Blakely said she'd played it for a semester, and rich people like the Theriots bought expensive shit because they could.

He walked past Pansy, who sat at the counter watching two older ladies pick up ceramic dogs that came from France or England and cost more than a week's groceries. Pansy always worried about frail old ladies dropping things.

"Later," he said to Pansy, who swiveled her head to try to find the two old ladies who'd disappeared.

"Yeah," she said, not really paying attention.

Sunshine and traffic met him as he stepped onto Magazine Street. Busy today because it was Friday. People liked to shop on Friday if they wasn't working. The Queen's Box got as much business as it did Saturday. Tre jogged across the street toward the club, which had a new window in place with *Blue Rondo* drawn in the center. Things looked tight at the club, and Tre had a feeling the smoothness Dez brought would translate to customers.

Excitement stirred in Tre's stomach at the weight of the case in his hand…at the thought of losing himself in the music. He'd tried to forget the feel of the horn in his hands, the big mellow notes spilling out when he applied just the right amount of air, small puffs balanced with sustained breaths. He'd buried the hunger for music when he sold his second-hand horn, but he'd done what he had to do. Big Mama had been in the home for a month and no check came from the government. Instead the money had gone to the nursing home for her care, so Tre had no other choice. He'd sold his true passion so Shorty D had what he needed for school.

Dez had restored the old bank clock on the outside of the bar, and the hands told Tre it was four o'clock. He'd always loved this part of the week best—people were in good moods and Shorty D never had basketball practice. He had a few hours before he had to go home. Before reality bitch-slapped him back into line.

He pulled open the door to find several guys setting up on the shiny wood stage. He didn't see Dez, but Reggie Carney, the big-ass left guard for the Saints, sat on the edge of the stage, cradling a beer.

"Yo, it's the man of the hour," Reggie sang out.

Something in Tre's stomach sank. He didn't need nobody putting no pressure on him. He just wanted to relax and blow. Wasn't an audition. Just fun. "Don't know 'bout that, Mr. Carney."

"Call him Reggie or shit for brains. Either one," Dez said,

coming in from the back room carrying an amp and a loop of cords.

"Watch it," Reggie growled, taking a draw on his beer before pointing it at Dez. "I usually take a man's head off for calling me shit like that."

Dez grinned. "But not the man who's going to make you a name in the jazz scene."

Several of the other musicians snickered, but didn't stop tuning their guitars and double-checking pickups.

Dez turned to Tre. "Get set up over there. We're not doing any definitive sets. Just getting our stuff up and running. We'll have plenty to tweak, so nothing's going to sound tight."

"Cool." Tre nodded, setting his case on a table shoved to the side of the stage.

Trying to look as if it was no big deal, he opened the case for the first time. There beauty sat, shining like a new box of Christmas ornaments, but much sweeter and more expensive. The sax was tenor, as expected, with a standard finish. The coolest thing was it was a Yamaha 62 series, which meant he could make adjustments on the stack. Excitement flipped through him as he lifted it from the velvet and pulled out the package of unopened reeds.

Hands near a tremble, he cradled the horn in his arms as he fitted the mouthpiece and pressed the keys to get the feel.

The rat-a-tat of the drums and low, plaintive whine of the trombone accompanied by the bright tone of the trumpet made him feel as if he'd stepped back into skin that fit him. As Tre lifted the horn, he imagined the zip, completing his transformation. No longer was he a delivery boy. He was master of the horn in his hands, ready to command.

No one said anything. Just moved into place, the intense focus on their instruments message enough. Dez settled on the futuristic piano, his long fingers gliding along the keys in a series of complicated runs. Five minutes later, the drummer, his face froglike but his licks hot, hit his stride, then the guy on trombone and the dude on trumpet jumped into the bass line and harmony of the electric guitars. Dez nodded to him and Tre joined in on "St. Thomas" in the playful tone Sonny Rollins had made famous.

The music drenched him, and his rustiness flaked away as he became what he was meant to be. Consuming and powerful, the notes flew from his horn. Tre closed his eyes and lost himself in one of his favorite songs.

The last note faded and he opened his eyes, realizing no one else played.

He pulled the horn from his mouth and blinked at the musicians frozen in place, staring at him as though he'd dropped from a spaceship into the middle of their session. The cymbal trembling beneath the still drumstick became the only sound in the club.

Shame washed over Tre.

He'd forgotten himself, allowed the music to overtake him. He wanted to tell them it had been so long since he'd played. Explain to them he wouldn't do that again. That—

Reggie Carney stood up, his mouth slightly open, but not as wide as his eyes. "Holy shit."

Dez started laughing. "I told y'all. I did."

The other musicians shook their heads, smiles creeping onto their weathered faces.

"What?" Tre asked, lowering the horn, uncertain about the reactions around him.

"You're frickin' incredible," Reggie Carney said, circling him like a hound circles a treed coon. "Why the hell aren't you playing this thing every day?"

Tre felt tears prick his eyes, and a lump clogged his throat. "Just got it today."

Reggie Carney smiled. "Hire him. He's the best thing I've heard since Drew."

Dez nodded. "We'll talk."

Tre didn't know what either of the men meant. All he knew was that a new door had opened for him, one he thought nailed shut, and his heart beat triple time.

Yeah, Tre Jackson was back where he belonged.

CHAPTER FOURTEEN

ELEANOR STRAIGHTENED THE PLATES on the antique sideboard, and hummed a song by Elton John, which had been spinning over and over in her mind since she'd heard it earlier that morning.

"Someone's happy this morning," Pansy trilled, bringing the two matching plates Eleanor had been looking for to complete the bright spring display. Not many customers toddled about the store and none were in sight.

"I am happy," Eleanor admitted, taking the yellow-swirled porcelain salad plates from her friend. It had been almost two weeks since she'd taken Dez home, and *happy* was the exact right word.

"I hate to tell you 'I told you so,' but I told you so," Pansy said, moving a rooster and hen salt-and-pepper-shaker set to the second shelf before eyeing it critically. "Dez has been good for you. You've shed at least five years off your face and maybe added a few pounds on your backside."

Eleanor fought the urge to crane her head so she could see her behind. "I haven't gained weight. In fact Dez and I went running this morning before work."

Pansy shrugged. "You look better than you have in years. You look happy and I can't tell you how much that lifts my heart."

Moving the salt-and-pepper set back to the bottom shelf, Eleanor turned. Her friend's eyes twinkled in true Pansy fashion. "I wish you'd share that tidbit with my daughter."

"Is she still being a little shit?"

"She's being Blakely."

Pansy walked back toward the register, where her afternoon coffee sat. She waved at Mrs. Finebaum, who came every Friday to look. The woman never bought. "I love that child, but she's a spoiled bitch sometimes."

Eleanor winced, even though she knew Pansy's words were tinted in truth. If she stepped back from her emotions, she could see she did Blakely no favors in protecting her so well from the ugliness of life. In trying to heal Blakely from the damage done by her father's death and the scandal that followed, Eleanor had enabled her daughter, had created a bit of a monster who thought whatever Blakely wanted, Blakely got.

Life didn't work that way, which her privileged daughter would eventually learn. Blakely wanted Eleanor to be what she'd always been—the self-sacrificing mother with no life of her own. Blakely was the world Eleanor should revolve around…even if she wasn't talking to her mother. Obviously, the girl hadn't forgiven her mother for winning Dez's attention. Didn't matter Dez wouldn't be interested in dating a college freshman even if Eleanor hadn't been in the picture. To Blakely, it was a ripe, fresh wound in her pride.

Earlier that week, Blakely had canceled the spring break vacation she'd planned with her mother, giving a fabricated excuse of friends not being able to go. Instead Blakely would go with Margaret to New York City. Eleanor hadn't been able to get her rental deposit back, so now she was stuck with a three-bedroom condo in Seaside for three days.

"Don't call her that, Pans," Eleanor said without much conviction, her happy mood dampened by the imminent trouble brewing on the horizon.

"Why? If it walks like a duck and quacks like a duck…"

After looking around to make sure no customers could hear their conversation, Eleanor straightened her business cards sitting beside the checkout. "She'll get over it and regret her actions."

"Yeah," Pansy said, stilling Eleanor's hand with her own thin one. "She'll get over it when you stop taking her crap. You need to tell her how you feel and help her see her behavior is petty and selfish."

"I did. She obviously doesn't care. I'm losing her, Pans."

"Bullshit," Pansy said, clutching Eleanor's hand and forcing her gaze to her own. "Blakely's aligning herself with Margaret because she knows it drives splinters beneath your nails. And Queen Margaret loves it because that's what she's always wanted—to separate Blakely from you. It's a total power move and Blakely's playing right into her hands, but that girl is still the same girl you raised. She's worth fighting for."

"I'm not giving up. Just not pushing. I can't force Blakely to accept I'm dating Dez. She'll have to come to terms with that on her own, and if she loves me, then she will," Eleanor said.

"Okay. Maybe pushing would be bad, but don't take her crap and don't stop doing what you're doing with that prime piece of real estate."

"I'm not. Dez and I are enjoying a friendship."

Pansy snickered.

"Okay, a bit more than friends, but it's nothing serious. Just two adults doing adult things."

Pansy smiled. "That's my Eleanor. Don't give an inch. You deserve some happiness."

Eleanor withdrew her hand and slapped both of them together. "Exactly. Now, I have to hit some garage sales tomorrow. You wanna come with me?"

Pansy wrinkled her nose. "I don't like getting up at five-thirty in the morning. It's indecent."

"Come on. We haven't gone in a long time and we always have fun. Plus, you're better at digging out the good stuff than

I am." Eleanor knew praise was Pansy's biggest motivator, and she wielded it to her advantage. One of the best places to find smaller items for her store was at local garage sales and estate sales. In a city as old as New Orleans, filled with the descendants of immigrants from all over the world, there was much to be found on the lawns of old neighborhoods. She and Pansy often went on treasure hunts, armed with coffee, beignets from Port of Call and the *Times-Picayune*.

"Maybe," Pansy conceded, which meant yes.

"Great, I'll pick you up at five-thirty and bring you a coffee."

Pansy made a face, but the anticipation of adventure shone in her friend's eyes. "Fine. With extra cream."

"I'm heading over to Blue Rondo. Dez said he's going to do an impromptu jam today and I want to hear Tre play. Dez said he's good."

Pansy nodded, picking up a decorating magazine. "Later, alligator."

Eleanor pushed out the door, the familiar bell clanging an easy comfort, and headed over to the jazz club. By the time she reached the opposite sidewalk, she could hear the faint sound of music being played. The door was unlocked so she entered just as the horns joined in on the rollicking tune.

For a moment, she felt like Alice down the rabbit hole.

Tre didn't look like the silent delivery boy any longer. He wagged his head to whatever invisible beat pulsed in him, his cheeks puffed out, his eyes closed and his fingers moving light speed over the keys of the horn.

Strange in a wonderful way to see such transformation.

For a full minute she watched, none of the band noticing her appearance as they wailed, rolled and rocked a song she'd never heard before.

Reggie Carney caught her eye and nodded in acknowledgment as he sat in one chair, feet propped in another, drinking in the sounds emerging from the stage. Eleanor glanced around the club that would open in two weeks' time.

The place looked good. The sign she'd found for Dez hung above the bar as if the room had been designed around it. Gray walls the exact color of Dez's eyes were a perfect palette for the cobalt-blue, mustard-yellow and pepper-red of the accessories. The classic black tables were good contrast for the polish-aged bar tricked out with black foot rail and hammered tin tiles tripping visually back to the golden age of jazz. Leafy palms flanked the huge mirrored bar, helping to soften the corners. Eleanor didn't know how long they'd last in a bar, but they did bring an upscale look to the space.

Overall, the place appeared nearly ready.

And then her eyes found Dez.

The man played the piano exactly as he played her body—with consummate skill, long fingers exacting the perfect response, eyes closed as he pulled from the instrument exactly what he needed.

It freaking turned her on, and for once, she understood Pansy's initial response all those years ago…though it bothered her to remember it.

Yes, Dez Batiste was sex on the piano—slow, seductive and rising in tempo with hot, naked notes reaching to an intense peak.

Eleanor nearly fanned herself watching him work the instrument.

Finally, after several minutes, the last jangle of the cymbal faded.

"That's what I'm talkin' 'bout, baby," the drummer crowed, his drumsticks clacking as he tossed them onto the stand next to him.

Reggie clapped, and Eleanor joined in, drawing the men's attention. Dez's smile felt like butter on warm bread, and her stomach flipped in response. Oh, that man could smile something sweet.

"Batiste Blue sounds legit, my friends," Dez said.

"I like the name of the band," Eleanor said before turning to to Tre. "You're amazing. Like a whole 'nother person."

Ducking his head in true Tre fashion, he nodded. "Thanks, Mrs. Theriot. And thanks for the horn."

She patted his back, wishing for more ease between them. She'd always been able to foster a decent relationship with the employees who'd come and gone over the years, but not with Tre. He held himself so far from people. She understood—she'd done the same far too long. "I wish I had known you had such a God-given talent. I would have made sure you had a sax before now."

He pulled away, his eyes briefly showing he didn't need her pity. Eleanor tucked her hand into the back pocket of her jeans, wishing she didn't always say the wrong things to her delivery guy.

Dez caught her gaze and his eyes shone with understanding. No misunderstanding there. In fact, for the past few weeks, she and Dez had found an easy existence. When Dez didn't have a gig in the evening, they watched TV and ate ice cream before retiring to either his bedroom or hers to make love. A few times, they'd not even had sex, just lain beside one another sharing dreams, tales of elementary school and hopes for one another. Falling asleep in Dez's arms had become habit quickly.

"Mutually exclusive friends with benefits" worked pretty well, yet she knew even as she tried to keep her distance, she fell harder and harder each day for the man who smelled clean as Irish Spring soap and slurped his coffee each morning.

And that didn't sit so well with her.

Not the slurping coffee…but the love thing. That wasn't supposed to happen. She was supposed to keep emotion away from the mutually beneficial relationship, but she felt herself sliding into love…and that scared her. Because he'd said he didn't want anything serious either.

She didn't think she'd be able to stay friends after they ended things. It already hurt to think about.

"Okay, that's a wrap," Dez said, standing and flexing his shoulders in a long stretch drawing her attention away from heavy thoughts, and to his awesome physique. When would she stop noticing how sexy Dez was?

Probably never.

"So you wanna go Sunday afternoon?" the bass player asked, unplugging his instrument. "We probably need a few more practice sessions before the big opening."

Reggie folded his arms. "Tom Windmere wants to sit in on the next session. Wants to hear y'all because he's interested."

Dez narrowed his eyes. "Why is Tom interested?"

"I saw him a few days ago, and he said he watched you guys play at the Priest and Pug, and is thinking about adding to his client list. Just wants to—"

"I don't need Tom nosing around and disrupting things, Reggie." Dez closed the lid over the keyboard a little too strongly. The other musicians paused and watched the exchange.

"He's not going to disrupt. Just asked to sit in. No big deal."

Dez shook his head. "I'm not cool with that, but I'm not going to deny anyone here the shot."

Eleanor saw Tre lick his lips nervously, dark eyes unreadable. "You mean Tom Windmere?" he asked. "The dude who manages Ridiculous D and Trombone Sonny?"

Reggie nodded. "Yeah."

Dez eyed his business partner, dawning rising in his eyes. Eleanor realized this wasn't about Dez. It was about Tre.

"Fine." Dez nodded, busying himself with flipping switches on the stacks of amplifiers that perched like huge guardians on either side of the stage. "Tell him to come… tomorrow morning."

Reggie nodded, shooting Tre a glance, and the boisterous energy that had first greeted Eleanor when she'd walked in vanished like a fart in a wind. Tension seemed knotted between Dez's broad shoulders, and though she didn't know anything about Tom, she at the least understood bad blood remained between Dez and his old manager.

Fifteen minutes later, she and Dez were alone. He handed her a cold beer and sank back onto the piano bench with a sigh. He studied the shiny lacquer, tracing one lone finger along the edges of the closed keyboard.

She moved toward him, resting her hip against the curve of the piano. "You okay?"

"Sure," he said, not bothering to look at her.

It was a sign he was not okay, but she wasn't going to push him. Like every man she'd ever known, Dez would talk about what was bothering him when he was ready and not before.

"You want to do something tonight? We've been low-key, and that's been good, but it might be nice to go to dinner."

"Thought that's how you wanted it. Casual," he said.

"Yeah, but we can be seen together." She stroked the back of his hand, not liking the distance suddenly between them.

He glanced up, his gray eyes raw. "Can we?"

"You think I don't want to be seen with you?"

He shrugged. "When I suggested going for pizza last night, you said you weren't hungry."

"I wasn't. For pizza. I wanted you."

Dez shook his head. "Sorry. I'm in a crappy mood. Probably should go home, have a beer and watch the Celtics."

"Alone?"

"I don't know. Reggie sprang that whole Tom thing on me and everything in my past slammed me."

Eleanor remained quiet, studying him. "What did Tom do to you?"

"Nothing. That's the thing. My whole career has amounted to nothing. Once I was Tre, you know? Young, raw and talented. Tom jumped on me like a hen jumps on seed, and he convinced me I would go somewhere in this world."

"But—"

"But Katrina washed it all away, and after that, Tom didn't seem to bother. All the publicity mired down and Drew was on tour getting lots of attention for his first album. We split ways and I gave up music."

"What do you mean?"

"I mean I gave it up. I evacuated to Houston and took a job in a bar. I gave up on my dreams. Couldn't write music anymore—it was as if the floodwaters drowned my muse. So I decided to be a regular guy. Met a girl, bought a house and managed her father's three restaurants."

Jealousy sprang inside Eleanor. Dez had been in a committed relationship. She hadn't expected to hear he'd been in love, that he'd been settled with a mortgage and a whole other life. She'd always assumed… Well, she hadn't actually thought about Dez and his life in Houston. It had been a hole she hadn't bothered filling. "So what happened to bring you back home?"

His mouth twitched into a bitter smile. "Me. I happened. After a while, walking our dog, Peanut, fighting with Erin over money, over the best kind of beer and over whether or not I should buy one of her daddy's restaurants, I checked out."

Checked out? Eleanor knew about checking out, but she'd never walked out. She'd never given up on Skeeter and Blakely. "You left?"

"No. I'm not that guy." He looked at her, his eyes intense. "I didn't physically leave, but mentally and even spiritually I withdrew. But that made things worse. She and I unraveled.

and we weren't going to find any common ground again. Erin was young, insecure, wanted a baby, a ring, a new Jaguar. It wasn't what I wanted, and restlessness made a home in me. I finally realized I hadn't really given up on my dream, I simply needed time to heal, to grow into a man."

Eleanor didn't know what to say. Her name had been Erin. Was she beautiful? Charming and sexy? Doubt gnawed a hole in her heart, and her self-confidence nose-dived. "So, you're over this woman?"

"That's the problem. I was over her when I was with her, and that wasn't fair to her. Erin's passionate, and very much spoiled by her daddy, part of a big Latino family with ties to the Cardenas family. Erin got what she wanted, except me. Our life was tumultuous and, honestly, considering who her father deals with, I'm lucky I came out without concrete shoes. But Jose knew his daughter. He came to me, told me to leave, gave me money to cover what I'd paid for the house and the engagement ring. Tacked on severance pay, and that was the end."

"You were engaged?" Suddenly she felt nauseous…and panicky. It became painfully obvious she really didn't know Dez. Sure, she knew he didn't like strawberry ice cream, but he'd been engaged to a crime lord's daughter.

Dez's smile was hard. "Yeah. Shoulda seen the ring. She had to have a three-carat square diamond. Sweated every month when I got the bill in the mail. But that was Erin. She wrapped people around her pinky so she could get what she wanted. Sort of like Blakely."

"Blakely's not like that," Eleanor said, rushing to her daughter's defense as she always did because it was genetically coded in a mom's DNA to defend and excuse.

Dez arched an eyebrow.

"Okay, I suppose my daughter isn't above manipulation… and pettiness. Since Skeeter isn't here to defend himself, I'll blame it on him. She had to have gotten it from his side of the family. In fact, truthfully, she did get it from his side of the family. Vipers."

Dez gave her a flashbulb smile and propped his forearms on the keyboard's lid. "Makes perfect sense to me."

Eleanor knew many of Blakely's problems were caused by a mother who tried to make up for what Blakely didn't have—four years of therapy helped Eleanor see she wasn't responsible for Skeeter's death merely because she hadn't been available enough, and also that *she* was responsible for some of Blakely's issues because she had been *too* available.

Now Eleanor reaped what she had sown. She could only hope the true sweet nature and integrity her daughter also possessed would win out. If only Blakely would let go of her anger... Eleanor shelved the nagging problem and refocused on Dez. "So this piano? Did Erin buy it for you?"

"Nah, once her father cut me a check, she and I split. I think she was relieved, but I was still adrift, just like after the storm, but with more dough in my pocket. I knew I had to walk away, but I wanted it to be on my terms. Pride is dangerous, you know."

"I know."

"So there was this dude who came into the restaurant, and before I stopped managing the place, he'd begged me to come play the Fazioli. He was a good guy, but I never went. A week before I moved back to New Orleans, I got a call from his attorney. He'd passed and left me the piano in his will. Made me feel like crap that I never went to play it for him when he was alive. But when I went to his house to meet the movers, I sat down right here on this very bench and cried like a baby."

"Oh, Dez," she said, stroking his forearm.

"It was the only time I ever cried since the storm. I'd balled up all that grief and tried to pretend I was someone else, but it came crashing down. As I sat there looking at this gorgeous instrument, I realized I had to come home."

Dez stood. "I actually dreamed about Blue Rondo one night. It was cool. I had this vision and when I woke, I had a new purpose. It was like I took my dream and shifted it on its axis, and I thought that was enough…until a few moments ago."

"Because Reggie invited Tom to come hear Tre?"

His eyes flashed with dark regret. "Yeah, it wasn't about me. It was about a new guy, a guy who has more talent than me. It made me feel so…"

He shook his head.

"I know what you mean," Eleanor said. "Sometimes I feel the same way…like I have this big part of my life I wasted on doubt, on being satisfied with mediocre. It's not a good feeling, but it's a human one," she said.

Dez pulled her to him, tucking her under his arm. He smelled like a sporty antiperspirant and a unique spicy scent all his own. She inhaled him as his head descended and he kissed her.

It was a kiss he'd never shared with her—open, honest and tender—like a gift for her understanding him.

Dez pulled back his head and stared down at her, gratitude warming those pretty gray eyes. "How'd you get so smart?"

"Years of regret. I've learned to be honest with myself. You scare me because when I'm with you, it doesn't feel so casual between us, and I'm not sure I'm ready for that. Honesty makes it easier for me, so saying things out loud sometimes doesn't make me weak or silly. It makes me—"

"Mine," he said, kissing her again, this time with the same passion he'd always shared with her.

And for that honest moment, it was plenty.

CHAPTER FIFTEEN

DEZ WATCHED AS HIS FORMER manager observed Tre, and the
envy he'd admitted to Eleanor days ago stuck and twisted
in his craw…whatever a craw was. Jealousy was not a good
feeling, but he had to be truthful with himself and own the
feeling. Some of what Eleanor had said made sense—living
honestly gave a person a sort of freedom.

The other guys in the band bobbed and swayed their heads
in time with the music, each giving way to Tre as if something inside each man identified he couldn't touch the talent of the nineteen-year-old blowing a secondhand horn as if
he'd been sprouted from the heavens a fully formed musical
genius. Even Dez was in awe as they hit certain parts of the
song, Tre showing a command of the saxophone rarely seen
by well-paid, seasoned veterans.

Layers peeled away from the quiet unassuming boy, and
he became a ballsy, sexy magic man who could drop a girl's
panties with the heat of the notes emerging from the brass
horn. Dez knew this from experience. Some cats could tran-
scend and become one with the music, and everyone around
felt the sacredness of being in the presence of someone who
could take things up a notch.

"God Almighty," Tom breathed when they finished "A
Night in Tunisia." "Never heard anything like that. Who's
been working with this kid?"

Dez shrugged. "I have no clue. He already played when
I met him."

Tre dropped the saxophone against his stomach. "Miss Janie Belle James taught me to play when I was five. She was my next-door neighbor and her daddy was—"

"Acre 'Birdman' James," Tom finished, shaking his head. "Fried at Angola for raping a white woman, but played the saxophone like a damn pied piper."

"No, sir," Tre said, shaking his head, his voice grave with an edge of anger. "He didn't have nothing to do with that woman. Just worked at the store she worked at. Everybody know it, but white people in the '40s don't care about getting it right, just shutting people up, so Birdman took it. But he taught Miss Janie the tenor and alto, and she was better than me."

"I'll be damned." Tom whistled, a smile appearing on his face. To Dez, the man might as well be rubbing his hands together and swirling a nonexistent mustache. Eagerness trembled the air. "What else you got? I want more."

"Dez, let's play your new song," Big Eddie said, clacking his sticks together impatiently. "Need something smooth to follow, and the sax solo you wrote is perfect for this kid."

Dez shook his head. "Not ready yet."

"Let's just play what you got," Big Eddie insisted.

Dez sighed. "Coming Down to Eleanor" was the most intimate, sensual piece he'd ever written. Big Eddie had caught him playing part of it on Friday and he wouldn't let Dez put it away. Everyone looked at him. "Fine. Here's the sheet music. I got two copies, but y'all should be able to follow along."

"Wait, you've been writing again?" Tom asked, shifting his chair so he faced Dez. Excitement still hung off the man.

"Just one song I've been fiddling around with," he said, passing a few sheets to the guitar players. "Horns are out except for Tre."

"I'm glad to hear that, Dez." For once Tom sounded sincere, and shades of what they once had edged into his voice.

Dez didn't want to be swayed by Tom, but it had been so long since he'd felt good enough. For a moment, he remembered what it felt like to be desirable…to be good enough to make it in an industry that left teeth marks.

Something gathered inside him, mixing fear and longing into a pulsing energy. He needed to calm his jittering nerves so he jumped up, grabbed a bottle of JB and poured a shot. It went down rough, but he didn't care. It was as if he'd been sucked back in time and his first song sat on the music stand. A new beginning felt possible. Not just for Blue Rondo, but for him as a songwriter and musician.

Champ laughed. "Damn, boy, you act like Satan's got you by the collar. Might as well pour me a shot, too."

Dez poured out a shot and passed it to Champ before settling down on his bench, rolling his shoulder. He recalled Eleanor's words about honesty. "First one I've written in almost eight years."

Big Eddie grinned. "It's the best damn song I heard in eight years."

Tom pulled out his phone. "Mind if I record a sample? I might send it to Terry Burton. He's looking for an R & B groove for a new kid he wants to break out. Might make you some money off this."

Dez shrugged. "I guess, but if there's interest, Terry comes to me. You owe me that much."

Tom's gaze flickered, but he nodded. "Of course."

"Okay. Let's roll it easy like Lionel Ritchie. This is our Sunday morning, boys."

Dez played a little of the melody and looked up. "You got it?"

Everyone nodded as Big Eddie set the beat and the guitars came in establishing rhythm as Dez's fingers stroked the keys, soft, plaintive. When Tre joined in, all threads of doubt flapping around inside Dez wound together tight…perfect.

Like Eleanor.

Dez sang the words from memory, closing his eyes as he put his emotions to the music, plucking out all she made him feel as he lowered himself to her, savoring the satin of her skin, the sweet delicious moans he caught with his lips, as he rested his burdens on Eleanor.

The whine of the sax stirred the emotions, and Dez's voice, carrying the sensation of making love to a woman, shone reverent on stage, before ending in a whispered plea—to remain his soft spot to rest, the place where he found his inspiration to move forward.

As he ended the final chords, Dez realized moisture filled his eyes, accompaniment to the passion flooding his soul as he sang his words to the woman who'd given him back the gift he'd lost—the gift of music.

Tre lowered his horn. *"Daaaamn."*

Dez refused to blink away the dampness—couldn't believe such feeling had risen to the surface and poured out of him. And the entire time, Tom had been filming.

He observed his former manager tapping on the screen of his phone with the exhilaration of a kid on Christmas morning. The man's pudgy fingers flew. Finally, he glanced up. "That's the best song you've ever written, Dez, and you've written some good stuff. Why did you ever stop writing?"

How could he explain it hadn't been his choice? How could he explain this woman across the street, this innocuous-looking woman with her funny sweaters and too-safe world had sparked something in him that had opened the floodgates? It didn't compute. It didn't make sense.

But it was the God's honest truth.

Eleanor had become his muse.

"You have my number, Tom?"

"No. Give it to me. If he likes this sample, you might need

to cut a demo. But we'll talk more soon. You can sell this. I know it."

Dez shrugged away the pride he felt at Tom's words. His former manager wouldn't have bothered if he hadn't thought the song good, but Dez didn't want to fasten hope to himself; it felt too much to carry. He had a ton to do in a short amount of time—the club would open soon and his to-do list was long.

He wasn't ready to have this song out there yet. Still needed some tweaking, and he wanted to share it with Eleanor before he let anyone else hear it. Seemed only right since it was intimate, echoing her name, telling the world how she made him feel, and "exclusive friends with benefits" didn't cover a corner of what he'd laid out for the world to hear.

On a rational level, he hadn't been able to vocalize how deeply he'd grown to care for her. She'd needed time, and he'd been willing to give it to her because he wasn't going anywhere anytime soon, but he knew she'd been leaning further and further into him over the past few days, deepened by his sharing the past of Erin, Houston and his inability to write.

Now he had proof she'd helped heal him—in a beautiful song honoring all they were together.

But was she ready to hear how much she'd come to mean to him?

"ANOTHER CUP, ELEANOR?" Margaret asked, holding up the silver carafe of fresh-brewed coffee.

"No, thank you," Eleanor said, casting another questioning look at her daughter, who sat demurely on the damask settee in the parlor of the colossal Theriot mansion on St. Charles. "I'd rather talk about why I'm here. And why my daughter is sitting on your sofa and not on the one at her sorority house in Oxford."

Blakely shifted her gaze away.

Margaret settled her bony bottom onto the blue wingback chair and drew her lips into a thin line. "I'm sure we'll get to that, dear."

Dear sounded like poison dripping from her mother-in-law's lips, and Eleanor felt instant sympathy for Snow White...even though the girl was fictional. Viperous mothers-in-law gave evil stepmothers a run for their money.

"Okay. Can we hurry through whatever else you wanted to say? I have plans tonight." Eleanor crossed her legs and leaned back, determined to appear unbothered by her daughter's ambush in Margaret's formal parlor. When Eleanor had gotten the cryptic summons, she'd thought it was about Blakely's legal woes with the drunk and disorderly, which hadn't yet been put to rest because the policeman Blakely had assaulted was threatening a lawsuit. But, no. It was something else altogether.

Margaret's smile was strained. "I rather think that's the problem...your plans for the evening."

Here it was—the showdown she'd been anticipating for the past two weeks. Time to defend her relationship with Dez.

"I don't see a problem. Why do you?"

Margaret's silver bob never moved when she turned her head. It was like that thing Darth Vader wore...but silver. "You mean a great deal to me because you carry the Theriot name and you're the mother of my granddaughter."

"Yes, I am, but I don't see how that translates into your meddling in my social life," Eleanor said, glancing again at her daughter, who had taken a sudden interest in the pattern on the expensive rug.

"Because who you associate with reflects on us," Margaret said, lifting one dark eyebrow. Her icy blue gaze remained arrogant and aloof. "Did you ever think about that when you chose a man to diddle?"

"Diddle?"

Margaret kept her eyebrow cocked. "Or whatever it is you're doing with that man."

"Careful, your snobbery is showing. You wouldn't want to show bigotry around common people like me. Word might get out and sway the vote against a Theriot…if they knew how you truly felt."

"Oh, please, Eleanor. Sniping doesn't suit your nature." Margaret sniffed and sipped her coffee, her gaze holding Eleanor's in an unspoken challenge. "And everyone knows we're Democrats and friend to the common man."

Eleanor almost rolled her eyes. "Okay."

"Mom, what she's saying is that Dez isn't the right guy for you to date. He's just not who you go with." Blakely tossed her hair over her shoulder and finally looked at Eleanor.

"Go with?"

"You know. You're, like, a mom. You wear really weird clothes and you're almost forty years old. You don't fit with Dez."

Eleanor shook her head. "You mean I'm not cool."

"Exactly."

Eleanor gave a bark of laughter. "Margaret Blakely Theriot, you really ought to be ashamed of yourself. What exactly have you two been up to? Discussing my private life, trying to manage me to fit in your world?"

"It's not like that," Blakely said, shaking her head, her face so young, so pretty and so very scary at that moment. She looked so much like Margaret, and it was hard to marry that image to the one of the girl Eleanor had raised—the girl who had run a lemonade stand in their yard, who had dressed up like Alvin the Chipmunk for Halloween and who had walked demurely down the aisle of their church in her communion veil. How had that girl become the kind of woman who would scheme to take away any piece of happiness Eleanor might grab?

"That's what it sounds like, honey. So what is this? Why did you come home? To—"

"It's called an intervention," Blakely said, aggravation narrowing her face.

Eleanor blinked. "What?"

"An intervention. Like on TV. You're acting crazy, Mom. Grandmother said some women act this way when they hit middle age, so you need to see what everyone else sees. An older woman dating someone inappropriate."

Margaret, God help her, nodded in agreement.

"Wait, let me get this straight. You two have cooked up an intervention for me because I'm dating Dez?"

The doorbell rang.

"Reinforcements," Margaret said, placing her cup on the antique coffee table and rising. Her low-heeled pumps squeaked as she glided ramrod-straight from the room.

"Reinforcements?" Eleanor echoed, twisting her body toward the double doors that led to the foyer. She then looked down at the whorls in the expensive rug, and wondered if she was dreaming. This whole deal was *C-R-A-Z-Y*. Capitalized and emphasized.

"Here we are," Margaret trilled.

Eleanor's mouth dropped open. "Mom? Dad?"

Her rotund mother delivered the gentle smile she reserved for students who forgot their lunch money. "Hi, honey."

"What are y'all *doing* here?"

"Margaret asked us to drop by," her father said, his dark eyes flintlike, his posture erect. "She's very concerned about you." He leaned against the back of the wingback her mother settled upon.

Bill and Tootsie Hastings could have graced a Norman Rockwell painting. Her father, with his long, studious face and grim mouth, and her mother, with her fluttering hands, dumpling cheeks and beauty-salon copper hair were the epitome of middle-class America. They ran Hastings School for the Gifted on the sunny shores of Lake Pontchartrain, eating, sleeping and breathing the Spartan way—Faith, Honor and Service.

They weren't horrible parents, but they hadn't been very interested in their only daughter. Nor in their granddaughter, especially when Skeeter insisted Blakely attend Sacred Heart Academy, rather than their own private Christian school.

"Honey, we understand how painful these few years have been. Losing your husband was very tragic," Tootsie said, reaching out and patting Eleanor's arm.

Eleanor didn't know what to say. They thought she still mourned Skeeter?

"Of course, it's been hard. It's been hard on us all," Margaret added, silently holding up the silver carafe, offering Bill and Tootsie refreshments as if this were an afternoon tea… in the 1950s before women burned their bras and found their voice. Maybe the two older women had inhaled too much Aqua Net and had brain damage. Her father had no excuse. She couldn't believe they were confronting her about Dez and her dating life over freakin' coffee in the drawing room.

And they all looked at her as if she were an overwrought fool who needed guidance.

"I'm fine," Eleanor said. "I don't understand why any of you feel the need to meddle in my dating life."

"It's because of who you are dating, dear," Margaret said.

"Ah, yes," her father said, accepting coffee from Margaret, "the street musician."

"He's not a street musician. He's a business owner who happens to be a talented, well-respected pianist."

"Honey, he didn't even finish college," her mother said, tilting her head like a small bird, mouth in a moue. "Who you associate with does impact your daughter. Remember that."

"This is ridiculous. There's no reason you two had to come

all this way into the city for something as silly as this. I'm a grown woman…a grown woman far from middle-age insanity," Eleanor said, glancing over at Blakely, who remained quiet, refusing to meet her mother's eyes.

"Oh, honey. We had an optometrist appointment for your father. We told Margaret we'd stop by for coffee and to see if we could talk some sense into you," Tootsie said, shooting a look at her husband.

Her father nodded. "We're not opposed to you dating. It's only natural you'd want to have a social life. You're still a young woman—"

"I'm glad someone thinks so," Eleanor muttered.

"—we just want you to choose someone who is better suited for you. Someone who is settled, has a good job and—"

"Plays golf?"

"Well, that's not a requirement, of course," her father said, pushing his glasses up his nose and crossing his arms. "We feel this younger man with such a colorful background might not be the best choice. We do have Blakely to think about."

"And the Theriot family name," Eleanor said.

"Now you're making sense, Eleanor," Margaret said, a pleased light emerging in her cold eyes. "I know you miss Skeeter. We all do. Porter and I don't expect you to mourn him forever, but we do expect you to have some standards."

Hot anger flooded Eleanor, and the kernel of dislike she'd hidden for many, many years exploded. "Oh, do you? Well, I expected some standards, too. I expected your darling son not to stick his pecker in the most convenient place. I expected to mean more to him than his schlepping the secretary."

"Now, now, Eleanor. We'll have none of that. Blakely is present," her father said.

"Really? I didn't see her. Look, Dad, she's part of this. Don't think Margaret dreamed this whole thing up all on her own. My daughter is mad I'm dating a man she wanted for herself. Don't think this is about me dating. It's who I'm dating."

"I didn't want to *date* Dez, Mom," Blakely said, tossing her hair over her shoulder, making it understood exactly what she wanted to do with Dez…at least to Eleanor.

"Blakely's old enough to know her father cheated on me. That he wasn't some golden wonder boy who was the victim of some evil woman. He brought what happened on himself," Eleanor continued.

"How dare you!" Margaret yelped, slamming her coffee cup onto the table. "He did not deserve to die by that floozy's hand."

"No, he didn't. But I was a victim, too, something you conveniently forget. His selfishness took away more than his life. He stole a father from our daughter, and a husband from me. I loved him, but I knew who he was, and he wasn't some paragon of virtue, so you need to stop treating him as if he was the tragic victim. And I'm not spending my life being a martyr. I'm moving on. Dez is part of that, and I'm sorry none of you like it. But it's not your life. It's mine."

Blakely faced her, tears trembling on her thick brown lashes. Guilt pinged in Eleanor's stomach, but she squelched it. She meant what she said. Blakely couldn't stir up trouble and not expect to hear the truth. "Mom, it's not just your life. You know that."

"It *is* my life. I've spent the past twenty years—hell, the past thirty-nine years—trying to please everyone but myself."

She gave her parents her attention. "First I worked to earn your love and acceptance. But I never was as good as the students whose pictures you strung up and down the school's hallways. I did everything I could, but it was never enough."

She shifted her gaze to Margaret. "And then I met Skeeter. I thought he was the sun and the moon, but he was just a man. I made gourmet dinners, raised his daughter, ever mindful of the Theriot standards. I worked out so I was thin, smiled when signaled and mastered the art of conversation so I could be the epitome of a politician's wife. And look what it got me.

"And then I worked to be the perfect mother," she said to Blakely, "with homemade cookies sent on snack day, clean uniforms for soccer and late nights finishing up school projects.

"The only thing that belonged to me was the Queen's Box. *I* didn't even belong to *me*." Eleanor thumped her chest. It was dramatic and over the top, but she meant it. "I feel empty and ashamed I spent so much time trying to be someone else."

Margaret cleared her throat. "We understand everyone has shortcomings and feels insignificant. Even I have times when I doubt myself."

"Do you?" Eleanor asked, shaking her head. "I'm glad to know you're human, because I've always wondered."

Margaret narrowed her eyes.

"I don't appreciate your attempt to meddle in my life, and I don't give a goddamn what you think about me, Dez and our relationship."

"Really, Eleanor Grace, must you use such language?" her mother asked.

"Yes," Eleanor said, "I must. Because I mean it. This is my life. Mine. If I want to marry Dez, I will. If I want to sleep with him, I will. If I want to move on to dating other 'street' musicians, I will. My. Life. And Dez makes me happy."

Eleanor grabbed her purse and stood.

"Mom, I'm going to move in with Grandmother and Grandfather for the summer."

Blakely's words brought Eleanor's exit to a halt. She stared at her daughter. "You're moving in with your grandparents?"

Her daughter's declaration cut across her heart as fiercely as a sword. She nearly staggered at the thought of Blakely aligning herself so firmly with Margaret. This was it. Game over. Margaret had won.

Blakely looked directly at her, her gaze apologetic as much as it was resolute. "It will be easier. With all the parties going on and Justine's wedding, Grandmother needs my help."

Eleanor swallowed, trying to rid herself of the rawness in her throat. "Fine. You do that."

And then Eleanor left without saying goodbye to her parents, without thanking Margaret for the coffee and cake, and without the girl she loved more than she loved life.

Because she had to.

The words she'd said to those she held dearest were the truest she'd ever uttered. She'd lived her life as a shell, bowing and scraping to others, and she had tired of being a martyr. She'd lived half of her life for other people. The other half belonged to her. She wasn't being selfish, but she wasn't going to dance to anyone else's music any longer. Eleanor owned Eleanor.

The thought of Blakely choosing Margaret and the snobby Theriots over her...well, there was no description for a heart broken so badly.

But Eleanor would own her pain just as she'd owned her decision to claim a new life. She couldn't go backward in life, and she couldn't keep treading water.

The deep end was a scary place, but she would keep swimming.

CHAPTER SIXTEEN

TRE STUDIED HIMSELF in the store's mirror. He wore a gray jacket with dull silver zippers across the front. It looked edgy and cool. Like something Dez would pick out as opposed to the gangbangers lining the streets in his hood.

He glanced at the price tag. $79.00.

But it was thirty percent off.

He'd unfurled his shoebox money earlier that day, hating to steal from his education, but banking on the fact he might be getting a break in life.

"So shall I ring it up?" the sales guy asked, lifting his plucked eyebrows. His blond hair was moussed into a faux hawk, and Tre thought he might be wearing blue eyeliner. He didn't like the way the dude had touched him, straightening his collar and saying things like, "This really looks nice on you."

"Yeah. Uh, it's on sale, right?"

"Oh, yes, sir. Thirty percent off, but if you open a charge card, you'll get an additional fifteen percent," moussed-up boy trilled.

Tre almost laughed. Charge card? Yeah. When pigs flew. "Nah. Just cash."

"Very nice," the man said, clicking his loafers, making Tre feel a little uncomfortable. Who clicked their heels together like that?

Ten minutes later, Tre was back out in the mall, shouldering the plastic bag holding his new jacket that he'd wear for the debut of Dez's club next week. Nervousness flapped around inside him with excitement. He couldn't believe how his life had changed in two weeks. Playing with Dez's band Batiste Blue. Crazy.

Cici, Shorty D and Kenzie were waiting for him down by the Easter train. Shorty D acted as though he was too cool to ride and would only go to take Kenzie on it, but Tre knew his brother liked the silly bunny train.

Tre took his time getting to where his family waited, stopping here and there, and checking out fly shoes behind the shiny glass of the stores. He rarely came to the mall out in Metairie. When you don't have no money, wasn't no use in coming out to look at what you couldn't buy. But Shorty and Kenzie needed shoes, and with him and Cici pooling their money, they'd have enough to get what was needed.

"Hey, where you been leaving me with these kids for hours? Damn, Shorty 'bout to drive me crazy wantin' them shoes," Cici said, shaking her head. Her big hooped earrings shook like ornaments on a skinny Christmas tree.

He didn't say anything, just flicked his gaze over to where Shorty D sat on a bench, pecking at Cici's phone with Kenzie next to him, sucking her fingers and watching the train go round and round. Cici was supposed to text him when she found the shoes Shorty D wanted, but he'd received no texts... except for one from Alicia.

"What'd you buy?" Cici asked, plucking at the plastic. "A jacket? Don't a fool like you know it's too hot for wearing a jacket this time a year? We live in New Orleans."

He ignored her and walked over to Shorty D, wishing he'd left Cici at home. But he'd been afraid she'd go out again. She'd start talking about DJing again last night. Had called her girls—sissy bounce rappers and DJs—asking about the clubs needing talent.

"Tre?"

He turned to find Alicia standing behind him, dodging other shoppers as they chased squealing kids stampeding toward the train.

Something inside him sank, even as his heart skipped a beat. He hadn't thought she'd actually come to the mall. He wasn't ready for her to see the real him. To see Cici. To see him in the role he sometimes resented.

He wanted to be the man he'd been under that Pontchartrain moon, when his lips moved hungrily over Alicia's. When he'd felt like a man, and not a babysitter with Kenzie's snot on his sleeve.

"Hey, what's up?" he said, rubbing his sleeve against the back of his pants and grabbing the phone from Shorty D, who shouted, "Hey!" Tre handed the phone to Cici.

"You didn't answer your text. Can't believe I found you—it's crowded this afternoon," she said, dropping her hands onto the knees of her tight jeans and smiling at Kenzie. "Hey, Kenzie. You remember me? You going to come play with me on Monday?"

Kenzie didn't stop sucking on her fingers, but the little girl's dark eyes studied Alicia who turned to Shorty D. "And who's this handsome man?"

Shorty D rolled his shoulders and stood, intentionally letting his jeans bag. He slid a worldly gaze over Alicia's shiny hair, ruby-glossed lips and green jacket and inclined his head. "Shorty D. What up?"

Alicia turned to Tre with laughing eyes. All he could do was shrug. Shorty D was Shorty D. "His name is Devontay, but we call him Shorty D 'cause he's cool like that."

Shorty D grinned and gave him skin. It made Alicia laugh. Which made Tre's heart clinch up. He really loved the way she laughed. Loved the way her eyes danced and her hair curved at her collarbone.

Cici sidled up. "Who you?"

Tre shot his aunt the look—the one that said *shut up*—but Cici didn't get no messages ever. She did what she wanted to do and always had. Big Mama had shed many a tear over Cici. Tre refused to hope the woman would change, but he couldn't ignore her this time. "Cici, this is Alicia Laurence. She works at the school we takin' Kenzie to on Monday."

"She don't look like no teacher," Cici said, her black eyes greedily drinking in Alicia's clothes, nails and extensions. Jealousy flamed before she looked away.

"Well, actually I'm working on my certification. My aunt's the director of the school, and all the teachers there are certified. I'm working as an aide. It's a wonderful school, and I know Kenzie will like being around the other children."

"She don't like other kids."

Tre saw Alicia look at Cici, who held herself defensively, petulantly, like Shorty D when he didn't get the kind of cereal he wanted, and he saw the dawning in Alicia's eyes, and for a moment, the pity.

Something hot flooded him. He knew it to be shame. If he was Alicia looking at him with his ragtag crew of snot-nosed kids and cranky former addict, he'd run the other way.

But Alicia remained, her gaze finally catching his. She reached for his hand. "You all done here?"

"No, we ain't done. I still gotta get my shoes," Shorty D said, walking toward the Foot Locker, not bothering to wait on anyone else.

Tre made a face. "Almost. I still got things to get, then we going to visit Big Mama. It's bingo night at the nursing home and I told her we'd stop by."

"I'm good at bingo," Alicia said.

Tre kept one eye on Shorty D and scooped Kenzie off the mall bench. "Yeah?"

"Yeah. I think we can all fit in my car."

Cici finally gave Alicia some attention. "You got a car?"

Alicia nodded. "I'll give you a ride, if you want. I've been wanting to meet Tre's grandmother."

He hadn't even told her much about Big Mama and she wanted to meet her? What did that mean?

Alicia was like dark glass—he couldn't see inside her—yet he liked the mystery about her. She surprised him. Just like on that bus, giving him her number, giving that gift to a little three-year-old. Being a stranger had not stopped her from wanting to make right where there was wrong.

"Well, ain't nothing much to my mama but a big attitude," Cici said. "She gonna like you, though. Anyone that'll come see her in a place smelling like pee will be liked."

"Hey, Cici, why don't you go on ahead and get Shorty his shoes? Here's fifty dollars. Can't spend no more." Tre pulled the money out of the ragged envelope and handed it to Cici. "Alicia and I'll watch Kenzie out here."

Cici had the money in her pocket before he could blink. Ten short clacks of Cici's high heels and he stood with Kenzie still in his arms and Alicia sinking onto the bench. She patted the spot next to her.

He sat, shifting Kenzie on his lap. His niece plopped her fingers out of her mouth and stared at Alicia. He stared, too. "Why you come here tonight?"

"Why do you think?"

He didn't know. That's why he'd asked.

Thing was, he'd never been this way over a girl before. Alicia made him feel like good things were possible, because ever since she'd come into his life, things had gotten better—a second job, a school for Kenzie and a shiny new horn sitting in a case on the end of his bed, waiting for him to take hold of a new future. "I don't know what to think. I ain't been with a girl like you."

"A girl like me?"

"You know, a girl whose daddy's a preacher. A girl who's already been married before."

Her brow crinkled. "Did I kiss you like my daddy's a preacher?"

"Nah, I'd say opposite."

"Good, 'cause I meant it that way. And my being married was what I told you. Stupid. That's behind me. I don't hold on to that."

For a moment, they were both silent, watching a group of teenagers skulk past, followed by an older man and woman who held hands, looking confused yet somehow content. Tre wondered how that would feel—contentment. To date, it had only been a word on a vocabulary test.

"So we like together?" He turned to her, wanting to touch her, and see if she was as warm as she looked.

Alicia searched his gaze. "I don't know. I think I know the man you are, but I'm still scared you just a player who's gonna break my heart."

"I ain't never been a player. My life's been too real for all that."

Alicia sat still as death, only her gaze roaming over him, as if she sought the lie leaking out of him. But he'd told the truth. He'd been with girls, but that had been like two buses stopped beside each other before eventually glugging off, rambling for better road. He couldn't remember a single girl who'd ever made him put on a jacket, go to church and sweat more than her old man preachin' in the pulpit. He'd never wanted a girl to sit beside him on a bench at the mall. Never wanted to be good enough for a girl like Alicia.

"Okay, if you mine, you mine. No playin'." Her mouth set, reminding him of Big Mama's...except he'd never wanted to taste his grandmother's lips. These strawberry-glossed ones he did.

"Didn't I just say—"

"And when you introduce me to your Big Mama, you say I'm your girl."

"You sure are bossy."

Alicia held out her arms to Kenzie, who, for the second time in her life, went to a perfect stranger. "That's a girl-friend's job."

He grinned and she smiled back.

Tre decided Alicia's smile was a slice of heaven he'd hold on to tight.

DEZ WAS LATE picking up Eleanor for their date that night, which he hated because it was their first date as a couple. He was taking her to the Three Muses for dinner, and then to Bigmouth Blues Bar, where his friend hosted Kermit Ruffins and the Barbecue Swingers. Both places were on Frenchmen Street, genteel enough for Eleanor but edgy enough to suit him. He usually stayed away from the Quarter, where the music felt sanitized.

He rang the doorbell three times before knocking.

Finally, she opened the door and he nearly fell off the step.

"Wow," he breathed as she pulled the door closed behind her, keys in hand. She wore a tight, short sheath of black, kinky-looking black net stockings and a pair of bright yellow shoes…no, not yellow…chartreuse. He'd almost picked out globes for the light fixtures in that very color. "You look amazing."

Her smile wasn't soft. It was fierce. "Thank you. I've been waiting to wear this dress for almost a year. The shoes were a spontaneous purchase this afternoon, and I might need your elbow to walk."

Dez stuck his arm out, glancing a kiss on her silky cheek. Eleanor had pulled her hair into some sort of knot with little pieces of fiery red sticking out at odd angles. A huge yellow daisy pin perched in the center, probably an antique piece.

Resembled something his aunt Frances might have pinned to her wool coat. "I'll carry you if you need me to."

They walked side by side down the front porch steps. Darkness had fallen and the flickering gas lamps softened her face, but even with the shadows playing hide-and-seek, he could see something bothered her.

Was it him?

Did she have reservations about becoming more official, dining in public restaurants, meeting his friends? Had uncertainty pulled her away and made her cautious? He'd told himself to be patient with her. Even though she was older than him, she was vulnerable, like a colt leaving the comfort of its stable.

"Is something wrong?" he asked. Honesty. She said she wanted it, so he wouldn't shy away from it. "If you'd rather not go out, we can order in."

Opening the wrought-iron gate, she teetered toward his car. "No way. I bought new shoes I can't walk in. We're going out. This is an official date, mister. You're not wiggling out."

He jogged around to the passenger side of the car and opened the door, stilling her by laying a hand on her arm. He searched her eyes. "I want to go out, but you seem…upset."

Her green eyes hardened. "I'm fine. This is what I want. You. Me. Dinner. Dancing. Making love in that soft bed up there."

Dez rubbed a thumb against her bottom lip, and those hard eyes softened. "You sure?"

She gazed deep into his eyes. "Being with you is the best thing I've done in a while. I need you, you understand? This has to be right. Has to be worth it."

Dez answered with a soft kiss at her jawline. "I'm not sure what you're getting at, but every moment I've spent with you has been worthwhile, lady."

Her eyes delved into his. "And that's exactly why you're

what I need." She clasped the hand he held at her jaw, squeezed it and then climbed into his Mustang.

Fifteen minutes later they searched for parking in the Faubourg Marigny neighborhood between the Quarter and Bywater District. The tight streets were lined with bright, happy Creole cottages, and held firm to a funky vibe. Close enough for tourists to discover, far enough from the souvenirs to remain authentic, the area had become a mecca for artists and musicians, many of whom congregated on Frenchmen Street, the heartbeat of the music scene.

Finally, scoring a tiny spot, Dez helped Eleanor from the car. She peered down the dark street. "I'm thinking I should have bought those sensible sandals."

"You kidding me?" Dez said, raking her with his gaze, admiring the curve of her hips in the tight dress, and the way the band beneath her breasts pushed them up, deepening her cleavage. "You look so damn hot all the men are going to be wondering how those yellow shoes would look hooked behind their neck."

Eleanor inclined her head toward two men walking hand in hand across the street. "Not all men."

"Touché," Dez smiled, remembering the area was also a mecca for gay men and women. A rainbow flag hung on the porch the two men passed, and something about the tilt of one man's head, the way he walked, pinged Dez's memory. "Hey, that looks like my old college roommate. Karl!"

One of the men turned, peered at them in the darkness and broke into a smile. "Is that my man Dez Batiste?"

Karl jogged toward them, his nearly bald head shining in the streetlights. Whoever he'd been walking with followed. Dez held Eleanor's arm and helped her off the curb. "In the flesh."

Karl gave him the complicated handshake he'd invented

their freshman year followed by a chest bump. It's how he and Karl rolled.

"How's it goin', brother? Haven't seen you in forever." Dez tucked an arm around Eleanor and extended a hand to Karl's friend.

"Oh, it's going," Karl said, introducing his partner, Miles. Dez introduced Eleanor, enjoying the feel of having someone like her at his side. After several minutes of catching up—including discovering that Miles worked for an architectural firm and raised French bulldogs—they moved together toward the infamous street.

"Y'all should come eat with us," Miles said, shoving his hands into the pockets of his pressed khakis, giving them a shy smile. "We have a table upstairs at Adolfo's. They can seat four as easily as two. I mean, if you want."

Dez slid a glance to Eleanor, who already nodded. "I'd love that," she said. "I want to hear about Dez's college days."

Karl grinned. "The X-rated version or PG-13?"

"Oh, definitely X-rated." Eleanor laughed, and at that moment Dez's heart squeezed so tight he thought he might choke. She was so damned gorgeous, fit him like no other. It was so like her to turn their romantic date night into a spontaneous dinner party with his old friend. Classy, wonderful…all things Eleanor.

This was why he lov—

His mind clamped down on that thought. He couldn't be there yet. They hadn't had enough time together to build something that articulated the commitment of his heart.

Let go, breathe, live and don't overthink.

Tucking Eleanor's arm into his, they followed a man riding a bike with a trombone attached to the handlebars toward Apple Barrel, a blues dive below Adolfo's.

The place was crowded, and the music trickled into one's soul. Dez ordered the grouper stuffed with crawfish and crusty garlic bread, and filled his mouth as he watched Eleanor charm Karl and Miles. Karl gleefully shared tales of crashing a sorority party and dressing up like a washer and dryer for Halloween. Dez remained good-natured, happy to see his old roommate, to see the love he shared with his partner and to see how easily his Uptown girl fit in with two gay guys in the nontraditional area of New Orleans. Everything felt so right—the way the lights caught the fire in Eleanor's hair, the clank of the forks, the food, laughter and frolic. All good.

Eleanor caught his gaze as they made a final toast, clinking glasses together and calling for health, wealth and old friends around every corner.

"And to new beginnings," Dez said, warming at the smile she gave him.

"Hear, hear," Karl said, taking a swig and lifting his glass again. "And to happily ever after."

They all raised glasses of Malbec, the tinkle of the crystal accompaniment to the happiness curling around him. Earlier the night had felt stilted, Eleanor's mood pensive, but now she seemed fine.

An hour later after leaving his friend with promises for getting together in the near future, he passed Eleanor another glass of wine as they stood, one foot in Bigmouth Blues Bar, the other in the weathered New Orleans street because there was not a table to be had in the place. Even the bar was three-deep in bodies.

Eleanor leaned against the door frame, bobbing her head to the beat of the music tumbling out into the streets. It was loud. Too loud. He grabbed her hand, pulling her through the crowded room of people riveted to Kermit and his band, and toward the courtyard just beyond the aged wooden doors. A fountain gurgled in the moonlight, the perfect background for several pairs of lovers talking low and a group of college-aged girls staring at their phones' glowing screens.

"I want you to myself," he said, nuzzling her neck.

She tilted her head to give him better access. "You have me."

"Do I?" he asked, curving an arm around her waist, moving his body so they swayed to the music, which had gone from riotous to smooth and mellow.

"This is nice," she said, slightly off balance. She'd drunk almost three glasses of wine, and had a soft, hazy expression that made him want to kiss her, taste the wine off her lips.

"Is it?" he said, taking her right hand and humming to the old standard, finding the rhythm.

No one looked askance at them—to spontaneously dance wasn't out of the ordinary in a place like Bigmouth's. In fact, a few other couples made good use of the music, too.

Eleanor felt good in his arms, a nice fit. Her hair, which smelled like clean, fresh air, tickled his nose, and her cheek nestled into the groove of his neck.

"You smell good," she murmured, her left hand stroking his shoulder.

"I've been known to shower on occasion."

Her gaze found his and instead of the expected desire within the green depths, he found profound sadness. His brows drew together. "Eleanor?"

"Oh, God, Dez. Blakely hates me."

ELEANOR FELT SLURRY...and filled to tip top with achiness. Probably the tears she hadn't cried after Blakely basically turned her back on her...after everyone she cared about, sans Margaret, virtually drew a line in the dirt in regards to Dez. The "intervention" that afternoon made the depression she'd finally pinned under thumb three years ago pop onto her periphery.

Those old feelings had wrapped round her, making her look at her bed with the eyes of the old Eleanor. What would it hurt to curl up and hide from the world? She could refuse her pain the light of day and perhaps it would shrivel and dry up.

But no. Hiding wasn't the answer. Fighting was.

She deserved to have a life.

Plain and not so simple.

So after a few hours alone in a house that echoed, she'd grabbed her wallet, hopped in the Volvo and drove to Saks. She bought a pair of shoes that cost so much she'd fought down vomit at the register.

And she could barely walk in the damn things.

She'd wanted tonight to be good for her and Dez. She'd hung her black fitted minidress with the satin tuxedo stripes on the back of her closet door two nights ago, ready to make her and Dez legitimate in the eyes of the world.

She wanted to be with him in every way, especially in a public way. Maybe she wanted to take them to the next level. Maybe she wanted to not think about labels and parameters.

But the "intervention" had sucked the joy out of it.

"Blakely doesn't hate you, babe."

"She does. She's moving out this summer. Wants to live with her grandparents."

She had to give Dez credit. He only missed one dance step. "Why?"

"Blakely, along with the rest of the family, thinks I'm going through a midlife crisis."

"Because you're with me?"

She nodded, her grasp tightening on his back.

"But I'm not that much younger. It's not like I just graduated high school and you're robbing the cradle."

"I know, but they think I've gone crazy. In fact, this afternoon they staged an intervention."

"An intervention? Wait," he said, stepping back a tad so

he could see her. "Is this about more than age? Do they have a problem with the fact my grandfather was black?"

"Oh, no. The Theriots are Democrats," Eleanor said, heavy on the sarcasm.

He made a face, and she could see exactly what he felt. She'd never had to go through that—racism, discrimination, being thought less of because her skin didn't glow in the moonlight. God, she loved his skin. "Eleanor?"

"I don't know. Maybe a little. They're of that generation, but mostly their protest revolves around your being a street musician."

"I'm not a street musician."

Eleanor gave a harsh laugh. "I know that. You know that. My family? Not so much."

"What did you say?"

"I told them to kiss my ass. I'm not dancing to their tune anymore." Eleanor pulled her hand from his, no longer moving. The world spun anyway and she wished she hadn't had so much wine. It made her not as careful with her words, and she needed to be careful. But too late, she'd uncorked the bottle. "But—"

"But?"

"It makes things harder, you know?"

"What things?"

"Me and you. From the very beginning, I had all these doubts. Some had to do with the fact I'm older and whiter, but most of it was about how different we are. Blakely nailed it when she said we don't go together."

"The hell we don't," he growled, jerking her back into his arms. She stumbled in the ridiculously high heels and fell against him. Dez's lips met hers in a punishing kiss, as if he could force the doubts from her head with his lips, with his determination. He finally lifted his head, his eyes raw with pain. "Why am I not good enough?"

Eleanor shook her head. "Don't you know you're too good for me? Too young, too ready to conquer the world with your music. I saw you play. You thought everyone watched Tre."

"They did."

"He's brilliant, but the emotion, the passion you bring to your art…it's amazing. I watched you and all I could think was, 'This man will break your heart, Eleanor,' because I'm just a pit stop for you."

"How can you believe that?"

"Because I know. You're destined for great things. I see this in you, and I'm not ready to go down that road. I'm just starting over, Dez."

"I am, too. That's what Blue Rondo is—coming home, starting over, making something good out of the shit life handed me."

"Yes, but it's different. You live boldly, rolling the dice. You're young, single and unencumbered. If Blue Rondo fails, you'll move on, taking your music with you. Even in these past few weeks, you've changed. You're confident."

"And you're not?"

"Yes, in a way, but I have a daughter, a family, a business that has to survive because I don't have anything else in life."

"You're doing it again. Throwing up barriers."

She stepped back, her hands seeking the support of the ancient brick wall. "You're damn right I am."

For a moment, they were both silent, no longer touching, something more than mere air between them. The damp of the night crept in and Eleanor wrapped her arms around herself.

"This wasn't supposed to happen," she said finally.

He hooked a brow—a dangerously sexy eyebrow that made her want to forget the obstacles she dug up and tossed in front of them.

"I wasn't supposed to feel this way about you. You were supposed to be the guy who pulled me out."

"Pulled you out?"

"Of the numbness. You were supposed to be a sexy, hot rolling stone who didn't make me—" She stopped, pressing her hand over her mouth. "Look, never mind. I'm half-drunk and emotional. I think I have PMS or something, and I'm making these molehills out of mountains. Or vice versa."

"Things are serious now."

It was a statement. Not a question.

"Yeah, but I know how things will end. We're not a happy ever after, Dez. That toast we made with your friends was a lie."

"Eleanor," he said, stepping toward her. She flung her hands up, hitting his chest. "Stop thinking so much. Right now we're having fun."

"No, we're not. Don't you get it? I'm falling for you, and it's not—" she choked on the emotion; jerking her hands up, she pressed them to her eyes "—fun. You're supposed to be a good time, a guy to help me get over being pathetic. But, joke's on me."

She couldn't stop the tears. They came and she angrily wiped them away. Her inability to control her feelings pissed her off. Dez watched her with conflicting emotions on his face as a world that cared little about their tears, fears or tangles moved around them.

"Shit," she said, sagging against the wall. "Everything is shitty right now. Blakely, my family, me going all psycho. I want to stop, but I can't."

"Sometimes love happens."

"Love?" she chirped, trying to rein in the rollicking panicky feeling in her gut. "You know what? I don't want to talk anymore. Forget about this. It's the emotion and wine. Not a good mix."

Inside the club, the band struck up a fast beat and the doors flew open. Several people stumbled out, their chatter and laughter almost sacrilegious in the severity of the night, in Eleanor's realization she couldn't prevent herself from falling in love with Dez.

Dez placed both hands on either side of her head. He didn't kiss her, and she didn't blame him. She was soggy, but he did level gray eyes at her. "You said being honest with one another is the only way."

"I didn't say only way. I said something about, you know… I don't remember. But being honest isn't always the right thing, especially when you end up looking like a fool. I should be able to handle dating without turning into a whacko."

His eyes puddled into velvet. "You know you're much more to me than a friend and a lover, don't you?"

"That's what scares me."

"Why?"

"Because the last guy I loved took something sacred and crushed me and then left me behind to deal with an assload of crap. I was stalked, belittled, talk-show fodder and it made me—"

"A survivor. Not every guy is Skeeter. You can't apply that to all of us. It's unfair."

"Why not? Everywhere I look love doesn't last. I'm a prime example. You're a prime example. Things go to shit all the time."

"But we survived."

"I know. But it's very, very tenuous. So, feeling this way about you paralyzes me, Dez."

"So if things don't work out between us, you'll wither up and die?"

Would she? She'd been through so much after Skeeter was killed—erecting walls to protect herself. Clinging to a safe world made sense…until she'd pretended to lock herself out of her store, and the cracks had started. Bricks fell to the ground and she stepped outside, blinking into the sun, feeling again.

But now that the walls lay in ruin around her, enemies assembled, and she stood naked, something deep inside prodded her to erect a new fortress. "I don't know."

"Well, I do. You're strong, just like this city. Storms will come, but you will endure no matter how much it chips away and reshapes you."

Eleanor nodded. "Sorry for ruining things tonight."

"Not to toss your own words back at you, but you're human."

She grasped his hand, determined to salvage the night, to do what he suggested—stand strong. "You're pretty smart."

"For a street musician who digs old ladies."

His teasing was exactly what she needed. Time to bring lightness and sexiness back to their night. "Speak for yourself. I'm working this dress with no support hose, and I'm ready for you to check out the new lingerie I bought today."

She tugged his hand to the back of her thigh where the garter held the fishnet stockings. He slid his hand beneath her dress and cupped her bare bottom. It was as forward as Eleanor had ever been while up against a wall outside a club.

"Mmm," Dez growled in her ear, trailing one finger toward the inside of her thigh. "I like this nonexistent lingerie."

She smiled. "Take me home and I'll let you see it."

CHAPTER SEVENTEEN

TRE TOOK THE 40-ounce malt liquor from Grady and leaned against the cool metal of the Charger. Crazy Eight and some dude they called Hoops lit up a blunt and passed it back and forth as rap music boomed from the car radio, heavy on the bass, making the car hum beneath Tre. It was bumpin' and made him feel chill.

"So you gonna go back to playin or what?" Grady asked, taking a draw on the drink he held in his hand. He and Grady had played horns together in school. Grady had played the trumpet, not as well as Tre played the sax, but good enough to earn him a spot in the Lil' Brass Rebirth Band. Of course, those years were behind both of them, but every now and then they talked music, and Tre was reminded of a time when they had been friends. Before Grady rolled with the 3-N-Gs. Before life got hard.

"Yeah, got a gig across from where I work. Pays pretty good if tips roll in."

"Cool. That's what you need to be doin'. That's your future, cuz."

"Yeah, it's with Dez Batiste. Remember him?"

"For sure. He's tight on those keys. Always thought he was cool."

"Yeah," Tre said, keeping an eye on his front door. He'd returned from the nursing home two hours ago, dropped off by Alicia with a sweet kiss. He'd stepped out on the porch, wanting a reprieve from Cici and the kids, and Grady had spied him and held up a beer. Usually, Tre would ignore his former friend, but tonight he felt good. Like bad luck couldn't touch him. So he'd walked over to hang for a while.

"Yo," Hoops said. "Let's bounce and roll over to Biggie J's. He got bitches crawlin' all over his crib and I need some honey, ya know?" He opened the car door.

"You wanna go to Biggie's with us?" Grady's dark eyes glittered a challenge. "We just gonna chill, dog."

Tre glanced back at his house, and then at the guys testing him. He didn't want to seem like a bitch, but he also didn't want to go to Biggie whatever's crib. Grady and his boys ran into trouble often and "just chillin'" could turn into something not cool fast. "Nah, I better bail. Got stuff in the morning." Like church with Alicia.

"Whatever."

Something inside Tre flickered at the unspoken rebuke in Grady's eyes. Tre hadn't been nowhere but work and his house in a while, and Grady said they was chillin'. Probably gonna smoke blunt and drink. Get crunk. No big deal. "You know, maybe I'll roll with you tonight."

"Cool," Grady said, draining the forty and pulling his keys from his pocket. "Let's head."

They all climbed inside the car—Grady and Crazy Eight up front, Hoops and Tre in the back. Dr. Dre rapped old school on the radio as they pulled away, and Tre settled back against the leather, reaching for the cell phone he kept in his back pocket, but it wasn't there. Damn. He'd left it on the counter at home.

They rolled slow 'cause that's how Grady liked it. He could see his friend's head move side to side as he surveyed the hood. Crazy Eight's shoulders were tight and he reached under the seat and pulled out a piece.

Tre's gut tightened. "What Crazy Eight doin' with that?"

Crazy Eight turned, white teeth glinting in the darkness. "Keepin the peace, boy. We ain't gettin' jumped."

Grady's eyes met Tre's in the mirror. "Chill, dog. We ain't lookin' for trouble. Eight likes his nine out, that's all. Never know."

Tre tried to relax, but with a dude holding a gun, he couldn't. They'd only gone three streets over when Tre knew he'd made a mistake. He should ask for them to put him out. Better to walk the streets. What if they got pulled over by the cops? Weed, guns and beer. Not to mention any of the dudes in the car could have a warrant out. Tre had screwed up when he'd climbed in. He was stupid.

"You making me jumpy," Hoops said, puffing on his blunt. "Here."

He passed the blunt to Tre. "Nah, man. I don't roll that way."

"You don't smoke?" Hoops drawled.

Tre shook his head and looked out at the hood passing beyond the glass. As soon as they got to Biggie's whoever the hell he was, Tre would walk to a bus stop and go home. Thank God he still had his bus pass in his back pocket.

"Ah, naw. Look at this shit." Crazy Eight waved his piece toward a house on the corner. Someone stood out front, hand in pocket. "You think he stupid or something?"

Grady's eyes met his again in the mirror. "Look, cuz. We gotta stop for this fool. He owe an OG some serious cheese and hadn't paid up. Been talking to a snitch, too. We got business, you dig?"

Crazy Eight slid a round in the chamber and hopped out as Grady slowed. Tre clutched the seat as he watched the homeboy in front of the house take off toward the stairs, scrambling like something in a cartoon.

"Shit, this fo real," Hoops laughed, taking a drag on the blunt as Crazy Eight start yelling at the dude running.

"Get your ass out here," Crazy Eight called as Grady put the car into Park but left it running. "You know you owe. Get your punk ass back out here."

"This ain't my beef," Tre said to Grady, leaning up. "Let me out."

"Where you gonna go?" Grady asked, opening up the center console and pulling out a Desert Eagle. "Look, this won't take long."

"No, Grady. This ain't me."

Grady opened the door. "Then run, bitch."

Tre climbed out, one foot hitting the pavement as gunfire burst out on the sagging front porch of the Central City house. Leaping toward the sidewalk, Tre twisted to see Grady climbing out behind him, gun in hand.

Tre didn't think. He ran.

Bitch or not, he wasn't part of whatever Grady and Crazy Eight had going down. The glow of Hoops's blunt shone through the tinted window of the Charger, and that was the last thing Tre saw as he sprinted toward the heavy bushes surrounding a house down the street. The bushes ran right to the edge of the cracked sidewalk—a perfect shield to duck behind to avoid the battlefield sprung up in the middle of New Orleans.

Gunfire spat at the night, lighting up the darkness as Tre ran as fast as his legs would carry him toward somewhere far away from Grady and whatever went down behind him. Shouting erupted. More gunfire.

The sidewalk was uneven, and Tre tripped over a root, sprawling onto the pavement four houses down from where Grady's car was parked. The headlights were still on, engine running. Grady stood beside the closed door of the car as more gunfire, this time from an automatic, sounded, then Grady wasn't standing anymore.

Tre's friend pitched forward, blood spurting, flying into

the air, like on a video game. A silent scream emerged from Tre's mouth as the Charger absorbed a volley of bullets, the metal punctured with a line of holes. Glass flew as shouts sounded around him. Men yelled as a car engine fired nearby.

An old Lincoln Continental burst out of the house's drive, tires screeching, stopping for whoever it was who stood on the porch holding what looked like a Tec-9. The dude shouldered the gun and jumped inside as the car shot by Grady's Charger.

Tre felt small rocks beneath his hands pushing into his skin, the sting of cuts from his fall, the cold shrouding him. The woody stem of the bushes poked into his cheek and the buttons of his collared shirt bit into his neck.

What he didn't feel was anything inside him. He was cold, empty. Just like that night years ago.

And then like water in a bathtub when the plug is yanked out, he was sucked back into darkness.

In that moment, he fell through time, and there stood his mama with eyes of sadness watching him and Shorty D. And Shorty D, not as he was now, but as a toddler, snot-nosed and baby sweet. And G-Slim, hard and determined to kill. And that night. That night Tre ran…just like he ran this night.

Always running from death.

He slammed back to the present as doors to the houses around him began to open. In the clear cold, he heard the sirens.

Run, Tre. Get up and go. Pretend this night never happened, just like you pretended the other night had never happened.

In. Out. Breathe.

But Trevon was no longer an eleven-year-old boy. He was a man, and though he wanted to forget all the bad in life, he knew he couldn't run from it.

He stood as a few other people pushed their heads out their

doors into the night, like turtles finally brave enough to see what had gone down on their street.

Tre brushed himself off and walked back to the Charger. He didn't want to go, but he did. Grady had been a banger, but he'd also been his friend. They'd thrown the ball together in the street, shot hoops, eyed pretty girls and created music together. Tre wasn't the man Grady was; he was the man he'd promised his mama he'd be. He was the man Big Mama had raised. He wasn't perfect, but he wasn't going to turn his head the other way, not when Grady might need him.

As he approached the Charger, Tre saw his friend face-down, his gun about a foot from him, blood pooling under his chest. Grady's face was turned away from Tre, eyes open. Tre knew he was gone. He didn't touch anything. He caught sight of Crazy Eight lying slumped at the foot of the old house's steps. Another man, maybe the one Crazy Eight chased, lay half in the open door, half out. Not one of them moved.

Then Tre heard a moan from inside the car.

Hoops.

He jogged to the passenger's side as an older man crossed the street, approaching the car as if it contained a bomb. Tre looked at the man who wore a faded Hornets shirt and appeared scared stiff. "Call 911."

"Already did," the older man said, eyeing the car. "Someone still in there?"

"Yeah," Tre said, opening the door. "I'm going to see if I can help."

"You with them?" the man asked, still on guard, shifting his gaze up and down the street.

"No, sir. I'm definitely not with them."

DEZ STIRRED as the phone rang. He didn't want to give up the dreams, the piano beneath his hands and something to do with a recording contract and a hungry dog sitting outside the bar, but the ringing was insistent.

He shifted in the bed and felt Eleanor solid against his back.

"Phone," he muttered, flopping an arm over, inching toward the edge of the bed.

"Mmmm?" she said, rolling onto her other side.

He pushed into a sitting position, fumbling for the wireless sitting on the mirrored bedside table. He found it, pressed a button. "Hello?"

"Hello? Mrs. Theriot?"

He passed a hand over his face and glanced at the alarm clock. 1:45 a.m. "Eleanor."

She stirred, blinking as he flicked on the lamp. "What is it?"

"Phone," he said, shoving it her way.

Even though sleepy, her eyes widened. Never a good call when it came in the wee hours of the morning. "Blakely?"

He shrugged.

"Hello?" she said, turning panicked eyes to him. He tried to portray calmness, but it was hard with his eyes still not adjusted to the light.

"Wait a sec. You're talking about Tre? Trevon Jackson? A shooting?" Her eyes widened.

Dez slid out of bed and grabbed his pants from the fancy armchair, and then searched for his shirt.

"Of course. I'll be there in a few minutes." Eleanor hung up the phone and pushed a hand through her tousled hair. "Tre's in trouble. There was a drive-by shooting and he was involved somehow. They have him down at the station. He asked them to call me."

Dez buttoned his shirt. "You don't have to go. I'll take care of it."

"No, he's my employee and he called me. We'll go together," she said, throwing back the covers, wearing nothing but the skin the good Lord gave her. A small part of him wanted to sweep her back into bed for one more round of finding the good in life in Eleanor's arms. But the rest of him knew they had something to do—help a young man who had nowhere else to turn.

Ten minutes later they backed out of Eleanor's drive and headed toward downtown.

"I didn't know Tre was involved in gangs," Eleanor muttered, her hair in a crooked ponytail, which made her look cute in a slouchy way. Street light streaked by, throwing stripes on her sleepy face—it made her look sad…something that she hadn't been able to shed even during their intense lovemaking. He sensed her pulling away, but didn't know what to do about it. Just like Tre, Eleanor was accustomed to going it alone. With Blakely pulling crap, her parents standing across the neutral ground from her, and the enormous history of being a Theriot, Eleanor prepared for a storm. She latched the virtual shutters on her emotions…because she was scared.

He understood. He'd done something similar after his recordings were destroyed, but instead of shutting everyone out, he'd tried to become someone else, to become a regular guy. And he wasn't a regular guy, no nine-to-five guy, and he never would be. Suburbia felt like a prison. "I didn't see any signs he was in a gang. No tats, no colors, no vibe coming off him. If anyone were to ask, I'd say he wasn't involved, but sometimes we don't know people the way we think we do."

Eleanor slid her gaze to him as he took the exit off I-10. He wondered what she thought, but was too afraid to ask. He probably didn't want to know.

They pulled into the police station, and as they climbed the steps to the front glass doors, Dez took Eleanor's hand in his. She squeezed his hand and looked over at him. "Thanks for coming with me, and thanks for caring about Tre. He's not easy to know."

"Who is?" Dez asked.

She stopped. "You're saying weird things. Did my honesty scare you earlier?"

"No, but I think it scared you."

Eleanor shook her head. "No, honesty doesn't scare me. Falling in love does. I don't want that in my life. I don't want to feel that…"

"Vulnerable?"

"Yeah. Probably makes me weak, or maybe it makes me a fool, but I feel what I feel."

Dez shrugged. "Yeah, you do, but I don't think it's a good enough reason to run."

"I'm not running, am I?" she said, her green eyes flashing in the yellow glow of the station lights. "I'm here."

"Why?"

"Why am I here?"

"Yeah. If we are such a bad idea, why are you still sleeping with me? Why are you still holding my hand?"

She dropped his hand. "I don't know. If I were smart, I'd stop. We both agreed this was not a forever thing. It's tearing me and Blakely apart. Causing my parents to side with the Theriots, something that never happens, by the way, but I can't stop. I can't let you go…yet."

He didn't say anything because her admission tore a hole in his heart. But she was right. If they were going to stay buddies who took mutual pleasure in each other, it should be easy to stop. He'd always been able to walk away when things got too complicated.

So why wasn't he?

They'd both gotten what they wanted. He'd gotten his muse back and Eleanor had stepped into the dating world with flirting, romance and hot, dirty sex. So why weren't they finished?

He knew the answer.

She knew the answer.

But neither one of them wanted to talk about where love would take them because it was a path neither had thought they'd take. Uncharted territory.

So it was easier to ignore it.

"Let's talk later. Tre needs us right now," he said.

Eleanor nodded and started up the steps again…but she didn't reach for his hand.

ELEANOR'S EMOTIONS WERE tangled like jungle vines…and she felt vaguely nauseous. Three glasses of red wine left a girl dried out and woozy. Loving Dez made a girl feel as if she were stuck on a roller coaster. In fact that might be part of the nausea—Dez and the ride she was on with him.

She'd dug her heels in with her family over Dez, but she wasn't sure if it was the right thing to do.

Why draw a bath if you were planning to shower?

Forever with Dez was implausible, so should she fight so hard for him when there was no need?

It's not about him. It's about you.

Yes, voice in her head, very true.

Dez opened the station door and she walked in, squinting against the fluorescent lights, tucking her conflicting emotions about Dez into the background. More important issues were afoot. She could dwell on where she was with Dez later.

The desk sergeant peered up from whatever she studied behind the high desk. "Can I help you?"

"Uh, hi," Eleanor said, fretting with the threads coming loose on her purse strap. "We're, uh…"

"Trevon Jackson? They brought him in an hour ago?"

The officer held up a brightly polished nail and flipped her thick dark braid over her shoulder as she picked up the phone and pressed buttons. "Clancy? Trevon's attorneys are here."

"Oh, we're not—" Eleanor said, stopping when Dez jabbed her.

The officer pressed a button and pointed to a wooden door with a small glass window. "Go on back. Jim Blanchard will meet you. He's the detective on this case."

Dez held her elbow and they walked through the door. Several empty cubicles met them, but coming down a hallway was a burly man in tan trousers and a button-down shirt rolled up at the sleeves. Sticking out his hand, he said, "Blanchard. Follow me."

So they did.

Eventually they ended up in a small conference room with scuff marks on the linoleum, and faded green walls. Tre sat at a table, head down, hands covering his closely cropped hair. Something the color of red wine stained the sleeves of his shirt, making Eleanor wince. When the door clicked shut, he looked up.

"Oh, Tre," Eleanor said, sinking into a plastic chair near him, her heart aching at the fright in the boy's eyes. "What happened?"

Dez jerked his head toward Tre. "We're not his attorneys as you well know, but does he need one?"

The detective shrugged. "Don't know. He said he'd talk about the shooting, but he wanted to call Mrs. Theriot first. I'm guessing this woman is her."

Eleanor nodded. "Yeah, I'm Eleanor Theriot. Tre works for me."

"And for me," Dez said, leaning against the painted cinder-block wall. "What's going on? Has he been arrested?"

"Not yet. We're not sure exactly what his involvement is, but as you can tell by his shirt, he was there. He knows something. And he needs to tell us what he does know." The detective's words were hard as he directed his attention to the boy slumped at the table. "Now."

Tre shot Eleanor an apologetic look. "I'm sorry to involve you, Mrs. Theriot. I didn't have nobody to call. Cici ain't the right person for sure." He spread his hands, a tremor evident in his voice.

"You did the right thing. We're your friends." She tried to convey that in her gaze. She touched his forearm. "You know we care about you."

He nodded as the door opened and a slight man with a receding hairline slipped in. An African-American with a suit that looked straight out of *GQ* magazine, this man seemed to be playing the role of good cop. He stuck out a hand to Dez. "Reuben Clancy."

Then to her. His hand was dry and warm, and for some reason she trusted him. She figured it was designed that way. Have gruff and lumbering greet them, and suave and sincere butter them up. Or at least that's how it worked on *The Closer*.

Clancy sat in the empty chair across from Tre and opened a folder. "Okay, Tre. Time to talk. We helped you by calling your people, now you help us. We got three people dead, and one gravely injured. The boy is on the operating table as we speak."

Tre's eyes flickered to Dez before he centered them on the light switch. "I'll tell you what I know, but you got to give me a deal."

"A deal?" Eleanor squeaked, jetting a glance at Dez, whose eyebrows had drawn together. "You need a deal?"

"I don't know. But I know I gotta be out. I gotta work, take care of Shorty D and Kenzie. She going to school on Monday."

The black detective tapped the table. "Let's see what you gotta say."

"No." Tre shook his head. "I can't stay in here."

Eleanor drew Tre's attention to her. "If we need to get an

attorney, we will. If you've done nothing wrong, we'll make sure you don't get screwed."

Tre stared at her for several seconds, exploring those words, testing them in his mind. Finally, he nodded. "I didn't do nothing wrong."

"Okay, then. Tell them what happened so whoever did do something wrong can be brought in," Dez said.

Detective Blanchard pulled out a tape recorder and pressed a button. He recited the date, time and the case number and then looked at Tre expectantly.

Tre's voice, methodical and calm, put together a picture of terror. Eleanor's blood ran cold at what she heard. She'd known Tre lived in a rough part of New Orleans—she'd seen his address on the employment applications—but she hadn't visualized the danger he and his family faced every day. His life on the streets of New Orleans was lived a mere fifteen blocks from her own Uptown address…but so very far from her safe world. When Tre finished his account, he hung his head. "I never should have gone with Grady. Don't change nothin', but I wouldn't be here. I wouldn't have seen my friend bleedin' in the street."

Detective Clancy's eyes were flat. "True, but your quick response with the passenger in the backseat may have saved his life."

Tre looked up. "Yeah, but what kind of life is that?"

Dez cleared his throat. "You think there's no value in saving that dude? No value in you? Me?"

"I didn't say that."

"You implied it. Some of us are born in the streets, but that doesn't define us, Tre. We have choices. Your friends had choices. That life's sometimes hard is no reason to think it's not worth doing."

The detective clicked off the recorder. "Tre, I know tonight was hard on you. I've been out in the world long enough to understand some guys feel like the police don't care about what happens in the streets, but you're wrong. Every person matters. Your friend Grady might have made some mistakes, but he mattered. We'll do our best to find who did this. That's our job. Your job is to take the gifts you've been given and use them. I'll do my job. You do yours."

The other detective signaled Clancy and jerked his head toward the door.

"If you folks will excuse me." He picked up the recorder, closed the folder and followed the larger detective out of the room, the door snicking shut behind them.

"Sorry," Tre said, spreading his hands, catching sight of the blood on his sleeves and frowning. "I messed up tonight."

"Yes," Eleanor said, folding her hands and studying a ragged nail that needed filing. Funny how the most mundane of things struck a person in odd moments, like sitting in a police interrogation room. "But you also did a lot of things that were smart. Like leaving when you could. Going back when you were needed. We all make mistakes. It's how we handle living with the repercussions that's the measure of our character."

Tre studied her. "That sounds like something on a poster at school."

"Maybe that's where I got it."

Dez sank into the chair the detective vacated moments before. "You're not in trouble."

"I was an accessory or something. I was in the car. They pin that shit on people."

The door opened. "Mr. Jackson?"

"Yeah?"

"I need to get some contact information since you are a material witness and then you'll be free to go. Please write down your address, your place of employment and your home and cell phone numbers. Can you do that?" He passed a legal pad to Eleanor along with a pen.

She handed it to Tre with a smile. "See?"

Relief washed over Tre's young face as he took the pad and pen. "Sure."

The door closed again as Tre scratched the needed info on the pad. After he clicked the pen closed, he looked up. "Thank you for coming down here. Not many people would do that."

"You have a poor opinion of people, don't you?" Dez said.

Tre shrugged but said nothing.

"I get it," Dez said, studying the boy who was more man than boy. But at that moment, all Eleanor could see was a child, a frightened child who'd seen too much of the underside of life. "You haven't had much reason to expect people to care about you, but if you'd stop squeezing yourself into what you think you should be, you might find you can be more than expected. You might find happiness. You might find a family."

As Dez's words fell on Tre, they also fell on her. Was he killing two birds with one stone? Had he meant those words as much for her as he had meant them for Tre?

Tre stood. "When life shits on you, it's hard not to want an umbrella."

Dez nodded. "That's a good analogy, but if you're always carrying an open umbrella, you'll never feel the sun on your shoulders. I don't know about you, but I like the way the sun feels on my face. It's okay to put down the damn umbrella."

"I did. I called y'all, didn't I?"

Eleanor pulled Tre into a quick, hard hug. She released him and stepped back. "I'm glad you did."

For once, Tre didn't look pained. "I am, too," he said.

CHAPTER EIGHTEEN

SEVERAL DAYS AFTER she and Dez had picked Tre up from the police station, three men were arrested in the triple homicide. The man Tre had called Hoops was still in critical condition… and Dez hadn't called.

Eleanor sighed as she packed a few boxes to send to the Salvation Army. Two sets of dishes and several vases hadn't sold in over two years, and with a new delivery expected from her English buyer in a few days containing dishes, Eleanor didn't have the room to store the others.

Dez.

Her heart thrummed when she thought about him. He gave her space, she knew that, but still something inside her wanted him to demand more of her. Part of her wanted to be pushed into a corner in their relationship.

But it wasn't his style to push her. He dropped hints, talked about growing and stretching, but he didn't push.

She'd set the parameters and he'd played by them, but they both knew it had moved beyond friends with benefits long ago. Hell, they'd been past that when she'd declared the designation. Still, she missed him, wanted him to darken her doorstep and demand she forget her doubts.

"Your phone has been jittering like a june bug," Pansy called from across the room. "Want me to get it?"

"No, it's probably Margaret again. Or my mother. She's feeling guilty about falling in with the Theriots, but I'm not ready to talk to her yet. I'm still pissed they showed up for that dog and pony show."

Pansy walked over and set Eleanor's phone on a nearby table. "What about Blakely?"

"What about her? I haven't heard the first thing from her other than a message asking me if I'd pick up her monogrammed pillowcase from LaBourge's and mail it to her. And that request was delivered with a condescending, you're-such-a-horrible-person tone."

Pansy tsked. "Maybe I need to talk to my monkey girl. She needs a come-to-Jesus meeting."

"Don't. I worked hard to instill the right ideals in her, so if she can't realize what she's doing on her own, then I've either failed or—" Eleanor grabbed the phone dancing on the surface of the table.

"What?"

There had been ten phone calls in the past thirty minutes—five of which were from Blakely. Two messages awaited her in the queue. "What in the world?"

"What?" Pansy said, craning her neck trying to see over Eleanor's shoulder.

Eleanor punched the button and Blakely's voice rang out. "What in the hell, Mom? I mean, really? It's not bad enough you're dating the guy I had dibs on, but letting him tell everyone about your sex life? Oh, my God. I'm so humiliated."

The connection clicked.

"What does that mean?" Pansy asked, cocking her head at the phone like a dog when it hears a weird noise.

Dread curled around her gut as she pushed the next message.

It was Dez.

"Eleanor, you need to call me when you get this message. I can explain."

"Oh, my God," Eleanor breathed. "Explain what? Blakely said Dez told people about our sex life?"

"That doesn't sound right," Pansy said, crouching by the boxes Eleanor had been packing, and tucking the ends into each other. She grabbed the packing tape. "He wouldn't do that."

Just then the tinkle of the front doorbell sounded and both women stilled, a sense of foreboding in the air. Pansy dropped the roll of tape and headed toward the front of the store. "What's going on?"

"I don't know, but it doesn't feel good." Eleanor followed her friend, dropping her phone into her apron pocket and wiping her sweating hands on the sides of her jeans.

A young woman stood in the middle of the aisle wagging her head from side to side as if she searched for someone. She wore a tight wrap dress, nude heels and her hair bore natural highlights…or the hand of a really good stylist.

"Can I help you?" Pansy asked.

"Oh, yes," she said, with a big smile. "I'm looking for Eleanor Theriot?"

"For what?" Pansy asked, her shoulders rising defensively as she propped hands on her hips.

"I'm Natalie Primm from the *Times-Picayune*. I'm a feature writer for the Living section and wanted to talk to her about a piece on her and Dez Batiste."

Eleanor stepped from behind Pansy. "A piece? On…what?"

The woman swept her from head to toe with a discerning look. "Mrs. Theriot, I remember you from that whole nasty affair with your husband."

Eleanor didn't say anything. Just stared back wondering what in the hell had happened in the past hour or two to bring a reporter to her door and so many strange calls to her cell phone.

The woman held out a hand as if they'd met at a social

mixer. "Nice to meet you. Hope you don't mind me dropping in without an appointment. This whole thing is fascinating, and with the song going viral, I knew I had to be proactive."

"What song? I don't know what you're talking about."

The woman's blue eyes grew to the size of the robin's eggs in the spring display behind her. "You mean you don't know?"

"Know what?" Pansy asked.

"The song by Dez Batiste? It's gone viral on YouTube and everyone in the music scene is talking about it."

Eleanor's mind scrabbled trying to make sense—Blakely's irate call, Dez's tone of urgency and this woman talking about something viral? "A song by Dez? Maybe you've got the wrong person."

"You are the wife of the politician who died in that murder-suicide thing, right?" The woman—uh, Natalie—flipped through a small notebook and pulled her smartphone from her purse. "Eleanor Hastings Theriot? Married to Skeeter Theriot? Dating Dez Batiste, the musician?"

Eleanor nodded, wondering if Natalie would consider mutual friends with benefits as dating. "Yes, but I'm not sure about this thing on YouTube. What do you mean? Song?"

"Here," the woman said, tapping a few buttons on her phone and extending her hand. Both Eleanor and Pansy moved toward her, watching as Natalie tapped the little curvy arrow.

Suddenly the screen came to life and Eleanor could see that the video had been filmed inside Blue Rondo.

"Look, that's Tre," Pansy said, pointing at the screen, taking the phone from Natalie.

"That's his name?" Natalie asked, pulling a pen out and scribbling on her notepad.

"Shh!" Pansy said, shushing Natalie with a hand as Dez began playing something slow and soft. Eleanor watched enraptured as the camera focused first on Dez, whose head bobbed as he did his thing, fingers moving deftly over the keys, summoning forth the music. Then the guitars joined in, and finally, Tre lifted his horn, the wistful moans from his instrument rousing and evocative.

"That's so pretty," Pansy whispered, enthralled.

"I know, right?" Natalie said, craning her head toward the phone.

Eleanor and Pansy stood, silent as stone, watching the jam session on the cell phone screen. The music Dez played was haunting, and when accompanied by Tre on the saxophone, sent shivers up the spine…and back down again. But it was the words Dez crooned that made the fine hairs on the back of Eleanor's neck stand up. Words about skin sliding against skin, the delicate beauty of two becoming one and of soft places to come home to—evocative, soulful and sexy. And then came the chorus…with her name in it.

"Oh," Pansy said as Dez talked about the peace he found when he made love to Eleanor. "Wow, I think he's talking about you."

"You think?" Eleanor swallowed hard, her heart beating strong in her ears.

Dear God. He'd written a song about making love to her.

Something tore lose in Eleanor…not the warm fuzzy feeling that should have flooded her when a gorgeous man sang about the way she changed him, healed him…but rather something cold and slithery. Something reminiscent of how she felt when she'd been blindsided by a dead husband and irrefutable proof of his unfaithfulness. Something reminiscent of a time when reporters stalked her, acquaintances poked their long noses into her business with the hope of sniffing out something deliciously titillating. All those horrible, horrible feelings of betrayal in her past slammed into her, leaving her an open throbbing nerve.

How dare he do this!

The man had taken the healing beauty of what they'd made

together in the downy softness of the night and shared it with the world.

The song ended and Eleanor was paralyzed. The phone slid from her hand, but Pansy caught it, and handed it to the reporter who smiled at her like a jack-o'-lantern.

"Awesome, isn't it? Can't believe you didn't know about it. Total new element to explore in this story," Natalie Primm said, her young face brimming with excitement as she pocketed the phone and clicked her pen. "Now can I get the name of the guy playing the sax? He works for you, right?"

"Yes," Pansy said, casting her gaze toward Eleanor, eyes wide and cautious, "but I think we need to regroup a moment."

Natalie frowned. "And who are you?"

"I'm the manager." Which wasn't exactly true, but at that moment Pansy was exactly who she said she was. Eleanor couldn't "manage" words much less the situation.

"Okay, I'd like to do an exclusive interview. I tried calling Mr. Batiste, but he said he's not taking questions. Maybe if you say you're willing to talk about this deal, he'd climb aboard. People *are* very curious."

Pansy shook her head. "Look, I understand wanting to scoop stuff, or whatever you media types call it, but this isn't going to happen right now."

"Why not? This isn't a bad thing. It's good. That's why the song got hot so fast. People are talking about it on Facebook and Twitter. Not to mention the way those two guys play. Why not let New Orleans get a glimpse into two of its most fascinating citizens, two people with a rough past who have found renewal? It's got such a feel-good slant."

"No, it's not perfect, and it's no one's business," Eleanor said, finding her voice, forcing her anger and disappointment down and finding the calm exterior she'd used for the past five years. She'd be damned if she let on how hurt she was at

seeing Dez reveal in his soft baritone something so persona
as making love with her.

Natalie's face darkened. "Are you hiding something? I
that what this is?"

Eleanor pointed at the front door. "No, and you can leave
now. I'm not answering questions about some random video
If anyone asks, I have no comment."

The reporter shrugged. "Fine. People will draw their own
conclusions."

"They're welcome to do so," Eleanor said, turning on he
loafer, walking to her office and closing the door. She didn't
bother saying "boo" to Pansy. She didn't care that she'd been
rude.

She leaned against the door.

Okay, Eleanor. Breathe.

With trembling hands, she clutched her stomach, which
cramped at the thought of thousands of people watching Dez'
tender admissions, soaking in his soul-stirring ballad of sex
tenderness and restoration. "Dear, Lord. Why did he do this?"

She walked to her chair and sank into it just as the phone
rang. She stared a moment before lifting the receiver. "The
Queen's Box."

"This is Monty Gale from the *Gambit*. I'd like to talk to
Eleanor Theriot, please."

"She's not available."

"I'll leave a message."

"She's not taking messages," Eleanor said, replacing the
receiver. She shook her head as if doing so would make the
past fifteen minutes disappear.

No good.

How many more people would call? Not that many peo
ple watched YouTube, did they? When they said videos o
pictures "go viral," that was fluffy stuff like barfing dogs o
overweight people tripping and landing in whipped cream o

something. Why would someone care about some guy singing about making love to someone?

But she knew magic lay in Dez. She'd seen his face, the dampness in his eyes as he bared himself emotionally. He hadn't looked at the camera, but had lost himself in a private moment of revelation. The potent combination of such a beautiful, masculine man pouring forth tenderness was seduction in itself.

And then there was Tre with his phenomenal ability.

Add up those things and it was easy to see why people wanted a piece of that moment.

Flashbacks overwhelmed her. Once again a man had thrust her where she didn't want to be—in the spotlight. She'd had no choice in the matter, no recourse. When people claimed a piece of Dez and his music, they took a chunk of her. As sure as they pried a clam apart and poked the creature within, so she, too, felt the point of their sticks.

The door open and Dez stood before her.

"Eleanor."

She refused to allow tears. "Yes?"

"I know you're pissed."

"Do you?"

For a moment, he looked clueless. Stereotypical helpless male. It was a look she knew well because Skeeter had plied it with the craftsmanship of a professional moron. But Dez wasn't a moron. "Wait, you're not mad about the video thing?"

"What do you think?"

"You're mad."

"Along with hurt and embarrassed. I pretty much feel like a jackass."

He shut the door. Clad in worn jeans and a faded long-sleeved shirt that fit him like second skin, Dez didn't look like a man who'd used and abused their intimacy. On the contrary, he looked like a model on the cover of a magazine.

Again, she was reminded of an Aztec warrior, golden an splendid. But those feelings were short-lived when she re membered he'd revealed to the world the most intimate de tails of their relationship.

He crossed his arms, legs akimbo. "Listen, I had no ide this would happen. Tom wanted to record the song becaus he knew a producer looking for new material."

"That's nice. So how did it end up on YouTube? In fact how did I not know you were writing about me...about how good we screw?"

"That's not what that song is about. Did you even liste to it?"

"Oh, yeah. I heard it."

"It's about more than sex."

"Mmm...so you say."

"It is." A frown gathered between his eyes. "Look, Ton called me several hours ago to explain. His teen daughte found the video on his phone and sent it to a few friends be cause she thought—well, that doesn't matter. It steamrolle from that point. Just one of those things that happen."

Eleanor felt the panic tear at her. She held no control ove what had happened...she wasn't even a bystander. She hadn' known anything about the song, and that made her feel pow erless.

"And it's not all bad. A lot of good things could come from this accident," he said.

"For you."

"No, not for me. Wait, do you think I did this on purpose?

"I would hope not. My daughter saw that video, Dez. Sh heard you talking about sliding into me. Can you see thi from my side?"

"Of course, but Blakely's grown. I'm not trying to capital ize off this mistake, but I'm smart enough to realize there' nothing I can do about it. It wasn't supposed to happen, but it did."

"No, none of it was supposed to happen, was it?" Eleanor looked down at the calendar on her desk. March 9 was circled with a little sunshine on it. She'd written *beach* beneath little waves. She took a Sharpie and scribbled over the sunshine that mocked her. "This was all a big mistake."

"What do you mean?"

She gazed up at him. "From the beginning I knew you and I were too different. This only proves it. We're on different wavelengths."

Dez sank onto the edge of the damask chair with the carved angels sitting vigil. "So what? You're breaking up with me because of this video?"

"Maybe ending us is for the best."

"Seriously? One rocky spot in the road and you're out?"

Eleanor shook her head. "Don't you get it? To you, it's easy. You've spent your life moving on from one thing to the other. This is no big deal because you can profit from it. For me, I'm out to dry. On all levels."

"That's a pretty harsh accusation. I'm not moving from anything."

"Don't you dare imply I'm in the wrong. You allowed this to happen. You let him film this thinking you can get back what you once had, but you forgot there were other people involved. You forgot you dragged me along for the ride." Anger burned in her. How dare he flip the tables and make her seem irrational? She hadn't a hand in what had gone out to YouTube or wherever, but she did have enough sense to stop the bleeding.

'Cause that's what she'd been doing…allowing her passions to leach out and cloud her judgment.

Eleanor Hastings Theriot wasn't meant to be with a hot, young musician. That was the tempo beating out in her head.

Foolish, foolish woman—that's what she was. Chasing after something she couldn't have, trying to grab hold of a different Eleanor. She should have known she couldn't handle Dez…couldn't handle something so exciting and passionate.

Her only recourse was to protect herself. No one would blame her for calling in the troops and reforming behind battle lines.

Dez regarded her with such sadness. "I can't believe you're ready to toss everything over this. Are you that scared?"

"Don't make this my fault, Dez. I'm saying what needs to be said. It's the only sensible thing to do."

His laugh was bitter. "Sensible? That's gotta be the dirtiest word in the book of love."

"Whoever said anything about love? We said from the beginning this would be good as long as we were both comfortable. I'm not so comfortable right now. So, yeah, I think it's inevitable. We're not forever, remember?"

"Who are you?" His voice vibrated with pain.

Her heart broke into a million, bajillion pieces. Never had she felt such utter devastation. Never had she not known what to do. Every cell in her body screamed to shut her damn mouth, drop to her knees and crawl to him, apologize for her weakness, but her brain, that rational part of herself that had gotten her through some hard years, overrode her impulses.

Dez studied her for a few moments, his gray eyes moving over her face as if he dissected her. It felt so familiar, yet so intrusive, she shuttered her expression and tipped her head down to study the calendar again. March 9 with its waves and blotted-out sun met her eyes yet again. Three days away. Maybe she'd go to Seaside after all.

Alone…with Nutella and lots of Oreos.

She needed time to process the past month, needed distance from her life here in New Orleans. This whole thing with Dez had happened too fast, and now things lay in ruin—

her relationship with Blakely and her intentions to begin a
new life of fun, frivolity and dating. She'd screwed everything up by falling for Dez.

And now everyone knew.

"I'm not a coward. I'm pragmatic. Being with you has been
good, but we got what we needed from one another, right?
You're writing again. My feet are wet." She looked up at him,
wanting him to understand the way she felt. It wasn't as if he
were in love with her. Better to end it now rather than have
her fall even more deeply in love with him. Nothing good
would come of their continuing. She had always known this.

For several moments, he didn't say anything. For someone
who wrote music, he was awfully uncommunicative.

"Are you going to say something?" she asked.

"Guess there's nothing left to say except I'm sorry you
aren't strong enough to bear the scrutiny. We had something
good and you're throwing it away because you're scared to
let go of who you were. Very sad you choose a safe, empty
life over me."

"I'm not afraid. From the beginning you said you weren't
interested in anything serious. Remember? How has that
changed? Don't pretend we were going to end up together
on a forever sort of basis."

"So you lied the other night when you said you were falling for me? I thought we were headed somewhere more than
the bedroom, Eleanor." Dez hardened before her eyes. Gone
was the tenderness, gone was the pity. Anger had grown in
its stead. "Guess you got what you wanted—hot sex."

"I believe it was mutually pleasing."

"Jesus, Elle. When you get dirty, you go all the way."

Her heart ripped into jagged throbbing pieces. "You were
good at teaching me dirty."

For a moment they stared at one another.

"You're too busy clinging to the rules according to Eleanor

Theriot, never wondering what life could be if you stopped listening to everyone around you and listened to your heart. You're not the woman I thought you were." He grabbed the doorknob.

"Wait," she said, not knowing what to say today any more than she'd known what to say to the same declaration weeks ago. Things happened too fast. The world was against her loving Dez…and she couldn't see risking her heart with a man who couldn't protect her…who didn't have her best interests at heart. She kept seeing the video of him at the piano in her mind, kept hearing Blakely's voice.

You don't belong with him.

"I thought I was a stop, not a destination," she said.

For a moment, they both froze. Dez with his hand on the doorknob, her staring up at him, confused about what he expected from her.

"I shouldn't have to tell you how I feel," Dez said. "I showed you every second I was with you I wanted you. How can you be so obtuse?"

She spread her hands, shaking her head. "I've never done this before. You know that. You're the first guy I've been with in years so how can you expect me to know how love goes?"

"Did you listen to the song, Eleanor?"

She thought back to the song she'd seen on the tiny screen moments before. She'd been so shocked by the suggestiveness, by her name, she hadn't truly listened to the meaning behind the words. "Yeah, I heard my name and…stuff. But honestly, it was hard to process the message."

"Exactly. Look, in regards to the song, you can lay your fears to rest. I won't do anything with it, and people will move on to other videos, other news. But as for us, I'm done."

And then he walked out.

Eleanor tried not to break down.

Done.

Dez had said they were over.

This was what she wanted, right? She had pushed against Dez and love as soon as she realized she'd fallen for him because love couldn't exist between them. What she'd had with Dez was what she'd intended—an introduction back into a new world. One day she'd look back and feel relief, know he'd dodged a bullet. *Sensible* wasn't a dirty word…it made sense to let Dez go. To get back to who she'd always been.

Ending her relationship with Dez was smart…for the best.

Even as she acknowledged this, she knew he'd been right. Fear made her run, hide and throw up defenses so she wouldn't get hurt. The video had given her the reason she needed to end what she had with him.

And she also knew she'd tossed love back in Dez's face like a child lashing out at a loved one in the throes of a nightmare. Eleanor was wrapped in fear.…

And nothing but a chickenshit.

She might hate herself more now than when she'd found out Skeeter had been screwing Shellee.

The door squeaked open and her heart leaped.

But it was Pansy. "You okay?"

Eleanor shook her head. "No."

"Anything I can do?"

"Watch the store for a few days?"

"Is everything okay? Dez looked—"

"No, it's not okay," Eleanor said. "I'm either the savviest woman—able to anticipate forthcoming heartache—or I'm the biggest dumb ass in the world."

Her friend's eyes were as soft as the blue quilt hanging in the vintage linens section of the store. "Oh, Elle, hon. What have you done?"

"I've done what I've always done. I've protected myself."

"I'd say something clever here, but you'd probably throw something at me, and I happen to know that Swingline stapler is heavy. So, I'll just be your friend and run next doo for muffins."

Eleanor put her head on her desk and cried as the doo clicked closed.

CHAPTER NINETEEN

TRE STOOD IN FRONT of the dilapidated housing project, and swallowed fear. Only a few units had remained after the storm hit seven and a half years ago, and the building where his mother had died was one of them.

For whatever reason, some politician thought this particular unit could be turned into a set of offices for the Housing Authority, but it had never happened. The other projects around the city had been torn down, and the office repurposing had gotten bogged down in red tape, so here the old unit sat, sad, decaying, but stalwart against the elements.

No one had lived in them since Katrina...other than the occasional vagrant who was rousted by patrols. Rusted padlocks refused outsiders entry, but there were always ways to get past locks when one lived in the streets.

Tre could easily get inside.

If he could make his feet move.

Maybe the old T-shirt hiding the things he'd taken would still be inside, hidden beneath moldering carpet in the floor of the old front closet. Or maybe some street person had already found the hidey-hole and added the stolen goods to his cart of cans and worn clothing.

Tre hadn't a clue because every time he got within a block of the place, he started shaking so bad he could hardly move. Didn't matter what he told himself—that the memories should be gone by now—he still shook like an addict detoxing.

Hard, cold fear sat like an iron ball in his gut, but after

facing what he had over a week ago, after staring down death and knowing he could do more than run, he'd found the courage to face his past. He wanted to do it for the woman who'd cared enough to sit beside him at that police station and refused to allow him to go down for something he hadn't done.

He'd feared her all these years, even after he'd gone to work for her. He still couldn't figure out why he'd walked into her store that day months ago. He'd had no intention of applying for a job. No intention of engaging Eleanor in any way. But it had to have been a God thing—that's what Big Mama would say.

And walking into the Queen's Box for the second time had changed his world.

Now it was time to give back to her what he'd taken in desperation.

Because it was time to move on. He'd grabbed on to hope with both hands and he wasn't letting go of a future for himself.

Night was a cloak for activities no one wanted anyone to witness, but it was also a dangerous time on these particular streets. Years ago, Tre had worried about his bright T-shirt standing out in the darkness. This time a wiser Tre had worn dark clothes and old sneakers. He carried an empty sling backpack he'd scored at a health fair and Big Mama's .38 Special in the waistband of his jeans.

If he got picked up with a concealed weapon, his phone call would have to be to an attorney rather than Eleanor. Of course, his boss had been in Florida for the past several days....

Tre circled the abandoned building, his ear cocked for any weird sounds. Hearing nothing out of the ordinary, he slipped toward a bottom window that looked to have been jimmied and carefully camouflaged, likely by a homeless person, or maybe even some kids buying and selling drugs.

Tre pulled himself through the window, grimacing as it creaked, and cast a quick glance up at the flaking fire escape, which he'd climbed down years ago, holding Shorty D like a football, ignoring the gunfire above him.

He balanced for a moment, wincing as the metal window stop pressed into his stomach, before sliding into the building and landing with a thump on the warped subfloor.

"Shit," he said, breathing in deep, but wishing he hadn't. The room smelled musty with mildew, though he could see the place had been mostly gutted. Tufts of green shag carpet still clung to carpet strips along the wall, and plaster hung from the ceiling. In one spot, he could see up to the second floor through a yawning hole, the splintered wood resembling fanglike teeth.

Not wanting to spend any more time than necessary, he pulled a small Maglite from his pocket, sprang to his feet and spotted the doorway leading out into the hall.

When he shone his light to the right, he breathed a sigh of relief.

The stairs were intact.

Even though he wanted to get the hell out, he took a moment to breathe, begging the panic to stay curled in a ball in the pit of his stomach. If he couldn't control the anxiety, he might freak out.

As he approached the stairs, the memories slammed into him.

Get your ass upstairs, Tre, his mother shrieked, her voice full of suffering, full of fear.

Tre shook out the memories as he climbed toward the place that haunted his dreams each night.

Run, bitch. G-Slim's voice echoed in the stairwell.

"Go away," Tre whispered to the ghosts, putting one foot in front of the other as he climbed toward the third floor.

But everything he'd tried so hard to suppress roared back.

The screams, the cursing, the sound of the gun, but most o
all, he heard his mother screaming for him to run.

He hesitated on the second floor, trying to control th
short puffs of air pushing from his lips into the darkness. H
felt cold all over.

In. Out. Breathe.

You can do this, Trevon. In, out, breathe.

Sucking in the stale air, he continued until he stood out
side the door to his old apartment. The hall was empty an
covered in pieces of plaster and old bottle caps. A scurry o
feet indicated mice were the only residents. Otherwise, eeri
silence surrounded him like a heavy cloak.

"This is it," he whispered, reaching for the doorknob, sum
moning all the reason he possessed.

*This is not the past. You are not a boy. You are a man, *
man with a future, the man your mama wanted you to be.

He turned the knob, but the door was locked.

Tre nearly laughed aloud at the irony. He'd done all this—
faced his giants—and the damn door was locked. He hadn'
thought about that. But he'd come too far to turn around, s
he lifted his foot and kicked in the door.

The crack sounded uncannily like a gun firing, and Tr
closed his eyes for a moment.

Then he opened them because now he needed to be quick
That sound could have been heard from outside, and wh
knew who lingered around the old block.

Not G-Slim.

He'd died right where Tre stood, or at least that's what th
police report said. Big Mama had demanded an accountin
of her daughter's death and Tre had pored over the report th
detective had given the family. G-Slim had bled out from
gunshot wound to his leg. Talia had shot him, nicking hi
femoral artery, but then G-Slim, or maybe one of his homies
had shot his mother. Five times.

Talia Jackson had died in front of the old couch.

Tre's eyes moved to the spot and his stomach clenched.

Sweat pooled at his back and he felt his heart ratchet up, galloping as though he'd run a race. He knew it was an irrational fear, a sort of post-traumatic stress symptom like soldiers got after war. PTSD. Yeah, he'd gone through the same kind of hell right in this room.

Clearing out all he'd felt then and now, Tre crept to the closet. No door was attached, and the apartment's carpet had long since been torn out. But the subflooring in the closet was intact. Tre dropped to his knees with a thud and felt for the chipped wood that allowed for the tip of a finger. Using the flashlight, he found it easily. One yank of the stubborn wood, and it lifted.

Tre shone the light around the inside of the hidey-hole.

Empty.

Disappointment punched him.

Damn, he'd hoped. The thought of recovering what he'd taken from Eleanor had weighed on him for so long. He'd somehow thought it could make everything right again. If he could give Eleanor back her past, she could move on with her future…and Tre could move on with his.

But it was unfinished business that would stay unfinished.

Tre sat back on his heels for a moment before crawling forward and swiping the light toward the front of the hole.

There.

A piece of brown flannel.

He reached inside and tugged, pulling out the old bundle he'd shoved inside seven and a half years before.

"I'll be damned," he whispered, tugging his backpack off his shoulders and pulling open the drawstring. He shoved the bundle into the depths of the bag, reshouldered it and rose. With one last swipe of the flashlight around the place that haunted him, Tre walked out of the apartment.

Ghosts had been met and dealt with, and as Tre descended the old stairs of the housing project, which contained the last vestige of the past holding him back, he knew a new tomorrow was on the horizon.

And as he climbed out the window and dropped to the hard ground beneath his old world, the first rays of the morning sun unfurled over the city.

ELEANOR HAD JUST POPPED the toast onto her plate and sat down facing the sliding glass door that showcased the Gulf of Mexico, when the doorbell rang.

"Ugh," she moaned, running her hand through her bed head. "Who in the hell?"

She padded past the rental house's bright kitchen, grimacing at the gritty sand on her bare feet. How did it get in? She vacuumed each day before bed, but still sand coated her feet.

She twisted the lock and the door pushed in.

"Oh, my arms," Pansy said, shuffling toward the counter with an armful of bags brimming with what looked to be junk food.

"What are you doing here?" Eleanor said, the door still open, bright beachy rays filling the foyer.

"I'm bringing the Oreos, chips and hot sauce...oh, and tequila."

Eleanor slammed the door. "I don't drink tequila."

Pansy started pulling things from the bag. "Well, you should. Makes your clothes fall off."

"Not what I need," Eleanor groused, heading back to her toast and the tropical motif living/dining room with the amazing view of the ocean.

"Ha, that's kinda the problem, huh?" Pansy cracked.

Eleanor ignored her and bit into her toast.

"But I bet you enjoyed every minute of sans clothes with Mr. Dez Batiste."

"Don't," Eleanor warned, wondering why her friend thought she could show up with junk food and be welcome at Eleanor's pity party. It was by invitation only. Exclusive. Private. Intended for one sad sack.

"Don't what? Talk about Dez? Talk about taking clothes off?"

Eleanor banged her coffee cup. "Did you drive all that way to poke sticks at me? By the way, I'm totally fine."

"Yeah, you look it," Pansy said, slamming cabinets and rattling crap in the pantry. "I came because it's time to kick your ass up between your shoulder blades. I've given you a couple of days to sob and throw yourself into the ocean."

"Well, you can turn right around and go back. Just leave the chocolate-covered raisins."

Pansy walked over to the table. She wore capri pants and a long-sleeved hoodie with starfish on it. She looked ridiculous, but somehow like home. Eleanor liked Pansy's zaniness…and she loved she had a friend who would drive five hours to bring her crap that should never be put in anyone's body. "Hell, no. Half those raisins are mine."

Eleanor pushed the plate of toast away. "Screw toast. Where are the cheese puffs?"

Pansy grabbed the bag and tossed it to her. "So I've been thinking about you, my friend."

"Oh? About how I screwed the pooch on this whole 'stepping outside' myself?"

"You screwed a dog?" Pansy cracked, snagging a few puffs.

Eleanor gave her the look.

Pansy smiled. "Seriously, I have been thinking about you and this whole mess you've gotten yourself into. And I've come to a conclusion."

"Do tell."

"That day before you met Dez, you said you wanted to get back the old Eleanor. Remember?"

Eleanor shrugged.

"But here's the deal—you don't want the old Eleanor back, honey."

"That's what you drove to tell me?"

Pansy sat back, licking the orange off her fingers. "Yeah. I did. Because you're punishing yourself for being who you are. But it's not too late to change. It's not too late to grow up."

Eleanor shook her head. She'd spent the past few days doing some heavy thinking. When she left New Orleans, she'd loaded up all the old family albums she'd painstakingly put together in her scrapbooking group. She'd spent hours trimming, cutting and pasting the albums together, striving for perfection, but had never really looked hard at the life within.

Then she'd driven to Seaside, picked up her key, groceries and wine, and dived into sand, surf and memories. As she turned the pages of her life, the tears fell and a strange thought lodged in her brain—she'd been so angry, so traumatized by Skeeter's betrayal and death she'd never mourned the man she'd married and loved for nearly fifteen years. As she touched the pictures of them young and in love in Scotland, or the tender pictures of Skeeter holding his newborn daughter, the tears had fallen, mixed with sobs. She saw pictures of herself with Blakely's soccer team, wearing her little Ralph Lauren polo dress and Tory Burch sandals; her and Skeeter at cookouts, wine in hand, and Christmas at the Theriots', smiling, faking happy. It made her terribly sad for the Eleanor in those pictures.

But wading through the albums had been necessary.

Finally, after two days of memories, crying and fighting the depression that dogged her, she'd let go of the anger. She'd taken the plain gold band, snatched from her jewelry box before she left home, and flung it into the depths of the Gulf of

Mexico, satisfied it would sink into the sands with lost gold doubloons and relics.

Eleanor had finally grieved her past.

She hadn't gotten to the present and future just yet.

"You're right," Eleanor said, picking up her coffee mug. "Let's go outside."

Pansy pulled the door open. The *whump, whump* of waves pounding the sugary sands of Seaside Beach greeted them. People frolicked in the cold water, determined to taste the ocean on their spring break. A few people strolled along the shoreline, searching for shells as children dogged their vanishing footsteps.

Pansy inhaled. "Ah, so restorative."

"Yes, e.e. cummings was right—you find a piece of yourself here."

"Yeah, whatever, but I have some more thoughts."

Eleanor sat because Pansy would have her say. Better to let her get it out so they could move on to watching sappy movies and eating Little Debbies.

"First, it's okay to be scared. It's okay to want to step back from a relationship. I understand."

"Thank you," Eleanor said, trying not to smile at Dr. Pansy McAdams, relationship therapist, no PhD or any other degree. She supposed Pansy's lessons were given by life.

"You've lived your life trying to please everyone around you, and when you engaged in a love affair with a young, hot, ethnic musician, you broke away from pleasing people and instead pleased yourself. And then when all those you loved, except moi, got pissed at you and tried to punish you, things got heavy. It was harder to be the woman you thought you wanted to be."

"Yep," Eleanor said.

"And then when Dez basically poured out his heart in a song that everyone got to hear before you, it was like a dam broke, and you reverted to the old Eleanor. You shut down. Closed the windows. And ran."

"I didn't run. I'd already paid for this place and I needed a vacation."

Pansy eyeballed her.

"Okay, I ran. I'm weak. I'm stupid. I hate myself."

"I wasn't going to go that far."

"Why not? It's true. I effed up in a big way. I took something genuine an amazing man felt for me, tucked away my own feelings for him and pretended everything away. And, guess what? I'm not better off. Blakely still hates me, my parents think I'm cracked, and, well, I could give a rat's ass about what the Theriots think, but—"

"Aha! There it is. Giving a rat's ass. That's the difference. Why do you care what anyone thinks, Elle? If Dez loves you and you love him, what's in your way? Your own insecurities? You're going to let uncertainty and old wounds ruin your future? Dictate your life?"

Eleanor didn't say anything. What could she say to that? Pansy was right, but it didn't fix what was broken...which was her relationship with Dez.

"Baby," Pansy said, "no one likes a pansy."

"Huh?"

"Not me, the euphemism thing. A wimp. A patsy. Someone who gives up without a fight. Are you that girl? Are you the old Eleanor?"

"No."

"Good."

"Look, I wanted to be bold, to carve out the life I wanted to live, but it was harder than I thought."

"No shit. Sometimes life's hard. Thing is, there are no rules for life. The people around you who try to tell you there are rules are the biggest liars on the planet. There's no right man, there's no right car to drive, there's no right job to have. You do what makes you happy, and you don't destroy others' happiness in the process."

"I made others unhappy when I chose to love Dez."

"No, you exposed their own insecurities, their flaws. No one was destroyed when you fell in love with Dez, and there should be no shame you earned his love in return. The idea of his song out there, something so beautiful and intimate, isn't something to be ashamed of. It's nothing like what happened with Skeeter. What Skeeter did was ugly—there's nothing ugly about what you've shared with Dez."

Eleanor swallowed her tears. "I know, but I panicked."

"Everyone makes mistakes," Pansy said softly. "In fact, there's someone with me who wants to talk to you."

Eleanor's heart skipped a beat. Had Pansy brought Dez?

"Mom?"

Eleanor turned. Blakely stood inside the open doorway, her blond hair blowing back from her face.

"Blakely," Eleanor breathed, her hand clutching the stretchy yoga shirt she wore. "Baby, what are you doing here?"

"Pansy and I had lunch yesterday, and afterward I told her we should come down to see you."

"Oh, God," Eleanor said, looking at Pansy. "Who's minding the Queen's Box?"

"Eddie and Tre," Pansy said, turning to face the ocean breeze, pointedly—and politely—tuning Eleanor and Blakely out.

"Mom, can we take a walk?" Blakely asked.

"Of course." Eleanor opened the wooden porch gate as Blakely pulled off her boots and socks. Rolling up her jeans, her daughter followed her down the stairs onto the boardwalk. Minutes later they sank their toes into the white sand.

Blakely reached out and took Eleanor's hand as they headed west, away from the rising sun. Just like she'd always done when they walked at the beach. Eleanor's heart lurched and her throat became scratchy. How long had it been since Blakely had sought her touch?

A long time.

"I'm surprised to see you," Eleanor said, lifting her gaze to her daughter's beautiful face. Blond peach fuzzies curled around her face as her hair whipped behind her. Blakely's eyes were the same shade as her father's, crystalline blue with dark rings around the irises. Her stubborn jaw was square and her nose aquiline and slightly haughty. She was a true beauty.

"I am, too, because I was so mad at you. So embarrassed."

Eleanor sighed. "So why are you here?"

"Well, it's strange, but after I heard that song, something stuck inside me. Everyone, like, heard the song. All my sorority sisters remembered Dez and then he used your name. They're not all fluff, you know. They figured it out quick." Blakely clutched Eleanor's hand tightly.

"But strangely the song made me think, like, heavy stuff. And then I went with Grandmother to New York, and every time she mentioned you, she belittled you. I guess I've always ignored it, but this time I really listened. It was crazy. Like she wanted to plant thoughts in my head about you. Horrible things about how Daddy should never have married you, and about how stupid you were to date someone like Dez. She said ugly things, and the more she said them, the more pissed I got. And then I started thinking about how you'd lived these past years. All the stuff you did for Daddy, all the stuff you did for me, even tolerating Grandmother because I wanted you to."

Something incredible bloomed inside Eleanor—rare and fragile—a new understanding within her daughter.

"I started to see you not as my mom, but as a person," she continued, finally looking over at Eleanor. "I'd never done that before. To me, you were always Mom. You baked stuff and made sure I did my homework. You kissed my boo-boos and stitched my straps on my prom dress when they broke. I didn't really get that you were like me."

Eleanor smiled. "I don't think we ever see our moms as people. Or, maybe we do, but it takes a while to see beyond our own perspective."

"Yeah, but I sort of did that, and it was an epiphany. I started seeing you…and then seeing me. That made me feel pretty shitty. I've been a total bitch about Dez, about Grandmother…just the whole thing. Even wanting that purse and trying to guilt you into buying it. I haven't behaved the way you raised me."

Eleanor squeezed her hand. "That you've realized this makes me believe I did a pretty good job in raising you."

"I'm not perfect, that's for sure."

"Neither am I, but I think we need to give ourselves permission to accept our flaws. Pansy just reminded me we all make mistakes, we all do stupid things. It's part of being human, but we have good friends and family to remind us of what is important, to smack us back in line."

"Yeah," Blakely said, pausing to kick at the waves, as she'd done as a plump eleven-year-old on that beach in South Carolina, before the hurricane came, before Eleanor lost her store, her marriage and her grip on the woman she was.

But no more.

Eleanor was done with the past, and having Blakely realize her role in weakening Eleanor's determination to move forward only strengthened her resolve.

She would go to Dez.

He was her future.

No more fear.

Just holding on to the good stuff for as long as she could.

Blakely turned to her. "I'm sorry how I've acted. I can't promise I'll be the most supportive daughter ever, but I'm not going to hold you back, Mom."

Eleanor pulled her daughter into a hug, inhaling her sweet scent, her heart bursting. "Of course, I forgive you. I want us to be close, but I realize relationships aren't ideal. We'll both piss each other off, and we'll both have to forgive each other because that's what family does."

Blakely squeezed her. "I think Dez loves you. You should go get him, Mom."

Eleanor bit her lower lip. "You think?"

Blakely lifted her perfectly plucked eyebrows. "I *listened* to the song. Love is pretty obvious."

CHAPTER TWENTY

TRE STOOD OUTSIDE Eleanor's office in his black pants, white shirt and new tie, hands shaking, gut clenched.

It shouldn't be a big deal.

He looked down at the cardboard box in his hands.

Felt big, though.

He knocked on her door.

"Come in," she said, loud enough for him to hear, but not all shrieky like Cici.

He poked his head in. "Uh, Mrs. Theriot, can I speak to you?"

Eleanor sat behind her desk, wearing a black dress and red, red lipstick. He'd never seen her looking that way. She looked exotic, like someone from the past who shimmied around in those weird dresses, like in *The Great Gatsby*. "Hey, come on in."

He closed the door. No need in Pansy knowing anything about what he'd done in his past. "Uh, I need to talk to you about something, and I need to give something to you."

"Sure. You want to sit down? You look nice, by the way. Nervous about playing tonight?" She smiled, but her eyes looked weepy. As if she was afraid everything around her might shatter. He knew she and Dez had broken things off, and he hated that. They both seemed happy together, like him and Alicia. Kind of meant to be.

"Yeah, I sort of feel like I could throw up."

Eleanor smiled, but it didn't reach her eyes. "To be expected, I guess, but I've heard you play, and something happens to you when you're up there. You become someone else."

He nodded, shifting the box from hand to hand.

Eleanor regarded him expectantly.

"So, um, you remember when I came in back before Christmas?"

"Sure. I was so glad to see you because I'd gone a whole two weeks with no delivery guy."

"Yeah, so that wasn't the first time I'd been in your store."

Her eyebrows lowered and her nose scrunched. "Okay, so…"

"I came by every now and then to check on the store, and I saw the sign. Don't know why I came in and applied for the job. Guess I wanted to see everything was okay inside the store or something."

"Tre, you're not making sense."

"I came to the store during Katrina." He dropped his head. He couldn't look at her when he said it. "I took some things."

"You mean you looted my store?" Her voice sounded weird, as if she was choking on a chicken bone.

"Yeah."

Silence squatted between them. Finally, he peered up at her.

"Well, this is unexpected," she said, looking as though she didn't know what to say, how to react.

"I didn't break the window or nothing. It was days after and my mama was sick. She kept throwing up and looked bad. Everything we had was ruined except for some peanut butter. No water to drink. Shorty D cried all the time, so I told her I'd go get some food somewhere. I walked over this way. People had guns and were guarding the food, but the window of your store was all busted and stuff. I came in to look around and found this."

He set the shoebox on the desk. Lifting the lid, he pulled out the old ragged brown shirt.

"That's Skeeter's old corduroy shirt," Eleanor said, her eyes on the bundle. She seemed as though she was in shock. "Where was that?"

"It was bundled inside a cabinet in the back. I didn't know what it was. Once I saw, I thought I could sell some of the stuff to get some food. I just took it."

"Pansy said she'd hidden the box." Tears trembled on her dark lashes and Tre felt as if someone had kicked him in the gut.

"I took it back to our place at the Magnolia Projects. When I got there, a bad dude grabbed me. He tried to take it, but my mama showed up with a gun."

Eleanor's eyes widened. She ripped her gaze from the bundle to his face. "What?"

"I just want you to understand why I ain't never give this back to you. I couldn't go get it. 'Cause it was where my mama died that night."

Eleanor clutched her chest and reared back in her chair. "What? You mother died that night?"

"G-Slim was meaner than a snake. He hated my mama and he shot her. I'd hidden this—" he pointed to the bundle "—in a false bottom in our closet. We use to use it for drugs and guns."

"Oh, my God, Tre. This is—"

"Yeah, it's okay."

"No," Eleanor said, shaking her head. Her goldish-red hair wisped out and she looked kind of panicky. "It's not okay. Tre, my Lord, that's terrible. I can't imagine what you went through."

He didn't say anything because sometimes he couldn't imagine it either. He'd spent a lot of time blocking it out, but the memories were fresh. They still hurt, but there was healing, too. Something inside him had found peace, like the beast that had slumbered had awoken and been silenced at last.

"So how did you come by this?" she asked, gesturing toward the bundle. "I thought all the projects were torn down."

"They was, but my unit had been saved to be used for something. They didn't do nothing to it, though. I couldn't go inside before. I wanted to go get it for you, but I couldn't. Like I got a physically sick feelin' when I went close to the place."

She rubbed her eyes as though she had a headache. "So why now?"

"Because I faced death the other night, and those things you said to me about the measure of character and stuff sat on me, and suddenly I knew the way I could close the door on who I used to be. I had to go back, face the past and make things right. I had to go get your box."

Eleanor reached a trembling hand toward the bundle. Tre leaned forward, picked up the ragged brown shirt tied with twine and placed it in her hand.

She brought it to her desk blotter, grabbed the scissors and cut through the twine. Carefully she parted the fabric, unwinding, until the box emerged.

It was black and shiny, trimmed with gold fancy embellishment with a strange-looking little bird on the top. Didn't look all that special, but he supposed owning something a queen once owned made it distinct.

Eleanor exhaled, running a finger along the edge, a sad smile on her lips. "Doesn't look like much, does it?"

"It looks like a fancy box."

"Marie Antoinette and all upper-class women of the day were fascinated by the Orient. This box was made in Japan, Kyoto to be exact. It's black lacquer with twenty-four-karat-gold and lapis-lazuli embellishment. This is a nightingale." She tapped the top of the box where the bird sat against a spread fan.

Eleanor opened the box and pulled a few things from within. Some pins and watches. "Pansy braved the winds to come to the store and secure things. For some reason she didn't put this in the safe. She said she forgot about it. As she left, she pulled it out, wrapped it in Skeeter's shirt that hung on the back of my chair, and put it in the upper cabinet in the back. She thought it would be safe."

Tre shook his head. "I'm sorry."

Eleanor laughed. "I can't believe this box is sitting here. I'd mourned it and all it represented for so long, but you know what?"

"Huh?"

She closed the box. "It's just a box."

"You don't want it anymore?"

She looked up, as though catching the disappointment in his voice. "Sure, but not because of what I lost. Because it's given me something new."

He didn't understand what she meant. She'd gotten a far-away look in her eyes.

"The past is a tricky thing. You have to hold on to the good stuff and banish the bad. For a long time I thought the loss of this box caused the bad things in my life, which is totally silly, but the mind sometimes clings to the irrational so you can explain why things fall apart. But this—" she lifted the box and focused on him "—it represents the future. It brought me you, and even though you won't stay my delivery boy, you're part of my family."

Tre felt something scratch the back of his throat.

Eleanor brushed a hand across the box and smiled. "Thank you, Tre, for bringing this back to me. For teaching me that letting go of the past is necessary to claim our future."

"That sounds like another poster I saw in school."

Eleanor laughed. "I should have worked for a greeting-card company."

Tre stood. "So we good?"

"We're good," Eleanor said, coming around the desk. Her skirt was short and she wore really high heels. Tre had never seen her look better…except for that sadness in her green eyes. "I'm ready to claim my future, but I might need your help. You game to help an old woman?"

"Depends on who the old woman is," he said.

"She's me and she's determined."

"I guess I'm trapped. You're my boss and I gotta do what you say."

"I've always liked you, Tre."

Tre smiled. "It's my charm and wit."

SHE CAME.

Dez looked up from the piano as the hostess seated Eleanor at an empty table near the stage.

And she looked dangerous in the same short black dress she'd worn that night on Frenchmen Street, but this time her hair brushed her shoulders, her legs were bare, and the strappy red shoes that would give foot-fetish dudes a hard-on matched her ruby lips. A long strand of glowing pearls lent her a glamorous patina. She looked like Rita Hayworth, like a goddess.

Eleanor tilted her head toward a waiter as he handed her a glass of champagne, and Dez refocused on the keyboard beneath his fingers as they played a new take on an old standard.

Why had she come?

The place was packed—people sat at every table, their lively faces lit by flickering candles in votives created by Pansy's husband. Specialty drinks flowed as white-jacketed waiters swarmed out of the kitchen with specially prepared heavy hors d'oeuvres. The hostess in a tight black dress, a bun at her neck and jeweled glasses, lent the right first impression as she escorted guests to their tables. The bartender shot the shit with guests who wanted more drinks and weren't willing to wait. Reggie glad-handed with a smile as big as the Superdome.

Dez had looked out minutes ago and thought opening night perfect…except for Eleanor not being there.

Weeks ago he'd imagined her beside him, smiling, as he greeted patrons. He would look dapper, and she elegant in a suit of pink or purple or whatever the hell color…but the key thing was she was beside him.

But that night he'd stood alone when the doors had opened. And that had pissed him off.

Fine. He owned loving her, but he didn't have to like it.

Shaking his head, he tried to tuck those thoughts away, tried to pretend his heart hadn't throbbed with disappointment. Dez was a survivor. He'd get over her by throwing himself into the club, ensuring his dream came true. He could stand alone because he'd done it time and again.

So he refocused on his music. Pretended the woman he loved, the woman who'd rejected him because she was an effin' scaredy-cat, wasn't sitting mere feet from him, looking like a 1930s pinup girl.

She'd probably come to support Tre.

Dez glanced over at the young musician holding the crowd in the palm of his hand as he wailed, and recalled the conversation they'd had earlier, recalled the way Dez had made peace with himself.

Tre had come in looking like a new man. "Yo."

Dez extended a nod. "You ready, bro?"

Tre's dark eyes glittered. "Yeah, and my girl's coming tonight. I'm jazzed, dude."

"Aren't you bringing the swagger?"

"Yeah, and Tom Windmere's coming, too. That's my two people on the list."

"Tom?" Dez looked up from perusing the list.

Tre kept his eyes down. "Yeah. Uh, I signed on with him." He lifted his eyes, brown eyes that were apologetic.

"Good," Dez said, reaching out and clasping Tre's shoulder. "That's a good move. Tom's a good manager and can do things for you."

"But what about you? What about Eleanor's song?"

"First, I'm my own man, Tre, and I've made peace with myself. Writing music and playing here in my club is what I want to do. I don't want to go on tour or do session work, but for you, it's a good move. You have the talent to make it."

"But so do you."

"I'm not saying I don't, but I like the niche I've carved, and I want a home. My old man roamed all over the world, never did find a place to rest. I don't want to be him. I have a place I belong, and it's here."

"Cool, man. That's cool."

Dez smiled. "Yeah, it is. And as for that song, I'm leaving it alone. It brought me back and gave me something I've needed for a while, but that's it."

And an hour ago, he'd meant every word he said to Tre. He wasn't playing that song, no matter how many people had already requested it. When he'd said he and Eleanor were over, he meant it.

But now with her sitting so close, he felt that ache so keenly—it ripped through him.

So close yet so very far away equaled torture.

As he played, he focused on the music, telling himself he scanned the crowd merely to gauge interest, to make sure everyone dug his groove. But his eyes kept finding her.

She never looked to catch his gaze.

Yeah, game over.

They ended the song and hearty applause broke out. Time for a break. He needed to check with the chef. Reggie said something about the shiitake mushrooms being spoiled and thus inedible, and then he needed to greet several of the merchants who'd shown for the opening. He signaled to the guys they'd take a break, but Champ smiled and shook his head.

Dez stood, but just as he turned to the audience, the band started playing…her song.

Eleanor's song.

He blinked and shot Eddie a look, but the drummer kept right on with the soft beat, a grin on his face.

A smattering of applause broke out and Dez had no choice but to sink back upon the bench and put his fingers to the keys.

Shit.

He'd told Eleanor he wouldn't play it. Daring a glance toward her, Dez nearly struck the wrong chord.

She watched him, a sweet smile on her face and tears shimmering in her eyes. Giving a thumbs-up to Tre, who managed a wink, Eleanor turned her full attention on him.

Something swept over him—a realization.

She'd arranged for the band to play the very song that had her scampering away over a week ago. So why would she coerce them in to playing something she'd been embarrassed of?

The intro faded and the time for him to sing the lyrics rose. He jerked his gaze back to her as he started the first verse, crooning about all she'd made him feel. Her gaze caught, held his, and something passed between them, something strong and true. And then he knew, as the tears trembled on her lashes, fell on satin cheeks.

This was Eleanor's apology.

Because she wanted him more than she wanted her reputation, more than she wanted to please the others in her life, more than fear of the future.

This was her way of saying she needed him.

Wiping her cheeks, she focused on him, her smile no longer a mystery. He'd endured a week of hell, of heartache and anger, but everything in her smile flipped his world to right side up again.

I'm sorry, she mouthed.

His answer was to grab hold of the emotion, close his eyes and sing to her. Reverence poured from him as he sang about loving her. He begged her to feel it, for all to know of what she'd given him.

And when the last note faded and he opened his eyes, the world came back to him. At first he flinched at the riotous clapping. Several people hooted and the hum of voices drowned out the final shimmer of the cymbal. Dez looked at Eleanor…but she wasn't there.

He stood, whipping his head from right to left, searching for her, but she'd left.

Then he felt movement, and turned.

Eleanor stood behind him, a smile on her face. "Hey."

Dez didn't return her greeting. Instead he swept her into his arms and kissed her.

Champagne and coming home—that's what Eleanor tasted like. She twined her arms around his neck and kissed him back, laughter welling inside her as she held him tight. Around them the world applauded.

Finally, he broke the kiss and gazed down at her. "You came back."

"Because I love you," she said, reaching up and wiping what had to be red lipstick off his mouth. "I do. I never should have run. I should have been strong enough. I should have been the woman you expected me to be."

Dez kissed her again. Around him, his band set down their instruments as traditional jazz piped through the speakers. Everyone still watched them, but he didn't care.

"You're going to get lipstick on your collar," she said when he finally came up for air.

"I don't care. I want your mark on me. And I want my

mark on you. You're mine and that's all I really care about right now. Stay with me."

"I'm not leaving, and I'll never run again. For a while things were cloudy, but—"

"You looked for the sunshine?"

"It was always there, Dez. I just couldn't see nor handle what you'd come to mean to me. But now I'm ready. Not just to date, but to love again."

He grasped her hand, jogged down the three steps of the stage and then swung her into his arms. "Then let the games begin. We're moving forward together."

She hugged him. "No games, baby. Just something real this time."

"Deal," he said, turning to accept the congratulations of his guests. Blue Rondo was open and Eleanor was by his side, and if that wasn't a happily ever after, he didn't know what was.

* * * * *

Look for the next book by Liz Talley set in New Orleans, LA! Coming in October 2013 from Harlequin Superromance.

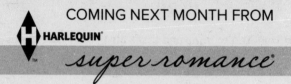

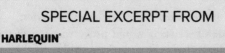
"That was a surprise." Ro's voice was soft but Miles heard steel
in its tone.

He traced her cheek with his fingers. "I'm not sorry I had
to kiss you."

"You did it to keep the wing staff from seeing us, didn't you?"

"Yes."

"Is this how you usually run an explosive ordinance op,
Warrant?"

"Out in the field, the guys and I don't do much kissing." He
saw her lips twitch but no way in hell would she let him see
her grin. Ro was so damned strong. He knew it killed her to

let go of her professional demeanor, even in civvies.

"No wonder, because it would prove way too distracting. I hope you don't plan a repeat maneuver like that, Warrant."

"I do whatever duty calls for, ma'am."

She glared at him. She didn't usually show this kind of heat, and it took all his control not to haul her onto the bike and take off for his place.

"What we're doing will not call for that kind of tactic again, get it?"

"Got it," he replied. She'd enjoyed it as much as he had, he was sure of it. But this discussion was for another occasion, if at all. "It's time to get to work, Commander."

Will this *really* be the last time for that kind of tactic? Or will circumstances keep pulling Miles and Ro together? Find out in NAVY ORDERS by Geri Krotow, available July 2013 from Harlequin® Superromance®. And be sure to look for other books in Geri's WHIDBEY ISLAND series.

REQUEST YOUR FREE BOOKS!
2 FREE NOVELS PLUS 2 FREE GIFTS!

HARLEQUIN

super romance®

More Story...More Romance

HSR13R

Love Western?

Harlequin® Superromance®
has *the* Western romance for you!

Once a Champion by Jeannie Watt
AVAILABLE IN JUNE!

Betting on the Cowboy
by Kathleen O'Brien

A Texas Hero
by Linda Warren

The Ranch Solution
by Julianna Morris
ALL 3 AVAILABLE IN JULY!